THE GIRL IN THE MIRROR

SARAH GRISTWOOD

The Girl in the Mirror

Harper
Press

**FT
Pbk**

Harper*Press*
An imprint of HarperCollins*Publishers*
77–85 Fulham Palace Road
London W6 8JB
www.harpercollins.co.uk

Visit our authors' blog: www.fifthestate.co.uk
Love this book? www.bookarmy.com

Published in Great Britain by Harper*Press* in 2011

1

Sarah Gristwood asserts the moral right
to be identified as the author of this work

A catalogue record for this book
is available from the British Library

This is a work of fiction. Names, characters, places
and incidents are either the product of the author's
imagination or are used fictitiously.

ISBN 978-0-00-737904-0

Typeset in Horley Old Style by
G&M Designs Limited, Raunds, Northamptonshire
Printed and bound in Great Britain by
Clays Ltd, St Ives plc

Mixed Sources
Product group from well-managed
forests and other controlled sources
www.fsc.org Cert no. SW-COC-001806
© 1996 Forest Stewardship Council

FSC is a non-profit international organisation established to promote the
responsible management of the world's forests. Products carrying the FSC
label are independently certified to assure consumers that they come
from forests that are managed to meet the social, economic and
ecological needs of present or future generations.

Find out more about HarperCollins and the environment at
www.harpercollins.co.uk/green

I grieve and dare not show my discontent
I love, and yet am forced to seem to hate;
    I do, yet dare not say I ever meant;
    I seem stark mute, but inwardly do prate.
I am, and am not; I freeze and yet am burned,
    Since from myself my other self I turned.
    My care is like my shadow in the sun –
    Follows me flying, flies when I pursue it,
Stands, and lies by me, doth what I have done;
    His too familiar care doth make me rue it.
No means I find to rid him from my breast,
    Till by the end of things it be suppressed.
    Some gentler passion slide into my mind,
    For I am soft, and made of melting snow;
    Or be more cruel, Love, and so be kind.
    Let me float or sink, be high or low;
Or let me live with some more sweet content,
    Or die, and so forget what love e'er meant.

Elizabeth I

Sometimes I think that I can feel the garden, like a prickle of awareness on my skin. As if sight – and smell, and sound – were not enough and I want to wrap myself in it, like you wrap yourself in a fur on a winter's day. I suppose those times should come most often in the mayday, the hay day, when the roses and the fleur de luce and the honeysuckle are in flower. When, in the knot gardens of my childhood, gillyflowers jostled strawberries, with the fruit already beginning to show. When, in the great gardens where they bring even the meadows within their walls, they're already scything the bloomy purple grasses, fine as the silk tassel on a nobleman's cloak. I have always loved the garden then, of course I have, but sometimes I thought I loved it better earlier, when the pinkish apple blossom and the green-white pear first begin to break out on the grey lichened branch, or before that, in the time of violets and Lenten lilies. When the grass is sparser and the great trees are still bare, and things bloom with less of a rash and threatening luxury. Or earlier still, when the first snowdrops show above the frosty ground; a promise, but only of the most modest kind. The kind of promise in which one can trust, without too much uncertainty.

I forgive the garden the dog days, the sullen weeks between the hay and the harvest. I forgive it, even though wet days leave the tired plants spoiled and leaden, and on dry ones the gardeners have to trail twisted rags between water tank and root; and sometimes the change comes so suddenly that the ground steams, as though the earth were no more than a giant stew pot. I like the fact that the garden, then, is not for everyone; only for those who will come on its own terms, at the beginning or the end of the day. The weather has dried leaf and bud, and from childhood I remember the thrill of dead husks yielding life between the fingers – the sharp oily strength of lavender as it's crushed. I've seen other ways, since, to deceive the heat – gardens with canals big enough to row a boat around, planted with overarching trees for shade. But it's still the smell of lavender, every time I open a linen chest, or turn over in new sheets, that brings the garden close to me.

Every husbandman loves the first sniff of autumn, when the golden days light up each separate leaf. Days when the bite in the air goes hand in hand with the sunshine, like the claws emerging from a velvety cat's paw. Even in winter – when the only colour comes from the tied bundles of the onion tops, and a trace of gilding on the rosemary leaves left over from the last visit of the queen's majesty, when they dip sticks in honey and sweet wine and put them in the hives to keep the bees alive – the garden was always my place of safety.

Except when it wasn't. Except when it was a place of puzzlement, of mystery. Of a dead bird thrown over the garden wall, of a warning given, cryptically. Of a man's teasing face as he dodged between high dark hedges, laughing out at me. Of not knowing what or where my place should be.

The garden in May-time is a place for lovers, with flowers dotting the grass like stars in the sky. The garden in autumn is a place of maturity. In early spring, perhaps it's for the children, who will crouch down by each new flower and give it the tribute of a wondering eye. I used to crave the early springtime, but now it's roses and cherry blossom, great lakes of bluebells and the lush smell of the new shrub, the lilac, they have in the garden on the Strand that fill all my fantasy.

When I was a child, the garden seemed a magic place. Not so much for the miracle of the annual rebirth – perhaps only adults, who've understood death, can appreciate that – but for its smallness, its perfection, the low clipped hedges of the sweet herbs dividing and defining a bright tiny world, safe and ordered as it should be. I've seen other gardens since that aim at more than safety. Where plants are brought from strange new lands, and bright jewels are painted into the walls of an aviary. Where statues spell out subtle messages, where fountains run with wine, and hidden water jets spring up to soak the unwary. These too I am learning to love.

Fashions move quickly: there was a time, not so long ago, when every man at court dyed his beard bright red, they say. Fashions change in the garden also – but then, everything changes. It's the one thing gardeners, more than anyone else, should know with certainty.

Everything changes. Even me.

Jeanne

The English Channel, 1583

We'd been on the boat for all my lifetime, or so it seemed, suspended in an eternity between black water and black sea. The sailors hadn't wanted to set out in this weather, that much I'd understood, but the shouting mob of passengers, desperate to get away, and the fists waving money had persuaded them. There'd been no cabins left, but Jacob had settled us on deck, said it would be easier that way, and I'd almost believed him – until we cleared the harbour from Antwerp and the first freezing slap of a wave washed over me. Then the lurching began, and the strange feeling in my belly, and though I knew that five years was too old to be a baby, I started to cry. I would have cried for Maman, but I knew that was no use. I knew by now that, however much I wanted her, she couldn't come to me. Because we hadn't been on this boat forever, not really, and before the terror here there'd been the terror at home, where things ought to have been safe, behind us in the Low Countries.

What I remember most is the moment before it started – a pause in time, like the pause of a bee hovering in the air, before it crawls into the bell of the flower. It had been a mild day, almost sunny, and I remember the flat warm light on the canal waters, and a moored boat rocking, and the blue of my new dress as I walked slowly, brimful of pride.

Then out of nowhere my mother had been there, snatching at my hand. 'Run!' she panted. 'Run, Jeanne, that's right, quickly.' I looked sideways at her, consideringly, and I did run, but not that fast. I could almost have thought it was a game, if it weren't for the little mewing sounds she was making as she tried to catch her breath, and the fact that her grip on my arm was hurting me. It had been weeks and weeks that she hadn't wanted to play any games, or to do anything that meant moving quickly, but now she was a pace ahead and tugging me along, despite her huge swollen belly.

We'd almost reached the canal water by the bridge when she stopped, as hard as if she'd run into a brick wall. 'Oh, *mon Dieu*. Oh God protect us, they're here already.' I didn't know who she was talking to. 'Maman,' I said clearly, 'where is Papa?'

She looked at me almost as if I were a stranger. Or as if I were a grown-up, maybe.

'They got him,' she said, as if she wanted me to remember. 'They came to the silk merchants' district first. Everyone knows where the chief Protestants live in this city.' While she spoke her eyes were casting around. 'There!' she said, and stumbled sideways down an alley. I followed, but I didn't move as fast as she did. My petticoats were in the way, and I didn't understand why we were running, anyway. At the corner I paused as I heard a man yell. A man with a curved metal cap on his head, and something long and shining in his hand. He yelled again, with a sound of triumph in it. He was pointing at me.

As we reached the end of the street Maman was banging on a door. I knew the man who opened it; I'd watched him talking with my father, though he'd never spoken to me. 'They're coming, they're coming, you can get away, you've got money, if you can only get up north there'll be a boat to take you away. You won't be on the list, Jacob, they won't stop you, you'll be all right, only you must take Jeanne.' She was talking so fast she sounded as if she were crazy, like the old woman in the house next door. Maman always said her wits had gone awry. Jacob was slinging his bags round his shoulders. He must have packed them already. His head jerked up, like a bird when you startle it. The man in the tin hat was rounding the corner, leisurely, and I could see that he was laughing, I could see his black beard and his dark eyes. At that moment my mother doubled over, clutching at her stomach, and giving a gasping little cry.

'Go!' she hissed at Jacob, fiercely. As he darted away round the corner she sank down against a wall. Whoever lived in that house had been doing their washing, and the sheets were all hung up to dry. My mother pulled one down right over her, almost as if she were hiding, but that's silly. 'Go, go.' It was as if she were screaming in a whisper to me. For a second I hesitated, then I dashed round the corner. From the dark of a doorway a hand reached out and Jacob grabbed me.

'Shhh –' Then, as if to make sure, he clamped his hand over my mouth. From behind us I could hear soft thuds, like the blows a baker gives to the dough, and voices in a foreign language, and my mother's voice crying 'No!' and a scream cut off. I would have run back but Jacob was holding me. There was a horrible rasping, gurgling sound, then the voices were moving away. For what seemed like long minutes Jacob held on, until at last he released me. There was a pile of white and red where my mother used to be. The corner of the sheet had fallen over her face and below it … I gazed, uncomprehending. I couldn't understand the glistening mass of red tubes and bags, like something left over on the butcher's counter, as being part of her in any way.

'Dear God in Heaven,' said Jacob behind me. I could hear someone retching, but it was him, not me. I was staring at a strange small figure, like a deformed doll or like a devil in an old wall painting, lying bloody on the ground beside my mother, and at the hilt of the knife standing up from her belly.

Beside me on the boat Jacob half reached out a hand, but uneasily. As if he were trying to comfort me, but didn't quite know how. Maybe he didn't know about children. Or maybe there wasn't any comfort. When he touched my blue dress it was slimy and stinking, from when I hadn't been able to lean over in time, and I'd just been sick down my own front until everything inside me was aching. Around us, I could hear other people crying and moaning but I was tired, so tired, and as I slid down to sleep the dreams took me.

My dreams were full of jolting, and the running, the not being able to run fast enough. Not the blood, or only occasionally. After that there had been the squeak of the cart wheels, and the cold of the night air, and me not understanding yet that it was no use to cry for my mother, and Jacob telling me to hush, we weren't safe yet, and the piles of still, silent shapes by the roadway. Another child screaming on one high note, and the sound growing and fading as the cart moved closer and then slowly away. A man pinned to a wall – if I did see this, or did I imagine it? – pinned there with spikes, and his hands and his feet lying a few yards away. Other people, people who weren't dead or dying but who looked away as we passed by in our little island of catastrophe.

'Bloody Papists,' the man next to me had muttered, but Jacob hushed him.

'That's not the way.' Later, remembering, I realised he sounded almost resigned, as if none of this were a surprise to him. As if, when he'd opened the door to my mother, it had been just the latest chapter in a long unfolding story.

A long time later there had been warmth and a fire, and a strange woman trying to persuade me to eat, even while she was crying quietly. I took the bread and pretended to mumble it, and some kind of unconsciousness overcame me. When I woke the next morning, trying to understand where I was, I could hear Jacob talking with urgency.

'... can't keep her. What am I to do with a five-year-old?' he was saying. 'If you'll take her, I'll leave you half the money.' The woman was protesting when I sat up, and they saw me.

Then there were more nights, and more carts, until Jacob said we were getting near the sea. He'd begun talking to me by now, though I didn't always understand him, and he said he'd decided to go right away.

'We fled once before, after St Bartholomew's Day,' he said. 'France to the Low Countries, frying pan to fire. What a mistake that turned out to be! The north's trying to hold out but, mark my words, the Spanish will soon be all over this country, and their Inquisition with them. There's only one boundary I trust, and that's the sea.'

Jacob had settled me on the deck, propped up against his bags and with his cloak over me. There was something hard sticking into my back, and cautiously I poked my hand inside the sack. My fingertips felt a book, but fatter and somehow more bumpy than a book ought to be, and between the pages strange shapes, thin and scratchy. Then the ship gave another lurch, and once again, though I'd retched until my stomach was empty, the sickness overcame me.

As the storm began to slacken and a grey light dawned, for the first time we could see each other clearly. Jacob was gazing at me almost in horror, as if he'd never seen anything like me before, and I gazed back at him defensively. I could smell that there was sick in my hair, and my dress was filthy. Jacob cast his eyes around the weary huddle of other passengers, rummaged in the sack where he kept his money, then went over to the nearest family. They had two little boys with them, and the youngest was staring at me, his thumb in his mouth. They didn't look happy, but they looked better than me. Jacob came back with some clean shabby clothes. The rough breeches felt strange, but then everything now was strange to me. Jacob told me we were going to London – 'though sometimes I wonder why. A vile climate, and the English hate foreigners like poison. But there are people I know and there's work I can do, and there's no doubt it's a great city.'

It didn't look great, through my bleary eyes. The voyage had been so slow it was almost dark again when we clambered from the big ship into rowing boats, and then up a shingle bank. Broken crates of cargo were all I could see, with piles of reeking oyster shells and a stink like the privy. But there was a large man talking to Jacob, not in the French I'd spoken at home with Maman but in the Flemish I understood just as easily.

'… safer this way than docking nearer the City. The authorities sympathise with refugees in theory, but the sheer numbers are making them queasy.' His well-fed face turned to acknowledge me. 'But I'm sure you'll soon make a home here,' he said to Jacob, 'you and your boy.'

PART I

To every thing there is a season,
and a time to every purpose under the heavens;
A time to be born, and a time to die; a time to plant,
and a time to pluck up that which is planted;
A time to kill, and a time to heal, a time to break down,
and a time to build up;
A time to weep, and a time to laugh; a time to mourn,
and a time to dance.

Ecclesiastes 3:2

For it is an old saying. The pot or vessel shall ever savour
or smell of that thing wherewith it is first seasoned.

A Werke for Householders, Richard Whitforde

Spring 1584

'Are you John or Jan?' He was eight or nine, older than me, and sturdy with the gap-toothed, scrawny sturdiness of the London streets, but though his feet were apart and his chin thrust forward, and the scabs and the bruises spoke him a fighter, he was looking at me with curiosity rather than hostility.

'I'm Jeanne, Jeanne Musset,' I said honestly, pronouncing it the French way my mother had taught me.

'That's what I told Diggory. I told him if they called you Jan, it meant you'd come from the flat countries. Is it true they have to dig ditches there to soak up the sea?'

I nodded dumbly, and he seemed to realise I was too shy, or just too uncomprehending, for there to be any more interest in me. But from that moment I had the acceptance, or at least the tolerance, of the boys in the street. The other boys, I should say.

I'd arrived in England in boys' clothes, and boys' clothes were the next set bought for me. I'm not sure Jacob ever declared to himself a decision to deceive. Simply, he had no framework in which to imagine the rearing of a girl. Later I understood that he could just about envisage the company of a boy, a younger Jacob. An apprentice, you might say. And I suppose, without any conscious sense of reluctance on my part, I set about becoming what he needed me to be.

That was one thing I learned in the garden where we went on summer evenings and on Sundays. Plants can adapt to the most extraordinary conditions – a geranium forced to bloom in winter, blanched celery grown up without light, or an espaliered pear tree. The garden didn't belong to us, I learned. Like many others, Jacob rented his little patch of land, just outside the City. Like the others he grew cabbages and radishes, frilled parsley and gooseberries, and from the last tenants we had inherited a fine russet apple and a walnut tree. But he also grew flowers, and rarities when he could get them – new shades of double primrose, or martagon lily.

As a child, I loved our Sundays. 'Their gardens are the best thing about the English,' Jacob said grumpily. Even he would warm and soften as he packed the earth around some young seedling with a tenderness he was never able to show me. But he did set me free to run along the rows of twining peas and small jewelled strawberries. There was a seat made of packed earth and turves, which he planted with low growing periwinkle, and sometimes, if he were working late, he'd perch me there when I got drowsy. I was allowed to trample the heaps of good-smelling cuttings, of hyssop or thyme or rosemary; to pinch the dead heads off the gillyflowers, and stick my fingers into the foxglove bells.

'Watch out for the bees,' the fat market-women would tell me, smilingly, and I'd listen to the humming from the skeps on the wall, before I ran off again to chase the butterflies. Outside, in the street, I'd seen little girls playing with scraps of cloth on sticks, or twisting handfuls of straw into dollies. But in the garden there were no girls or boys. There was just pretty.

I'd pick snails and caterpillars off the leaves, and fetch water in a copper pot from the well that served the gardens. I began to notice that different plants grew in different ways, and sometimes, if I sat near Jacob's feet of an evening when he read his gardening books, he would pass them over to me. Once I saw that he was looking down at me, oddly. 'Your mother loved gardens, too,' he said quietly.

I remembered it, because it was so rarely either of us spoke of the past, or of my family. It was as if a kind of shyness held us both in thrall. Greedily, silently, over the years I hoarded every tiny detail Jacob did let slip, and secretly, in my mind later, I would add another minute piece to the jigsaw puzzle of my family.

Sometimes, in our garden, he'd grumble that in this country the grass grew so lush it choked all the flowers, and as he set me to pull up the fat emerald clumps, I fancied I could remember a shorter, spikier turf under my fingers, and a mead where the flowers shone out more brightly. Once, wishing perhaps to praise me for picking out the Latin name of some strange flower, he said it would have made my father happy.

As I grew older, just occasionally, he'd tell me stories from his own past – or that part of it which touched on the plants and the gardens. That book I had felt on board the ship was his greatest treasure – a *hortus siccus*, a whole garden of dried plants arranged according to their form, the Continental way. I learned that the great adventure of our age lay in understanding the way a weed grew, just as much as in travelling over the sea. This was one field where we of the new religion led the way, he told me proudly. He'd studied botany at the great university of Montpellier in the south of France, where many fled from persecution in the north. Though at first I understood little of what he told me about it, gradually the names of the men became familiar to me – Andrea Cesalpino ('He works for the Pope now. Pity, a pity …'); Charles de l'Écluse, who ran the emperor's botanic garden in Vienna, with his elegance and his generosity; Matthias de l'Obel with his orderly mind, classifying plants by the shape of their leaves and the way they grew from the stem or the tree. I liked it, when Jacob showed me how that was done. There was something about the sureness of it that pleased me.

Several of the great plantsmen were living in London now: Master de l'Obel visited us from time to time, and he and Jacob would chew over the plants and gardens they had seen until they came alive in my memory, too. They seemed to avoid anything more personal, however intently I might listen for it. Flemish gardens had more rare plants than any in Europe, Master de l'Obel said once, 'But who can live in a land watered by blood?' Then, catching me listening, he quickly changed the subject.

Jacob knew several of the other plant collectors here – James Garrett, the Huguenot apothecary, and Master Garth, whose connections with the southern Americas brought many rarities his way. They even passed some business to Jacob, but he was too uncompromising a man to fit for long into that or any other community. The few people who really made up my world came to me in other ways. There were the Hills, who rented the bigger patch of land beside ours, with cherry trees standing sentinel in the rows of herbs, and a pool and, most magical of all, a curved shape of willow like a tiny house with a vine growing all over it, and bunches of hard little grapes like beads hanging from the ceiling. They had a daughter – fourteen, almost grown up – who told me how to use the sops-in-wine and helped me play games with the cockleshells that edged the border. Master Hill was well to do, and though occasionally he grumbled his family would bankrupt him some day, more often he liked to boast that they had a garden that would do for a fine lady. Master Hill was a man of connections, Jacob said, and once he bought his wife a present that made me stare at it, round-eyed: the shape of a cocklolly bird, made all from living rosemary.

Master Hill paid Jacob to keep his accounts, and to write his letters neatly. So did other businessmen, one by one, and not all of them Dutch or French, though it helped that, besides the Latin, he spoke three languages easily. Four, in the end, for he came to teach himself Italian, and in doing so to teach me. He hadn't the time or the patience to school a child in the rudi-ments, so I learnt to read and recite, and figure, at the petty school. I learnt to write there, too, but Jacob said it was a vile, clumsy hand they were teaching me. He said it to the dame, who announced the next day she wanted no more to do with me. So I stayed at home, and imitated Jacob's beautiful curling writing, and ran loose in the shelves of his growing library as if in a row of peas. He was friends with all the booksellers around St Paul's, and when he went to see them, he took me.

He made more than enough money to keep us both decently, if not luxuriously. He even made enough to employ Mrs Allen, the Dutch-born widow of a local seaman, to cook us one hot meal a day and to keep the house neat. Mrs Allen must have known my secret – though in truth it never seemed as dramatic as that word implies. Just once, I remember, when I was begging to go back to school like other children, she did look me right in the eye. 'And what about the first time they take your breeches down for the birch? Have you thought about that?' I dropped my gaze. It was the sort of thing neither Jacob nor I ever thought about directly. But she in her turn never said anything straight out, perhaps from respect for Jacob – 'such a man of letters', as she called him, a trifle breathlessly – just as she never said anything about the packed bags he always kept by the door, even after we'd been in England for years and developed a cautious acquaintanceship with the idea of safety. But it may also have been because she, too, was unable to envisage any other solution for me. If I were to be a girl, then I would need to marry, and who would want a girl with neither dowry nor family, with no idea how to sew or to make herself pretty? Looking back now, I'm grateful to Mrs Allen. Looking back, I think of her affectionately. And looking back, I think there might have been mothering there, had I been able to take it. But I was a child who'd learned, the hardest way of all, that safety lay in self-sufficiency.

Still, it was to Mrs Allen I owed the few festivities I knew – the old rites and revels that grow from the blood and bone of this English country, and that made me less of a stranger than I might otherwise have been. It was she who, in the first bright days of February, would take me to the English church to see the procession of candles on Candlemas Day. They didn't hold with

such things at the stricter Dutch church where Jacob took me –
'Papist nonsense,' they used to say. It was she who sent me out
with other children begging for treats on St Valentine's Day. 'It's
one thing we can do right in this household, just like everybody
else,' I heard her say firmly to Jacob, and he stopped protesting
and turned away. She took me out into the fields, to look for
blossom on the first of May.

Sometimes, too, she'd take me to the playhouse. One of her
husband's cousins was in the business and he'd leave word with
the doorman so we could get in for free. Sometimes, after, she'd
take me behind the scenes, where the kings and villains became
men with traces of grey hair gummed on their face and paint in
the corner of their eyes – but still, men whose voices carried
across the room, men whose air and gestures made everyone else
in the room look paltry. Men in velvets and in lace, even if both
were a little shabby. And with them the boys, the shrill-voiced
pieces of vanity who'd don petticoats and act women in the play.
I looked at those boys with a mixture of fear and the most burning curiosity.

There was one old actor, Ben, who took especial pains with
me, showed me the tricks of posture and paint that made young
into old and boy into girl – or, I suppose girl into boy. It was only
later, as I grew, that I wondered how he had known that these
things would interest me. But perhaps he just liked children.
Children liked him, certainly. Ben had been to sea, when the
acting work would not support him, and he had fabulous stories
to tell – of lands where the waves flashed amethyst and turquoise,
where emerald green birds with clamouring wings but no legs
sucked the honey from scarlet flowers all day, and of the serpent
hiss of hard rain beating on a tropical sea. I'd take the stories
home to Jacob, like a bartering tool, and sometimes I could sting
him into telling me tales of his old life in the south, where bushes
of rosemary grew so high they used the branches for firewood,
and clouds of pomegranate blossom glowed against a blazing
sky.

By and large it was, I suppose, a lonely life, but I didn't mind much. It was easier that way. As I grew older, I watched the young girls begin to blush and giggle as they filled their dresses, and the young men stare and swagger on their way to the butts, out past the laundresses on Finsbury Fields, and I knew neither was for me. I didn't go to the butts, though the law said all boys should practise archery; I suppose here as elsewhere our foreignness protected me, explaining any differences away. It was not quite true, I'd found, that the English hated foreigners – not the Londoners, anyhow. What they really hated were those native-born English who were different in any way. For almost ten years, after we first arrived in England, I lived among them as a mouse lives in the wainscoting. Glimpsed, sometimes. Cursed at, occasionally. But on the whole, peaceably.

Winter 1593–94

You could live well here, if you chose to, within a network of others who had fled to Elizabeth's England, some fleeing the Inquisition's long arm, others simply to make money. It was easy to forget we were strangers in a strange land. Until something happened to remind you, and anything you'd learned about safety had to be unlearned, painfully.

I must have been turning fifteen when Jacob came home one day, his face bleached.

'I've just seen Roderigo Lopez,' he said. It was a mark of his anxiety that he was confiding in me. 'Of course, it's all an absurdity. But mud sticks, and these days, you never know what nonsense is going to get you into trouble.'

Indeed, that year had been far from easy. First we heard that the Spanish had another Armada on the way – terrifying for everyone, to be sure, but anathema to those who'd seen what the Spanish were doing in the Netherlands, from whence came bloodier stories every day. Next we heard that the winds had changed, and we were safe – certainly through another winter. But then came news that Henry of France, our Protestant hero, had turned Papist as the price of holding on to his country. He said Paris was worth a Mass: he should have heard what they said of him, the grave old men with their neat ruffs and their wine cups, in the Huguenot community. Even the plague had been worse than usual, so that people started talking about the great epidemic thirty years before, when one in four Londoners died. Jacob said the ordinary people, in their ignorance, were blaming 'strangers' – immigrants, like us – and keening over the wickedness of the country. Even the playhouses had been closed. But this was something different, apparently.

'Roderigo should never have got across Lord Essex – never!' Jacob exclaimed angrily, as I knelt to stoke up the fire. 'That's a young man who doesn't forgive a slight – yes, and a young man in a hurry.' I was sorry. I didn't know much about the Earl of Essex, no more than I did of any of the grandees whom the other boys ran after when they rode through the streets, half in admiration and half in mockery. But I liked Dr Lopez, who'd always been kind to me. Jacob said he'd been a Jew once, but he'd become a Christian many years ago when he'd first come to this country from Portugal – 'Had to, naturally.' He eyed me with a rare impatience when I looked at him blankly; yes, I knew, of course I did, that no one practised the Jewish faith in this country. But the fact was, I looked at the world around me – the world of people, not of books, or plants – as little as might be.

When Dr Lopez was appointed the senior doctor of St Bartholomew's Hospital, and even the queen's own physician, Jacob said, it reflected credit on us all. Showed you could do service to England, even if you were born across the sea. 'Shows that at least here you can get along, if you'll just try to fit in and live quietly.' As a child, all I knew was that, when Dr Lopez came to visit, he brought a bag of comfits for me. And as I grew, and Jacob let me stay up to listen to the grown-ups' talk, I liked the way his cheeks creased up and his white beard trembled as he banged his beaker on the table so that the drops splashed red, and I liked to hear his stories.

Yes – he had told some about Lord Essex, maybe. Or at any rate a young noble patient who was suffering half from the spleen – 'If he was a girl, we'd call it hysterics, but he thinks it gives him a hold over her majesty!' – and half from some unnamed disease, the thought of which made the older men purse their lips slyly.

Perhaps now Jacob thought that it was time the men's conversations ceased merely to pass over me like a ripple of water. Perhaps he just wanted to talk with somebody.

'Lord Essex has got wondrous great these last two years. What, not out of his twenties yet, and a privy councillor already. And the favourite companion of the queen's majesty – aye, and one who dares to slight her and say her nay in a way his father, God rest his soul, would never have done. The old Earl of Leicester, who married Essex's mother, and brought this boy on as though he'd been his own flesh and blood,' he explained impatiently. 'Myself, I think that's why the queen keeps him so close, for the old lord's sake, but of course there are those who say –'

Mrs Allen came in then, so I didn't hear what others say, though naturally I could guess. It sounded silly to me – the earl was in his twenties, after all, and the queen must be more than sixty. I didn't hear, then, what Dr Lopez had done to annoy Lord Essex, except maybe talk too freely. But I was of an age by now to pick up scraps of information when anything interested me.

Advent didn't bring us many callers – who sent out invitations to dine, when you had four weeks of fast days? – but when visitors did come on business I kept my ears open. I learnt that Lord Essex was white hot against the Spaniards, and anxious to lead an army off to war and make his fame that way. I learnt it was the Cecils, old Lord Burghley and his son, who were leaders of the peace party, and the queen, reluctant to spend blood or money, leaned their way in terms of policy. And that Lord Essex, pent up at home, was seeing Spanish spies under every bush, and claimed Dr Lopez – our Dr Lopez – had given house-room to Spaniards, or men in Spanish pay, plotting some dangerous conspiracy. Then Christmas came, and the feasting and the frost fair, and I forgot it all for the moment.

Christmas wasn't out when Dr Lopez was arrested. It was only the first of January, and the news spread like a sickness from feasting house to feasting house, quenching each little light of merriment as surely as if it had been touched by the plague, and as swiftly.

'They've taken him to Essex House. But Lord Burghley and his son – you know, Robert Cecil, the hunchbacked one – have been sharing the interrogation. They're reasonable men, the Cecils. He'll be out before Twelfth Night, you'll see.' It was our most cheerful neighbour, a dapper tailor once from Le Havre. Jacob glanced at him sourly.

'Reasonable men, you say. Are reasonable men going to fight with Essex over the welfare of a foreigner, and a Jew at that? What have they found to charge him with, anyway?'

It was three days later when we heard. For two of those days Lord Essex had sulked – the Cecils had done the right thing, after all, they'd declared Lopez innocent, and the queen had believed them, to the earl's fury – but on the third he had been busy. Lopez had been whisked into the Tower, and the earl set about declaring, beyond all doubt, a treasonable conspiracy, a Spanish plot to poison the queen, as her doctor could do so easily.

Terrified and confused, Lopez himself seemed half to agree. ('Of course he agreed! They showed him the rack,' said Jacob indignantly. I saw one of the other men there, another foreigner, rub his shoulder as if an old wound pained him, and stir uneasily.) Lopez had actually agreed he'd once taken Spanish pay, but only on the instructions of English agents, to lead King Philip astray. But that was back in the days of Walsingham, the old spymaster, and now Walsingham was gone, and couldn't say yea or nay.

'Take heed of that,' Jacob said. 'It's hard enough not to get caught up in intrigue, if you're a foreigner in this country. But the men who try to hire you will leave you in the lurch – by dying, if they can't do it any other way.' Privately he told me he had not the least hope; something about a job Lord Essex wanted for a friend of his, and the queen had given it to someone else, on Cecil advice, so that she'd want to soothe Lord Essex by yielding to him in some other way.

After the doctor and his associates were arraigned and sentenced, the little tailor took some comfort in the fact that the queen couldn't bring herself to sign the death warrant at once.

'She knows it's wrong, she'll let them out eventually.'

'She knew it was wrong with her cousin, the Scots queen, but she still signed. Eventually –' Jacob imitated the little tailor. 'She's the queen, isn't she?'

When the news came that she had signed, he grew ever more gloomy. Lopez was to be tried and hanged, he said, on Tyburn tree. It was from the streets that I heard the full story.

'Hanged all right, but not till he's dead, or not unless he's very lucky. Then they'll cut him down alive and hack off his privities, and slit open his belly and pull his guts out before his eyes.' One lad with a lazy eye seemed to know all about it. 'Sometimes, if they like him, the crowd yell to the executioners to leave it, to let the man die first, at the end of the rope, but they won't do that for a Christ-killer, you'll see.'

'Anyway,' another boy chimed in, 'they say Jews are built differently.'

The night before, Jacob told me he was going to watch. 'I have to, the Lord knows why. Somewhere in that howling crowd, there has to be a friendly eye. But you're to stay home – do you hear me?'

I nodded, my eyes fixed on my plate. In the last weeks, the dream had been coming back to me. It wasn't of the knife, or the hilt in the belly, not precisely. It was the running, and the knowing that I couldn't run fast enough, and that they were going to die because of me. The next morning, I pretended to be asleep as I heard Jacob leave. In his absence I tidied his desk, and cleaned out his inkwell. I was going to sharpen him some quills, but the knife disturbed me. Instead I set myself to copying the various pages of figures he had left me – for I helped him in his paid work by now – and tried not to count the time passing slowly. In the end, the suspense got to me – and the curiosity. I had to know. I had to see.

I left the house as quietly as a mouse leaves its hole with a cat there to pounce and, slipping surreptitiously from corner to corner, made my way towards Newgate, where the Holborn road leads west. It was one of those days, again, when everything seemed to move slowly. When each familiar sight of the streets struck me with unusual clarity. I suppose everyone in London can't really have gone to see the sight, but that's how it felt to me. As though I were a ghost – one of those spectres they used to paint for the casting down into Hell, mouth ever open in a silent scream – moving through an empty city. I saw Master de l'Obel, his face full of distress, but he did not see me.

Past the looming bulk of Ely Place, past the great chains across the road, to seal the way to the City when necessary, and soon I was in open country. In this dank weather the fields were just a sludgy mass of brown, cold and uninviting. Starting out so late, I was far behind the mass of the crowd, but the state of the track showed how many had gone before me.

I hadn't realised it was such a distance. I'd been hurrying my steps, to try to catch up, and I'm not sure what it was that halted me. Maybe the smell brought back on the wind, or the sick low roar of the people pressing westwards ahead of me. I don't really know what it was – the fire must have smelled like any other, even if they had lit it to burn the doctor's privates, and the crowd was noisier for the football match every Accession Day. Maybe, as I started to find myself among squabbling families, and carts full of people as cheery as on market day, it was the look I saw on the faces of those others who were flocking that way.

In the end I never even reached Tyburn. Just as well, maybe. I heard later that Dr Lopez died shouting out that he loved her majesty better than Christ, and that one of the men who died with him tried to fight off the executioner, and they had to hold him down to slash his belly open. Up until now, I'd only half understood things Jacob tried to teach me – about quarrel, and dispute, and the passion of belief. About how it made men do things in God's name that in fact the Creator would weep to see. I hadn't understood why – when Mrs Allen nagged him into getting me ordinary school books – he'd snatched the discourse on rhetoric back at once, having caught me showing off for her admiring eyes, imitating the kind of rhetoric class real school-boys had every day. At the time, I felt reproved for my vanity, but later I came to understand more clearly what Jacob had muttered under his breath about convincing and convicting, and about the wrong-headedness of teaching children that the important thing in the world was to prove their point, however blunted it might be.

Now I did understand, as I saw citizens' kindly faces alight with a brutal glee. I stood there in the muddy track for a moment, cursing myself for folly. Then I turned back, and half ran towards the familiar streets. At the empty house I bent over the desk, trying to ignore the chill sickness inside, and took care not to look up when Jacob returned, his tread slower and heavier than when he had gone away.

I had other things to concern me, as I grew older. In my mind and in Jacob's I was a boy, but my growing body heard a different story. Quietly, as she sat with our mending by the fire, Mrs Allen had made sure I'd know what I needed to know, though always imparting her information with the casual air of one who is talking for the sake of it. Never as if these were things that I might need to know personally. By the time I first bled I knew what to expect, though the pain like a knife grinding in my belly brought the dreams worse than usual, and I was glad that I did not bleed frequently. And that my shape stayed thin and unformed – slim enough in a stripling, but what in a girl you might have called scrawny.

Autumn 1595, Accession Day

Sometimes, when Jacob was out, I'd slip on my cloak and go down to the Thames, and wish the waters could take me … somewhere. To some other destiny. I heard Mrs Allen telling Jacob, in that comfortable way, that all young people were sometimes as wild as March hares, and I suppose it was true.

If I'd been of another disposition, it might have taken me to the bear-baitings, or the executions. If I'd been a proper girl it might have taken me to a boy's arms. If I'd really been that boy, it might have taken me to the stews. As it was, it took me towards the court, for the jousts on Accession Day. Ascension Day, I almost said, when in the days of the old faith they celebrated the Virgin Mary. But now the altars and the blue robed, sweet-faced statues were gone. We celebrated another virgin queen, and after more than three and a half decades on the throne, in truth she seemed as much a fixture in the sky.

The tiltyard lay to the northwards of most of the palace buildings, though close enough that you could see its yawning doorways, close enough you could feel the beast's hot breath down your neck. Close enough that the turrets and pennants loom like a fairy-tale castle. Other children heard fairy tales as something delightful, sweet as sugar comfits, but to me they were always frightening, with their world of things that were not as they seemed, of unknown possibilities. I knew you went to the tilt-yard not just for the fights, but for the masques and pageants and stories they used to dress up the fact that times had changed, and knights no longer really fought each other with spear-tipped poles under codes of chivalry. I was scathing of all that; the very young feel scathing easily.

This – I told myself, as I jostled along with the crowd trying to get in at the gates, squeezed by a merchant's wife with a picnic basket on one side, and on the other by a courting couple who couldn't even keep their hands off each other until they found a seat – was modern London, where you could buy anything from a Spanish orange tree to a copy of an Italian play, where every householder had by law to hang a light outside, so that the night streets were almost bright like day. Where the queen's own godson had invented a flushing jakes, so that after you'd evacu-ated, a stream of water carried your filth away ... But it was good, just for the moment, to be swept along with the crowd. To smell the damp sand of the arena, and the farmyard aroma of the horse lines, where the chargers were shitting with eagerness and fear.

The only place I could get was high up in the grandstand, so that what was going on below had an air of unreality, like some-thing seen at the play. But I was happy enough to gaze down at the courtiers who were coming in last of all, to the seats beside the arena, furred and cloaked against the November air. Mulberry and tawny, sulphur yellow and ox-blood red, their very velvets seemed to warm the day.

At one end, the royal gallery still stood empty, fluttering with silks in the Tudor colours, green and white. The crowds were beginning to cheer some arrivals – clearly well-known person-alities. The man beside me, a burgher as broad as he was tall, could see my ignorance, and was only too happy to enlighten me.

'That's Ralegh,' he said, 'see, the tall one? That's the queen's cousin, well, kinsman, Lord Howard the Lord Admiral, with the white beard. Look, that's Master Cecil, Lord Burghley's son – I daresay the old man will stay away, I doubt he's got much taste now for a tourney. But Robert Cecil, he's a rising man – and a sharp one, they say.' There were no cheers for Robert Cecil, I noticed. In fact there were even some jeers as he took his place. He was a small man, I saw, and almost twisted – hunch-backed? – in some way, though for all that he managed his slight dark figure gracefully.

'Ah,' my neighbour said on a grunt of satisfaction, 'here she comes, the queen's majesty.' Now there really was cheering. I peered downwards, hungrily. I hadn't expected to make any-thing out, but as the stiff tiny mannequin advanced to show herself, I found I could see quite clearly. See where the blaze of jewels caught the winter sunlight, see the bright red fringe of curls around the white oval of her face. Around her clustered the young maids of honour, with one or two older ladies.

Jacob and his friends, talking of an evening, had nothing but contempt for the court – a nest of carrion crows grown fat, they said, of maggots feasting on decay. But even they would hush their wives when any of the talk – 'Of course it's a wig. My sister's husband's a perruquier, and he says she's bald as an egg underneath!' – came close to touching the queen's dignity.

'She may have her vanities as a woman,' they'd say, 'and why shouldn't she? But she's given us close on four decades of quiet – aye, I know things haven't been so good this last year or two, but she can't help the weather and the harvest, can she? Just look across the Channel if you want to see how bad things could be.' And then they'd break off, with a sidelong glance at Jacob, and at me.

Something was happening, down in the lists. A herald on horseback, dressed in red and white, had trotted into the arena, and was making the circuit of its brightly painted wooden walls with something in his hand held high.

'It's a glove – they always do it,' said my knowledgeable neighbour. 'They put word out that Lord Essex would be sending early, to get a gage to show he rides in honour of her majesty.' Indeed, the jewelled figure at the window of the royal gallery was holding up her hand, to acknowledge the tribute graciously. But the play wasn't over, so it seemed. As the herald left, a good-looking youth in the same bold colours took his place in the arena, and looked around until he could be sure he had all eyes. He struck a pose, and began to declaim, though high up as we were the wind whipped his words away.

Three figures followed him, and knelt at his feet, in dumb show asking him to choose between them. The first, a soldier, was tall and armoured. It could have been anyone. It could have been Ralegh. The second drew a ripple of laughter from the crowd. It was barefoot in a hermit's robe, but my neighbour hissed in my ear that the long beard and the staff were those of Lord Burghley. The laughter grew louder as the third figure, in a statesman's dark clothes and waving documents of policy, leant sideways to hump one shoulder high in the air. I couldn't make out Robert Cecil's face, but he seemed to be bearing it quietly.

As the actors took their bows, to roars of approval, my eye was drawn to the end of the lists. A knight was watching there, in red-and-white livery. 'The colours of love,' said my knowledgeable neighbour and I stared – I wouldn't have put him down as a man for heraldry – until I saw he had a printed bill, like they might hand out for a play.

The knight's helmet was still off; I could see his hair and beard were tawny, and that his face was turned not towards the players but to the queen's majesty. As the actors left the lists, he bowed his head to let the squire put on the metal headpiece, and snapped the visor down. Both knights were ready, their great heavy lances resting on the ground, waiting for the sign. It was the queen who gave it – an arm held up, a glove fluttering down, and the slow thunder of the horses' hooves making the ground groan in sympathy.

It was Essex's opponent who fell, and a great sigh went up from the crowd; I knew men were running in from the sides, and that he wasn't hurt, or not seriously. But my eyes, now, were on the royal gallery. I was too far away to see properly, but in my mind's eye I saw the tiny figure tense, the hand clench on the window frame as the great metal spikes steadied to hit home. I knew now what I'd come for, and I'd found it in the queen's majesty.

'Something more than a man – and something less than a woman,' Lord Burghley had quipped, famously. Something else, at any rate. Something else, like me.

But I'd learnt another lesson, and one I put aside, uneasily. The queen watching Lord Essex was like Mrs Allen, waiting for a letter from her son, on business across the sea. Or Kate down the street, watching her man clambering drunk into the wrestling ring on fair day. Hopeful and fearful, proud and angry. A woman, for all she was queen, and statesman, and old, and majesty.

Cecil

Autumn 1595, Accession Day

I'll laugh about it later with Lizzie. I hold on to the thought of her forthright face, I imagine what Lizzie would say if she were here. Lizzie will say anything to anybody – ask her how much she paid for her gown, and she'll answer you honestly. When I first saw her at court, I asked my cousin to find out whether my disability revolted her, before I asked if she would marry me. She reminds me of it – regularly – and every time she does, I could swear the twist in my shoulders grows slightly less. I know a little of the ache goes away. She says she married a man, not a set of muscles. If she were here, what would she say?

I do not say, my time will come. I see a future with Lord Essex riding high: I see a future without Lord Essex in it. I plan for all contingencies: that is what my father taught me. If my father were here, if he'd been well enough today, he would be brushing off the mockery as though it were no more than a few drops of rain on his miniver collar. When we meet in the hall tonight he may speak of it, but only if there is need.

He may say, it's good that Essex is going too far, the queen doesn't like her officers mocked too publicly. He may say, one of our men in place should be told to feed his lordship's vanity. Or he may wear that disapproving look, that puffs out the pouches under his eyes and makes his years hang heavy, and say that we should damp down all comment, a period of quiet would be good for the country.

On the whole he is unlikely to say anything: as he grows older and his hand starts to shake, he assumes everyone will agree with him and I do, actually. How would I not, when he trained me so thoroughly? The one thing he is certain not to say is, Don't let it hurt you. Flattery is for fools, vanity is for women, that's what he'd say.

Thank God for Lizzie.

My ruff feels too tight around my neck but I know better than to lift a hand to ease it. There are too many eyes on me, watching for the least sign of discomfiture. I can see Southampton grinning spitefully. I remember him as a child, always trying to keep up with the older boys. I can see Francis Bacon, his profile turned away from me. He's never forgiven us for that business over the Attorney General's office, he's linked his fortune to Essex's chariot wheels, and it will be like the clever fool he is if he gets dragged the wrong way. But he won't entirely be enjoying this – the same blood runs in the veins of both our mothers; at rock bottom we are family.

In the convoluted world of the court, there may even be some who believed we Cecils had a hand in writing Essex's little story. My father has been painting himself as a hermit for years, asking leave to retire and tend his garden. And one thing we all learn at court, a veil of enmity can cloak allies as easily as a show of friendship cloaks enmity. They may think I have the subtlety, or the courage, to make fun of my own misshapen form, to consider the sting was a price worth paying to have made the queen laugh out loud.

I should be flattered by their thoughts, probably.

Essex himself is riding around the ring, that victor's lap of honour where they hold the horse's pace down so its oiled hooves flick up the dust contemptuously. As he passes he looks at me with a hot urgent eye. It was always that way, ever since he was young, one of the aristocratic orphans, like Southampton, raised in my father's house. He'd do something outrageous, and then he'd come to peer at you, in his tall gangling way, looking for – what? Shock? Approval? Envy? Reassurance that you'd forgive him, come what may?

Perhaps now it is my jealousy he wants, for me to acknowledge that my feeble arm could never even bear the weight of his lance, so I give it to him, dipping my head a little and smiling slightly, like a fencer courteously acknowledging a hit.

Smiling is easy: my father always taught me to praise in public, and criticise secretly. Sweetness is easy: it is easy, actually, as I look at Essex, but why? Absurd, irrational, but there is something in the sight of that tall, trotting figure that melts some of the sore frozen core in me.

Perhaps that is something I will not say to Lizzie.

Jeanne

Winter 1595–96

Around Christmas Mrs Allen's cousin, the theatre man, sent word he wanted to see her. They'd been given a gift of clothes from some grand lady that needed altering to make players' costumes, and she was clever that way. She took me along to help carry the bundles, and I went with more than usual alacrity. I was feeling restless since that day at the tourney – as if my little hole in the wainscot were no longer enough for me. It was not to the theatre we were to go today, but to the great lady's house in Chelsea. The troupe had been hired to put on several shows during the festivities. It was the first time I'd actually been inside such a place and I looked around, wide-eyed, as we stepped inside the high, red-brick walls, welcoming but imposing too. When we mentioned the players, the porter nodded us through, albeit grudgingly.

'Straight through the court and over to the right,' he said. 'Don't go bothering the gentry!'

They were just ending a rehearsal when we got there, and I left Mrs Allen muttering with pleasure as she pawed through a heap of finery, lifting a scarlet doublet that hadn't worn too badly. I went in search of old Ben, and found him carefully wiping paint from his face – a face more lined than it used to be. Another, younger, actor stood nearby. I almost said, young actor, but the truth is I found it hard to tell an actor's age then, and I still do today. All I know is that he was slim, and brown, and pleasant looking and that Ben, who seemed preoccupied, eyed him from time to time almost hungrily.

'Martin Slaughter' – he made an actor's gesture, introducing the younger man to me. 'Take our young guest to see something of the place, why don't you? It'll get you out of my way.'

The slim man made me a light, almost mocking, bow. 'Shall we?' As we passed out into court again I asked a shade anxiously if Ben was all right, and before replying he paused slightly.

'More or less all right. All right for this season, anyway. But an actor's life isn't easy as you start to age. The best parts are mostly for men in their prime, and the pretending gets harder every day.' He turned the conversation, gracefully. 'But, here, I'm being a poor host – even if my ownership is distinctly temporary. It's too cold outside – let's take a turn in the long gallery.'

'Are we allowed?' I was anxious here. It was all strange to me. The room was not so much, compared to some I've seen since, but at the time the floor seemed an ocean of polished oak, the walls a glowing forest of oil paint and tapestry.

'Oh, yes. Of course, we bow low and turn tail if her ladyship appears, or any of the family.'

'Who owns this house?'

'Lady Howard, no less – the queen's own cousin, or at least her father was – and her husband, naturally. You'll have heard of him – Lord Charles, the Lord Admiral, one of the ones who saved all our bacon in Armada days. Off to save it again, when the spring comes, if it's true what they say about the Spaniards eyeing the French ports, and another Armada on the way.' I was dumb. Though I had more cause than most to fear the Spanish, the politics of it all still meant little to me. Martin Slaughter must have seen it.

'Look, here's a portrait of Lord Howard –' And we began to walk the length of the painted images in the great gallery.

As we walked, we talked – or Martin did. It was only later that I wondered, a little, that he hadn't asked anything about me. At the time, I just accepted it gratefully. He told me how he'd wanted to be an actor, since being taken up to the local great house once as a boy.

'It was her ladyship's father's place – old Lord Hunsdon, he is, the Lord Chamberlain, it's him whose mother was the queen's aunt – and he's always been a real patron of the players, licensed his own troupe. They put on a performance, because the queen was come to stay. And my father, he worked in the estate office, wangled us in to watch from the back, and that was it, a few dramatic speeches, and all I wanted to do was join an actors' company. In the end my poor old father had to ask whether the Lord Chamberlain's Men could find a use for me. I was with them until my voice began to break, playing the ladies, and then they tried to put me to work with an ironmonger, but I wouldn't stay. I picked up work where I could find it, but for a while, with the plague, it was a bad time for the play. We all had to find another way to feed ourselves.' Briefly, his eyes clouded, and a tiny silence fell. I felt I should offer a similar account of myself, but I didn't know what to say, and in a moment he picked up again.

'When my old man died and left me his savings, Master Henslowe was just moving into the Rose, with a new company. Under Lord Howard's protection, it is – he and her ladyship, they've been good to me.

'So now I'm a sharer in the Admiral's Men, and everything is dandy! But of course, you'll have heard all about us.'

I stammered, until I saw that he was teasing me.

I tried to ask him something of what an actor felt – whether it wasn't a thrill, to be someone else every day. To my own surprise, I found I was waiting for his answer, quite as if it really mattered to me. There was a pause before he answered.

'Yes, of course it is. You can be a lover, a lunatic, or a poet. You know what it's like to be a girl as well as a boy, and that's quite something – wouldn't you say?' He wasn't looking at me.

'It's as if you get to look at the world through different eyes – or through the eye slits of different masks. You know, you can almost wind up despising those who only experience life one way.

'But of course …' He paused again. He'd turned away and was gazing down the gallery. '… of course, the most important thing is that you get to take the mask off at the end of the day.'

Katherine, Lady Howard

Spring 1596

The queen's furs should be sent to the skinner soon for beating, and stored away for the season in their bags of sweet powder. I must check whether we've enough summer hose from the silkwoman: the woollen stockings can go back to the hosier, to have their feet remade against next winter. The dresses of tawny and brazil colour that did for the cold should be put away; the peach satin furred with miniver, the russet satin nightgown and the robe striped in silver and *couleur du roy*. In their place come the lighter garments; the carnation-coloured hat embroidered with gold and silver butterflies, the yellow satin petticoat laid with silver lace to ripple like the sea and the velvet in light watchet blue trimmed with silver roses.

I had a dress that colour as a girl, with fine streamers off it to look like water; in my father's house at Hunsdon, it was, when we all put on a masque to represent the rivers of England, because the queen was coming to stay. Still, I have finer dresses now, even if they do not look as good on me.

At court, of course, the queen's ladies may wear only black and white, and I regret that occasionally. But I wear what I want to in my own house, needless to say. (Twenty years – more – First Lady of the Bedchamber: there is no way any lady in the land can raise herself higher by her own efforts, and efforts there have been, make no mistake, her majesty's cousin though I may be.) There's one dress the queen says she'll give to me, in the dark brocade suited to a middle-aged lady, and one of my own that should be given away in turn, though I've given enough to the players this season already.

Perhaps there is something to be said for keeping one's mind on the practical. It holds the fear at bay. Seven years ago, the Armada summer, it was almost easier, oddly. With invasion planned we were all in danger, every one of us, all London throbbing with the knowledge of how vulnerable we were, how close to the sea.

This time it's different; it feels like a foreign war, this alliance with the French to drive the Spanish out of Calais and keep the Channel free of Spanish fleets, and with my boys, my girls, my own shrinking skin safe out of it, I have time to fret about my husband Charles as I sort taffeta and embroidery.

Mind you, some of Charles' preparations have been domestic, too, in their way. You don't take six thousand men to sea without victuals, prepared to sit there in the Channel for months if necessary. They've been at it since Christmas, almost, and knowing what to do with all those barrels of biscuits and salted beef was one of the more foolish worries they had to face when it looked as though the queen had cancelled the expedition again, as she has done so frequently.

Charles wrote to me that he felt like a merchant whose goods didn't sell on market day. I'm inclined to doubt – though that may be prejudice – Lord Essex worried himself unduly.

Essex: I can't think of him without remembering that masque last Accession Day. All about him, and about how he can do the work of a statesman and a soldier too, I suppose he thinks the queen should give him both the Council and the army. As if it had been he, and not my Charles, who led the country against the Armada.

But seven years is a long time at court; that's all but forgotten today. Well, not forgotten by the queen. She lives in the past a lot these days, and one can see why. The present bare of ease, and the future no ally. But I've always told Charles, it's no use thinking he can just sit back on his victory, not if he still means to have any part to play. Well! No cloud without the lining, as they say. We may be sailing to war again, but at least it gives Charles an opportunity.

Seven years ago, our family were allowed to sit out the danger at my house in Chelsea: it was young Essex who was held at court to keep the queen company. Now he's challenging Charles for control of the army, and I'm needed here at court today.

The queen has been maddening: even Lord Burghley says so, and I may agree without disloyalty. Everyone else believes that war is necessary. When the City merchants were told at Sunday sermon that London needed to raise troops, they rallied a thousand men before the end of the day. And there's Charles and

Essex sitting at Dover, and the ships all ready, and the quays stacked with supplies called up from the surrounding counties, and the queen says it's off – and on – and off again.

Not, mind you, that I don't understand. These are the kind of nights that make me positively glad it was one Boleyn girl, not the other, wrested a wedding ring out of old King Henry. Great-aunt Anne, not Grandma Mary. Charles used to joke – in the early days, when we still had our own night-time secrecies – that he was glad to be in bed with Mary's side of the family. Ambition in the Boleyn blood is like a sleeping dragon and you never know what will wake it, but the Boleyn blood didn't run as strong in Mary, or so my father used to say. Not that the Boleyn girls weren't half Howard; and not that my Howard husband is really so far above the fray.

That business with the report: too childish of Essex to have done what he did, scrawling his signature so large at the bottom there was no space left for Charles to add his name. Either of my boys would have been whipped, if they did anything so petty, and so I told my sister Philadelphia when she tried to excuse Essex's folly. But for Charles to take a knife and cut the paper apart ... My lord Essex needs cutting down to size all right, but not like that. And then Charles had to go and write to Cecil that he wanted to resign his charge and only serve her majesty as one of the common soldiery. Cecil will damp it down, thank God, but some whisper will get through, and while half of me wants to be cheering Charles on, the cautious side knows better. We know what can happen to the ambitious, in my family. Ambitious women, especially.

Maybe it's just as well that I am here at court, to limit any damage there may be. But oh, I can't wait to be at my house at Chelsea, where the pear blossom will be green-white against the wall and the birds will be coming back with the spring to wheel above the river. My house, with the silver that would once have graced an abbot's table and some of the fine tapestries my father has given to me. A better house than my sister Philadelphia got with her husband; Lord Scrope's northern castle may reek of ancient nobility, but don't tell me it isn't draughty, whatever work they did there in her mother-in-law's day. My house in Chelsea, that the queen granted to me, directly. Other women in this world can only make their way by marriage, but I already had a position to bring my husband, like another dowry, on my wedding day.

One of the younger maids comes scuttling round the doorway. The queen is calling for me. As I approach she looks up from her writing desk with a smile like sunshine, one of those smiles for which one would forgive her anything. She beckons me over, and displays with a flourish the paper before her. It's a letter she is composing, to Essex, and I brace myself, momentarily.

'I make this humble bill of requests to Him that all makes and does, that with His benign Hand He will shadow you ... Let your companion, my most faithful Charles, be sure that his name is not left out in this petition.'

'My most faithful Charles,' she repeats, extending her hand to me, and obediently I bend to kiss it as I sink down into a curtsey.

Jeanne

Summer 1596

The summer agues came badly this year. Many fell sick and died between dawn and dinner time the same day. Yet Jacob had seemed much as usual, grumbling over the news from court, and the cost of kitting out Lord Essex's sally against the Spanish, all in the name of foolish glory. I thought nothing of it when he complained of the heat one morning; it would indeed be a warm day. I was out all morning, delivering documents he'd completed, and when I came back in, Mrs Allen turned a tear-blotched face to me. They had sent for the physician, she said, but ... I brushed past her and went to where he was lying on the bed. He didn't look afraid, he looked angry. His breath began to rattle before the doctor arrived, and an hour later he was dead.

I told Mrs Allen to go home, and I was alone in the front room when the shop door opened and a solid, florid-faced man came in. I knew him, he was Master Pointer, a nursery gardener, who put a lot of work our way. He was talking of business and I gazed at him stupidly. I felt death should have put a mark on the door. When I told him the news he was genuinely sorry, but after a moment I realised he was sounding me.

With Jacob gone – what a loss, his deepest sympathy – what would my own plans be? He would still need someone to deal with his letters, someone who knew the names of the plants, and he was sure many of Jacob's other clients would feel the same way. Of course, of course, it wasn't the moment … But we understood each other before, with a squeeze of the hand, he left me. The past and the future were bleeding into each other, and it was making me dizzy.

We buried Jacob quickly, as the law required, and I was touched at how many came out, with the sickness all around, to pay their respects. They all spoke to me with kindness, but I wasn't sure I understood their sympathy. I'd had my great sorrow in the Netherlands, a decade before. No one ever spoke to me of that, and I'd learned to lock it away. Now this new frost of loss fell on ground already frozen: I would mourn Jacob, but not too deeply. He'd have understood that – like me, since the Netherlands, he'd kept part of himself locked tight away, and I'd never presumed to give him more affection than he was happy to accept from me.

I owed him as great a debt as one human being can owe another, and never to try to grow too close was the only way I could pay. Children understand these things instinctively. Now, as an adult, or something near to it, I understood that the framework of my life had changed, but that I was not wounded in myself, or no worse wounded than I had been already.

He left me all that he had. Forty pounds – I was amazed, but we had always lived frugally. I'd have to quit the house, of course, but I'd be able to find rooms easily. The officials of the borough came to see me, since I'd not reached legal maturity, but were only too ready to accept there was no need to worry.

Mrs Allen came to help me move out, and I thought she was looking at me curiously. It was only later that I realised she'd half felt she should offer a home to me. It had never occurred to me, and the idea withered unspoken away. But on the last day, as we said goodbye, she seemed again to be struggling with what to say.

'Remember, in this world, a woman does whatever she has to do to get by. *Whatever* she has to do,' she said at last, and it was with an unexpected pang I watched the back of her plump worsted figure walk rapidly away.

I found myself doing a strange thing the following Sunday. The lease of our little garden would end with Jacob's death, and I had to go there to find the caretaker and hand back the key. But before I did that, I set to work, as though he were beside me. I clipped the hedges and cut back the herbs, selecting the strongest to leave for seed. I sowed carrots and beet as though I'd be the one to eat them next year; searched out the seedling of the cowslips and bear's ears and transplanted them carefully. The double daisies had been Jacob's favourite and, when I left, Heaven knows why, I took a pot of them with me. I clutched them to the chest of my boy's doublet as I walked through streets ringing with the news of Lord Essex's great sea victory, and realised that for the first time the news, the crowds, the little decisions of every day were things to which I would answer as myself, and no longer as Jacob's protégé.

Cecil

Autumn 1596

I felt sorry for Essex, briefly. He had come back from the sea aglow with victory. He and Charles Howard had planted England's flag on the Continent again, in a way we never hoped to see, the King of Spain's fleet smashed at Cadiz so that Calais itself was freed as a sideshow, or nearly. I remember and salute Charles' joint command of the campaign, but that's something Essex himself will have managed to forget quite easily.

He'd landed on the south coast and ridden to court, so hot foot he was lame from a fall along the way. Instead of the hero's welcome he expected, he found the queen dressing him down before every giggling maid and gawping serving man, for all the world like an errant schoolboy.

Why, in his vainglorious pride in victory, had he let the Spanish treasure fleet sail by unmolested? Why, having once taken Cadiz, had he simply sailed away? What became of the fifty thousand pounds his exploits had cost her majesty, and where was the recompense to be? I could see the red creeping up under the square beard – a folly, that, it will never please her – his lordship had grown on the voyage home, and I could hear the queen's voice cracking with fury.

The irony is, it wasn't Essex's fault, or not entirely. Not in the short term, anyway. Fast as he had ridden to the court, we'd had a faster report from a serving man on board: he'd wanted to go hunting for the treasure fleet but the other, more experienced, commanders had brushed his views away. Commanders like Ralegh: now he'll know how to make a gain from Essex's disgrace, and another from selling his share of the booty.

Of course we won't say as much, or not precisely. But I believe my father will try to calm the queen's displeasure. We take the long view, naturally.

It is a great task, at court, to prove one's honesty, and yet not spoil one's fortune, and the role of peacemaker befits an honest man. Even my father won't succeed in curbing the queen's rage: already, she's declaring she'll have no victory celebrations in this city. But when the real facts of the Cadiz debates seep out, as in the end they will, the queen will remember that we Cecils did not attack her favourite (still, her favourite?) too bitterly. And Essex will bask in her favour again, and being Essex he will boast of his favour, immoderately. The suitors will clamour for his voice to the queen, and he will clamour for their requests, loudly. And every voice that huzzas him in the streets will come to fret her majesty.

'Men of depth are held suspect by princes. There is no virtue but has its shade, wherewith the minds of kings are offended.' So says my clever cousin Bacon: clever in everything except his conviction that he will be able to steer my lord Essex into prudence and make his own career that way.

Princes fear, Bacon says, that clever men may be able to manipulate them, popular men may overshadow them. Brave men are too turbulent and honest men too inflexible. Who – I asked him once – are the men that will thrive? If he'd ever stop to listen, I could have given him the answer. The men who make the prince's problems go away. They'll thrive. Well, for a time, at least.

Bacon urges Lord Essex to courtiers' ways. Never complain of past injuries. Never stand on your dignity – you have none, compared to her majesty. Learn the subtle ways of flattery – invent a pressing reason to visit your estates, then cancel the proposed journey on the grounds that you can't bear to be away. Study her majesty's moods and trim your suits accordingly, and don't disdain the advice of those most close to her, even if it's only the maid who's waiting by the door when they take her chamber pot to empty.

This to Essex, who has a hundred moods of his own and can't master any. Can't even dissemble them successfully. Who has

never understood that his virtues may become vices to the
queen, who mistrusts a soldier because a battlefield is the only
field where she cannot lead her country. Her majesty has always
made her weaknesses into virtues: look at the way she, a spinster,
held every prince in Europe in thrall to her very availability.

At first, Essex's follies charmed the queen – his passionate
conviction, his inability to flatter, his impetuosity. But now? He
is blamed for his insatiable pride: but without his pride who
would he be? Who would he see, when he looks in the mirror
each day? Not that he does look in a mirror frequently, if that
beard is anything to go by. With his pride, how long can he
survive? It is a matter that has to be decided, a question not only
of policy, but practicality.

Jeanne

Autumn 1596

I'd found a room easily enough, and a decent one too, fires and
laundry included. There was a dent in the wall where the last
tenant had made the bedstead rock, but it was no dirtier than it
might be. The landlady sniffed when I ran my finger over the
cupboard checking for dust, and said young gentlemen weren't
usually so pernickety. So I put a touch of accent into my voice
and said that in my country we were used to having things clean,
and I heard her going down the stairs and muttering 'damn
Frenchies'. Her little brown-and-white dog stayed behind a
moment, wagging at me curiously.

With Jacob I had always lived up on the northern fringes of
London, but now I had chosen a street near Blackfriars, hard up
by the City's walls, not far from the western suburbs and the
great palaces on the Strand – not that I imagined, then, they'd
concern me directly. It seemed a world away from our old home,
but it still had enough immigrants in it for safety.

I swept the landlady an exaggerated foreign bow and went out to buy myself some necessities. Candles enough to write by, a painted cloth to cover the marks in the wall, a posy of marjoram and lavender to take the mustiness away. At the nearest cookstall I bought a pasty, big enough I could share it with the dog, and an orange, and a small flask of Rhenish, and went home and called myself happy.

Well, content.

Well, lucky.

Yes, by comparison with those I'd known – and those I saw on the street around me – definitely lucky.

The work, and the money, were the easy part, oddly. For that I have Master Pointer to thank, and my thoughts do thank him every day. He first sent for me before Jacob had been buried three days. He did it with apologies, but his affairs, he explained, were at that point where he had to take the turn of the tide or else … I warmed to him, not only because he took trouble to explain to me, but because something in his urgency, his hot desire to catch the tide of the times, raised an answering warmth in me. I soon learned that while simple fruit trees and hedgings might be the core of his business, he was passionate about new plants and opportunities, and sold slips and seedlings to many of the nobility. It was no strange thing, of a Sunday, to see ladies and gentlemen strolling around his gardens out at Twickenham to inspect the latest rarity. Once, I even saw the stooping figure of Sir Robert Cecil, leading by the hand two small children, as grave and as slight as he.

'Look at this! Look at this, Master Moosay!' – this was Master Pointer's version of Musset. I peered at two small, rather hairy, leaves which he assured me would soon sprout a flower the like of which had only been seen in the palaces before, but would soon be in every garden. The goal, I learnt, was novelty – novelty, and the charm of bloom when no bloom used to be.

'Think of it, we'll soon have borders as bright in August as they are in May.' Though some of the new plants, from lands far beyond the sea, came direct to England, others went first to the growers in the Netherlands or Italy, whom he regarded with a blend of comradeship and envy. With a few such, he had struck up a deal, but to keep it going required a skill in languages beyond him. That is what Jacob had done; that I could do easily. I'd been working for Master Pointer a few weeks when he found I had another useful ability.

From a child I'd loved to draw, though with Jacob it was always the words and the thought behind them that would be taken most seriously. But one day, Master Pointer was labouring to dictate me a description of a seedling – 'two leaves like heart shapes, spring direct from the stem, and veined like – like – like the ribs of a ship?'

'No, it's more like this, surely?' Hastily I sketched out what I meant, and he gazed at me thoughtfully.

'I didn't know you could do that,' he said. From that time on, his catalogues went out with my line drawings, printed from etched blocks of wood, and kindly, he said that it increased his sales. He said it was a lucky chance that had shown him my skill. But I think Master Pointer was one of those men in whose genial warm presence people, like plants, did understand their capabilities.

Cecil

Spring 1597

I always knew the meal was never going to agree with me. They don't keep good cooks at Essex House: for all his grandeur, his lordship is served but carelessly. I don't suppose he even noticed – from a boy, I remember him just cramming what was in front of him into his mouth, and that only when the waiting men nudged him that they wanted to take the plates away. Gulping down the mouthful with his eyes fixed where his speech was directed, intent on winning your response to whatever he was trying to say. I doubt Ralegh cared for the food either, though I saw him drinking deep.

But then none of us were there for our stomach's sake, were we?

The puzzle of the court is how one day's enemy is the next day's friend: more unexpected, surely, than a friend lapsing into enemy? My clever cousin Bacon says 'love your friend as if he were to become an enemy, and hate your enemy as if he were to become your friend': he was so proud of the thought, he showed the letter to me. Does even he know what he means, I wondered. I have become more irritable since Lizzie –

His mother, my aunt Anne, told her sons when they first came to court that anyone who spoke them fair was doing it to serve their turn. 'He that never trusteth is never deceived.' 'It is better to suspect too soon than to mislike too late.' 'As a wolf resembles a dog, so does a flatterer a friend.' 'Don't write letters that can be held against you, don't speak without looking to see who can hear, and then not openly.' I get impatient with the flood of warning sometimes, even though I have forged my career by following the maxims attentively. They translated the sayings of Erasmus in my grandfather's day: 'It is wisdom in prosperity when all is as thou would have it, to fear and suspect the worst.' What, are we never to be happy?

Lizzie and I were happy.

The strange thing is that Essex's father was as full of good advice as mine, or as Lady Anne: I suppose we all react differently to the medicine. Now it's Ralegh penning advice for his son. Which is why he was here tonight, in a way – Ralegh needs both our help if he is ever to get back his captaincy of the Guards. The queen has never forgiven him for having run off with one of her maids of honour, and less so than ever now that they've started a family.

Essex needs all the help he can get, too, if he's to persuade her majesty to finance another voyage against the Spanish. And I?

Well, it's true there's the business of the Duchy of Lancaster. The chancellor's post would come easier if no one were opposing me too actively.

And of course, I am committed, always, to seek unity: I must send to Charles Howard tomorrow, make sure he understands there is no threat to him in this rapprochement with Essex. He's doing an Achilles at the moment, still baffled that the people see Essex as the sole hero of Cadiz, but his wife is a lady shrewd enough to ensure he doesn't sulk in his tent too long.

All the same, as I climb into the litter for the brief ride home, the old black mood sweeps over me. The whole question of the chancellorship of the Duchy wouldn't be so tetchy if we hadn't been there already with the Court of Wards, but Lizzie was so pleased when we won it for her brother, in the teeth of Essex's man …

Lizzie.

Two months, almost to the day, since the doctors told me there was nothing they could do, and I had to open the bedroom door and go inside to meet her eye. I have spent a lifetime dissembling, but I couldn't do it this time. In the end, it was she told me, with the ghost of her old briskness, we had a lot to agree together, and not to cry. She wanted the children brought up away from the bad airs of the town. She did not say, away from the corruption of the court, and from a father who has to wallow in it every day, but it's true they're better off at my brother's in the country.

She said when I wanted her I was to go into the garden, and there by the good grace of God she would find me. She said if God didn't want to allow it she'd be having a word with him. She made me laugh, even then, actually. I went to the garden this morning, to Lizzie's favourite rose tree. It's covered in leaf shoots of stinging green – not long till the first buds are on the way. I gripped its trunk so hard, I was glad when the thorns pricked me. Oh, Lizzie.

Back to the business: it's one thing she said to me then. 'Work will be your salvation. You'll see.' Give me the work, spare me the sympathy. I cannot take the sympathy, although Charles for one wrote very kindly. I really feel something like friendship for Charles, beyond even the alliance of necessity.

This thing with Essex won't hold, of course it won't, but we can probably get Ralegh his captaincy. I say 'we', but in truth the queen may give it less because it is Essex who requests it than because she wants a firmer hold on one of Essex's allies. It would never do if he and he alone held the loyalty of all the fighting men. Essex will probably get the money for his new Spanish voyage: the queen will hate it as much as I do, but it is needed.

Whether he'll get her gratitude for whatever he brings home will be another story. Be sure that any news of her displeasure will be for my father or I to carry. It is our job, but it will fuel the fire of Essex's suspicion, as if any fuel were needed.

Even Ralegh writes: 'Whoso taketh in hand to frame any state or government ought to presuppose that all men are evil, and at occasions will show themselves to be so.' The face of treachery is the devil's face, in the form we see among us every day. But Essex spends his life peering through the bushes to trace the devil's grin in the bark of an old tree. He knows every man is against him: in the end, they will be. I suppose it is his way of imposing order on the world. Less frightening, perhaps, than knowing his failure, like his success, is his own responsibility. As we pull up, the thought sends me into the house even more lonely.

Jeanne

Summer 1597

I wasn't unhappy in the next year or so, or not precisely. Master Pointer's was a kindly family, and his wife thought I was young to be alone in the world. I did not, unless I chose it, need to dine alone of a Sunday. And Master Pointer introduced me, carefully, to some of his gardening friends, always on the understanding that his work came first, that I was his discovery. But sometimes as I sat around the well-stocked table, a wave of unreality swept over me, and I watched them as wonderingly as I had watched, once, when a cousin of Mrs Allen's had taken us to see the wild beasts in the Tower menagerie.

What had these people to do with the past I'd known? What had they to do with my real identity? Even if it hadn't been for my secret, I'd had a family once, and look what happened. The way I lived was the only safe way. And dear God, where was this closeness going to end – with the suggestion I might marry one of their friendly daughters, and bring my skills into the family? And the next Sunday I'd make excuse, say I had to see an old friend, though in truth I would spend the day alone, wandering round all the gardens of London.

The gardens were my salvation, you might say – lucky there were so many. But the gardens were my danger, too, with their siren song of what might be. Master Pointer sold plants to many of the grandees, and he made sure that sometimes I went along with the delivery, to walk around and increase my knowledge as much as might be.

'They won't mind – they'll be flattered someone wants to admire their taste. Show them one of your drawings if they query you,' he said shrewdly. I remember a garden by the London Wall, close to sunset one late June day. A gardener was settling the new plants in, as tenderly as if they'd been new babies. The light had sunk to that low pitch when the blues sing clearly, and the yellow in the leaves makes each flowerbed a mirror of the sky on a sunny day. The roses were almost over, but a hint of their scent hung under the honeysuckle, and the air had cooled just enough to make you nostalgic for the morning's heat. It was an evening for the touch and laughter, and dreams. For lovers … For a heartbeat, I almost felt the touch of skin on skin, and here was I, walking alone with a scrap of paper and a stick of charcoal, exploring a business opportunity.

That's where I understood that some change had to come. That however lucky I'd been to survive so far, survival was not enough for me. That I couldn't go on forever, like some lying ghost, haunting the fringes of some happy ordinary family; and nor could I push myself into the ranks of the plantsmen in my present identity.

I couldn't just step back; I'd been Jan too long, and there was no way for Jeanne to live and make money. As a woman alone and without family – a woman neither child nor wife nor widow – there would be no place for me. I'd still be a freak, an anomaly.

I couldn't see the way to change clearly, and yet change there had to be. And as I walked ever faster in the golden light, staring without seeing at the heartsease pansies, the thought of that Accession Day came back to me.

Every one of the great lords was a garden maker. Apart from anything else, it was known to be one way to the heart of the queen's majesty. And Master Pointer sold plants to many of the grandees, but there was one family who truly loved their gardens. Time was, Lord Burghley had competed with the old earl, Lord Leicester, as to who could make the most dazzling fantasy. When Master Pointer spoke of the experiments at Theobalds, Lord Burghley's country showplace, he did so with a glow of purest envy. Lord Leicester was long dead, and Lord Essex who had inherited his great house on the river had no name for being a plantsman, hadn't the money for it, maybe. And Lord Burghley was failing, and begging the queen every day to let him retire. But his son Robert Cecil also loved a garden – a fair amateur of plants, said Master Pointer, respectfully.

The Pointers spoke of the nobles with a kind of familiarity. The summer Jacob died, I'd heard that Lord Essex had led a great expedition against the Spanish at Cadiz, and that Master Cecil had been made Secretary of State, and heard of them as things outside my own life. Now, for the first time, I began to wonder if, in that wider world, there might not be a tiny chink of a place for me.

The Cecils had a town house too, of course. Great tubs of the sharp Seville orange trees went there in bloom, once Master Pointer had nursed them through the winter, and the new nasturtiums with their hot colour, and the latest strain of auriculas, striped and pinked like a town buck on May Day.

A stream of gossip fed back in return, and though Mistress Pointer wanted to hear about the family, it was their garden plans that gripped her husband. I learned that Sir Robert used his contacts beyond the seas to send him the newest seeds or slips from foreign nurseries. Master Pointer spoke longingly of great books he'd been shown in Sir Robert's library, 'Ay, and he said he'd be having them translated, so I could read them too, one day. God's breath, the Italians know a thing or two – did I tell you the tricks they play with water, they've a few toys like that at Theobalds, as well – but for my money, if it's the plants you're looking for, you still go to the damn Frenchies. No offence, lad,' he'd add belatedly.

I'd never forgotten the little dark statesman who, at the joust, had taken insult so quietly. I found thoughts of that day were coming more frequently. Since I'd moved to Blackfriars, I saw the court crowds in the streets every day: young men whose clothes were stiff with embroidery, once the queen's fool and once one of her ladies, in a misty blue gown trimmed with silver lace. They gave me the sense I'd had sometimes when I went down to the river and looked at the sky – a sense the world was larger than it seemed to be, and with more varied possibilities.

I could no more have approached one of those swans than I could fly. But the ugly duckling with the damaged wing, the sober man of work who did the queen's business night and day – well, given Master Pointer's connections, a move towards him might just be a possibility.

It was a September day and in the orchard the apples were ripening, while the heavy pear-shaped quinces perfumed the air around them. The emblem of happiness, I thought – I was young enough for superstition – and after all, what was I going to do that was so extraordinary? Only go with Master Pointer's men when they took the pots of lavender held back from blooming early, and report to him how the vines he'd sold to the Cecils were fruiting, and see whether the new hazels were thriving in the nuttery.

It would be the purest chance if Sir Robert actually spoke to me, even if he did happen to be walking in the garden, as he did frequently. And if I did take my sheaf of sketches with me – well, nothing in that, surely?

Burghley House was a rambling comfortable building on the north side of the Strand, poised between the palace at Whitehall and the City, opposite the old Savoy. Kings had lived there once, but today its grandeurs were in ruins, while a poorhouse camped in the wreckage. The rich, odorous stew that was a London crowd grew even thicker and more exotic as one drew near, for all that the Strand held the palaces of the nobility. Deep-water sailors from distant countries eyeing liveried men at arms, cutpurses skirting the ordinary citizens just trying to get through the working day. No wonder Burghley House showed the street a long line of thick brick walls, with only three small windows to break their solidity. The Cecils were still near the people – of them, in a way – and this was a bustling place of business as much as a gentleman's private residence, but that didn't mean they took stupid risks.

A porter's lodge stood in the middle of the wall, but Master Pointer's men turned into another gateway. To the west of the house, the palace side, lay the service quarters and the vegetable beds, and the back way up to another arched gate which led out to the north and the open spaces of Convent Garden, where the monks or their servants used to tend their own beds and orchards in the old days. I walked and I wondered, along clipped hedges and gravelled pathways. I was on Master Pointer's business, wasn't I? And in any case, the afternoon would have encouraged an anchorite to linger.

The grass had its brightness back, after the summer drought, and the soft warm light brought out the reds and greens, making a little miracle out of the trees. In its plan perhaps the garden wasn't as modern as it might be. I could feel the taste of old Lord Burghley. But it had still its element of fantasy. A mound rose up from a sunken garden, a man-made hollow and a man-made hill, and the winding path up to the summit guided your feet clearly. The plants themselves were extraordinary. One great flower had been left to form a seed head more than the spread of my hand across, and I was drawing it for Master Pointer when I sensed a presence beside me.

He was alone, but he must have moved lightly – his feet on the gravel made no sound as he approached. He was dressed in black – we'd heard that his wife had died recently, for I remember eager talk about whether it would be appropriate for the Pointers to send a gift in sympathy.

Perhaps that accounted for the lines that already showed on his face, but I suspect they came there naturally. It was the eyes that struck me, cool and grey under high arched brows.

He held out his hand. 'May I see?'

Dumbly, I passed over my sheaf of drawings, barely remembering to jerk down into a bow, and he leafed through the pages, those brows raising slightly.

'Impressive. Do you work for Master Pointer? In what capacity?' He gestured me to fall in with him as he walked on. 'My constitutional. If I'm taking you from your art, you must forgive me.' He knew I'd come in his way on purpose, of course, but he was a polite man – polite in his soul – and he didn't let the knowledge intrude.

As he walked he questioned me – my skills, my situation – and I answered him with a sense of inevitability, so completely had it fallen out as I had dreamed it. Though it was my penmanship first caught his eye, it was my languages that seemed to interest him most. He'd ask me for the names of plants in French and Flemish, as well as Latin, as we passed by. He spoke to me of the great plant hunters from earlier in the century, of Turner and Gesner and of Mattioli before them, and of who was like to take up the mantle of Plantin in Antwerp, now that his great printing centre under the sign of the golden compasses had passed away. He spoke of his own commission to John Gerard, the surgeon and collector who'd had the ordering of the Cecil gardens, to produce the first great English Herbal in almost half a century. I was devoutly thankful to Jacob, and to all the evenings, since his death, I'd spent in solitary study.

'I may be able to find a use for you, Master – de Musset?' Of course he pronounced it correctly. 'If Master Pointer can spare you, naturally. Come and see my steward tomorrow.'

When I went back next day, I didn't see the steward, I saw Sir Robert himself. But I was then too new to the game to realise that was extraordinary.

Cecil

Summer 1597

I walk in the garden more and more these days – even when it's wet, even when it's too hot for comfort. It's the only thing that makes the pain go away. Well, not go away, but step back a single pace, still snarling, like a dog when you pick up a stick and wave it menacingly. Round the beds, like a soldier on a route march, ticking off the success or failure of each plant in my head, like nature's own litany. Rosemary for remembrance, the last seed heads of the heartsease pansy … Lizzie would give my bad arm that little shake that seemed to loosen more than it hurt me and tell me I was a secret sentimentalist, for all the rest of them thought I was so canny.

Lizzie.

I'm not alone in the garden this time, though usually the gardeners absent themselves now. I suppose one of the secretaries has tipped them off, tactfully. There's a boy – at least, he looks no more than a stripling, brown-haired and neat, without being finicky. He's standing in front of the Marvel of Peru, and he has a paper and a stick of charcoal in his hand, but from a certain self-conscious stiffness in his stance, I know he's waiting for me.

I would have gone over anyway. Always know everything that's happening in your household – and for your household, read the whole country, or as much of it as you can manage. That's another thing my father taught me. And, never ignore any thing that comes to you. You never know where you'll find an opportunity.

I hold out my hand for the paper he is working on. 'May I see?'

He hands over his sheaf of drawings, silently.

'Impressive. Do you work for Master Pointer? In what capacity?' I gesture him to fall in with me. As we walk I question him, and I believe he answers me honestly. There is something held back, of course, there always is. If there weren't, he would be too simple to be of much use to me, and I can use him – on the garden records, certainly. New plants are arriving every day. Gerard's indisposition is likely to be lengthy, so the physicians say, and it would be a crying shame if our records were to remain incomplete, and his book left with only English eyes to admire it. I ask the boy for the names of plants in French and Italian as we pass by. He speaks Flemish too, which is less ordinary. It only takes two sentences for him to tell me why.

It carries me back ten years to that first journey, my first taste of a diplomatic mission, and me barely past twenty. I'd gone to the Netherlands in an older man's train, to see if Parma could be bought off, with the great Armada on the way. It hadn't worked – no one ever thought it was likely to – but the time bought was something. What I remember most wasn't the negotiations, nor even the hard riding that made my shoulder ache, but the inns where they served up half a herring as a feast, and then stood around to watch as we ate it, and the miserable state of the country. That was when I truly understood that peace in a land matters more than anything. That it is worth dying for – or arranging others' deaths, if necessary.

I should like to help this boy, apart even from the question of his use to me. Never dismiss your kindly impulses – they can be as useful as any other, so my father used to say. My father used to do a lot of saying, before age made him as twisted as me, as twisted as Lizzie just before she –

'Come see my steward tomorrow,' I tell the boy. Pointer won't make any trouble – he'll understand the value of a friend at court, to make sure all the Cecil business doesn't go any other firm's way.

There's a discreet bustle by the house. I've dallied too long, and someone needs me. I set my shoulders as I turn back – as set as my shoulders are able to be. I will take our business off my father's hands where necessary, and when business fails me, I will keep my mind firmly fixed on the trivialities. The gardeners should be getting the seeds in now, if we're to eat green vegetables again before May: folly to say you can't plant before spring, just because that's how it was done in their grandfather's day.

But sometimes I think that the two weights, my work and my grief, will be enough to crush me. Now, though, there's the faintest breath of relief – a tickle, at the corner of my mind's eye. I'm not sure what it was but there was something – something about that boy.

PART II

I am melancholy, merry, sometimes happy and often
unfortunate. The court is of as many humours as the
rainbow hath colours, the time wherein we live more
inconstant than women's thoughts, more miserable than
old age itself and breeding both people and occasions
that is violent, desperate and fantastical.

Letter from Robert Devereux, Earl of Essex,
to his sister Penelope

We princes are set on highest stage, where looks of all
beholders verdict our works; neither can we easily dance
in nets so thick as may dim their sight.

Letter from Elizabeth I to James VI of Scotland

Jeanne

Autumn 1597

'You won't be needing livery – the secretaries don't. Just wear something neat, dark and discreet. No ruffs,' the steward added, sharply. I nodded, as if curbing an inclination to finery, though the truth was I was only too glad to be let off an accessory that would have to go to an expensive laundress every few days.

'Here – you might want to take this, though. You'll find it's something of a passport.' It was a metal cloak badge with the Cecil crest, and as I pinned it on I felt at the same time a small tug of vexed pride, and a tiny glow of warmth. It seemed I had not just accepted a post, I had joined a community.

That had been six weeks ago, and I was finding I liked this new sense of family. I'd kept my own room in Blackfriars for the nights, of course. It wasn't as if sharing with three other young male clerks was really a possibility. But I found that more and more often I was getting up early in the morning to walk along Fleet Street and break my fast in the hall at Burghley House, not just for the fine white manchet bread the steward occasionally let slip to our table, but for the company.

I suppose I'd always assumed that I'd stick out like a sore thumb in any group I tried to join, but on the clerk's table everyone was an oddity. There was one old man, with his delicate small paws and twitching mouse's face, kept on for the beauty of his calligraphy. There was one gangling youngster with a lantern jaw and spluttering speech, who read seven languages fluently. There were two silent watchful men who rarely spoke of the day's business, though one had a passion for part singing and the other for archery, and they carried an air of warning about them. The music lover was one of the best breakers of cipher in the country, I was told quietly.

Not all the business in the Burghley household was open for all to see. But there was nothing secret about the job laid down for me, in between the routine tasks I'd be given, translating and transcribing whatever was necessary. All the world knew that Master Gerard was about to publish his great Herbal, and dedicate it to Lord Burghley. This was my first chance to read it, in the original copy, and of course I did so avidly. Some of its information seemed strange to me – I'd heard Jacob and the other herbalists speak of Gerard's work before, and not always kindly – but Master Pointer had said that such a book, and written not in Latin but in the vernacular tongue, would be a great help to the industry. And Gerard's vivid descriptions of the yellow loosestrife in the meadows towards Battersea, of the kidney vetch growing on Hampstead Heath, brought plant-hunting expeditions with Jacob back to me.

But Master Gerard's health was poor at the moment and, as new plants arrived every month from abroad to be added to the records of the Cecil gardens, he couldn't get out to sketch them easily, or to quiz the gardeners about their care. What's more, Sir Robert had no intention of letting this new light of knowledge shine only in his own country. The Herbal was to be translated and finely bound up, with coloured illustrations and new additions wherever necessary, and then sent out to foreign dignitaries; a minor tool of diplomacy. It was a specialised task, which set me a little apart from the rest of the under-secretaries, just as surely as the small closet, with its window over the garden for a clear light, where I was allowed to spread my paints and papers.

I felt so spoiled I was almost scared of it – half drunk with the freedom to borrow any book from the great library. For the first time in my life, in fabulous hand-tinted editions, I saw the plants from foreign countries spring to life in shades of saffron, cinnabar and verdigris. Maybe it was because Sir Robert's rule over the household was so complete that I suffered no open signs of envy. Or maybe mine was a private pleasure, and the others didn't envy me.

Sometimes I thought of Jacob, and wished that he could see me. Sometimes I thought what Jacob would say, if he could see the Herbal: I knew Master de l'Obel had begun to correct Master Gerard's work, before its author took it back, indignantly; and truth to tell I wondered, I did wonder, when I read his description of how the barnacle geese that flock here each year spring from the shells shed by a Scottish tree. But in our age of marvels it might be foolish to query – it would certainly be foolhardy. I bent my head to the translation, industriously.

I was sent to make my bow to Master Gerard, of course – in this house they did things courteously. His brief glance made it clear he wouldn't expect to be seeing too much of me, but if he felt any resentment, he didn't show it. The only person in the house who seemed openly to disapprove of me was the nominal master himself, old Lord Burghley. He wasn't there all the time – everyone knew that for years he'd been begging her majesty to let him retire, and that his greatest pleasure now was to ride around Theobalds, his country estate, on a mule, or to sit and watch his gardeners from the shade of a tree. But sometimes I would hear the clunk of his stick, and turn to see his small eyes fixed on me. Like a lot of old people, he had the habit of talking to himself aloud and once, 'I suppose Robert knows what he's doing,' I heard, as he glared at me.

I ventured to mention it to the old clerk. 'Don't worry,' he said, twisting his hands below his pointed face, so that I almost expected to see whiskers twitching above a grain of corn, 'he's like that with everybody.' And even for Lord Burghley, it seemed, in the end it was enough that Sir Robert had a purpose for me – just how good or useful a one would become clear eventually.

Katherine, Lady Howard, Countess of Nottingham

October 1597

There are patches of time when too much seems to happen, so that in the end you feel punch-drunk, like a cheap fighter in the ring at the end of fair day. It was only yesterday, the twenty-third, that the queen paused on her way back from chapel, and handed to my husband the patent that made him Earl of Nottingham – and me the countess, naturally.

Of course we knew that it was coming – the queen herself had been in a little ripple of amusement when she beckoned me to walk to chapel with her that day. But even so there is something about the moment: I couldn't step from my place in the queen's train to be beside my husband, but after so many years of marriage, I could still feel his joy. The ceremony was all it should have been – I wished my father were alive to see. He once said these things were the nearest a gentleman could get to the drama, and of course he loved a play, and players – Lord Hunsdon and his Lord Chamberlain's Company.

The earls of Shrewsbury and Worcester presented Charles, Sussex bore the cup and the shiny new coronet, Pembroke lent his robes and Robert Cecil read aloud the patent he had drafted, with a convincing gravity. Time was, no doubt, when any Howard would have been glad to see a Cecil done down, when we'd have stared at the idea of any friendship between these jumped-up pen gents and the old nobility. But one must try to move with the times, and new enemies make new allies. And of course these days, it's hard to tell who is the old nobility. Look at my family – which means her majesty's. And Robert Cecil, unlike others I could name, has always behaved with respect towards my husband and I.

So the next morning should have been good, and ordinary, surely? Maybe I would have had a chance to enjoy my new honours, maybe I would have gone around the court a little, to savour the greater depth of the bows that greeted me. Maybe – for one has, after all, experience in this world – I would, underneath, have felt a little flat, as often one can do after the event, but I'd sent for my sister Philadelphia and surely, at the very least, I could have enjoyed having her see me in my day of glory – she may have been grabbing everyone's attention ever since she was in the nursery, and her husband may be the tenth Lord Scrope, but he isn't an earl, and entitled to wear the purple, is he?

Well, enough of that. Everything was in train for my husband to preside over the new session of Parliament today. Instead what happens? A galloping messenger to say Lord Essex's ship has been sighted off Plymouth, so we'll have him trying to explain his latest folly, and trying to take the gloss off our new honours in any way he may. Oh yes, and as if that weren't enough, they say a Spanish fleet is once again on the way.

Of course the two things are tied together. Essex's job was to smash the Spanish fleet in the harbour, and ensure our safety. Instead he sets off on a wild-goose chase, all around the seas.

For Essex to disregard his orders is no new story. Sometimes when I reckon up his transgressions, I am frightened at the tally. None of the others, not even his stepfather, would have dared break the rules so frequently and I cannot help worrying, as on a sore tooth, at how the queen has let him do it with impunity. Whether her indulgence has become a habit, whether it's that his battle cry seems to sound with the voice of half the young men at the court, and the sheer clamour makes her weary? Whether, even, the noise makes her doubt her own judgement or whether – my mind just touches on the thought – there is (was? is) something about his young man's urgency? Something she allows herself to feel, and just for a breath I remember a time when feeling seemed easy.

Anyway, as any politician knows, the outcome is half the story: oh, you don't get to be queen's lady all these years without being a politician, in your heart. Essex was to have gone after Spanish treasure, yes, but only after he had destroyed the Spanish ships in their harbour. Then again, if the fleet had failed to sail, as fleets had failed before, if the treasure had proved rich, then maybe he would have been forgiven, even by the queen, though I for one would have kept the tally. Instead we have still a fleet to face, and barely a groat of prize money.

I knew it was bad when the boy came so early to say Burghley himself was waiting to see her majesty. He's an old man now, and you wake early as you get old, but to face the day is another story. I knew it was bad, since he was here so that Robert wouldn't have to be. Bad news rubs off on the man who brings it, and it's only when you've been together as long as Burghley and the queen that you acquire a measure of immunity.

We sent word the queen would see him as soon as we'd dressed her, but he'd have known as well as I do that wouldn't happen quickly. She sat still while we adjusted her wig, and pointed out where the white paint on her chest was looking patchy: I had the feeling she was jibbing, like a nervous horse, at having to face what might come this day. She made us try on three different gowns, until I for one could have screamed with the tension, but I think she put on strength with the finery. She signed me to stay as the girls left, and Burghley gave me a terse nod as he came in.

It was brusquely, almost with a sense of familiarity, that he said a dispatch had come in and that all the rumours are true, another Armada really is on the way. We had, after all, been here before – what, three times since that first appalling time, since Leicester's death, since Tilbury? I swear, the first thing I felt was pure exasperation. Dear God, does Philip never learn? If he's so sure he's doing God's work, does he never ask himself why God's winds don't allow him to succeed, once in a while?

But of course it's serious, it has to be taken seriously. The more so for the fact that every year, every false alarm, tires us as much as it must tire the poor starved and taxed Spanish peasantry. We have more ships than we had before Tilbury, but we also have less energy. And all I could think is, why now? Why couldn't they, why couldn't fate, have just given these few days to me? As we pace the Privy Garden so fast the girls hustle to keep up with her majesty, I am in a bustle of anger that makes the crisp October air seem hot to me. I'll admit that stupidity has always irritated me, even with my children when they were young.

If these messages are true, Spain's fleet will be on the seas by now, while Essex let their treasure ship pass by, full of bullion from the Americas, through a sheer stupid piece of vainglory. It's the thought of that bullion that'll be working in the queen, making her anger rise up like bile, even more than when we first heard the tale of Essex's folly. It's the Cadiz voyage all over again, but worse – too serious, the possible results this time, for anyone to forgive him lightly.

We don't know it all yet, and the queen won't let her real anger out, not immediately. Like wine laid down, time only ripens the taste of her fury. But I'll admit the fatigues of the last few days are getting to me. The crunch of the gravel under my boot only echoes the harsh sound in my head, and when the girls lag behind to giggle or exclaim over a late flower, I take it on myself to call to them not to be so lazy, and not delay her majesty.

Cecil

Autumn 1597

The burst of friendship was never going to last. That was foreseen, naturally. But what has happened since the fiasco of this
last voyage has an air of irrevocability. Essex is sure, now and
forever, that Ralegh and I are his enemies: he will make it a self-
fulfilling prophecy. But more, he is convinced every man is
against him. Every woman too, maybe.

Even if he thinks it, fool to show it so clearly. The queen has
always been impatient with folly. But more than that, she is
growing suspicious, and you don't raise a Tudor's suspicion
lightly. I must try, again, to persuade Charles Howard to take
Essex's insult quietly. Yes, even though Essex is trying to get
them to reword the very patent of poor Charles' earldom, so
that Essex can claim credit for the whole of last year's Cadiz
victory. Yes, even though the queen wavers over granting
Essex another honour – what, Earl Marshal? – that would let
him outrank Charles' brief position as the premier earl in the
country. 'Your very patience shows your strength,' is what I'll
have to say. 'Believe me, the queen will appreciate you the
more that you were willing to put aside your own grudges for
the country.' Briefly, I toy with the idea of speaking to Charles'
wife, but perhaps no word of advice is necessary to that shrewd
lady.

What is it that Essex really wants? Just – just! – to be first in
honour with her majesty? Or – there are things it's treason to
think, or to say. Yes, even for a state secretary, who must consider
all things clearly.

Now he's sulking at Wanstead, his house in the country. More
folly – it's another of Ralegh's new aphorisms: distance breeds
suspicion. The prince is most mistrustful of the mighty subject
they cannot see. Absence magnifies your faults, and makes
forgiveness come more slowly.

Where there is suspicion, there must be certainty. Not action, not yet, but it will come. There is a man: Ralegh's cousin. I have begun to consider Ralegh differently. He bristled up like a country squire when one of the jesters had a touch at him the other day – oh, nothing so crude as a mockery of his Devon burr, but a strut of the walk that made the court smile knowingly. He looked baffled and angry, like a dog when it knows it's being laughed at – but all the same, I begin to have a new respect for his abilities. It was he who brought this cousin, this Sir Ferdinando to me. Ferdinando Gorges, what a name. I hope I never have to give it to her majesty. But the man has the touch of tarnish on him, the readiness for things to go badly.

The laying out of plans, the agent's consent, is like a seduction and, like seduction, it goes slowly. Small agreement by small agreement, until the final consent is a surety. Then a bargain that lies dormant like a seed in the earth: not knowing what the crop, or what the cost, or who in the end will pay.

The autumn is coming in. As I stroll in the garden to clear my head, the corrupt sweet smell of rotting leaves accompanies me. Often, I see the boy Jan sketching, and something about the nape of his neck, thin and vulnerable, almost reminds me of my daughter Frances. There is a figure waiting in the shadows by the door – one of the two secret secretaries. Of course, he wouldn't have sent a page this time.

'Sir Ferdinando is here to see you, Sir Robert.'

Quickly I nod. 'Good. Take Gorges to the study – I'll be with him directly.'

Jeanne

Winter 1597

Sometimes – quite often – when I was drawing in the garden, I'd find Sir Robert was by my side, and stopping to speak to me. He didn't spend all his time here, I'd learned – much of his work was done in the Duchy of Lancaster offices across the Strand – but he used to walk in these gardens very regularly. He'd rarely touch – he wasn't one of those great garden owners who had to know better than the gardeners did – but his dark eyes were everywhere, quietly. He'd always stop by the aviary, and scatter a handful of the seeds that were kept ready nearby. Sometimes he'd raise his eyebrows in invitation, and pass a handful of seed to me.

'Do you like the birds?' he said one day. I knew him well enough by now to be aware that his most banal questions were the ones with the layers of meaning behind them, but I had to answer.

'I'd like them better if they were free.'

He nodded, as if I'd said something intelligent – or maybe just something expected, and his was the intelligence, for having foreseen it so accurately.

'If we set them loose now they'd be back for their food next day – those the sparrow hawk had spared, and that hadn't been mobbed by their wild fellows.'

'At least that would be their decision.' I didn't know why I was arguing the cause of liberty so passionately. I didn't know why he was talking to me this way. But as he moved on, he gestured me to walk with him, our footsteps crunching on the icy gravel, our breath mingling on the frozen air. We must have looked like brothers as we walked there – he couldn't have been much more than a decade older than me – but his containment, and the experience that wrapped him round like a cloak, made me feel like a callow child and, childishly, I found myself blurting out more than I meant as he asked me more about my upbringing and my family.

'I'm sorry,' he said gravely, when I told him how my parents died, and he led me on to speak of them, as I had done so rarely. How my father had always said he wanted to become the finest silk merchant in Antwerp, and how my mother joked she wanted a house with a garden, where the flowers would be brighter than all his woven finery.

'And you? What do you want, Jan?' I stared at him, dumbly, all my newfound ease of speech, all the pleasure of reminiscence, vanished like smoke, instantly. It wasn't just the boy's name he'd called me – the reminder that, while I kept my secret, there could be no true intimacy with anybody. A reminder that, while I kept my secret, I couldn't dream a happy future with a girl's dream or a boy's. It was those things, but it was more. I'd never, you might say, allowed myself to want – not for anything more lasting than a sweet or a sunny day, or for the toothache to go away. I'd lived like the beggars in the streets, not wanting anything more than the food to get by. I felt inadequate, naked and ashamed, as Sir Robert stood there, eyeing me quietly. Then, with a slight twist of his lips and an inclination of his head, he allowed me to slip away.

They kept Christmas well in the great house. I'd found my way into the kitchens soon after I'd arrived. Even the dogs turning the spits were too busy to talk for long, but I don't think they minded seeing me, especially after the master cook stopped shouting at the scullions long enough to fling a thin foreign book at me and demand I translated a recipe – leg of lamb it was, in the French way, its meat minced with spices, suet and barberries, and stuffed back into the skin again. I thought it sounded nasty, but the cook was pleased.

I didn't care so much for the dairy, or the game larder where they hung birds of every size, ready to be stuffed one inside the other, from the quail to the turkey – nor even for the confectionary, with its candied mock flowers, its cloying marchpane and gilded subtleties. But they soon got used to me in the main kitchen and they'd tease me with tales of what I could expect in summer. Asparagus in a butter and ginger sauce, sweet potatoes boiled in wine, fresh sheep's cheese and French Angelot. Pies of artichokes with bone marrow and dates, and the crisp, watery cowcumbers, of which I had heard but never tasted. Against the outside wall, the gardeners sheltered pots of herbs, to make sallats for Sir Robert even in winter and dress the celery they'd nursed through the cold days. The smell of the rotting manure came up from the melon pits – 'Though if we're not careful the master will be eating them raw as soon as they're ripe,' the under-cook said, 'instead of baked in milk, the proper way.' The household laughed at Sir Robert's tastes, but they laughed affectionately.

Until I came here, I hadn't known that I was greedy. But now I was glad to know that the whole household would be welcome to the feasting, each of the twelve days, and if in so huge a house-hold the best dainties couldn't be served to all, we surely wouldn't go hungry. At this liberal season we were welcome to the roast meats, and the stuffed carp, the marrow with its toasts, the soft sugar suckets made from carrot and green walnuts, and the hard comfits of orange peel and caraway. And welcome to the company. The thought of hours spent alone in my little Blackfriars room, that seemed smaller and dingier than it had done, no longer held any appeal for me.

There were entertainments almost every day, though Sir Robert wasn't always present himself, and neither was Lord Burghley. The waits with their old songs, a troupe of Italian tumblers, and one night there was to be a play. They shut us all out of the hall that day, to allow the actors to make all ready, but I caught two page boys peeping through the window above, and sent them on their way. And then, I admit it, took just a single glance myself.

'Oh dear – the biter bit,' said a voice behind me, mockingly. I turned, to meet a wide mobile mouth twisted in a smile, and a pair of brown eyes that sparkled indulgently at me. There was nothing else remarkable in his features, nothing that would stick in the memory. And yet, somewhere, surely …? The same under-standing was dawning on his face, but he was quicker than me.

'Jan? Is it really you? Don't you remember me? Mrs Allen, and the scarlet doublet – oh, years ago, it must be.'

I did. I did remember now. The slim actor who'd told me stories of the great houses, the one who been kind to me. But it wasn't pleasure I felt now at the sight of him. That would come later, maybe. It was something more like terror. This was my old life come face to face with my new, and I wasn't ready, I wasn't ready. Fast as one of the counting house clerks clicking the beads on an abacus, my brain was running through what I'd said then, what he knew, whether there was anything that could harm me. I didn't usually feel like someone with a secret, so used to it had I become, but this had thrown me. No, it was all right, it was surely all right, he'd known me as a boy. Hadn't he? Had Mrs Allen ever said anything to her cousin, feeling that just that once, in that lax company, she could let herself go, and would her cousin have thought the story worth passing on to anyone else in the party?

Something of this must have shown in my face, and no wonder either, for he was grasping my arm urgently.

'It's all right,' he said gently. 'It's all right, Jeanne.' He said my name the proper way. 'The first thing you have to learn as an actor is that you are the person you decide to be.

'It's all right. Really.' He shook my arm slightly for emphasis, and moved to shield me as a serving man passed by. The pounding in my chest was slowing down, and I understood that yes, maybe it would be.

More of the memories were coming back. He'd shown me his face paints at that house in Chelsea after we'd got back from the long gallery, and he'd made me laugh, and he said he wasn't really a rogue and a vagabond, because he was a member of a regular company. His name had been –

'– Martin Slaughter,' he reminded me, and I looked at him in a kind of apology, for who was I to have forgotten such an exotic, while he remembered me? Except that he didn't look exotic as he stood there – just a brown-haired man with a malleable face, whose age could be anything from thirty to fifty. I remember he'd told me that there were two sorts of actors, and one played off their own personality 'and the other decided to be an actor because they haven't got a personality, and I'm afraid that's me. This way, I can be anybody.' I remembered now, I remembered him talking to me this way. Talking idly, as I'd thought, in this vein, and I realised he must have known then, or half known. It's just that I was older now than I'd been when I first met him, and I understood more of what lay behind his words.

We couldn't stand stock still outside the hall, not with the servants passing by. Instinctively I turned towards the garden, my place of safety, and he fell in beside me.

He asked nothing more just then, and I appreciated that. For a few moments we strolled, silently. I expect we looked like old friends, and I suppose we were, in a way. Or the nearest I had to an old friend, anyway. He told me he'd left the Admiral's Men that summer – 'Other fish to fry!' When he did put a question to me at last, it was with an air of hesitancy.

'So, what have you been doing all this time?'

I told him in two sentences, and he nodded approvingly. 'A decent man, Sir Robert.' There was something there I might have questioned – he'd spoken as if from personal knowledge, not just what any man in the street might pick up about a grandee. But I was still too shaken to think about anything except my own position. I thought probably I could trust him, but trust did not come easy to me.

Someone stuck their head out from a window, and yelled for him impatiently.

'I must go. But I meant it. I hope we meet again some day. I may be away for a time, out of the country' – he broke off, as if he might say more. 'But I think that we will meet, in the end, and you know all actors are a little fey.'

He smiled, and reached out a finger to tap me on the nose – playfully, as a man might to a boy. Then he turned crisply on his heel and, upright, walked away, leaving me standing there in the garden.

I made no move to follow him. This once, I would do without seeing the play. I thought probably I could trust him, I might even, in the end, find I was pleased to have seen him. But just at that moment I wanted only one thing – to be safely away.

Spring 1598

Sir Robert went away to France soon after Christmas, on what even the kitchen, never mind the clerks' room, knew was likely to be a bootless attempt to talk to their king. The unexpected peace France had negotiated with Spain left England at everyone's mercy, but why should their king care for that? The fact of Sir Robert's being away so long, following the French court round the country, left Lord Essex free to take over many of his powers and duties – 'so', as the old clerk said sourly, 'at least someone's happy.'

It was strange: since I'd come into the Burghley household, it was almost as if the grandees of the land had become part of the same extended family, they were talked of here so frequently. Lord Essex, holding the reins of the Council. Lord Essex holding the hands – 'and not just the hands' – of too many of the court ladies. Even the queen's reactions were canvassed, when the steward sent up our share of whatever strong ale was left over at night, though they, in this household, were discussed more cautiously.

As the weather started to warm, and the bulbs stirred under the ground, I found myself remembering Martin Slaughter. It was as if that conversation, with someone who knew both my identities, had made me look at myself differently. But like a shoot that is fooled by a false spring into rising too early, I pushed the thoughts away.

It was well into April when Sir Robert came home, and for several weeks he was so busy that I saw him only in the distance. The garden woke into life without him, though I walked and wondered, and a gardener told me fresh flowers were taken to his rooms every day. The bright purple and orange flames of crocus reminded me of Jacob, showing me a picture in Master de l'Obel's book. That all seemed far away, today.

They were proud of their new bulbs, Sir Robert's gardeners. I saw the Turk's Cap, the tulip, a clear red bell on a hard stem, and the first black-flowered fritillaries. The cooks had already begun to demand the first salad forcings, and the shoots off the over-wintered cabbages to serve with garlic – they'd be tasting green rampions cooked with bacon fat in the country. It was high May when a page came running to find me, with word the master wanted to see me in his study. I smoothed my hair as best I could, and tweaked at my cuff where the cloth was starting to fray, and pushed down the questions in my head as I followed the boy.

'Ah, Jan. Have you been well, these months? How is the work going?' So, not a reproof, then. That was something. And Sir Robert himself seemed eager enough to get to the point, past the preliminaries.

'I have an errand for you to do. I was speaking to my lord Essex the other day, and he was regretting that our cousins across the water didn't rate our arts more highly. Indeed, from the treatment I and my embassy had in France, you'd think they set our whole state of civilisation low … Or so his lordship suggested to me. I mentioned the task I'd set you, as one exam-ple of my own poor efforts at remedy, and he was gracious enough to say he'd be interested to see.

'He's at his hunting lodge in Wanstead, with my lords of Rutland and Southampton. Set out early tomorrow, and tell the stables to give you a decent horse: you should be there and back inside the day.'

He looked at me more closely, struck by a sudden thought.

'You do ride, I suppose?'

'Yes, sir. Badly.' In truth, my life in London had given me little opportunity. In my restless waking dreams that night, I didn't know which loomed larger – the impending tussle with the horse, or the man it was carrying me to see. The man who'd had Dr Lopez hung, the man who set my master at naught. The 'man of blood', as old Lord Burghley called him, whose violence and arrogance repelled me – but, the man who fought the Spanish as fiercely as if he'd been in the Netherlands with me, to see what they could do that day … Of course, when I got to Wanstead it was quite possible I'd only see the steward, who'd carry my drawings off while I kicked my heels in an ante-room all day. In fact, nothing was more likely; and that thought allowed me to sleep at last, uneasily.

The horse they gave me was a bit too decent. As I rode out through the lanes, and the beast twitched and baulked under my nervous hands, I was too tense even to snuff up the soapy scent of may. Wanstead was easily found, a square small house with a welcoming aspect, but as I rode into the courtyard I jerked the reins in sharp dismay. A group of men stood there, laughing at some joke, and the extravagance of their dress and gesture allowed no hope that these were mere retainers. The tallest turned towards me, his brows raised in enquiry. His long red hair and beard made him recognisable, instantly.

I stumbled off my horse and went into a low bow, the best my stiff muscles could manage.

'My lord of Essex – Sir Robert sent me –'

'Of course – the young artist who's to convince the French that, if nothing else, we know something about botany.' A groom had appeared at the horse's head, and a household official was advancing to deal with me as befit my station, but the earl waved him away.

'My lords, gentlemen, give us minute. Boy – a glass of ale for our visitor.' Later I'd learn that this was part of his charm – to treat an anointed queen as though she were any dairymaid, and a clerk as though he – she – he – were Queen of the May.

He leafed through my drawings once, and then again more slowly. 'You must see our gardens here – nothing to Lord Burghley's Theobalds, but I believe my father, my lord of Leicester, laid them out with some small artistry.' He turned towards a doorway in the wall, along with a dog, a beautiful silken creature, who was snuffing at me eagerly.

'Down, Caesar! How very strange – usually he only cares for women. You must have something unexpected about you, Master …?'

'Musset, my lord.'

He turned at that and began to question me as to how I'd arrived in this country. I don't know if I answered as carefully as I would normally. I was too aware of the dog, still snuffing – and aware, too, of my own body. Usually I pulled on my man's clothes without thinking about them either way. But now I could feel my breasts pressing against the stiffness of the doublet, as well as a strange tingling in my belly.

We'd passed beyond the knot garden – nothing exceptional, just as he had said, but still colourful and alive in the warmth of May. But he hadn't kept it well – off at the side I could see the hedges round his warren quite broken down, so that every fox in the country could help themselves to his coneys.

He moved towards the pleasaunce, stooping to throw a stick for the dog, which bounded eagerly off. It was a relief to be free of its questing nose – but absurdly, it seemed almost as though my chaperone had gone away.

The path was broken by a little stream. Disdaining the bridge at some small distance, his lordship made a long stride across it. I tried to follow but, stiff after the ride, stumbled and landed clumsily. He flung out an arm to steady me, then tightened his grip as I tried to pull away.

'I thank your lordship – idiotic of me …' He ignored my stammering words, but held me with a long questioning look, before at last he released me. I felt as if I'd been rooted to the spot, but at least he had now turned away. There were doves calling from somewhere in the trees, and he echoed them teasingly, 'Whoo-hoo', like a schoolboy. I thought the sound would always stay with me.

'There's a bank here where the gardeners used to plant the small strawberries. I wonder if there are any ripe yet? Yes – I see –' He turned back to me with a smile in his eyes, and something small and red in his fingers. As he held it towards my face, I opened my mouth, involuntarily.

My head was in a whirl. This to a boy, to a rival's secretary? It was almost as if my lord of Essex were flirting with me. He was a married man, naturally. Though there were wild tales my lord Southampton and he –

He set out at a run, back towards the house, tugging me after. I'd already noticed he was clumsy, with the leggy awkwardness of a colt in a field, but of course he far outstripped me. There was a wall of yew, separating garden from wilderness, and as he dodged through an opening, I followed as fast as my thudding heart would allow me.

The hedge was in fact two rows of hedges, with a dark pathway running inside, and a piece of leering statuary. I halted, confused by the sudden shadow, and from behind one of the bushes Lord Essex sprang out and seized me, laughing.

'I don't even know your name. No, not Musset.'

'It's Jeanne.' It came out, Jan, as it always did. My head was in too much of a whirl even to ask myself which name he'd heard. It was ridiculous, but behind my eyelids, tears were pricking at me. He saw it.

'I shall call you Janny. There, now we have been introduced, we can greet each other properly.' But this was no ordinary kiss of greeting, as his mouth came down on mine. The moment seemed to go on forever, as I felt my lips beneath his open slightly. 'Did you know you taste of strawberry?'

Still smiling, he turned away towards the house, and I ran after him, desperately. As he looked back he laughed outright, and his glance gleamed at me.

They came out from the house in search of him a moment later, and the steward led me away, no longer baulked of his lawful prey. I was offered a bench, and some refreshment, and I took them in a daze. I sat and watched, like a yokel at a play, as another hunting party rode up and two more young noblemen strode past into the house – my lords Rutland and Southampton, a page told me. Then someone brought me back my drawings, and the horse was returned to me. This time, as if it knew I had no concern to spare, the wretched animal went quite quietly. I even found his footfalls kept pace with the thoughts banging away at me. Did he kiss me because he thought I was a boy? Or because he knew I wasn't? I could hardly make out which of the two ideas most disturbed me.

Cecil

Spring 1598

We are reaching the days of cuckoo call, of quick summer show-ers, and of strawberries. Sometimes, when I'd walk in the gardens with Lizzie in these soft weeks before midsummer, she would put off the forthright air she wore for everyday, pick one of the damask roses and snuff up the scent with her mouth open. She said you got the smell better that way. I'd let my arm brush the front of her dress and smile to watch her stiffen and colour, and later, in bed that night, I'd tell her her nipples were like the berries.

I wonder if, up at Wanstead, they'd eaten strawberries, Essex and my young emissary.

She'll be halfway in love with him by now: it is some time, if I am honest, since I first began thinking of Jan – of Jeanne – as 'she'. But she will not need to fear discovery by the household at large: my senior staff and those servants who matter are too well trained to see what they are not required to see. This is a household where secrets are normal currency. We know everything and nothing; deal in reflection and illusion. We might as well be players, so accustomed are we to living in several different realities. A world of spies: the only true seat of privacy.

I passed her in the corridor the days after she came back from Wanstead, but she kept her eyes cast down, and hurried on past me. There was a blush on even the thin brown nape of her neck – Essex's work, presumably. I should be glad of it – you never get under someone else's guard without letting them under yours: a lesson for Lord Essex. And for me. The dance of seduction and betrayal is as intimate as the sex act, in its way. And the best traitors are those who have no intention of committing treachery.

High time my lord of Essex had something else to think about, from what they tell me. My absence in France gave him opportunities, and I may thank God and his own temperament he did not exploit them to more lasting effect. This Irish rebellion to be put down: he'll box himself into a corner there. Clamour that no one but he can do the business, and then find, like so many before, that no one does themselves good in that country.

Still, Essex didn't do badly while I was away, and the mission to France cannot be said to have crowned me with glory. It would be all to the good if something, someone – placed now, like a thorn, to fester later – were to throw my lord of Essex off his stroke, however momentarily. I would be sorry if it also threw out the balance my young garden artist holds, so very precariously. But there is no use to be had in thinking that way.

It's more penance than pleasure, this golden season, to walk in the garden lonely. No roses, no strawberries, for me now, though I find, as I step briskly towards the house, that I've snapped off a sprig of honeysuckle, and the gentle scent wreathes up to greet me. I find, whatever comes of it, I almost envy Jeanne her golden day: yes of course we had someone watching the walk, and the adventure in the yew trees. I hear of every incautious letter Essex is writing. He even dares to question aloud whether princes can do no wrong, whether subjects should bear wrong indefinitely. Folly! Fool to write it, certainly. Is he a fool to think it? The whole world seems to reel and I close my eyes, but as I open them a glance at the order of the beds in the garden restores me. I gaze down at the spray of golden trumpet flowers in my hand as the steward comes to tell me my father is not so well, again, and that the physicians would like to see me.

Jeanne

Summer 1598

No one at Burghley House saw anything out of the ordinary, but as spring rains soaked the hawthorn blossom, day after day, I hadn't been able to forget Wanstead, though I had tried. Told myself, as I dipped brush in paint, to colour in a drawing to be presented to some visiting dignitary, that at best, Lord Essex had just been amusing himself for an hour. At worst, he had been trying to gain an advantage over a rival's emissary. Jumping out from behind a hedge, like an overgrown schoolboy.

By day, in the damp green pause between spring and summer, I managed well enough. At night, my dreams betrayed me. I had no real fear his lordship would pass on my secret. My very unimportance protected me. But as June came in, I sensed the roses, and the strawberries, a little more keenly.

When I heard Lord Essex's name on the gangling clerk's lips, I started guiltily, absurd though it might be. Of course the story had nothing to do with me. Indeed, as I heard with mounting dismay, this was something to be taken seriously. A meeting of the Council, to discuss the running sore that was our governance of Ireland, and the appointment of a new Lord Deputy. The queen had announced her choice, Lord Essex had dared to argue, and grew angry that his views, he felt, were not being taken seriously.

'And then he turned his back on her! On her majesty!' The gangling clerk was a magnet for gossip, which he broadcast indiscriminately. This time he had all of our attention.

'What did the queen do?' It was one of the page boys.

'She boxed his ears. Yes, really. She shouted at him to go to the devil.' It was hard to know whether the murmur of disapproval was aimed more at the earl or the queen. A little of both, maybe. But the gangling clerk hadn't finished. 'No, wait, there's more' – as the old clerk began gathering his things to move away.

'Give over, lad. That's enough, surely?'

'He said he'd never put up with such an insult, and not from a woman, especially.' The young clerk was gabbling slightly. 'He said he would never have swallowed that, even from old King Henry. And as he said it' – he looked round importantly – 'he had his hand on his sword hilt. They say he even drew his sword – well, part drew anyway. The Lord Admiral, I mean Lord Nottingham, had to grab his arm, or maybe –' He faltered slightly and his stream of words ran dry. Even to say what had happened here required a kind of temerity.

'Where is he now?' We expected to hear 'in the Tower', surely.

'He's gone back to Wanstead.' Doubtless with Rutland and Southampton, his cronies. I tried to think of that smiling house and garden as the seat of rebellion, but found I couldn't do it easily. But neither could I still think of it as only a place of high shady hedges, and of strawberries.

Soon we had other things to think about at the great house along the Strand. When the fresh peas came, the cooks boiled them into broth; it was only the simple soups and pottages of his youth that could tempt the old lord as he aged. I still went down to the kitchens and ate the dishes they had promised me – the asparagus cooked with beaten egg, the apricots not yet crystal-lised – but I was one of the few in that house who were still greedy. And that, perhaps, was only because I'd learnt to keep grief, like love, at one remove: perhaps it made me less than human, but it was a lesson I'd learnt early.

Lord Burghley's health had been failing for so many years that it conspired to make him seem indestructible as one of those old hollow oak trees. But when the change came, it came quickly. As summer passed the height of its sweetness and stumbled towards the sparse dog days, the only whisper at the clerks' table was, 'How is he today?'

The physicians came, but he'd have none of them. He'd take only the odd garden remedy – a decoction of strawberry leaves and roots for his kidneys. The queen sent messages ordering him to rally. When they failed of their effect, she even came herself, and I was there with the rest as she swept in, bowing in the hallway. I lingered to see her come out again. I had a kind of hunger to see her closely. But as I dawdled there, I heard a kind of snuffle from across the room. It was the old clerk, crying quietly. I tiptoed silently away. There was no comfort I could give, but I could spare him, and the queen, my curiosity.

Katherine, Countess of Nottingham
Summer 1598

It's me she wants with her when she goes to visit Burghley. Well, of course, it would be. We're getting precious now, like any other rarity, those of us who remember the old days. And at the moment we're riding high, my husband and I. I should thank Lord Essex, really. Of course it was pure instinct made Charles grab Essex's arm, that day in the Council room, and he made nothing of it when he told me. Well, I don't suppose Essex would have gone further in any case. But Charles' action proves to have done us a lot of good, though it was sheer instinct, as I say.

Actually, maybe that is the point – that Charles' instincts were to keep the peace and protect the queen, before any calculation got in the way. Maybe the queen saw that more quickly than I. So I'm with her now at the house on the Strand – not as much to my taste as my house in Chelsea, but solid enough in its way. She even wants me with her in the bedchamber, though I stay in the background, beside the door. The man has the right to die in some privacy. When with her own royal hand she fed him his broth, I had to catch myself from jumping forwards. She was too unaccustomed to do it handily. Half a spoonful fell down onto Burghley's white beard, but I know she saw the tenderness with which Robert wiped it away. They have strong affections, one for the other, in the Cecil family. And perhaps it was something she needed to do, however untidily.

Afterwards, her face was damp with tears, and she called Robert to walk with her in the garden. She wouldn't want to go out in the street, and have the people see her that way. That garden is flattened by yesterday's downpour, and if the thought of another bad harvest, another hungry winter, fills me with a sick fury, I can only guess what it must be doing to her majesty. Nothing she can do, save declare more fast days, but the blame and the guilt will still stick. That is what it is to be a ruler, to have some power, and all responsibility. Like being a woman, maybe. Last autumn we all cheered that God was on our side, when he sent the winds against the Spaniards, but sometimes it seems that from us, too, he turns his face away.

There's a boy at an easel in front of a flower bed, so intent he had not noticed us until we were quite close. As he hears us at last, he starts up, bows, and backs away, Robert starts speaking about his garden, about the catalogue of plants he caused to be made, and is having translated for growers abroad, to our greater glory. The queen allows him half an ear, and I hope she appreciates the attempt at diversion, but she's listening only distractedly. Robert may be about to lose a father, but she is about to lose her past, the man above all others with whom she shared the years, and the only one left, or nearly.

I've thought, as I have to, of what this means for us, because Charles does not see these things clearly. Perhaps there is no harm in that: I like to think I have long made my deal, heart as well as head, with everything about the man to whom they married me, and a good marriage it's been, too – well, when you think I might have been given over to something like Philadelphia's brutish booby, Scrope. If Charles does not think of his advantage at this time, that's the very simplicity of temperament that allows him to work with Robert Cecil the more easily. Cecil's will be the planning brain, but as the queen's – now – oldest councillor, the one with the most years of service, my husband will have a certain new status, naturally. For a single second I allow myself the thought of how it might be to be married to a man who made the plan himself, or how it might be if I … No point for a woman to think that way. Behind the queen, her arm on Robert Cecil's, I climb the little garden mound, and stare out over the damp prospect. I doubt that, this time, the queen has been able to walk her cares away.

Burghley dying here, and in Spain the spies tell us Philip is going, too, of a slow putrefaction, with his coffin placed beside the bed to set his mind on immortality. Keep your friends close but your enemies closer; though the loss of Philip will be England's gain, I could almost swear we're mourning for him as well as for Burghley. I was too young to know much about the alarums when he first married Queen Mary, when our queen was still a princess, but as a child in her household I swear I remember her going to the court to make her curtsey to the new King Philip, and the red velvet gown she wore that day. Everyone else from those days is gone: Mistress Ashley and the rest of the ladies, the old Queen Mary herself, of course, Robert Dudley. The thought sends a breath of chill even through me, though I'm a younger woman than she.

When there is no one left to whom you seem young, then you are old indeed, they say. And, unless all the doctors are wrong, then in a few days' time, that's what will happen to her majesty. So don't think – don't think, I urge her in my thoughts, silently – that I don't understand why you can hanker after an Essex, in his youthful vitality.

Don't think I don't understand why to talk of the succession, as a childless monarch should, drives you into a nervous frenzy, like a dog that's been whipped so often for barking at strangers it only has to hear the gate now to run away.

If she were just my cousin, instead of the queen, I'd put my arms around her in the carriage home, and say something silly. Instead, I sit there reminding myself to make sure her ruffs go to the Dutch laundry since none of the English cleaners starch them properly; and thinking about whether I'll be able to slip away to Chelsea some time – I don't trust that new confectioner – to see they're preserving the summer fruits properly. I sit there with my eyes cast down, while she turns a still, hard profile away.

Jeanne

November 1598, Accession Day

Lord Essex had to come back to town, of course. He had to, to take his place as one of the black-cowled mourners at Lord Burghley's funeral. I'd been there too – we all were – though he didn't see me. The old lord would really be laid to rest in his own church at Stamford, up to the north, but her majesty had decreed that there would be a great mourning ceremony in Westminster Abbey. They had as many of the household there as possible, to do him honour – or 'to make a show', as the most malicious of the clerks put it bluntly.

No one had looked more sorrowful than Lord Essex, but the clerks weren't the only ones to whisper he was sorrier for himself than for the loss of Lord Burghley. Down in the kitchens they were shouting it, over the sound of the cleavers and the kitchen boys, that the trouble continued between him and the queen. He actually dared say he wanted an apology. And the real question wasn't just how they'd make up, or when – it was how we were all to go on as before, when a subject set his rights and the queen's on terms of equality.

They had to find some way. The news from Ireland was worse every day, and while Lord Essex was wanting to take an army, swearing he'd hang the rebel Tyrone from the country's highest tree, the queen was holding back.

'Well, you can't blame her,' the malicious clerk had said. 'She's never liked sending a man off to lead a war – shows who's got the balls, besides the question of money. But this time, if she gives Essex an army she must ask herself what he's going to wind up doing with it.'

I'd kept my head down while the talk was going on, but at night I realised that I didn't know, either, just what Lord Essex would do with his army.

This was no golden harvest year; the corn had been snapped up for the tables of the rich, and by October the poor were already baking bread of beans and barley. The weather had worsened sharply as autumn wore on, and when the odd day did come of chilly sunshine, we'd snatched at it like greedy children who'd known the gift of light would soon be seized away. As Accession Day approached, I'd told myself I might not go, for all we knew Lord Essex would be a challenger. But when it came to it, of course, I shrugged my shoulders and allowed the other young clerks to persuade me.

The crowds and the vendors were the same, and the awnings flapping in the wind overhead, and the sand underfoot. But I fancied I felt a special anticipation in the air. Everyone there knew of Lord Essex's quarrels, and I felt a prick of irritation at him for making himself a motley. Maybe it wasn't irritation so much as jealousy. I'd kept it close to my heart, that he'd been so open with me in the garden that day. But I'd come to realise that, like a beggar with his sores, he showed his moods to everybody.

I felt a tug at my elbow, and it was the gangling clerk. 'Come on – they say there's going to be something to see.' The grandees were beginning to arrive – my lord of Nottingham the Lord Admiral, a youthful earl or two, Sir Walter Ralegh the Captain of the Guard, with his men bravely decked out in plumes of orange and tawny.

But they'd hardly taken their places when a titter arose, from those nearest the gateway. They were carrying Lord Essex's scutcheon, with rows of men marching behind, decked out in … orange and tawny. Ralegh's colours. More men, taller plumes, and the crowd were enjoying it hugely.

I turned away, with a tinge of sadness. I knew, of course, that his lordship and Sir Walter were no friends, but this seemed so – petty?

I wasn't the only one who thought so. 'She won't like that. He won't do himself any good that way.' I started – I hadn't even noticed that the old clerk had joined the party. I craned round to peer to the royal gallery near at hand – this was a better place than I'd managed for myself when I'd come to the tilt as a lone boy, and I could see that the waiting gentlewomen were paving the way for her majesty. But of the champions themselves there was no sign. They were still hidden behind the bleachers, and on a sudden impulse I sprang up and raced back down the stairs, drawn as surely as if I'd been a fish on a line in the garden pond, and he playing with me.

I turned my back on the lists themselves, and dodged round behind the back of the stands, to where the squires and the grooms would be making the knights ready. Down at this level, the noise was overwhelming, with the shouting of the boys and the stamping and whickering of the restless horses, but Lord Essex was already mounted, a little apart from the crowd, sitting loose in the saddle as he waited, idly.

I slowed as I approached him, unsure what I could say. Unsure whether he'd even remember me.

'Why, hello, Jan. Have you come to wish me luck?' His squire started up, with a warning face, from where he'd been checking the point of the great lance, but Lord Essex waved him away. I was drinking in every detail of him. He looked tired – I'd heard that he'd been ill in truth, besides the diplomatic illnesses he'd used to get round her majesty.

'You're not wearing a favour this year,' I said idiotically. 'You haven't got her majesty's glove.'

'I haven't, have I?' It was stupid of me to have reminded him, at this of all moments, how everyone knew he'd lost the queen's favour, but that didn't seem to worry him. Quite the reverse. He'd seemed to be drooping a little when I'd come up, detached from the scene; more like a crusader knight on a tomb than someone who was going to spur his horse into those lists and win a crashing, snorting victory. But now he was rousing, opening up like a plant in the sun under the flattery of my memory.

'You've seen me joust before? Then you'll know the rules. And you're right – I should have a token. A knight should tilt for the favour of some lady.' His voice lingered on the last word and my breath caught, half in anticipation and half in fear. His dark eyes were dancing as he beckoned me closer. The smell of the sweating horse was in my nostrils as I came to stand by his armoured knee.

'Who do you suppose I should ask to give me one, my Jeanne Janny?' His voice was quiet, but alive with mischief as he gave me my girl's name, the French way.

I'd been out in the gardens that morning, and found a bush of early blooming rosemary. I'd tucked a sprig into my doublet, telling myself it was best to have some clean scent by, in case the smells of the crowd grew unhealthy. I couldn't have moved my fingers towards it, even had I dared. I was as paralysed as a rabbit in front of a snake. It felt as if I hardly breathed as slowly he stripped the metal gauntlet from his hand, and slowly reached out his long white hand towards me.

My eyes were still fixed on his face as dimly I heard the herald's trumpet sound. With a shout of alarm his boy sprang towards him, helmet at the ready, and I stumbled out of the way. As the great roan clattered past me I looked down at my doublet, at where the sprig of rosemary used to be.

Katherine, Countess of Nottingham

November 1598, Accession Day

I do not actually watch as the queen raises her arm and unclenches her fingers, letting the glove fall solidly to the sand, heavy with its embroidery. I merely make a mental note to see that, this time, they clean it carefully. How many Accession Days is it now? It can't be far off forty, though in the beginning we didn't celebrate them this way. Once, long ago, we gave her such a wisp of a thing to throw that the wind all but whipped it away, but after this many years we've learned how to do these things properly.

I can see the queen's hands clench on the railing as the hoof-beats take up their rhythm, and, reluctantly, I turn my attention to the joust. Long past the time when my husband might take part, and I thank God neither of my sons are competing today. It takes skill to get a horse straight into a canter from a standing start, but Essex knows his business – in horsemanship, at any rate. Bad luck, I know – the curse, on the curser – but I can't help half wishing him a fall. Not a serious one, naturally. Just enough to slow him down, to give a check to his career, and one for which no one could blame her majesty. Or say she was an old lady now, blind to genius and opportunity. One to make him walk cautiously for a few weeks. The way the queen walks today. The way I am beginning to walk myself – I can give a good decade to her majesty, but I swear I'm beginning to grow as old, in sympathy.

Then again, after all those births – five large Howard babies living – you'd be lucky if you were left walking as easily as you used to as a girl; it's the kind of thing the queen used to ask me about, once upon a time, when she'd keep me in her bedroom talking late into the night, and what was I supposed to say? They were all desperate for her to marry and produce an heir, and if it cost her life, well, so long as the baby was a boy … I told her the truth, the bad and the good, the so very good, but I don't suppose it made any difference to her, really. I don't suppose it made any difference, full stop. She may still have the figure of a girl, even without the whalebone stays. But no one could say she hadn't suffered in other ways.

When I glance around the younger ladies, the chits are all gazing at the tourney, with eyes like my lapdog if I hold a bone up, slowly. It's Essex, languishing his way around the ring again, needless to say. The queen has seen it too. Her thin lips are clenched under the paint, and the pale winter sun shows the lines on her face too cruelly. So many years of these chits of maids, with their follies and their fancies, it makes me weary. Thank God I'll be home for a few days soon, at my own house in Chelsea.

Cecil

Winter 1598–99

'Wish the king no evil in thy thought, nor speak no hurt of him in thy privy chamber; for the bird of the air shall betray thy voice, and with her feathers shall bewray thy words.' It says so in Ecclesiastes, and our best theorists agree. But the birds of the air may as well have help: especially since we can't yet be sure whether evil is wished to the queen, precisely. Indeed, when

Lord Essex declares he needs an army to take to Ireland, I'm not sure he himself formulates his thoughts too clearly.

My father said that there were three sorts of traitors: since he died, I've found myself mouthing his sayings more frequently. Those 'discontented for lack of preferments', those who couldn't afford to live quiet at home, and the bankrupt merchants. By merchants, he meant those buying and selling more than goods. By merchants, he meant anybody. Perhaps he was too sweeping, putting it all down to money. But in some ways, Essex is all three.

A conspiracy must be laid out and tended like a garden. A plot for a plot, but only schoolboys congratulate themselves on their word play. Nor, of course, would I use the word plot for the simple precautions I am taking: and I doubt Lord Essex tends anything carefully.

I listen to the rumours Essex has been in touch with Tyrone, just as I will later listen to the drone of the bees, which tells the keepers to get their skeps ready. I observe the wilting patch where the queen's affection for him has faded, and I consider whether anything else could be planted there more usefully. I see the weeds sown by his lordship's determination that his officers in Ireland shall be his men only – but these tares I shan't pluck up too quickly. I think of the snares the gardeners set, before the rabbits can get the young seedlings. And I think of how Lord Essex set himself up so none other could be given the Irish captaincy. I think of how he may be regretting it already.

Jeanne

Spring 1599

He wouldn't set out until after dinner, bound for Ireland with his army. One of the secret clerks broke his silence for once, to say that it would be a miracle if his lordship set out at all – but truth to tell, there wasn't much of a secret about that. Every ale-drinker in every tavern had been talking for weeks about how Lord Essex was having second thoughts. It wasn't just the impossibility of the job, though no Lord Deputy had ever managed to tame those wild Irish kerns. But they were talking, too, about how he'd told the Council he was armed before but not behind – 'Saying while he was gone, our master would stab him in the back! Quite openly!' It had been one of the pages reporting the tale, wide-eyed, in the kitchens, and the cook slammed his pot lid down with unusual vehemency. The old clerk said something damp-ing, when he heard, about getting the tutor to thrash some gram-mar into the boy – but the fact was, everyone had heard of his lordship's accusations. And I don't think I was the only one, even in our house, to have divided loyalties.

The day he was going dawned fine and clear – the kind of day you dream of as Easter approaches. The people would have a choice of blossoms, if the crowds wanted to throw flowers in his path as he left. The country women in the streets were already selling great balls of cowslips smelling like honey, and any chil-dren who ran out early to the woods could bring back the wreck-age of frail wilting windflowers and the last of the daffodowndillies.

No one actually said that we were all free to go out and watch that day, as Lord Essex and his troops rode out. Perhaps, in a Cecil household, it was the kind of thing you didn't really say. But as I looked around the hall at dinner, there were a lot of trenchers being mopped up briskly, and more of the fish than usual went back into the kitchens. It might still be Lent, but the scullions would have a feast day – if they themselves hadn't already tumbled out onto the streets.

Outside, in the Strand, as I made my way to Essex House, the crowds were behaving as though it were indeed a festival. The vendors were out in force, and from the queues and the nudges around the pasty vendors, I'd say the rules about needing doctor's order to eat meat were being broken pretty freely.

Indeed, there was a curious feel of lawlessness, as if this were a crowd that could turn nasty – as all crowds can, maybe. The army was drawn up in the fields beyond the Tower, and after he'd joined them, Lord Essex's path lay towards Chester, where the boats waited to take him to Ireland. He'd set out towards the village of Islington, not due west past the palace at Westminster, and the shadow of her majesty's authority.

They were coming. I could hear the shouts of 'Hurray!' and faintly, under them, the click of the horses' hooves and the chink of armoury. Whatever privations lay ahead – and I knew enough now to be sure this expedition wasn't flush with money – he'd make sure his personal guard made a fine show in their orange livery. And whatever sulks and furies lay behind, he'd greet the crowd smilingly. He went past in one long moment, the cool spring sunlight shining on his breastplate, decked out for battle already, as though he were going to have to fight his way through London. Maybe that was what he was trying to say.

'God speed your lordship,' people were shouting. And yes, they were throwing flowers in his way. But – perhaps it was only my imagination, but I fancied there was a faint undercurrent of mockery in the calls. A London crowd was a strange beast, savage, shrewd, and fickle – as strange as anything you might find in the Tower menagerie. We'd seen a noble young lord, tall and shining as a god, ride out on a venture of chivalry. But was it – did we think it – any more real than the feints and masques at the tournament on Accession Day?

Yes, the air was chilling. I looked north, the way the army would go, and black clouds were massing in the sky. 'That's a bad omen, sure enough,' said a workman beside me, cheerfully. 'They'll be soaked and sorry before they stop tonight.' Sure enough, a few spiteful drops of rain began to fall as I turned and made my way back to Burghley House.

Passing through the courtyard, I made my way into the garden, despite the moisture on the air. I'd be alone there.

Except that I wasn't – a small, dark figure stood by the aviary. From this angle his twisted shoulder showed clearly. I hesitated for just too long to be able to go back, then slowly moved towards him. I had a feeling he might welcome company. He turned at the sound of my steps, and I think his face lightened slightly.

'Ah, Jan. We'll miss him, won't we?'

I didn't know what to say. I was taken aback twice over. Once, that Sir Robert had seen my feelings so clearly. Once that he, whom everyone thought was Lord Essex's sworn enemy …

As he turned, and began to pace the gravel, I was used enough to his ways by now to fall in automatically. 'We were boys together – you knew that, surely?'

I nodded. It was one of the old clerk's favourite stories, about how Lord Essex had been made Lord Burghley's ward, after his own father died in Ireland (in Ireland!), and how they should have seen this coming, even in the old days.

'There's good as well as bad in that, and they neither of them ever quite go away.' He slipped a hand under my elbow. I'd seen gallants do it all the time, but from him, to me, the gesture was striking. 'His father was dead then, and he was determined to see his work finished. And now my father is dead too, and I …'

All I could do was bow my head attentively, while a tiny voice in my head whispered that this was a man who did nothing without a purpose, and why was he talking this way to me? But another, firmer voice spoke, telling me that sometimes conviction and convenience marched hand in hand. That whatever Sir Robert did to put stones in Lord Essex's path – I was no longer as naive as I used to be – yet all the same, this was still a kind of verity.

'We've both lost people, you and I. Oh, they've gone into God's care, of course, and we're still in the sinful world. Perhaps that's why, sometimes, I swear, it can make you feel almost guilty.' He wasn't looking for an answer, and I couldn't have made one easily. But as the rain began to fall in earnest, and he turned to precede me into the house, I thought that, for all its hidden secrets, that was the most intimate exchange I'd ever had with anybody.

Summer 1599

As the summer approached, with its odours and its whispers of plague – and its puffs of rose scent borne on warm wind too – I was told we were all going out from town, to Sir Robert's family home at Theobalds, and that the queen was coming to stay.

'Yes, I said "we". You're coming too,' the steward told me irritably. 'Her majesty loves a garden, and she'll want to see all the work that's been going on, whether it's in the flowerbeds or the library. What do you expect Sir Robert to do, if the queen asks him about a plant you've drawn – say we'll get back to her in a week or two?

'What' – as I began to stammer a feeble protest – 'you've got something more important to do? More important than maybe meeting with her majesty?'

I went back to my room that evening to pack my things with questions whirring in my brain. There were concerns – not least where they'd tell me to sleep. In a room with the other young men, all too probably. But there'd be ways. If need be I'd proclaim a liaison with a scullery maid and take myself off to sleep in a corner, out of doors, if necessary. And in any case, worrying was useless: clearly I had to go, or risk bringing questions on my head. In short, I convinced myself, surprised to find that, under the worries, there was a kind of excitement welling up in me.

I'd heard stories about the old progresses, the ones the court used to take each summer, travelling like an army on the move, with the baggage train stretching from one town to another, and teams of decorators working in relay to prepare each of the queen's stopping places on the way. I'd heard of whole new gardens thrown up overnight, of fireworks bought in from Italy, and entertainments so elaborate they put the hosts into bankruptcy.

This wouldn't be so grand. The queen was coming for the night, with just a small train, and only enough guards to ensure her safety. She knew Theobalds well already, and she might not now have the energy for spectacular festivities – though no one said that, precisely.

All the same, the fuss seemed extraordinary. We rode out of town, along roads lacy with cow parsley, accompanied by every book, plan of works and musical instrument that might possibly entertain her majesty; a case of spices, to aid the Theobalds cookery; and half the treasures of the Strand house to deck the royal bedchamber, as if Theobalds weren't furnished already.

Nothing to do with me, thank God. I could frankly enjoy the ride. The marguerites on the banks turned their faces to the sun; now we bruised a patch of rank-smelling wild garlic, now we passed an open space where campion and foxglove showed pink under the broom, or a meadow yellow with buttercups. The smell of the elder must have made even the bees drowsy. I'd never seen flowers growing in such profusion, all untended by any. Of course, the lords and ladies left London every summer, to get away from the pestilence heat brought to town, but people like me didn't have the opportunity.

I'll never forget my first sight of Theobalds – like something in a story. A forest of turrets, each flying a flag and guarded by a wooden beast, gilded brightly. Closer to, the magic changed, but it didn't diminish. This wasn't a house, it was a city. Parks and courtyards, stables and bakery. With no idea where in the world to go, I hovered at the steward's elbow, anxiously.

'Ah yes – Sir Robert says you'll need a little closet room to yourself to spread your papers. They'll bring you a pallet bed there at night.' Did his tone suggest he thought it a little odd for Sir Robert to bother himself so particularly? I was just thankful to have got so easily over one difficulty. The master wouldn't arrive till the next day, riding with the queen, and no one seemed to have any special task for me. I was free to explore – after all, gardens were supposed to be my subject, weren't they?

So much has been written about the gardens at Theobalds. It's all true, that's all I'm going to say. I saw pavilions and arbours, and meadows where wilderness had been tended to the perfect degree. Early roses beds, underplanted with periwinkle, pinks that scented the air (they scattered pigeon dung to make them grow larger, a gardener said), and pots of lemon trees. If Master Gerard supervised the planting of this, then I might begin to see him differently.

I saw the giant Peruvian marigolds – Flowers of the Sun, they call them – with their brown-gold heads two handspans across, their stalk the thickness of a man's arm, and I saw a whole bed of the new Turkish crown imperial, a ring of bright yellow bells on a thick stem, and inside each bell clear drops of honey. Just the way Master Gerard had described them in his book, I admitted grudgingly. If I spent much time here, I might start believing in the barnacle tree.

They sent plants to us in town, of course, but nothing like this; and indeed, compared to what I was seeing here, our city gardens with their honeysuckles and gillyflowers seemed like the most rustic simplicity.

We had a mound at the house on the Strand, but this mound here was planted with hawthorn trees, so that you walked up as if through a labyrinth, in mystery. We had topiary there, but here life-size hounds chased a deer across the lawn, all formed out of close-cropped box trees. The grass was so fine they must have been raking and scything it for an eternity. I swear, it even smelled different, as if it been manured with money.

I saw a network of waterways, with trees planted around them for shade, so a guest could be rowed on the hottest day. I peered down through the water, and bright-coloured stones like jewels winked back at me. I saw a lake so broad it was no surprise when a gardener told me it was called the sea. I walked and I wondered, and it was only at night, as I spread the bedding on my straw pallet – none of the servants had had time to spare – I realised I had not thought of Lord Essex all the long day.

The next morning we were up with the light. Preparations had clearly been going on for weeks – gardeners even forcing strawberry plants under glass, in hopes a single dish of berries might be ready early – but there was still everything for the servants to do on the day.

Old Lord Burghley had built a new bedchamber for the queen, after she complained her old one wasn't spacious enough, but the last time she came to stay, she'd chosen to sleep in the old one, just the same … They decided to prepare both, so as to be ready.

As the delivery drays rolled up to the kitchen, even the clerks got involved, clocking in each plate of cakes or present of pike sent from neighbours through the surrounding country. In the end I slipped away. I'd still hardly seen the state rooms in the house, and I wandered unheeded past painted walls and carved staircases, through the great chamber where the columns were carved as oak trees, covered with real bark and leaves. The birds came in and nested there and I don't blame them for being fooled. The whole house was like an allegory, a conversation where only the words were missing. Nothing was as it appeared to be. I was up on the roof when the cavalcade came on the Astronomer's Walk on the flat leads, and I paused there to watch, shrinking back behind a chimney.

She came on horseback, as she tried to do whenever her people could see her, but her stiffness as they lifted her down showed that she was weary. Sir Robert saw it too, from the speed with which he summoned a servant with a cup of cordial. But as they stood side by side, she was still taller than he. I could see why she called him her elf, or her pygmy. They'd dismounted in the courtyard, and she glanced towards the fountain in the middle. The first time she'd visited, with the whole court, they'd made it run with wine, both white and red, but this time she'd said she wanted no great ceremony. A gentle stroll, a little archery, a glance through whatever was new in Sir Robert's collection of curiosities. She walked, just where I'd walked the day before. She was pleased to admire; and I believe she admired even my illustrations, which I'd been told to spread out ready in the gallery. Sir Robert must have explained them to her himself; in the end, no one needed me.

In the evening the ladies danced for her; there was an acrobat; later there'd be a play. She seemed to enjoy it all, but looking around the court from my vantage point behind a pillar, I was struck by how young they all seemed in comparison, dare I say it, to her majesty.

Theobalds had always been Lord Burghley's house; Essex House had once been Leicester House, home of the old earl, Essex's stepfather, Robert Dudley. But all the men of the queen's youth were gone now, every one. Where once she'd had the fathers, she was left with the sons. I thought she must be lonely. And as I saw her turn her face aside a moment, the folds under the jaw sagging sideways beneath their mask of paint, I thought that for all she was treated as a goddess, there was one thing she could never allow herself to be, and that was simply an old lady.

The great chamber was stifling, but a breath of fresh air to one side showed me a doorway. Maybe I could wait in the quiet, at least until the start of the main play. I edged my way through and found myself in an ante-chamber, full of what looked for all the world like someone's upended laundry. Two doublets, a shirt, a stuffed parrot and a wig – with a start, I realised these must be the actors' props.

At the other end of the room a door opened and a man came in, in the great colourful suit of a braggadocio, all made up for the play. I began to make a quick apology, and turned back the way I'd come when, from somewhere inside the mask of paint, a voice said, 'Jan? Jan? I never thought I'd see you here.'

It was Martin Slaughter.

I'd never have recognised his face, those ordinary, malleable features were hidden so completely. It was his voice that gave him away. He told me later his looks were at once his blessing and his curse – not dramatic enough for a memorable leading man, but adaptable enough to keep him in work pretty regularly. I must have gaped at him stupidly.

'I thought I'd never see you again!' In truth, the last eighteen months I'd hardly thought of him at all, but that wasn't the thing to say. I settled for a more palatable truth. 'After you left, for ages, I went to every play. I did. I began to think you must have died.'

That mobile mouth twisted into the trace of a smile. 'Once or twice, nearly. I told you I might be away. First in the country and then abroad. I was forced to go, you might say.'

'Debts or some quarrel, I suppose!' I couldn't imagine why I was angry.

'Not quite, though the debts did for an excuse.' He'd always had the ability to convey much more than the words said, and I understood. I'd learned something these last two years, maybe. Actors often doubled as, well, messengers, agents – 'Call us emissaries.' I hadn't thought my face was one to show my thoughts too plain, but he seemed able to read me easily. 'It sounds so much nicer than spies. But what about you, Jeanne?' This time, he said my birth name. It was so long since anybody had named me properly. Well, except for Lord Essex – but the thought passed, swiftly. And this was different anyway.

I paused a second. He could see I had stayed in Sir Robert's employ. I did not know what else to say. But he came to my rescue: he was someone who knew the many facets of a life, and knew it couldn't be summed up easily.

'Here – let me show you something.' He took my hand, briefly, and tugged me towards a stairway in the corner. Up he ran, and up again, while I panted behind him. Whatever else they say about an actor's life, it must keep you fit.

'Martin, where in the world are we going?'

'You'll see – here.'

We were up on the roof, in a dream world, lit by a white cheese of a moon, so much a picture from a storybook it made us both break into laughter, then look away, shamefacedly. Tall chimneys twisted like barley sugar reared up to make a stone forest against the sky. Without a word we both went over, to lean against the balustrade, facing out over the garden to the country.

'You said you went to the plays for a while.' He paused. 'I haven't been away all this whole time, you know. I was playing in Southwark last summer, after I saw you.' Last summer, when Essex kissed me.

'I was ... busy.' I owed him more honesty, but I didn't know what to say. How could I explain what had happened – or happened in my head, since nothing important had happened in reality, and I was beginning to understand that more clearly every day. But again he surprised me.

'Perhaps I know more about it than you realise. These times with Essex have put all of us out of joint.' There was too much clamour in my head to wonder why Lord Essex's name had sprung to his mind so readily. I didn't want to know whether gossip had reached him from some part of the dark spy's world, or whether he was just speaking generally.

'You feel his pull, don't you? Well, of course – we all do, in a way. I've played men like him on stage, and I've always thought that they'd cause chaos in reality. But you must feel it, especially.' He paused a second, and I had time to understand that though we hadn't met these years, he must sometimes have been thinking about me. 'When you have to – or want to – deal in illusion, there's a fascination in anyone else who's living their own fantasy.'

He turned away with an air of conclusion, gazing out over the view, and began pointing things out to me. Disjointedly, I followed his lead, and began telling him my day's adventures. Indeed, I found I was telling what I'd been thinking in the hall, which I wouldn't have cared to do to just anybody.

'I know. We were waiting in the courtyard when they set off this morning – rode out here behind the royal party, like the tail of the dog. I thought the queen looked as though she hardly wanted to set out on yet another journey.'

'Couldn't she just have said so?'

'Not likely. If anyone tries to suggest it, she brags that the old and infirm should stay behind, that the young and active are for her company. If she as much as called for a litter instead of a horse the whole court would have understood, and every ambassador in the country would have sent home the news she was beginning to fail. They watch her the way the carrion crows do an old animal in the fields that's waiting to die.'

He had said the forbidden word. He had said, *die*. Of course everyone knew the queen's life couldn't go on forever; of course by now, most thought, if they didn't say, it was a miracle it hadn't ended already. Of course everyone asked who the next on the throne would be – the King of Scotland, my lord of Hertford's son? – and some felt the choke of a nightmare coming close when they thought of England seized by some great Catholic country. Some – like me. All the same, there was an air of unreality about the thought. For all except the very oldest nodding in the corner, Queen Elizabeth had been there forever, sure as the sun in the sky, and even if you grumbled about the weather, you never considered any other possibility.

Now, for a minute, gazing down on the chequerboard landscape below, I allowed myself to look at the future, like a soldier looking at a map of enemy country, a land full of dangers and opportunities. The way the gossipmongers in their cups did when drink had made them reckless, and men like Sir Robert did in all sobriety.

The way Lord Essex did, or so men said. They were saying ever more openly – I tried not to hear their talk – that the queen had good reason to fear sending him to Ireland at the head of an army.

It was as if Martin had picked up my thought. 'You know he didn't want to go? Not really. But he'd criticised every other candidate, he'd jeered at everyone else's policy, so he could hardly complain when they took him at his word. And now they're in a winning situation, you might say. If Essex pacifies Ireland, well then England has her victory. If he fails miserably – well, at the least it will take a little lustre off the people's golden boy.'

He paused for a second, as if wondering whether or not to speak.

'Of course, there are some – just a very few, the ones who don't usually do much talking, who say there's a deeper game afoot. They say it's one that the old fox used to play.' The jerk of his head around us said – as if I couldn't have guessed – that he meant Lord Burghley. '"Give them enough rope, madam, and they'll hang themselves sure as sanctity,"' he quoted, with his actor's mimicry.

'The old man even did it with the Queen of Scots – set the temptation in her way, then cut off her head when she fell for it. Like father, like son, they say. Maybe there's a reason for it, every time Sir Robert plays the peacemaker, helps Lord Essex's favour with the queen to go grinding on one more day.' He stopped. I must have made a movement, enough to let him see the thought distressed me. Yes, I had learned a lot those last two years, but the thought of such hidden wheels still frightened me. Perhaps one of the things I'd learnt was to believe Sir Robert acted for the best. Perhaps I shouldn't have trusted so easily.

'Ah well, I daresay that part isn't true,' Martin added more lightly. 'Maybe it's all just coming from her majesty. This queen's father said once that if he believed his nightcap knew his counsel, he would throw it in the fire, and no doubt she agrees.'

A ripple of applause came from the hall, and he turned his head quickly to listen. We were both a little relieved, maybe.

'The play! You should go –'

'No, that's all right, this is just the first act. I'm not needed until nearly halfway. But, listen, Jeanne –' He stopped again. His arm on the balustrade was very close to mine. For the first time since I'd known him, he seemed uncertain what to say. Then he seemed to shrug on confidence and gaiety, as he might don his costume for the play.

'We'll meet tomorrow. You can show me the marvels of Theobalds, and we'll find a few more together, maybe. Come now, you're not going to say no, surely?'

'No – I mean, yes, after breakfast, in the hall. Unless Sir Robert needs me.'

I found now my arm was brushing his. For a long moment we both gazed at the moon, silently.

When I found him next day, there was mischief in his face.

'Come on – I know what I want to show you. One of the gardeners told me.' I hesitated, but I'd already checked that I couldn't be called on for another hour or two – or probably at all – and there was really no reason not to agree. He led me down through the orchards, where a few petals still clung around the swelling fruit, and towards the great lake I had seen yesterday. Behind it, screened by a line of trees, there was a smaller pool, with fountains shaped like serpents and white with water lilies.

'They don't use it much now but they used to bathe here.' He flicked a smiling glance at me. 'I don't suppose we dare – dare we?' I felt sure enough of him now to smile as I shook my head. 'But that's not what I wanted to show you. Come – I got them to lend me the key.'

A little banqueting house stood at one end of the pool and he held the door open for me, ceremoniously. I stepped in past

him, as a lady might sweep past a gentleman, and gave an un-
ladylike snort of laughter. I was in something straight out of a
fantasy. I'd read about things like this – the gardens the emper-
ors had had in Rome – but now the story had become reality.
Above me, naked figures rioted across the ceiling. At my feet
huge carp rose lazily to the surface from great shallow tanks and
Martin – eager as a boy, proud as the proprietor – ran around to
show me the underwater gates that would release them, when
the house was closed, into the outdoor pond to swim free. A
tiny bridge, fit for a child, or for a queen's feet, led over the
water to a minute man-made island, where a stone table stood
ready for a feast.

'Now, that I didn't think to organise. I'm sorry.' But we sat
down anyway, one across from the other. He spread both hands
flat on the surface, like a man about to come to a point, and I
remembered how every movement of his seemed to mean something – how he made me feel as graceless as a landed plaice, flop-
ping in a fishmonger's tray.

'You know, I'd thought the Cecils were –' I made a
damping down gesture with my hands, less expressive than
any of his. Were order and safety, were the garden on the
Strand with its ordered patterns, was what I was trying to say
– not, too, the wonders, and the tricks, I had seen these last two
days.

'They are. But that's not all they are. There's a lot of things
about the Cecils you don't know.' I looked at him sharply. 'But
– that's not what I wanted to say.

'Jeanne, do you think of the future? No – for yourself, I mean,
not Essex or the country.'

I shook my head mutely. I tried not to think of it. I knew it was
easier for a girl to be a boy than for a woman to be a man of full-
bearded maturity. I knew I should be grateful for his concern,
but I felt shy in his presence suddenly.

'If I can help in any way –' He broke off, uncertainly. 'You
could always join an actors' company! Not much botanising to

be done, except the hedgerow plants along the road, but a talent with a pen might come in handy.' I laughed with him, relieved that the moment had passed. As we walked back to the house we talked idly, of the past more than the present. I asked after Ben, and he said the old actor had died, on the road, two years before. From the way he spoke, Martin had been with him on that last journey, and I was glad.

He said there'd been more than one time he'd seen me, in the old days – that once or twice he'd seen me with Jacob at the booksellers behind St Paul's. 'Do you ever go there now? I do, when I get the chance, of a Saturday.' He let the information hang in the air, as we turned back towards the house. We passed the maze, and he drew me inside it. You reached the centre easily: the path led just one way, and you had only to follow it.

'Lord Burghley's taste,' Martin said, inconsequentially. 'Did you know, now they're planting mazes where half the paths are dead ends? The whole point is to make you lose your way.'

The moment was over. He began to tell me of his travels as an actor, and of other great houses around the country.

When we got back to town, nothing there seemed to have changed, and if things had changed for me, no one knew it. We, Sir Robert's household, stayed some days at Theobalds, though the royal party, with the actors' company behind them, went back almost immediately. Sir Robert had things to order here: since his father died, Theobalds was now his property. The great house on the Strand had gone to his brother, and Sir Robert was preparing himself another across the street, hard by the Savoy, though in this close family the change of ownership hadn't altered the household, or Sir Robert's presence, to any real degree.

As we rode back to town the dog roses were opening in the hedgerows, though a sharp wind made silver waves on the seas of barley like the ripple of fur on a noble's cloak. London seemed stuffy on my return, and in that close stillness the thought of Martin Slaughter kept coming back to me.

PART III

… who seeketh two strings to one bow, they may shoot strong but never straight. And if you suppose that princes' causes be veiled so covertly that no intelligence may bewray them, deceive not yourself: we old foxes can find shifts to save ourselves by others' malice, and come by knowledge of greatest secret, specially if it touch our freehold.

Letter from Elizabeth I to James VI of Scotland

Weeds are always growing, the great Mother of all living Creatures, the Earth, is full of feed in her Bowels, and any stirring gives them heat of the Sun, and being laid near day, they grow.

A New Orchard and Garden, **William Lawson**

Jeanne
July 1599

I was happy in those next few weeks, and yet I was unsettled. I wasn't at ease. I'd always thought of happiness as something calm and reassuring, like a warm coat on a winter's day – the absence, for a while, of fear; a little pleasure, a new plant or a pasty; something interesting to chew on in my work. This was different. This was more like finding that a layer of my skin had been stripped away, so that everything I felt, I felt more sharply.

I went to the booksellers' row round St Paul's churchyard the Saturday after we got back, and it was thin of company. The poor scholars were still there, in their shabby black, and the foreign visitors too, but the young lawyers from the Inns of Court had gone home for the harvest holidays, and the gallants snickering over the latest Italian translations – the ones with the special illustrations, that the shopmen brought out from under counters, quietly – were likewise in the country. I spotted Martin Slaughter quite easily. Spotted him, and then stopped dead for a moment feeling oddly shy. Seeing him as a stranger might do, slight and inconspicuous with his brown hair and brown doublet – until, I thought, you noticed something quick and definite in his movements. A kind of gallantry … Or was that just to my eye?

I might almost have gone away that moment, but he turned and saw me – and beckoned, as if to an old friend, easily. He was leafing through a pile of new editions of some of the London plays, and expostulating on the cuts and errors in a way that made the bookseller eye him angrily. It was only later that I realised, looking back, he had been talking too much, too fluently – as if he were as nervous as I. He asked which stall I liked best, and I led him to the one with the great illustrated herbals, where a new barrel of the latest books came in regularly from the Low Countries. Afterwards, it seemed only natural that he should suggest we go to a nearby tavern, to sit outside in the summer warmth, and only natural for me to agree. It was the kind of thing I hadn't often done, keeping myself one step away from those around as I had had to, and it came to me, with quite a different kind of warmth, that with a friend, someone who knew my past, there might be new pleasures open to me.

We came to meet almost regularly on the booksellers' row, though always without acknowledging that there was any more than chance, without anything so close to commitment as an appointment. Books can be a path to anywhere and so they were for Martin and me. Showing him the illustration of a herb, or a way of growing, I told him about Sundays in the garden with Jacob. To talk of the publisher Christopher Plantin, Jacob's friend, who had died in Antwerp but whose illustrations lived on, was to talk of the Low Countries and of what had happened to the Protestant refugees who had remained there. Even now, I said little. But what I did say, I think he understood. Maybe it was his actor's craft, to feel dead or invented tragedies as if they lived anew. Maybe it was something of his own experience; though England had looked peaceful to Jacob and to me, it had known its troubles just as we had in the countries across the sea. These last few years, it seemed, one could remember that more easily.

Sometimes we walked; sometimes we sat, to watch the other people walking by. It was something I might once have dismissed as a waste of time, but for him it was a business to be taken seriously. He told me an actor must learn how to read the signs, so he can give an audience more about a character than mere words alone can ever say. He taught me to open my eyes – how this man walked bold, but had a thief's brand on his hand, how the sailors in from foreign ports looked about them with as much bravado as curiosity. I learned, I suppose, that everyone has a story.

Showing me the play texts, Martin told me of parts he'd taken, and a little of his own early years in the smooth fertile Hertfordshire country, a placid land that yet remembered dramas from when Catholic and Protestant princesses, Mary and Elizabeth, had squabbled over the territory. He told me tales, too, of life on the road – tales to make me laugh, mostly. I came to be aware of reticences – that there were things he was not telling me. But that was all right; I'd grown up with silences and with secrecies. Martin had shown me I was not alone in that, but open-mouthed frankness might still have disconcerted me.

And yet behind the pleasure of those Saturdays, I had a growing unease. Sometimes his question, about the future, came back to me. It was one of those things of which I had managed not to think, and done it successfully. He never mentioned it again – I came to realise he was handling me warily, as one might a half-tamed animal lest it suddenly run away. But there was still a kind of challenge, not in anything he said but somehow in what he was. In what he was to me. I greeted that challenge almost resentfully.

Sometimes we talked of the news on the streets – it was hard not to, in those weeks. As July wore on the reports from Ireland grew worse every day. They were raising more trained bands in the City. The tavern drinkers still cheered Lord Essex's eventual victory, but the more sober heads – Martin said – were setting their faces against further demands, and lamenting the monies already spent.

'You should hear his excuses,' Martin said once, with a flash of what looked like real anger. It was the kind of feeling he showed only rarely. 'In the spring his force wasn't ready to campaign, or so he said. In the summer he was too busy on other matters to march to where he's supposed to be. Now autumn's almost on us, and I suppose he'll be declaring we're past the fighting season, see you next year, and anyone could tell you how well that will go down with her majesty. Anyone but his lordship, anyway.'

He seemed well informed – I said as much, but he didn't answer me directly. I suppose every ale-drinker was a bar-room general, though I wouldn't have put Martin in that company. Some doubt must have showed on my face because 'Actors hear things,' he reminded me. 'And when you think how many times I've waved a sword on stage, I swear they could give me charge of a company!' I laughed, as I was supposed to, but it was a retreat, or so it seemed to me. And perhaps Martin's nerves were a little on edge. As we left the tavern late, and set out through the darkening streets – only a few weeks past midsummer, but the evenings were drawing in already – he stopped, and grasped my arm suddenly. I didn't know what he was going to say. For a single minute I thought he was going to kiss me – me, standing there in my doublet and hose. I wrenched my arm from his hand and almost ran down the street, calling an incoherent farewell behind me. I did not go to the booksellers the next Saturday.

Katherine, Countess of Nottingham

August 1599

I'd thought the rows were bad enough before he even went to Ireland. That'll teach me. He hadn't reached his ship before the complaining letters started, all about how he'd gone armed before but not behind, meaning that we'd be stabbing him in the back. As if we haven't had other things to think about while he's been away! It was the last of July or near when the report came secretly to my husband that the Spanish were on the move again, and he sent it on to Master Secretary. It was the very next day when another of Essex's complaints turned up: I suppose, to be fair, he could hardly have known it in advance, but it's hard not to feel that young man has always been his own worst enemy.

I knew the contents of that letter before the queen did; one learns how to arrange these things when you've lived in a palace as long as I have, but this time it was easy. The messenger was my own kinsman on my father's side, a promising young Carey.

Three months' campaigning and what had he to show for it? Nothing, not a single real victory. Oh, he complains the rebels fight in woods and bogs, skirmish and run away. They're armed by Spain, and more numerous than his troops, and he feels the lack of backing here at home. He'll have heard that while he's been away, Cecil has won mastership of the Court of Wards, and all that money Essex needs so badly.

I think Charles almost sympathises with him, oddly – of course they have both campaigned for her majesty. I can't say I do: a woman has different loyalties.

Well! Now at last the country has seen what my husband can do, I'm happy to say. Three days after that first secret warning, we all heard that a hundred Spanish ships were on the way, and as August broke the town was in a panic, chains down across the roads and closing the gates to the City. And who did they look to to defend them? Charles. Yes, even her majesty. Appointed lieutenant and captain general over all forces south of the Trent, with powers to defeat invasion and rebellion by whatever means he saw fit. Declare martial law, punish disorder at his own discretion, even make statutes, as long as they were necessary to govern the army. That's what the queen does when she really has confidence in somebody, I tell Lord Essex, silently. When she is certain of their loyalty. And the army Charles pulled together at Tilbury! Fifty thousand men and forty ships, all from nowhere in less than three weeks. That's what the people of this country can do when they actually trust somebody, for all Lord Essex is the one with the easy popularity.

Of course there were naysayers. At one point there were rumours the queen was dying; there were even rumours that Charles, if you please, had whipped up the panic, to show Lord Essex, the absent hero, 'that others could be followed as well as he'. My sister Philadelphia, always standing up for Essex, sniffed that Charles was always one to make a mountain out of a molehill – but that was after we'd heard that the Spanish fleet had sailed on by, to deal with the Dutch in another country. It's the fourth invasion scare in hardly more years, and I suppose it's got to feel like the boy who cried wolf. But of course my husband is right when he says that one fair day should not breed opinion it will never be foul weather again.

I told Philadelphia, what a pity her husband can't be here to help us – but then again, when you think of the turmoil Lord Scrope has managed to create in his governance of the Border countries … She blushed – we've both got the scarlet blush of the red-haired woman – and then I looked at her as if something had just caught my eye, and said what a pity that red hair like ours shows the grey so easily. Petty, in the context, maybe.

You'd have thought Essex might have been quiet, at least, while all this was going on. Maybe given us a little Irish victory. Instead, it was hardly a week later that the news came. He stood opposite Tyrone's army at last, and what was the outcome? A truce treaty! He should have brought us Tyrone's head on a spike, not splashed across a ford to shake hands with the enemy, in view of both their watching armies. And we're to believe that, in some mysterious way, it's for the good of the country? Tell that to someone who hasn't been watching court quarrels so long. My enemy's friend is my enemy. That's a maxim I learned from her majesty.

I didn't see the letter with that news. That one was brought not by a Carey but by Essex's man, one Cuffe. Still, the queen's anger knew no concealment, and I am left to wonder that his lordship shows his hand so clearly – or, whether the hand there now before him was quite the one he had meant to play? I'm not surprised that his friend Bacon warned him against Ireland, and has now abandoned Essex's cause entirely. And maybe, maybe, I'm not surprised that, when his lordship clamoured for the Irish job, Sir Robert Cecil helped to make it a possibility.

There was some satisfaction in knowing he didn't want to go, not really. But he'd bragged of being the right man for the job so often, he could hardly complain when they took him at his word. It was a winning situation, you might say. If Essex pacifies Ireland, well then England has her victory. If he fails miserably – well, scales and balances, it may take him down a peg or two. Every day, I find myself growing in admiration for Master Secretary.

It's barely a month later and I don't know what shocked me more – what happened this morning, or what I heard just now, as I came up through the pantry. We'd hardly got the queen out of bed when we heard the uproar, outside her very door. I remember we all froze there – her in her shift, with her hair, what there is of it, every which way, her wig on the stand, and the whalebone bodies laid out on the bed. There was one girl kneeling on the floor ready to roll the silk stocking on, another standing with the sleeves ready, and we all stuck as we were, like parts of the same clockwork toy run down.

As he stood there, the violence of the door slamming behind him made the dried cowslip blossoms dance in the bowl of white wine – nothing like it to drive wrinkles away – and I saw his eye light on a pile of stained brown bandages, like something off a mummified corpse. Soak them in solution of lady's mantle and it keeps the breasts firm, but I'll admit they don't look pretty.

Even Philadelphia looked thoroughly startled. I suppose, as much as anything else, it was the sheer incredulity. Almost half a century on the throne and now it comes, the sound we were always waiting for in the early days; the sound of men outside the door – shouting, angry.

He stank – that was the first thing I noticed. He must have been in the saddle since he landed from Ireland, and stewing himself into a muck sweat every inch of the way. But he went down onto his knees, babbling some nonsense about making her understand, and I hardly heard the words but the gesture would do, he was on his knees, no sword in his hand. I suppose it was then we all began to breathe again, just barely.

She's at her best in an emergency, of course – always was, from a girl. She held out her hand and she spoke to him kindly, and seemed not even to know what she looked like, she who manages these things so carefully. I think I admired her then as much as I ever have – to sit there as bare of grace as a plucked chicken and make believe she didn't feel diminished in any way. When she told him she would see him later he went away quite quietly, leaving her to face the day, and us to shut the doors on the whole court outside, gawping, as well they may. Oh, of course the insult to her hurts. I think we all felt it, even the young girls. To have her caught out like this, it lowers us all. In this world, a woman needs her mystery. They say the queen has two bodies: as a mortal, and as a monarch, one step from a divinity. What I say is, when your mortal body has just been exposed like this, it's hard to take comfort in a theory.

But, all of that, that's not what most shocks me.

As we stood for that moment at the open chamber doors, as they led Lord Essex away, I saw a man in Howard livery, and made sure he caught my eye. He slid out after Essex's party – we don't keep fools in our employ. I snapped at the girls to put the queen's combing cloth about her shoulders, and to use the box comb carefully, and that this time they might get a quill and clean the brushes properly. I was making more bustle than I had to, I suppose, but it relieved me. I waited long enough to see that Philadelphia wasn't supervising the choice of ribbons as she should. My sister has not the brains of a coney. 'Lady Scrope!' I said sharply, in public reproof, and she started, and signed to a maid where the ribbon knots should be pinned on the gown, for when the queen was ready. Then I said her majesty might wish to dress her head with the other pearl border, and made excuse to slip away. By now I reckoned the servitor and his news might be ready.

For the most part his words were reassuring. Essex himself, or so he claimed, had only ever planned to speak with the queen, though some in his party had talked more wildly. They'd met with Lord Grey on the way, so the man said, quite casually, and they'd tried to hold him back, to keep the advantage of surprise, but Lord Grey had got away from them and galloped ahead to the palace to warn Master Secretary.

The words seemed to burn into my brain. He'd galloped ahead to warn the Secretary, and what did the Secretary do with the warning? Nothing. How far ahead of the Essex crew had Lord Grey been? Only a few minutes, maybe. Yes, but how many minutes does it take, to run from the Secretary's chamber towards her majesty's, to call the guards – to shout a warning from one man to the other. It's not even as though we were in Whitehall – Nonsuch is a small palace, for all that it's so pretty.

Oh, I'm sure Cecil knew or guessed there was no real danger. I can't believe he'd have risked her majesty. But for all that I've said myself it would be best if the queen saw soon what Essex could do, for all that, this still shocks me. I'd thought myself so shrewd, so awake on every suit. Now I feel like a child, groping my way through a maze, while above my head others, more grown up than I, see their way clearly.

October 1599

There was a knot of serving men blocking the gravel path through the garden as I came in to work at Burghley House on Monday. Usually they kept their distance from the clerks, but today any hearer was better than none, and one of the more impertinent boys spun away from the group long enough to speak to me.

'Did you hear? They've got him at York House, just up the road, in the Lord Keeper's custody. Lord Essex, silly!' he added. He must have thought I hadn't understood, but behind the blankness of my face I felt as if all the barrels of the lock inside my head were suddenly clicking open. I hadn't thought much of Lord Essex these last weeks. Well, months, maybe. When men – when Martin Slaughter – spoke of him, even, it was almost as if they were speaking of a public stranger, as if there was a safe wall between the me I had become and the day at Wanstead, the moment at the tourney.

But I hadn't heard Martin Slaughter speak of anything, of course, since that August day, that evening in the alley. I hadn't seen or heard of him, and it felt almost as though those few weeks of companionship we'd shared had been swept away. If I were hiding myself, then events had helped me. No one could expect you to stroll around booksellers while London was preparing for a siege, and in the Secretary's house we were all too busy to go gallivanting, anyhow. On the heels of that reflection, I seemed to see Martin Slaughter's face, a faint look of hurt in his brown eyes. As I flinched away, my mind's eye fell greedily on Lord Essex's image, with the blind determination of a baby grasping at the breast. Only a few hundred yards away!

I knew I had to see him. It had been six months, almost to the day, since he'd gone away and now, as if to make up for the summer's disloyalty, my very gut seemed to have kept the tally.

I might not get into his presence. But I had to try, even if all I got to do in the end was to sit in the courtyard with the soldiers and their stories. If he'd returned in triumph, I might have been content to stand at the back of the crowds as they cheered, but he'd returned a captive, under the queen's displeasure, and that seemed to open a space for me.

A few drops of rain started to spit down as I turned towards the gate and I blessed them. They gave me the excuse to pull my cap low enough to hide my eyes. I'd have staked a guinea that panic stared from them as surely as from a doe's when the huntsmen hold her down and bare her throat for the knife, or a horse's, when they fit the headpiece on before the tourney.

The luck was with me. As I turned in to York House the porter's lodge was crowded with men and reeking with beer, and a bubble of frantic laughter rose up in my throat. Of course – they'd want, just like everybody else, to talk over the events of the last few days. The porter jerked a piece of sacking over the barrel as he turned towards me, caught out and ready to be surly. I just held up my satchel, bulging with papers, and let the badge on my cloak speak for me.

'It's all right – you can let him through. It's Master Secretary's boy.' It was a clerk of the house who called out from the back, and he added something under his breath that made the rest of the men laugh drunkenly.

The courtyard was still quiet – I thought that when my lord's baggage and his servants really started arriving, that porter had better put his head under the pump and get ready for the fray. I didn't know the house, but they'd have put him upstairs and at the back: honourable quarters – just in case he was back on top of the dung heap tomorrow – and far enough from the street that any supporters couldn't get to him too easily. A lad with a bucket pointed me to the right staircase, and the badge and the papers were enough to make the guard open the door. I stopped dead inside. I didn't even know why I was here, never mind what I was going to say.

He was alone, thank God. He showed no surprise at seeing me. I suppose the appearance of one of the Secretary's servants really didn't rank high in the surprises of these days. He just held out his hand, for the papers he supposed I'd brought. It was a minute before he even recognised me.

'Why – Jeanne.' He said it like a man waking slowly from a dream. 'Janny ...' I gazed at him dumbly. So much had happened in Ireland, yet on the surface he didn't look much different and that's what I blurted out, indignantly.

'Oh, Janny,' his eyes creasing up with laughter, 'ten months, and battles, and high politics and the queen's displeasure, and what a thing to say. I've had the Council on at me for three days now about Tyrone. Surely there's something other than my looks you're supposed to ask me?'

'Is it true, that you came back from Ireland without permission? And that you shoved into her majesty's chamber early and found her ...'

'Yes! Every bit of it! They hadn't even cleared away the pot she used to piss in. I felt like the fox who'd got shut in the hen house. Mistress Russell shrieked as though I'd violated the Vestal Virgins' shrine, and I thought my Lady of Nottingham was going to make the sign of the cross at me.'

'How did she look?' I seemed to have got stuck on a loop of trivialities, but it was what everyone wanted to know. When you've spent a lifetime gazing at an image of jewels and face paint, and being told it's an icon of beauty, the idea of pulling down the conjurer's screen and showing how the trick is worked brings out the wicked schoolboy in everybody.

'The queen? Old.' He'd sobered suddenly. 'If you want the truth, I wouldn't have recognised her at once – not from behind. They hadn't got her wig on, and there was just this short, grey stubble. In her nightgown, without the dress and the jewellery, it could have been an old man sitting there.' His eyes flicked up at me.

'You know she'll never forgive you.'

'What, for the treaty? No, I tell you –' He'd explained it all to the lords. He seemed to have forgotten he had no need to justify himself to me.

'Not the treaty – for having seen her like that.' He gazed at me uncomprehendingly. 'No woman would.' I could see him registering slowly that this was one area where I could speak with authority. But he shrugged it away.

'She always forgives me.' He jumped up and began striding around the room. An inkwell on the desk crashed to the floor: the very force of his convictions must make him clumsy. The guard stuck his head around the door in alarm, but Essex waved him off, ignoring the spreading stain on the floorboards. The servants would curse, when they tried to scrub that one away.

'She's got to forgive me.' He was off now, talking wildly, half to himself, about the queen's enemies, how everyone was against him but they'd all see, how he was the only one who gave a toss for the country. The words hardly registered, everybody knew the theme, and truth to tell it was hard to take it more seriously than when old Nan down the street used to start yelling about how the end of the world was nigh. It was the kind of thing they came on and roared in a play. But not for Lord Essex. His face was red, and he was sweating slightly. I smelt a strange acrid tang on his breath as he grabbed my shoulders and rounded on me.

'Whose sake brought you here? Is it for Cecil – or for me?' When I didn't answer, he shook me. I saw my master's face in my mind's eye, knowing eyes under those arched brows. It seemed to make no demands, to leave the judgement to me.

'Me. I mean, my own sake. I'm here for myself.' It seemed to satisfy Lord Essex – or at least, to make him lose interest in me.

It was time to get out. I didn't know what I'd come for, but I'd been wrong: this was a different Essex from the man at Wanstead, or at the tourney. And at any moment, someone was going to come along who wouldn't fall back in awe at the mere sight of a handful of papers. Someone who would query my presence later, in silken tones, to the Secretary. At the door, I turned.

'My lord – if there's ever anything I can do.' I didn't even know what I meant, but he seemed hardly to hear me, and just as well, maybe. Later, down the road in an empty wine shop, with a beaker of mulled ale to still the tremble in my legs, I remembered that promises of loyalty to Lord Essex had a way of coming home to roost. They should not be given lightly.

Back at work, Sir Robert set me to translating a new volume on herbs that he'd been sent from France, though the litany of vervain and tansy, mallow and chamomile didn't soothe me as it usually would. I was relieved that he didn't say anything about Lord Essex – but then why should he? It was only much later I realised the guard on the door probably took extra pay to keep his ears open, and the Secretary knew everything already.

As the days passed and autumn edged towards winter, and the chill began to stick out under the late sun like the ribs under an alley cat's fur, the tavern talk was still all of Lord Essex, and of how he was growing sicker in captivity, and whether he'd be out of custody for the tilt this Accession Day.

There came a Saturday when I couldn't resist the booksellers any longer. And in any case, I knew I was being silly. Had been silly, in the alley that day. And there were some references in that new herbal I didn't understand, and maybe I'd find something else that could help me ... At any rate, that's what I told myself.

My heart gave a queer leap when I saw his back in that brown doublet. Only a turned shoulder and a cap, but I had no doubt that it was he. I had time to notice the cloth was getting shabby before I reached him and, tentatively, put a hand on his arm. He spun around and for a second I saw warm gladness in his eyes before something more complicated took its place.

'Jan!' This time, he pronounced it harder than he usually did, so the boy's name came out quite clearly. The name everyone else called me. 'How nice to see you again. Master Cuffe, might I present Master de Musset?' I hadn't even noticed the man standing beside him – why should I? But now I found myself making a hasty bow to a lanky man in black, who barely acknowledged me. I had time to eye him while Martin was explaining that he and I had met here before, that I was a fellow book lover though our tastes differed occasionally. He was speaking as if I were the most ordinary acquaintance, but I couldn't blame him for that, after last time, I thought miserably. And how did I expect him to introduce me, anyway, me with my cropped hair and clerk's outfit? It might have been different if this Cuffe had been another actor, but somehow I knew he had nothing to do with that all-forgiving company. A pale face and somehow puffy under the tall-brimmed black hat, an air of self-consequence. Until his eyes fell on my livery button, he hardly looked at me.

'A pleasure, Master de Musset. Martin, shall we? That new place you promised to show me ...' And Martin was off behind him, with a stranger's hasty bow to me, and another hard look I couldn't understand. I was left standing there, more disturbed than I'd thought I could possibly be.

I walked for a while. I didn't know where I was going, but eventually I found I was circling the gardens outside the City. That wouldn't get me anywhere, and I needed to eat. There was a tavern where I'd been with Martin several times – after all, they knew me there, and I knew the food. And why shouldn't I dine there as well as anybody?

I'd have had no chance to turn and run, he was watching out, and he sprang up as soon as he saw me.

'Jeanne – thank God, I was afraid you wouldn't come. Look, I'm sorry –' But he broke off. Sorry for what, exactly? He seemed to realise that explanations would only get us into worse difficulties. With an air of lightness that was only slightly forced – he was an actor, after all – he began to talk of other things. The book he'd found, the unseasonable weather, and the news. Heaven knows, news wasn't hard to come by.

Everyone knew Lord Essex had fallen sick of the Irish flux; just as they knew Tyrone had taken up arms again in Ireland, at the end of the month's treaty. One of the secret clerks had said Lord Essex's illnesses came as easily as a whore's kisses, and for just the same reason – adding that, this time, if he were hoping to move the queen, it wasn't going to work. I opened my mouth to force myself to tell Martin Slaughter that – I couldn't go on just nodding about the harvest, and I had a dim sense that if we spoke of his lordship, Martin might somehow help me to make sense of the mixture of feelings that were in me. But he forestalled me.

'Master Cuffe, whom you met earlier – he's one of Lord Essex's men. In fact, he's one of his foremost secretaries. Professor of Rhetoric at Oxford, he used to be. It was who brought Lord Essex's last letter back from Ireland.' He was speaking not without effort, or so it seemed to me. And I was struggling to frame my reply.

'A responsible position – especially in these times.' I had to bite back other words. For God's sake, why? When I've heard the disapproval with which you spoke of Essex before, why are you cosying up to his man, and why now are you sitting here speaking of him in this guarded way? I couldn't stand it any longer. I'd had no training for this kind of thing in my life without society.

'I must go. I'm glad to have seen you, Martin.' He made no move to detain me. But he looked at me again, and this time I'd have sworn I could interpret it, as a plea. Or an apology.

One morning in early November, with the news from York House that Lord Essex was sicker, Sir Robert sent for me. I was to take a letter to York House, and give it into Lord Essex's own hand. I was ... He paused, as if uncertain what to say.

The study window gave out onto the garden. He stood there, gazing towards the river, though the day was too thick to see clearly. 'Tell me how he really is,' he said abruptly. 'I've got a doctor's report for every time he takes physic, but they're the stew without the meat. I don't doubt he's fretted himself into high fever by now, but is there any more to it? He always was one who could die of a cold for thinking it was a catalepsy, as our old nurse used to say.' I had almost forgotten that they had been boys together. But for Sir Robert the memories, good and bad, can't ever have been far away.

'Take him some fruit, as a token of my good will. Nothing raw if he's got the flux. Pears in wine? Or some of that quince jelly? Tell them to give you whatever you want. See if you can find anything in the garden, maybe.' He met my eyes briefly, and I might almost have thought he knew the pleasure the giving would be to me. Knew that the wide-eyed gabble in the streets, that Lord Essex was failing and the doctors despaired, had felt like something gnawing a hole in me. Hastily, Sir Robert gestured me to go, as if half ashamed of sounding so solicitous over the man who was supposed to be his enemy.

I ordered the pears, and the jelly, and a bottle of the cordial of red rose hips, and a dish of crab apples baked in honey too. The beds in the garden were dug over by now, but I found a few sprigs of a bramble blooming late, and grey lavender spikes where the scent still lingered, and the first blue flowers of next year's rosemary. Rosemary for remembrance. With fingers that trembled slightly in their haste, I bound them into a nosegay.

At York House, things were more in order than they had been. Lord Essex had never been allowed to have his own servants join him, but now he was attended – guarded – properly. I could never have bluffed my way in, as I did that first day. Even with Sir Robert's authority, I was stopped at the door by my lord Essex's doctor, who lifted the cloth from the basket I carried and sniffed at the content suspiciously.

'What do you want to do, boy – poison him?' The word hung in the air between us like an accusation, and the doctor retreated hastily. 'I meant, such indigestible foods, for a man in his lordship's condition …' He signed for a man to carry the delicacies away, no doubt to be enjoyed at his own dinner, but I clung obstinately to my little nosegay.

'A token of Sir Robert's goodwill.' The doctor nodded, grudgingly.

Inside the chamber, the air was foul. The servants had done what they could, but when the patient has voided, and voided again, the very hangings take up the smell of sickness, change the linen and the rushes as often as you may. The voice from the great bed was no more than a thread. 'Janny?'

I would hardly have known him, his cheeks were so fallen in. There were sores around his mouth, and his long hair hung limply. Under the watchful eyes of his attendants, he held out a hand for the letter, but his grasp was too uncertain to break the seal and he gestured me closer. His breath was hot and sour. 'Read it to me.'

The words themselves were nothing much. Sir Robert was grieved to hear of Lord Essex's illness – wished to assure Lord Essex of his prayers and his friendship – hoped Lord Essex would soon be restored to health, as to her majesty's most princely favour. He seemed to take them as routine – with disappointment, I thought, as a piece of mere court flummery. With a finger he brushed the flowers. 'For me? From Sir Robert? Really?' I shook my head dumbly. The ghost of his sweetest smile flickered over his face, and the bridle of pleasure seemed almost to lend him flush of strength. Absurd to think he could care that way for a mere nobody's affection, but he'd always responded like a shy girl to flattery.

'I give humble thanks to all my well wishers. Say as much to Master Secretary.' He turned his face on the pillow, and the doctor hurried forward officiously. I made my way out into the street with my head in a whirl. In the pride of his strength and his ambition, Lord Essex had been able to turn my mind upside down. Now for the first time I had a presentiment that his weakness might give him an even stronger hold over me.

When I went back to the house to make my report, they told me Sir Robert was at Whitehall with the court, and had left word I should make my report to him there. The corridors and the courtiers no longer held quite the terrors they once would have for me – I'd been here before, stepping soft behind some more experienced secretary. But I stuck close to the page as he led me through the maze. It was a rambling, old-fashioned rabbit warren of a place, courtyards sprouting literally hundreds of doorways giving onto poky rooms, the kind of rooms made for secrets – and for disappointment, it seemed to me. But as we thrust onwards into its heart, further than I had ever been before, the richness of the decorations made me gasp. It was like stepping into the pages of a missal.

I checked when the page passed before me through the great hall, and the guards' room, and to the doors of the very Presence Chamber. The boy, an impertinent scrap, contemptuously jerked his head for me to go on in. A throng of ladies and gentlemen were there, but among them to my relief I could see Sir Robert, talking to a middle-aged lady all in black, whose curls showed reddish under the back of her cap. Over her turned shoulder, he saw me. I knew him well enough to read his moods by now, and he was not sorry to come over and speak to me. I told him what I'd seen and he nodded as if to say, yes, after all, just what he'd known already, when there came a rustle of skirts and the click of heels on the floor and a sharpening of the atmosphere, as if the very air itself had sprung to attention, to tell me that this heralded her majesty.

I stood just inside the door, and lowered my eyes submissively. I tried to pretend I was part of the furniture, but of course she had no eyes for me.

'Ah, Lady Scrope, as festive as ever, I see,' she said in clear, cold tones as she swept past me, and the black-clad lady ducked her rusty head submissively. As her ladies followed hastily I heard an exasperated murmur – 'Philadelphia ...' – spoken exasperatedly.

I could see the flowery hems of the younger maids' skirts, and hear the hiss and bubble of their whispered chatter, but the queen and Sir Robert spoke together in low tones at the far end of the room. After a few minutes I grew bolder and peeped up under my lashes, only to find that the queen was looking directly at me. Drop my gaze as fast as I might, I was still hooked, like a fish on a line, by the power of that hard black eye.

Old she might be, and indeed, as she passed there had been the faintest whiff of decay. The image Lord Essex had conjured up for me had destroyed the illusion she was anything but an old woman, soon to die, and for the first time I truly understood the urgent squabbling, the need to secure a future, of those nearer at hand who lived with this knowledge every day. But nothing could take her force away.

I rode back to Burghley House behind the Secretary, behind the guards who went everywhere with him these days. These were hard times to be Sir Robert Cecil on the London streets, or even to wear any trace of his livery. Rumours of Lord Essex's sickness, of his close imprisonment, were on every corner and the people knew who they blamed. Mostly it appeared only in their sullen eyes, but occasionally some urchin, bolder than the rest, would catcall, or yell out something about 'pen gents' from the safety of the crowd. As we drew near the house, men were scrubbing at the wall and I cocked an eyebrow at a groom, enquiringly.

'Yes, another one, this morning,' he confirmed in an undertone. '"Here lies the toad", it said.' We were beginning to get used to the graffiti.

As we dismounted and the grooms came to the horses' heads, I would have melted away, but a motion from Sir Robert stopped me. 'Walk with me a little, in the garden,' he said. 'I need the fresh air to clear my head.' To most people there would have been little to see except the bare shape of the borders, but he looked at the clipped hedges and fine raised earth of the neatly turned beds with a true gardener's eye.

His servants knew his habits; even in winter, the sand on the paths was freshly raked, and there hadn't yet been a frost hard enough to make them bring the birds indoors from the aviary. A small bag of grain hung ready to hand and he flung a pinch to the twittering occupants, absent-mindedly.

'He's been writing to Scotland, you know.' No need to ask who 'he' might be. I suppose in a way it should have been no surprise. Everyone knew that, of all the contenders, the Scots king had to be the best bet to succeed her majesty. I daresay there wasn't a courtier or an officer of state whose mind's eye didn't turn that way. But even to say so aloud was treason, and for a private citizen to approach the head of a foreign power, in a matter of such magnitude, was worse than that – it was treachery.

'Are you certain?' I said it baldly, almost as if I spoke to an equal, but he didn't reprove me. Although he didn't answer, either, just passed me the grain and gestured at the aviary. A dozen sentences hung around my lips – Do you have proof? and Surely he wouldn't? and Now's your chance to crush him, if you want to – but there seemed nothing I could safely say.

After a minute he moved on, by the wall where in summer the peach tree bloomed, and where, on a warm evening, you could hear the laughing couples on the other side make their way up to the fields. Abruptly he paused, and though his grave face gave no sign, I felt his dismay.

A robin lay at his feet, its feathers bright as on the aviary birds, but a stick had been driven through its red breast, heavy enough to carry it over the wall, if flung with sufficient force. The man whose name was often made into Robin gazed at it a second, summoning his calm, then stepped back towards the house without a word. It was I, left behind, whose eyes pricked with a sudden burn of sympathy.

I grabbed the stick and would have thrown it back – but the more people who saw it, the more the insult would be a tavern story. Instead I seized a spade that a gardener had left and began digging a shallow grave, clumsily. I was too angry to think of the question I should have been asking. The news about Lord Essex and the Scots king – no doubt it was true. He'd never neglect such an opportunity. And Scotland was far enough away that maybe James would believe Lord Essex when he said he alone could rule the queen. Or maybe not. Everyone said the Scots king was canny. But – and it only came to me that night, when the call of the Watch had woken me – true or not true, prudence or treachery, why was Sir Robert telling me?

Cecil

October 1599

He's been writing to Scotland: well, of course he has. Cuffe must be putting something together every week, or nearly. Erratic in his behaviour Essex may be, but he's not such a fool as to ignore what any ploughboy in the field could see, that her majesty cannot grace the throne forever, that change must come sure as night follows day. And I'm sure he's loving it – a clandestine correspondence, with all its perfume of rebellion and of secrecy; a chance to preen himself again as England's saviour, and for a new audience which hasn't already seen through his games. James may take Essex at his own valuation – or nearly, everyone agrees that the Scots king is canny. But they also say good-looking young men can hope he'll look on them indulgently.

That could never have been my way to appeal to him. I would not want it to be. But any question of approach is for the future: for now, the faintest question of it is impossible. Ruination if it came to the queen's ears – though just occasionally the dizzying thought takes me, what if the queen is one step before me? What if she knows we are all calculating the future, and it's from the safety of that knowledge that she allows herself to indulge her folly? For it is folly, for an old and childless monarch to scream that to speak of her successor is to set her winding sheet before her eyes; and yet her majesty is the furthest thing from a fool; and so logically ... I push the thought away, for there is no profit in it. Even if I could safely send letters north I wouldn't do it; not to appear as second-best claimant to the king's attentions at a moment when he is dazzled by Essex, when Essex will have told him I am the enemy.

My father could never understand that I am a gambling man. I told him it gives me good access to the gallants at court to play, and to play high. He nodded, grudgingly. But one thing gambling has taught me: I know when the player who sits out a round may rise the winner at the end of the evening, and I know other things too. I know the value of a wild card, and that's what I have been offering Essex, ever since I sent Jeanne to Wanstead that day.

Oh, the chances of its paying dividend could never be rated high, but in this game you scatter your bread upon the waters and if one crumb in a thousand comes back to you as a loaf, you're happy. There are spies informing upon spies in the Essex household, but knowledge can never be too dearly bought, as Walsingham used to say. Not that the gathering of information is all of it, of course: information, disinformation; lies to draw truths, sprats to catch mackerel; and the faint fishy reek of scandal to be spread, maybe. We can use Jeanne's innocence as well as her isolation, and perhaps even the uncertainty over her sex.

I could have had no excuse to send a girl to Lord Essex, openly; but he would never have treated a real boy so, at the tourney. We can use Essex's charm as well as his vanity: use your opponent's own strengths to overthrow him, the sergeant used to tell the boys – the other boys – when they practised in the armoury.

You can always use charm, and in more ways than one. You can always use vanity. My father could count on Walsingham's spies: now Walsingham's daughter is married to Lord Essex, and I have to do things differently.

So: James. I do not move, I wait. I wait and see. It's what my father would expect of me. On his deathbed he laid it on me as a charge, to ensure a smooth transition for our country. But it was not rash action he had in mind: nothing ill-considered, nothing hasty. Rather an onward-looking gardener's eye, to see that the beds which hold the future's crop are dug and seeded carefully. Only – I do wonder sometimes, how it would be, to live in the present, unquestioningly. To know that the future is out of your hands, as surely as a gambler when he turns over the cards, or a milkmaid who's been with a boy, and can't do anything else but wait for the missed courses and the tender breasts that mean an unwanted pregnancy.

Jeanne

November 1599

Queen Elizabeth had sat on the throne of England since before I was born and I suppose we had all come half to believe the legend of her immortality. But sometimes, it's as if your eyes have been opened to a particular subject and suddenly, that's all you can see. Of course I'd thought about the future – the future after Queen Elizabeth – who hadn't? The ploughboy in the field maybe. But somehow, underneath the speculation, there must have lain a vague sense that these things were sorted out somewhere. That someone knew what the answer would be. The king of Scots, the Earl of Hertford's son, or my lord of Shrewsbury's niece. Even, God forbid, the Infanta of Catholic Spain, and that thought had seemed to bring it closer to me. Seemed almost to make me think that everyone had a part to play.

Now, not only did every tavern conversation half heard seem to contain an illicit whisper, but I truly understood for the first time how anxious, how ambitious, how afraid all the nobles were – the ones too highly placed to hide their heads in a crowd, the ones with most to lose. Yes, even – especially – the Secretary.

A new king, or queen, might seek new advisers. The race would be to those who had offered their support early. Yet who was more firmly barred from offering support than he who was tied to the old regime most closely? It must be like one of those baitings, where they tie the bear so tight he can't even fight against the dogs. Or one of those dreams, where you can see the danger coming, but it's as if you're mired in quicksand, and can't run away.

I said as much to Martin Slaughter, sitting inside the tavern, this time, driven in by the threat of rain. This was the first Saturday I'd seen him without Master Cuffe at his side (yes, I had been keeping watch) and I was determined to make the most of the opportunity. But it seemed to me, sadly, that we were glad, now, of a subject of conversation outside ourselves. As I spoke, he looked at me – what? I almost thought, contemptuously. That, or as if he felt sorry for me. I suppose I had been slow on the uptake. I suppose I didn't grasp as much as I should of the world around me. In my confusion, I almost said that his friend Master Cuffe must know all about that problem, but I bit the words back as they rose to my lips. Just as well I did – almost as I began speaking, a dark shadow materialised behind me.

'Martin – are you ready?' I don't think Master Cuffe even glanced at me. A tiny spark of anger rose in me. I didn't have much sense of my own importance, but it was too much to be ignored this way.

'You have an appointment, Martin? You should have told me.' Now Cuffe did flick his eyes down to me.

'Master Slaughter is taking a role in a very special new play,' he informed me, and my tiny bubble of pride was pricked, like the pigs' bladders boys blow up and explode on fairground day. He hadn't told me.

'Oh, you should have said. I must come to see it.' Now Martin looked embarrassed, quite definitely, and it was Master Cuffe who answered, shortly.

'It's a private theatre – near Blackfriars. You'll have heard of them, no doubt, but they're only for the gentry.'

Martin had leapt to his feet when Cuffe arrived. Now, silent, he allowed himself to be ushered away.

The news from York House was always worse. Lord Essex could only be lifted from his bed long enough for the servants to change the sheets soaked with black voided matter. Lord Essex was so sick his doctors despaired; and the preachers in the London pulpits offered prayers for his recovery. The queen didn't like that, so they said. She'd never been a woman who wanted to share her place in the sun, and now, when so much in life had left her, she clung onto the love of her people, jealously. But she sent her own doctors to him: teams of them – a sign she still cared, surely?

'A sign she prefers a man when he's beneath her, not on top,' said the gangling clerk, grinning bawdily.

Katherine, Countess of Nottingham

29 November 1599

I swear, now I see the queen in the cold winter sunlight, that black satin sleeve looks positively faded, and as I stand behind her chair, my face, I may trust, as expressionless as ever, there is an angry litany running through my head of what I'll say when I have the maids alone.

Must I go down into the park myself, I'll say, and pull the ivy off the trees? And then mash the leaves until the rinsing water runs dark – or is it just possible that one of you could see the laundresses do their work properly? I can see in my mind's eye the pout there'll be on each young face, but they won't voice their thoughts, not in front of me. Mind you, her majesty won't be wearing much more black this season, or not if I have anything to say about it. We've got enough crows at court already.

If Lady Essex wants to wear mourning while her husband is in prison, well, I suppose I've nothing to say. He is her husband, after all, and the poor girl with a baby on the way. But Philadelphia! What cause has she to go into mourning, pray? – and then to go round telling everybody Lord Essex's troubles have taken her joy in living away. I suppose I may be thankful she didn't take it upon herself to spell out to the queen precisely why she feels – I trust I have her words right – that while virtue and valour lie smitten to the heart, it is time to mourn for the country. I told her, if she wasn't careful people would be saying she was just another old woman fallen for a handsome young face, and she pretended to look shocked and to hush my mouth, as if I need lessons in discretion from the likes of her, as if I'd be meaning her majesty. And then she said, with that little dazzle of conscious daring on her face, the one she had as a child when she knew she was being naughty, that that's what the men do so why shouldn't we, and she hadn't seen Emilia around court so much recently. And I had to hold my hands hard not to slap her, for we all know my father had Emilia Lanier in keeping the years before he died but to mock like that at his memory ... And then she said, how is Charles, by the way? I told her, with forty far behind it was time to put off these young girl's tricks, and she said I'd never been young, anyway. My sister is a flighty woman. I was never able to be flighty. Those six years in age I have over her feel more like something she has over me. Six years, just the length of the reign of old Queen Mary, so that I grew up in the dark days, the burning days, when anyone with Boleyn blood in their veins walked fearfully, while she stepped straight out from the schoolroom into our own queen's first heyday. Any disturbance in the court sees her darting above it, zestful as a gadfly. It's enough to make me wish that husband of hers would come down from his precious northern castle occasion-ally and give her something else to think about: all these years of marriage she's had and just the one baby.

These last few weeks, the queen has been calling for Philadelphia to sit up late with her as often as for me.

I couldn't believe it when Lady Warwick told me where they'd been yesterday. I thought everything was as it should be. Tomorrow the queen will have her complaints against Lord Essex read out, and it will be Charles' chance to have his say. He'll be able to tell the world that if he'd had the army Lord Essex was given, he could have marched it clear to Spain, as he has so often said to me. I could have sworn the queen was as annoyed by Philadelphia's folly as I am myself: she's certainly been speaking of it despitefully. But then to go out on the river with just Lady Warwick, and to have herself rowed down to York House privately. Lady Warwick swears they didn't even get to Essex's sickroom, in the end, just walked in the garden with the Lord Keeper, and came away quite quietly, but that's almost worse in a way. Well, no, not worse, but it makes the queen look like a lovesick laundry maid, or one of those laugh-able suitors in the old songs who just wanted to be near their beloved and probably wouldn't have known what to do about it if they were wedded and bedded decently.

She'd said that if Lord Essex had been her own son she'd have had him shut up in the highest tower in England for his wicked folly. When the wife of one of Lord Essex's crew – Lady Harington, it was – tried to excuse her husband's part in it all, she said that no doubt Lady Harington was doing her wifely duty, but that she was the queen and she had her duty to her husband the country. Now this. It makes her look foolish. It makes me feel foolish, as if there are things about the queen I've failed to understand. As if there are things that are closed to me. And the worst of it is, I see Philadelphia's hand, even though she may not have been in the boat with her majesty.

What, my sister intercedes for Essex, and Essex has become the proposer of James, and next thing we know we have a king who owes his crown to Philadelphia's meddling? All my life I've been careful to stand a little apart, to ask few favours of her majesty. It is one reason why she trusts me. But this – I've tried never to have much truck with fear, or no more than any woman with children must do. No truck with the foolish fears, at least. We who grew up in the middle of this century knew there were enough real dangers to endure, without going out to meet ideas halfway. But now I find myself fearful, and I do not quite know why. I do not know which thought rattles me more: that the queen may still have a foolish heart for Essex, or that there may be sense in Philadelphia's folly.

Cecil

30 November 1599

I look on it as one of my advantages that I never make the mistake of underestimating her majesty – unlike so many others, unlike even my father, maybe. He spoke to her always as an

elder, however respectfully – I must frame my words more carefully. But care comes naturally to me. And I am aware that I
have never known for certain how much she is really – was
really? – under Essex's spell, or whether she dices with danger as
one leans over the side of a ship, half dreaming the next big crash
of the waves might carry you away. Or, as one stakes one's last
card at the tables, maybe.

When I said that to Lizzie once, she looked at me as if I were
missing something important – almost pityingly. I am reluctant
to take onto my back the burden of doubt such a thought would
load on me, but better that than really to have failed to understand. The queen has two bodies, and one is frail and mortal, all
too surely. If it is sense enchantment we are talking here, the
sheer power of his long body, then I can make reckoning,
whether or not I understand. And there are other things I do
understand: I understand that the queen, that any woman, has
fears that may be hidden from me.

I have never been a man who has much truck with fear; not
like Essex with his suspicious mind, and his imagination's
tyranny. Dangers are real and present and all around us, and I
see them clearly, as my father trained me to do. But by the grace
of God, rewarding our own uttermost efforts, we can prevail
against them and the world work out the ordained way.

Oh, I understand fear, as any effective statesman must do: I
have doled it out in judicious measure, as a doctor might a pill
– spread whispers about our enemies, had a witness shown the
rack – but its conquest, in myself, has been my victory. Still the
thought of the queen and Essex makes me uneasy, makes me
wonder what wheels have been turning where even I cannot see.
Makes me wonder – just faintly, in moments of fatigue, in the
night – whether I and my like have got things wrong, and that
thought does frighten me.

Jeanne

December 1599

The more word spread of my lord Essex's illness, the more the people in the streets grumbled he'd been treated harshly.

'Held in close confinement without even a trial, shows they know they've got nothing against him. Why, you wouldn't treat a dog that way.'

That must be why the queen had her complaints against him read out, and every member of the Council, from the Secretary to the Lord Admiral, had their bit to say. That he had mismanaged the Irish campaign, that he had wasted a fortune in public money, and made a shameful treaty with the Irish leader. But in the clerks' room I had to listen to even darker stories. I'd taken to dropping in there at the end of the day, with a flagon of warm ale from the inn on the corner. The old clerk cracked a scribe's joke about Greeks and gifts, but he let the spicy heat melt his discretion away.

There were letters – he said – decoded in the utmost secrecy, from agents in Ireland who suggested Lord Essex had been something more than clumsy. That it wasn't just Tyrone had been one too many for him, and that he'd let himself be manoeuvred into that foolish treaty – that the friendship between them was of older date, that when Lord Essex was sent to Ireland he already had an alliance with the man he was supposed to defeat, and maybe even ideas what he could do if he struck a deal for that man's army. I'd always seen him as a mouse of a man, with eyes grown rheumy and little wizened paws to hold his papers, and I'd come to grow fond of him over the months, but now I must have gazed at him as if he'd bared a rat's fangs.

'What, made a fool of you too, boy, has he?' He said it almost jeeringly, though his face was turned away. I answered something so pompous I could have learned it from a prayer book, about being horrified at such perfidy, and he bared yellow teeth and snuffled into his mug disbelievingly.

There came a day after the middle of the month when, having been out at Twickenham viewing a new consignment of plants Master Gerard had ordered, I was making my way back to the horse ferry near Whitehall through the clammy yellow light at the fading of the day. As I rode east it seemed to me that there were more crowds gathered than was usual for a week day and, now I thought of it, surely as I'd come up from the village to the south I'd heard the ghost of bells tolling on the wind. I kicked the horse to go faster, and leant forward anxiously. At the great house there was no more bustle than usual – or no more than I could be sure wasn't just my fancy, but I hurried to the clerks' room just the same. The gangling boy was there, with his loose wide mouth and the shiny-faced pleasure he always seemed to show in others' misery. He raised a mug in a mocking toast.

'What, you come back to join the mourning party?'

I froze. It seemed to me my face must have ceased to function the way it normally did, but luckily he went on, oblivious.

'You've missed a fine day of it, trekking all that way out after a few new daisies. Some fool spread the story his lordship had finally shat himself to death, and they've been ringing the bells all over London.

'Oh, it's not true,' he added, regretfully. 'But the rumours, and the counter rumours, and the wailing in the streets – you can guess how well that went down with her majesty. Sir Robert's been off to the palace, and I doubt he'll be back today.' He giggled, and drank again. It had become a funny story. I raised a hand, as if to gesture 'I give up' or 'Tell me another one', and turned away. I think I managed the ghost of a grin but it didn't matter, he wasn't really looking at me.

As I walked back to my lodging I was worrying, like a dog with a bone, at two distinct feelings inside of me. One was a shudder for what might have been. I'd had the tale with the truth, the fever with the medicine, but there was still a shiver there for what might have been. I was glad I had gone to Twickenham that day. But there was maybe, too, just a faint cold surprise, like a powdering of frost, that the thought of a world without Lord Essex didn't touch me more deeply.

The next day I found out what did touch me: nothing here I could even pretend to find funny. I was walking in to work in the morning when I recognised the voice behind me. Sure enough it was Master Cuffe, with Martin Slaughter a pace behind him, like a lackey. We all came to a halt, of course, and this time even Master Cuffe deigned to acknowledge me with a nod, though he went on with what he'd been saying to Martin.

'... and now everyone can *see*. Why, there were women sobbing in the streets as though it were the queen herself had passed away.'

Martin and I both blenched. No one who wanted to keep their ears spoke openly, in the streets, about death and her majesty in the same breath, but there was an air of barely contained excitement about Master Cuffe, and he swept on regardless.

'I told his lordship it just showed how the people feel about him, and as you yourself said, Martin' – he nodded, condescendingly – 'every actor knows there's one moment when he has to step out on stage and make his presence felt, and if you don't seize it you'll be stuck forever on the sidelines of the play.'

I looked at Martin in quick horror, but he wouldn't catch my eye. He was nodding at Cuffe, almost sycophantically. What had he been saying, what was this role Lord Essex was supposed to play? We'd talked about this, we both understood deep in our gut that what mattered in real life wasn't drama and glory, not if blood in the streets was the price you had to pay. We both agreed. Didn't we? Cuffe must have mistaken his meaning – sure enough, Martin was holding out a restraining hand and I breathed again. He'd explain that he'd only been talking for talk's sake, God forbid anyone should take it seriously. But no –

'Henry' – Henry? – 'not here. You never know who might be listening.' This was worse. This meant for sure they weren't just talking generalities. And then Martin put his hand on Cuffe's arm, to turn him away from me. From me. I went on to Burghley House deeply uneasy – yes, and more than uneasy. I was angry.

We shared a camaraderie these days, we Secretary's men. One or two of the brighter sparks even took to sporting a quill pen through the lacing of their cloak. Pen gents, were we, and despised by those who liked their lords all hot for death or glory? Well, we'd see who laughed loudest in the end, wouldn't we? I laughed along with that, too, and it wasn't altogether a lie. My thoughts of Lord Essex didn't permeate, quite, the rest of my life. They were like some dangerous animal I kept in another room, and had to feed occasionally.

The animal could live as well off curses as kindness; grew fat on disapproval and jealousy. As Christmas drew near, we heard Lady Essex had been allowed to see her husband – had hung around the court, dressed in mourning weeds, until the queen took pity. We heard his sister visited too; and if ever I'd fanta-sised making one in the group around his bedside, that news killed the foolish daydream in me. I'd seen her at court, swishing by in a fanfare of pearls and lace, and lawn so fine her beauty shone through it. She hadn't noticed me – another dun clerkly mouse – but it made me uneasy to be around that triumphant femininity.

There was no such sting in the thought of the old queen. That Christmas, as she feasted at Richmond there was talk of her taking a new favourite, Pembroke's heir; a new suitor in prepa-ration for a new century. She danced three or four galliards at the Twelfth Night celebrations, and I am sure I wished her happy. I wondered if Martin Slaughter would be celebrating with Master Cuffe, and in a mood of sheer self-pity, I wondered if I were the only one lonely.

Winter is the waiting season. Sometimes in London you can forget that, but it only took a few moments in the garden to remind me. The brown frozen beds preached patience. Wait – for the warmth, for the new shoots, for the turn of the year. It was as if the earth itself were holding its breath.

When the change does come, it comes quickly – in the earth, anyway. It was only a week after the melt of the snow before the first snowdrops showed their heads. I picked a few, when the gardeners weren't looking, and sniffed their faint powdery fragrance. Soon there would be a gleam of yellow in the stiff buds of the wild daffodils, the Lent lilies, and a touch of green – the buds schoolboys nibble for the first fresh taste of the season – on a sheltered hawthorn tree. It was still February when I found the very first of the fat sweet violets, their leaves almost as perfumed as the velvet flowers, were dropping purple heads. Soon they would make a pool under the mulberry tree.

'Amazing flowers, I always think. Something so lush should really come out in May.' I pulled myself together and bowed, hastily. Sir Robert had come up behind me. 'Have you ever noticed that these big scented violets actually come out before the little woodland sort? I'm sure there's food there for an allegory.' He went on with hardly a break: 'I shall be going to York House this afternoon.' He paused for a moment. 'I think perhaps you should come with me.' He sounded almost regretful – or perhaps it was just that he had phrased it oddly. But I wasn't thinking about Sir Robert, I wasn't even questioning why me, out of all the clerks who could take any notes more appropriately. As I dropped my flushed face in acknowledgement, my heart was beating too rapidly.

Sir Robert ordered a carriage, unusually, for such a short journey, and summoned me to sit with him, but he hardly spoke. When I ventured to peep sideways, he looked like a man with a lot on his mind. Just what, was known to everybody.

The queen had ordered that Lord Essex should face trial in Star Chamber, so that his faults, she said, should be plain to see.

Those who the beer had made pot-valiant said, instead, that this was his chance to prove his own case. Perhaps that was what was making Sir Robert look like a soldier in the cold light of dawn, when he knows the battle is on the way. I heard him sigh, as if he had reached a decision about something, but one he did not enjoy.

Lord Essex was no longer in his bedchamber. He was seated in the study that by rights belonged to the master of York House; and when Sir Robert was announced he paused before he rose, just long enough to make it clear that this was no more than a voluntary courtesy, to a commoner from a member of the nobility.

'Master Secretary – how kind of you to visit me. I am all the more grateful since the pleasure has been so long delayed.' It was the flourishing salute before a duel of words, but Sir Robert, I saw, was not going to play. He stood silent a moment, head slightly bowed, and suddenly I saw them as the boys they must have been – Sir Robert four years the elder, to be sure, but, with his slight frame and stooping back, outstripped by the other every day.

'My lord – I am happy to see you so much recovered. The more so since I have come to make your lordship a plea.' I stood three steps behind, lost in admiration, as the web of words wove round me.

He said he had no desire for the trial to go ahead. I could see Essex quickly casting around in his mind to judge whether this was a bluff, and deciding it was not. His nature, and his life, had made him see bogeys wherever he looked, but he was not a fool. Perhaps, too, that shared boyhood had given each some under-standing of the other. Or perhaps it just made it easy for Lord Essex to underestimate the Secretary.

The master was sketching a picture of the chaos that might follow the conflict of a trial. The rioting in the streets, the rumours in the night. And this was the beauty of it: no one could doubt the truth of Sir Robert's hatred of chaos, his conviction that the order of England must be maintained. It was not quite clear whether he was suggesting the rioters would be protesting or celebrating the queen's or the earl's victory ... It was not quite clear whether he was urging (begging!) the earl to put an end to the situation for his own safety, or for her majesty's. Both at once – the pill, and the pastille too, maybe.

He managed to suggest to the earl that – again – his country needed him: needed him first, of course, to set himself at liberty by putting an end to this comedy, but needed him, too, more fundamentally, needed the kind of man of action he had proved himself to be. The kind he, Robert Cecil, Robert Crookback, Master Secretary could never be.

I was ashamed, when I thought about it afterwards, but at the time, I fell for it completely. Ashamed, most of all, that I let my master, the cleverest man in England, convince me that he was a creature of no moment, just because his limbs were not long, and he didn't have the kind of charisma a street corner comedian might envy. But when the earl, wholly dazzled but still slightly doubting, glanced around the room for reassurance until his eyes lit on me, I know mine glowed back at him with an urgent plea.

I almost spoiled the point of the quill in my eagerness, when Sir Robert signed me to take down the earl's letter of apology to her majesty.

'The tears in my heart have quenched all the sparkles of pride that were in me,' he dictated, with moisture, indeed, brightening his eyes. The words were abject, but we were wrought up to a pitch, all three of us, where subjection seemed like glory. Yes, I still think, all three. The best tellers of tales believe their own story, at least for as long as their performance lasts.

It was enough. There would be no trial, no riots. For Lord Essex, no sentence publicly proclaimed – but also no public victory. As we walked back to the carriage, the letter safe in my satchel, I noticed my master was limping slightly, the slight cast to his shoulders more noticeable than usual. His lips were stretched into a smile that held as much of pain as pleasure. It was the smile of someone who has won, but who resents the means they have used to win the victory.

Any fool, in the wrestling ring, can down an opponent smaller than they, but the skilful can use their opponent's very weight against them. Can make a weapon of their own vulnerability. I realised afresh just how formidable Sir Robert Cecil was as an adversary.

Cecil

February 1600

There are things I do, and will continue to do, because I see that they are necessary. You use whatever weapons you have: that is what my father taught me, although I do not think, looking back, that he was ever forced to practise what he preached quite so completely. I do not think he was ever forced to display, like a leper's sore, the most shameful, the tenderest, place, in his whole mind or body. But I did it: it served its purpose, and I am sure I am only imagining that my shoulder is paining me.

But somehow, when we get back to the house, I find I do not want to have Jeanne near me. It is not her fault: she saw only what I arranged for her to see. But she seems to feel it too – she bows without a word and leaves, silently. A woman's tact, maybe.

I am positively glad to feel a hovering presence, and see one of the secret secretaries. A visitor, cloaked and come by the back way. In my present mood I am glad of what I might otherwise find dirty. At any rate, it's a matter of business and brains. Nothing messy.

He is unhappy at having come here. In a man less clever, I would call it sulky, but Francis Bacon's fast mind analyses even his own moods, and dismisses what is unnecessary. A shame that leaves him so ill placed to deal with the rest of humanity.

'I don't like it. It's dangerous,' he says.

'Oh, tush. We're cousins, we're both in her majesty's service, there could be a thousand reasons for a visit. And nobody saw you, anyway.' That's the other thing about Francis; he takes everything so seriously that he is the only man in whose presence I feel myself frivolous, or nearly.

'So you've done it.' He sounds grudging, and I allow myself to bow my head in acknowledgement of victory.

'He's made a good apology. There should be no trial, no pot boys shouting his praises in the streets, no public declaration of his guilt – or of the contrary. At least' – I check myself – 'not if her majesty takes it as I hope.' And from his sharp sound of alarm it's obvious he agrees with me. Her majesty's mind, and its incalculability. But I've long understood that Francis and I don't feel the same here, though he probably assumes we must agree. He sees only the weakness of the queen's way. He doesn't see the skill which uses her very defects so peerlessly. He sees only the flaws in her mind; he doesn't see its beauty, and I smile at him, now, a little sadly.

'All well and good, so far, but what comes next? Reinstatement? You know he's writing to James, secretly?' I shrug my shoulders and raise the corners of my mouth in a way I know will annoy him. What will be, will be.

'Robert, for heaven's sake! You must have a plan.' He eyes me, baffled, not sure if my silence is discretion or inadequacy. He can see there must be hidden layers of intention here, but that is as far as he can see. He does not know everything Gorges has told me. He does not know about the countess and the actor, and about Cuffe's malleable vanity. He does not understand the value of timing, the delicacy and the subtlety of it; that tomorrow, Lord Essex's plight may not seize the townsman in the tavern in the way it does today. He has infinite subtlety, my cousin, but his mind always circles a maze of its own making, and there are possibilities he cannot see.

My cousin Bacon does not know I am aware that his are still divided loyalties: that when he advises my lord of Essex, he does so only partly so that he can then advise me. Gratitude for Essex's past kindnesses does not weigh with him, naturally. But he is drawn, like an alchemist to gold, to the idea of being the brain behind Essex's party, and if that party brings the Scots king to the kingdom, he would love not to play second fiddle there to me.

That sharp mind registers that I am not telling him everything, that there is a door that is closed. He will worry at the problem, unwearyingly. He will make himself useful to my lord of Essex, and he will be useful to me. I pass on to talk with him of our gardens. It is one of the subjects of which I enjoy his mastery. It is the one on which we will always agree.

Jeanne

March/April 1600

Spring is the itching season. Nothing wants to wait for its right order: the days draw out before the warmth begins. And everywhere in the streets I seemed to hear a mutter, the same sullen rhythm that was beating in my veins. Soon after Christmas we'd heard Lord Essex was mending, by the end of January he had quit his bed. Now surely the time had come for the queen to forgive him. What was he supposed to do – stay shut up alone in York House until his beard went grey and the boredom turned his head? But down in the kitchens where speech was free they were saying, too, it was easier to get milk from a bull than forgiveness out of the queen's majesty.

There was a pale profusion of primroses, now, where the snowdrops had held place only days before. I saw them when I'd walk out into the fields – not anywhere near where the booksellers had stalls – on a Sunday. I saw the blackthorn trees turn white with blossom, and the first green fronds of cow parsley.

Around my feet there was a sprinkling of colour, though when I looked up into the high trees the branches were bare. The spring had not got into the bones of the land. It was too early: they'd still be feeling winter in the country. I noticed everything more sharply than I did usually, because every step I took, down lanes where new shades of green appeared every week, I was aware I was seeing what Lord Essex could not. Even this first faint fore-taste of the year made me feel his captivity. Or maybe it was that this time – this year – we all felt captive within the moody city.

But at least the queen had given permission – the doctors urged it – that Lord Essex should now be allowed to walk in the garden every day. And when I saw our gardeners plant new slips to fill holes in the lavender hedge – when I saw them take up the spent hellebores, and put in seedling of granny's bonnet, aquilegia, and young oxslip plants brought in baskets from the country – I imagined that he was seeing them too, just along the river bank, hardly a mile away.

Talking to imaginary companions is a game for a lovesick girl – or boy – not a secretary to a Master Secretary. But I had never allowed myself to dream when I was young, never known who I should dream of, and now, like the plague that hides away in the winter, only to return more strongly with the first heat, perhaps the infection came all the stronger for the fact that it came unseasonably.

I didn't see Martin Slaughter, and I told myself I didn't want to, not unless I could see him without his shadow Cuffe, the way it used to be. I was growing angrier with him in his absence, and had we met I might have told him so, but he made no attempt to see me. That made me angry too, and I'd never had the conversations with girls – or boys – that might have told me how there were some things not meant to go easily.

I hadn't seen Lord Essex either, though I did once succumb to folly. Just once, the impulse was too strong for me, and I tied up another tiny nosegay, sweeter and softer than the November blooms. I slipped into the courtyard of York House, and handed them to a young serving boy. 'For his lordship,' I said firmly, and the child eyed the badge on my cloak and nodded eagerly. I saw no sign of Cuffe, or of Martin, and I left no message, naturally, but for two days after, my stomach churned. It was dangerous, of course it was; what if anyone thought it worth their while reporting to the Secretary? In the event, no one asked me, but I knew I should never again indulge myself so stupidly.

It was only later that I realised, fearful though I had been then, that taking a token to a state prisoner had actually seemed less dangerous than thinking of Martin Slaughter too freely.

Sometimes the promise of the seasons is not fulfilled. Sometimes even the events of the year come out of order, and in the fierce grip of a backwinter the early shoots are covered by new snow. A few balmy days of sunshine were followed by weeks of rain, and a freezing wind that seemed to blow the buds back into the trees. No pleasure to be enjoyed in the garden but to kick the clods of heavy soil and watch the stunting of leaves that had unfurled too early. It was as if the paralysis that held us all had infected the land, so that not even the movement from the earth could progress properly.

We heard that Lord Essex had grown religious in captivity. Down on his knees, praying for forgiveness, sending for his old tutor from Oxford to talk of his immorality. Sending letters to his friends, urging them to repent in misery. Some of his supporters in the taverns said wisely that his lordship knew what he was doing; if straight appeal wouldn't move the queen, then maybe it would work this way. The woman who served the drinkers their ale, whose cheeks had grown rougher and her voice huskier over the last year, said in truth he had plenty to repent of. But her man had gone to Ireland in Essex's train, and had never come home again. For me, I had seen how fast his moods could change. He had no nerves to play this waiting game the queen imposed on him; he could easily have fallen into true despair, I told myself – it must be better that he should take this way.

We'd heard he was to be allowed home, to Essex House, though still in the conditions of captivity. Hard to know how he'd live there, though. He'd been told to dismiss his household, those two hundred men in their bright orange livery, and as April came in I often thought about what he might be doing now, racketing around all those empty corridors. It was enough to drive any man to misery. The old clerk told me it even worried our master.

'It's not natural to Master Robert, all this shilly-shallying. He can be slow and devious when he has to be, none better, but the trouble is, his mind is tidy.' He'd known Sir Robert since he was a boy, and when he talked of him, it was most often to me.

As Easter came and a few first stunted bluebells with it, and sharp gusts still blew the apple blossom from the trees, the old man told me there was a fresh source of worry – the coming of St George's Day. Lord Essex was a Garter Knight, of course – one of that select band who (so the theory ran) the sovereign had deemed most worthy. Now he'd written to Sir Robert that the rules of the Order decreed he should wear his robes on Garter Day.

'He's quite right, too. We checked,' the secretary who took care of these things interjected, fussily. So did this mean he should wear them in the Garter Procession? ('which would mean his being allowed back into public, to a degree'). Should he do honour to the order by dining in state in Essex House? ('All very well, but if we're not careful, that one could turn into some kind of private rival ceremony.') Or was he to wear them only in the privacy of his bedroom? I gaped at the absurdity. 'Oh, you may laugh, young man, but I'd wager you that's what it will come to, when Sir Robert asks her majesty.'

They knew a thing or two, those old men. Three days later we in the scribes' room heard that Lord Essex had been refused permission to join the court, or to break in any way the conditions of his captivity. Which meant ... 'A feast in all his splendour, and no one there to see!' It was one of the younger boys, this time, making a chant of it; a chunky, cheeky lad, on whom the ink stains under his fingernails looked like an anomaly. He didn't see any pathos in the situation, that's for sure, but I don't think I was the only one in the room to feel the diminution of the earl.

Even Master Secretary felt it, I found. Everything his father had taught him schooled him to cut down the too-tall poppy, for fear of spoiling the bed. Everything in him told him to shun the 'man of blood'. But still –

'Go to Lord Essex today, at dinner time. Take him a dish of those candied violets, with my compliments.' Sir Robert glanced up from his letter. 'He'll be pleased to see you,' he said. I stared at him disbelievingly. Of course he meant that Lord Essex would be glad to see anybody, anyone to break his boredom, since no visitor would be allowed save one who came direct from the queen or the Secretary. But to my greedy heart, it sounded almost as if Sir Robert were acknowledging a bond – I'd blush even to suggest it aloud – between the earl and me.

The present was in the kitchen, waiting and ready, and of course the sweetmeats weren't really the point, even though they'd bulked the violets up with squares of milk jelly, and confit of quinces, and a few candied roses the confectioner must have been hoarding: England's flower for England's saint's day. The silver dish on which they rested was worth a king's ransom – or an earl's, maybe. I wondered whether Sir Robert would have mentioned his present to her majesty. I wondered if, when he looked to the future, he ever thought of the possibility their positions would be reversed, and Essex would once again be riding high.

'We'd best send a guard with you, if you're carrying that,' said the steward, signing two burly men-at-arms to fall in behind me. He was wise: on the short journey over the Strand I saw that the street was packed, with everything from apprentices in crudely painted dragon masks to vendors with their pickled fish and their mutton pies.

Only Essex House stood quiet, its courtyard empty. The very façade seemed to stare at me reproachfully, and even the porter sounded almost grateful to see me. As my two guards turned gladly back into the throng, he bowed low at Sir Robert's name – word had got round, it was the Secretary saved the earl from the indignity of a public trial – and whistled up a boy to show me the way to his lordship's chamber.

They had taken most of the dishes away. Perhaps there hadn't been that many – he had never eaten with any great interest; his appetites did not lie that way – but he had obviously been drinking heavily. I could see a red flush where the white ostrich feather and the black heron's plume swept down over his cheek, and there was a splash on his velvet sleeve. He was indeed in all his finery.

'Why, Janny. How very good of you to visit me. I dare not hope it's for the pleasure of my company. As you can see' – he waved an arm vaguely around the empty room – 'that's a pleasure the rest of the world seems able to resist quite easily.' I stammered something graceless, about Sir Robert's wishing to send him a gift and the compliments of the day.

'Sir Robert, Sir Robert. Is there no end to the kindnesses I'm fated to receive from Master Secretary? Sometimes I think they may yet be the death of me. But come' – he seemed to pull himself together – 'I am being a poor host. Sit down and have a drink with me.' He pulled up a chair next to his own, and I subsided into it, uncomfortably. It was hardly proper, for a clerk to be seated by England's premier earl, but at this tiny table, at the end of his bedstead, there was no above and below the salt.

'That right. Now, have a drink, if there's any left – Aha, what have you got there? Another present for me?'

I blushed. It was true – before I left, I'd begged from the housekeeper a bottle of the new cowslip wine. Its sweet honey taste spelt the spring to me, the spring we'd shared only in my fantasy. But on the way I'd had time to realise how ridiculous I was – taking a country bottle to one of the greatest men in the land, for all the world as though I'd been visiting my old granny.

'A present from yourself, perhaps. If so, I'll drink it the more gladly.' He spoke more soberly, and with some gentleness. 'Here, let us strike a bargain. For the next hour or two, I'll forget that I'm the earl, or that Master Secretary hates me.' I looked up sharply to protest, that my master's overtures weren't feigned, that they weren't really enemies –

'Hush, no ...' He laid a finger on my lips. 'Let's forget, I said. And you – what do you have to forget, my Jeanne Janny? Or should it be, who?' I gazed at him dumbly. I was back in the maze, more than eighteen months before, that summer's day.

He was looking at me intently. 'There's something different about you. There's been somebody.' But now he took pity on me, or so I thought, and began showing off the Garter insignia. 'I suppose you know this story?' He gestured to the blue ribbon round his thigh, and I shook my head.

'It was old King Edward – Edward III, two centuries ago – at a court dance with his daughter-in-law, Joan of Kent. A beauty, so they say. In the pace of the dance step the garter holding her stocking fell down, and the courtiers sniggered to see her lingerie. King Edward picked it up, and said to them all "*Honi soit qui mal y pense*". I've always rather admired him for being so ready to spare embarrassment to a lady.'

He held out his leg towards me. 'I don't need to translate for you, surely? Not for Master, or Mistress, French Secretary.' I shook my head as he gestured me to look closer. 'Shame be on him who thinks evil.'

His finger traced the golden words embroidered on the ribbon, and as I bent forward his other hand smoothed down my short hair and closed around the nape of my neck, caressingly. 'Do you know how they make a brood mare ready for the stallion? If you're Master of Horse, you know all about making good foals. They bring in another horse, just to get her juices flowing, and then they take the poor beast away unsatisfied so that the real stallion, the bloodstock male, finds her receptive and easy. They call the other beast the teaser. Has someone been the teaser for me?'

His words hardly reached me, I felt only his body. I could no more have resisted than a fly in a spider's web as his lips came forward to meet me. I felt my mouth open under his. His breath tasted of wine, but his hand moved with deliberation across the front of my doublet, and through the rushing in my head I heard him give a half laugh as he realised just how firmly it concealed what lay beneath.

'A good disguise, by the Life. But I think the time for that is over.' He fumbled only briefly with the fastening before his hand slipped below. As I felt it close around my breast, my bowels seemed to be turned to water. 'Not a full rose here, just a little bud.' His other arm was around me, urging me up as he pressed me back towards the bed. I was leaning backwards against the pillows and he was kneeling over me, his hands tugging at his own clothing, when –

'No!' I hardly knew where the voice came from, but from the frenzy with which I was pushing at his arm, it had to have been from me. He gaped at me, too surprised to insist. It was only later I thought, too, that perhaps sex was another of the things for which he was not truly greedy.

'I can't! I mustn't ... Please – my lord – I'm sorry ...' I could see him rallying his forces, the wine beginning to leave his head. Recollecting the servant who could come in any moment, recollecting who had sent me.

'As you wish.' He said it thickly, with something of a grudge in his voice, but after a second he said it again, more clearly. 'As you wish.'

I was yanking my doublet closed with such speed I almost broke the laces. I stammered again, 'I'm sorry.'

He had himself under control now. It would, after all, be beneath him to show even if he cared, that he'd been discommoded in any way. 'Don't even think of it, my dear. It's of no consequence.' I must still have been looking stricken, because he added, wryly. 'I'm used to it, after all.

'Thank Master Secretary for his gift,' he called after me.

Back in the street, making my way home towards Blackfriars, without the guards this time, I wondered what he meant – used to the brush-off, or used to the preliminaries of love, cut off too early? Uncomfortably, I realised that, either way, he was probably thinking of her majesty. He'd said something else, too, about other men, and horses, but I couldn't think about that properly. As I cleared the corner of the house I saw a brown figure going in where I'd just come out and faltered a moment, shrunken into stillness like a woodland creature. I'd recognised Martin Slaughter but I hoped, I did hope, he hadn't seen me.

May/June 1600

I told myself I'd just been prudent. I told myself that I was lucky. If heartbreak had been the worst of it I'd have got off lightly; no one can walk the London streets without seeing the women and their babies. But in the days and weeks ahead I knew it hadn't been just prudence talking, when I pushed him away. It had been something deeper. If before *that* I was Jan, then who would I be after? And I did not ask myself whether, if Martin had been the man, I would still have reacted in the same way.

For a second my mind even hovered over the question of what the queen might have felt, why she had sent suitor after suitor away. Pushed away Leicester, and Hatton, and Essex; and only at the very last minute, some say.

I didn't see Lord Essex, and we heard no more, as the hawthorn blossom whitened and then grew brown and powdery on the branches, smelling like the kitchen on washing day. The real spring had come at last, as it always does, and in the gardens they had wild purple geranium, and fleur de luce and the yellow poppy. In the country the bluebells came properly, in lakes so blue it burned the eye, and then began to fade; in the lanes when I walked of a Sunday the greens – the dark green of reed, the pale green of barley, the sullen grey green of the nettles – made a tapestry. I registered each one with a kind of determination, because the truth was, the lanes these days did not mean so much to me. Just occasionally, I caught myself wondering whether they would matter again, if I were walking there with somebody. But I stopped, before ever there was a face on the figure beside me.

But I did seem to be seeing everything differently, as if someone had clapped a pair of spectacles over my eyes. I noticed the young men in the streets; and not just to be sure my impersonation didn't err in any way. I noticed the ladies; and how the sway of their huge bell skirts gave their movement a languorous rhythm, like the thrust of a man's hips.

I noticed the scars and the roughness on my own ink-stained hands, and I bought a salve of mallow and goose grease from an old herb woman. I rubbed it into my skin every night, though I had to wash the residue off me every morning before I went to my work, for fear the faint scent should betray me. Once, I even bought a musk ball, but I found the smell disturbing, and I threw it away.

Lord Essex continued in his imprisonment, but as the warm air came, and the rioting season, the people began to mutter. I wished I knew whether Henry Cuffe was still pushing his dangerous enthusiasms, and if so, what Martin had to say. The old clerk told me that Sir Robert had been urging his mistress to act decisively. Although, as he added with his dry, almost painful, smile, men had been urging action on this queen for more than half a century.

At last came news. The queen, who never said anything defi-nitely, had never quite put the idea of a trial away. So now in the first week of June there would be – not a trial, but a private commission of inquiry. This time it was the gangling clerk who told me, and I grabbed his arm as he stared at me, offended.

'Who'll be there? Can anyone go?'

'No, not anyone. Two hundred invited guests. But they'll always find standing room for Sir Robert's secretaries. What are you getting so het up about, anyway?'

It was to be held back at York House, and I would be there early. The milky midsummer morning was still at the cool of the day when I choked down some ale and a half slice of bread and made my way to the porter's lodge. Perhaps it was my satchel of papers did the trick again, or Sir Robert's badge, or perhaps the porter recognised me, but he nodded me through to the benches where the clerks sat, ready to take down the events of the day.

It was nearly eight in the morning when the commissioners shuffled in to take their seats at the long table, well over a dozen of them, shuffling their papers, their own clerks at the ready. Eight o'clock had struck when Lord Essex came in, escorted like the prisoner he was, and fell to his knees before them. I winced at the bang, and so did the old Archbishop of Canterbury. He asked if his lordship might not have a cushion. I suspect Lord Essex was a little reluctant to have anything take away from his dramatic effect, but he accepted it gracefully.

The first to speak was the queen's Sergeant at Law. He told of how the queen had discharged Lord Essex's debts before he went into Ireland, given him as much money again to equip his army, and yet despite all he'd lost for her would not have him proceeded against in a court of law, such was her gracious clem-ency. It was all as carefully rehearsed as a confrontation in a play.

At the end of it, Essex began to get up off his knees before they even brought the footstool for him to sit on. They'd briefed him well, and I thought, with rising hope, that it must be true: at the end of the day he would be allowed to rise to his feet and walk out free.

Next came the Attorney General, Sir Edward Coke, and he laid out the charges against Essex's conduct in Ireland precisely. Disobedience to orders, all along the way.

We all knew that it was true. We all knew the transgressions would have been forgiven, if only they'd led to victory. In fact, as Coke thundered away, him and his three categories of wrong – *quomodo ingressus, quomodo progressus, quomodo regressus* – I could feel a rise of sympathy for the earl.

'The ingress was proud and ambitious, the progress disobedient and contemptuous, the regress notorious and dangerous.' Yes, but we had the man himself before us, his long legs hunched foolishly on the low stool. They weren't talking about treason, surely, but about the kind of errors that are the stuff of humanity.

All day it went on, until the time came at last for Lord Essex to speak himself. He began calm, but his sense of his wrongs was too much for him and, as Coke tried to shout him down, he began to speak faster and more chaotically. 'At first I believed it when the queen said she meant to correct and not to ruin me. But the length of my troubles, and the increase of her indignation, have made men shrink away from me. Every chattering tavern-haunter says what he likes of me, my reputation is in the dust. I am thrown into a corner like a dead carcase, gnawed on and torn by the basest creatures on earth.' He was on his feet now, and glaring wildly around the room. 'There are those who envied me her majesty's favour, now they have grown used to hating me, they spread malicious stories about me ...' His answer came in Sir Robert's cool tones.

'My lord, this commission is not called to look into the terms of your custody. And your lordship is protesting more than the situation requires. You claim you never wavered in your loyalty to the queen. My lord, if you look at the charges against you,

you'll see none of them mentions disloyalty. One wonders why the thought of it weighs on your mind so heavily.' It might have been a veiled threat, but I hoped it was a warning, and Lord Essex took it so, sketching a nod of gratitude towards the Secretary.

'I have to thank Sir Robert for his reminder; and to ask this commission only that it should deal honourably and favourably with me. If my disordered speeches have offended any, blame my weak body and my aching head.'

After almost twelve hours in that close room, his was not the only aching head. Even the commissioners could hardly wait to conclude their business. Briskly, they declared Essex guilty on all the counts charged – guilty of folly, if not disloyalty – and declared that had this been an official trial he would have been sent to the Tower, but as it was he should return to his house to await her majesty's pleasure. It was clear the punishment had been decided already – the verdict too, presumably. We were almost exactly where we had been at the start of this interminable day.

As they led him out into the fading summer twilight, I saw he was indeed so tired that he was stumbling slightly. I felt a foolish qualm that there would be nobody who would see him looked after properly, but of course that was ridiculous. Servants apart, he had his sisters – and his wife, naturally.

Others were waiting, too. As I came out into the street, I saw an anxious party standing there, most of them in Lord Essex's livery. Cuffe was there, and – yes, I knew it. I sent a long accusing stare at Martin Slaughter, and this time he returned it, hardily.

Katherine, Countess of Nottingham
June/July 1600

It is my sister Philadelphia who brings Lord Essex's letter, holding it out as she sinks down into a curtsey so deep it's almost a prostration, picking her moment so we can all see. She always did have to have the starring part, even in the nursery games, and I always had to let her, because I was older than she. But I can't help myself, I crane round to see if I can guess from the queen's reaction whether it was worth the delivery, and perhaps she understands, for when she's finished reading she passes it over for me to see.

Essex writes of his longing to kiss her hand again – her 'fair correcting hand'? – in apology. He writes of how he'd prefer death to living in her displeasure, and denied access to her doorway. But somehow it's a letter all about himself – his situation, his regrets. It's as if he doesn't even see the living woman, just a symbol of power in paint and jewellery.

I understand, as they do not, that these are not the words to move her and before I catch myself I feel an urge to step forward with a word of instruction, to tell them how it used to be. When Christopher Hatton used to write, twenty years ago now, he used to write more passionately. They made us laugh, his letters, and I swear he must have composed them with a twinkle in his eye. But for all that, they were the letters of a man who knew the woman he was writing to. I think even Leicester would have admitted as much, though when she showed off a page from Hatton he half died of jealousy – his own letters could have been any farmer writing home, waiting in town for market day. Her health, his health, a grumble about the weather and a dollop of advice. Leicester's letters didn't breathe romance, they breathed domesticity. They were, if you like, a husband's letters and she used to tease him by telling him so. It was, I suppose, an unkind joke, when all Europe knew that her husband was just what he'd hoped to be.

Essex's letters are certainly a contrast. Eloquent, if you like that sort of thing, and the queen says as much to Francis Bacon, who smirks complacently, as well he may, since we all know he's been coaching my lord every step of the way.

'These letters breathe a proper spirit of regret,' she says. 'But perhaps, Master Bacon, you knew that already?' He is a clever man, undoubtedly, but I'd hate for her to let him think he was cleverer than she. Cleverer than we – we of the Chamber, the queen's closest, we bond together these days. 'And behind all his talk of love and duty, I can't but feel his real concern is for his income from the sweet wine levy.'

Bacon bows apologetically. A complicated man, like his cousin Cecil, but writ in darker colours, and even after all my years at court, to see him here as Essex's mouthpiece still astonishes me. It's only, what, a few weeks since he stood up at the hearing as one of his lordship's accusers and I'll admit he made his case eloquently. I remember seeing the earl himself, who'd been still till then, hunch a shoulder defensively.

Bacon had begun by reminding us that any existing bonds of loyalty to the earl should be put away. He'd certainly shed his own very easily. It was he who did most to expose the earl's real vulnerability. Whereas the others had talked of his mistakes, Bacon had spoken of his motives. He'd quoted a letter Lord Essex had written almost two years before, after one of those quarrels with the queen some might still have thought loverly. 'What, cannot princes err? Cannot subjects suffer wrong?' Such a challenge, read out in such a place, had made a creeping unease come over me.

Lord Essex must have felt the mood in the room, for he'd flung himself back down on his knees, and spoken out with what, like him or not, sounded like sincerity.

'I will never excuse myself from any crimes of error, negligence, or inconsiderate rashness – not as long as they are those of youth, folly, or my own manifold infirmities. But I must ever profess a loyal, faithful and unspotted heart, and a desire to serve her majesty. I would tear that heart out of my breast with my own hands if ever a disloyal thought had entered it.'

He might have left it there with his audience's goodwill. Abject repentance was a set part of the script; so was the protestation of loyalty. But no, he'd had to start to argue every point of his conduct in Ireland, while his audience fidgeted. Still, I suppose I could hardly grudge him his chance to speak out. By then it seemed every man at court had already had their say.

Every man at court. I see now, more clearly than ever I had before, that women must go about their business differently. And so today – later at night, when my chance comes – I am ready. I knew the queen would be restless: it has been a hard day. The business of giving audience, the endless suitors, the reports from the Treasury – this year, pray God, a better harvest, but so far it's not looking that way. Summer used to be the time of pleasure, but it seems now, what with one thing and another, we can hardly ever get away.

In the end she calls for a cup of Hippocras, though usually she drinks abstemiously. I linger while they serve it, arranging the ivory combs on the dressing table, putting the agate toothpick back in its holder, and sure enough she gestures the others to move further off, nods to me to stay.

She signs me to sit, and on a stool not a cushion. So, it is to be a conversation between cousins, though the ghost of Essex and his letters hover in the air like a third party. I know what I have to do; to bring the other ghosts of the past alive so she can see, see, that things are different now, that Essex doesn't have their love, their loyalty. I cast around for something, some memory, that will do it, and I see there's no need, she's ahead of me already.

Do I leave it at that? No. The point is worth the hammering. I know a brief stab of compunction as I think of Leicester with his gout and his vanity, and his arrogance on top and underneath it his loyalty. He took two of my brothers to the Netherlands with him as volunteers, and he brought them back safely; and this is his boy, the stepson he loved and brought to her majesty. I harden my heart: if Leicester trusted Essex to continue his own work then he shouldn't have, should he? It was as foolish as – well, as for the queen to think she can keep yesterday's relationships alive with the men of today. Not that this queen would ever allow one to couple her and folly … That's it, that's the point that will touch her. In this, she is like me.

'I'm glad your majesty showed Master Bacon you're awake to his games,' I say brightly. 'Lord Essex seems to think he can play the rest of us like a child pushing the counters around a tiddlywinks tray. Well, that's a young man for you, thinking the rest of us are as foolish as he.'

Jeanne

August 1600

The mood in London was sullen that summer. We rush to embrace the warmth when it returns, bringing the light and the liveliness of the land, but in July and August come the dog days, with the pest and the sweat, as if the earth were already tired of its own fertility.

This was a wet summer, too. The harvest would be bad again, the seventh year in a row, and there were those who said half openly it would not be good until a barren old woman no longer reigned over the country.

I went about my work, and dropped into the clerks' room when I could. Lord Essex continued in his confinement. In fact the custodian in charge of him had been withdrawn, we heard, but so long as he was ordered to keep within his house, it was still a kind of captivity.

When midsummer had been and gone but the long twilight hours encouraged lingering at the end of the day, I called in on the old clerk. This time, several people were there already, bent over the desk, and they looked round at me, I thought, almost with hostility. Only the old man himself made room for me.

'The lad's all right,' he said to the others. 'He's one of the confidential secretaries.' The stranger seated at the clerk's desk – a stranger with a sharp, swarthy face – nodded curtly, and bent to the letter he was copying. Inconspicuously as I could, I peered over his shoulder, and with a shock recognised Lord Essex's hand.

'What's this bit? I can't make it out,' the copyist said to the company at large, and that gave me the excuse to look openly.

'... you have believed I have been kind to you, and you may believe I cannot be other,' I read. 'I never flew with other wings than desire to merit, and confidence in, my sovereign's favour, and when one of these wings failed me I would light nowhere but at her feet, though she suffered me to be bruised with my fall.'

I looked a startled query at the old man, and silently he pushed another letter towards me. This one was written in a different hand. It was addressed to 'My lord' – Essex, I supposed – and it was signed ... Francis Bacon? 'But – at the inquiry –' I stammered confusedly. The clerk just jerked his chin at the paper.

'You'll see.' I read on, furiously.

'... I humbly pray you to believe that I aspire to the conscience and commendation first of *bonus civis*, which with us is a good and true servant to the queen, and next of *bonus vir*, that is an honest man. I desire your lordship also to think that though I confess I love some things much better than I love your lordship, such as the queen's service, her quiet and contentment, the honour, her favour, the good of my country, and the like, yet I love few persons better than yourself, both for gratitude's sake and for your own virtues ...'

It was an effort not to crumple the paper in my hand. This, to the man who had attacked him at the hearing? I was surprised Essex had replied so mildly. I looked back down.

'… I was ever sorry that your lordship should fly with waxen wings, doubting Icarus' fortune … of the growing up of your own feathers, no man shall be more glad.'

For one soaring moment I was captivated. What I resented most about Bacon's letter was the aptness of the analogy. Icarus, who made wings of wax and feathers to fly with the gods, but flew too near the sun so they melted and sent him crashing to his death on earth. But then I realised it wasn't the contents of the letter that had struck me so forcefully, nor even that Bacon seemed to be again aligned with Essex, though that alone might have made one dizzy.

'These letters – how did they come into your hands? Our hands,' I corrected hastily.

'You'll not have forgotten Bacon's mother was our master's aunt, before she married into the pig family?' While the other men glanced at me with renewed suspicion, I thought the old clerk was watching me with something like pity.

At the end of August, Sir Robert was one of those sent to tell Lord Essex he was to be set free. Only, that he must not come to court; he'd already been stripped of the Mastery of the Ordinances, and of the great office of Earl Marshal. The Mastership of the Horse was all that remained to him; the same that had been the start for Leicester, Robert Dudley. In my naivety, I thought that his liberty was the great good news, but the old clerk disillusioned me.

'When he was shut away, at least no one could get at him, but now the creditors will all want their pound of flesh, won't they? Yes of course he's got debts, haven't they all, but now how's he going to make any money, to beg favours and sell them on again? How's he going to keep his followers happy? He may say he's going to live retired in the country, but with the bailiffs at the door he can't do that very comfortably. And you've seen how they live now, the lords, you with your visit to Theobalds.' He nodded at me, amiably.

'It's true Essex never splashed out on houses like that. They always said he was the poorest earl in the country. But all the same, he can't just settle down in a cottage and tell his wife to do her own laundry.'

That was the general opinion, I found. The earl was writing a string of increasingly desperate letters to the queen. I saw them all, now that I was on the strength of the secret clerks' room, so to speak, and heard that Bacon had half dictated them, too, which made me feel strangely. It seemed Essex, like they all did, had lived off a tax – the right to take a levy off the people, if I looked at it honestly. A slice off the top of the duty paid on all the sweet wines to come into the country. Trouble was, his rights to it ended this year, and it would only be renewed by favour of her majesty. It was obvious by now that even he did not rate his chances highly.

Summer is the strolling season, they say, though there hadn't been much sense of freedom or pleasure this summer. But before the season was out came word we would all go up to Theobalds again: Sir Robert for his own reasons, and me, because of some plant that needed drawing, or so the chief clerk told me briefly. Packing my bags, I could have wept, remembering with what excitement I set out there last year. And of the hopes with which I returned. But in fact, the atmosphere in London was such that, even though the skies were still weeping as we left, I was – I think we all were – glad to get away.

I saw the fountains and grottoes, the lakes and waterways. The gillyflowers and snapdragons in their pots were all but over, yet I could see they'd boasted as many double flowers as they used to. The citrus trees, free of the seasons, still showed flowers and fruit all at once, like something out of a picture of Paradise. But somehow, this time, they couldn't touch me. Perhaps it wasn't only me – all festivities, that summer, seemed to have desperation in their gaiety.

I did not go back to the little pavilion where Martin had taken me. But the thought of it surely brought him to my mind because, as the rain drove me from the garden back into the house, I almost fancied I saw a familiar brown figure darting into another doorway. With the miserable wet outside I started to explore indoors – the galleries painted with the Knights of the Golden Fleece, with the arms of England's nobles and the products of their counties, the great cities of the world with their customs and their features; it was as if Lord Burghley had turned schoolmaster to instruct me. At last I drew near to the private apartments of the family – or of Sir Robert, I should say. I was just outside the door when it opened quietly. It was with a sense of shock that I saw Martin Slaughter come out – and at the same time, with a sense that I'd known it already.

For him, I think, it was much the same, but he gestured to me quickly. 'Not here.' I was reminded, horribly, of that scene with Cuffe, but Theobalds had other, Cuffe-free, memories. 'Meet me in' – for a brief second I thought he was going to say, the pavilion, but he would never be that clumsy – 'in the orchard.' A gleam of rueful humour. 'We should have it to ourselves today.'

In the orchard, the fruits were beginning to swell on the dripping trees. The rain had mercifully halted for the time, but I hurried under lowering skies. He was there waiting for me already – he clearly knew the paths better than I – and there was a look on his face I hadn't seen before, at once stern and naked. With the long grass at our feet, between the grey framework of branches, we faced each other like adversaries.

He stood there, silently. Perhaps he was more experienced at this than me. I spoke first.

'What are you doing here? They haven't announced a play.'

'I'm not here as an actor.' He paused. 'I'm here doing other work,' he said deliberately. We both remembered our other conversations, here, and elsewhere. He'd told me once that many actors do other work, travelling as they do all around the country. That they wind up as messengers, information gatherers, emissaries.

'What work?' I put it crudely but my brain was making calculations like an abacus. 'That's what you're doing, isn't it? That's why you're hanging round Lord Essex's house. You're acting for Sir Robert.'

He paused again, oddly. 'Not entirely. Not him only. I have Sir Robert's interests at heart, but also those of ... somebody.'

'Oh, why not? After all, that way you get two salaries!' I was becoming angry. 'I'm surprised you have any time left to devote to the drama. Or is it they aren't hiring you for the plays?'

He didn't visibly wince. He rallied quickly. 'I'll be doing some of those too. Not in the theatres – at Lord Essex's house. You know my lord of Southampton, his lordship's friend, is a great patron of the drama.

'Don't look at me like that, my dear.' The endearment came almost insultingly. It wasn't his normal style of speech, or it wasn't with me. 'You take work where you can get it, if you're an actor – my kind of actor, anyway.' He paused. 'And besides, just at the moment, Essex House is an interesting place to be.' I knew he wouldn't shirk the confrontation. Not finally.

What he did was take the initiative. 'You can hardly expect me to give you script and scrippage – tell you exactly what I'm doing, and for who. You could work out the important part for yourself, if you looked at it clearly.

'Just think, Jeanne. We've talked about this, haven't we? Do you really believe Lord Essex's way is the best way of running a country?' He didn't even wait for me to shake my head. 'And who are you working for, yourself? Who is it pays your salary? Never mind what little extra-mural visits you might make.' So he had seen me, on Garter Day.

'You're not wrong, and neither am I.' His face softened slightly. 'Look, don't think that I don't understand. This business isn't easy for anybody. And for you –' He stopped. I must have moved slightly. 'But the fact is, a number of people agree that, whatever plans Lord Essex is brewing, it would be best if they came to a head, quickly. So that everyone can see the damage, from the market girl with the pickled herrings right up to her majesty. Do you think that's wrong? Do you, really?'

'So that's why you and Cuffe –'

His mouth twisted. 'Master Cuffe is exactly what he appears to be. The more honourable of him, maybe. But Master Cuffe has Lord Essex's ear, and I –'

'Have Master Cuffe's,' I finished bitterly. 'As long as you fawn round him like a dog all day.' I didn't know quite why I was so angry, but I felt as if everything I thought I knew was crumbling away from me. 'And now Cuffe's been telling Lord Essex the terms of his freedom are an insult, that he shouldn't accept retirement quietly! Someone in the clerks' room told me. What is it you want to happen?'

'What do you want?' he flung back instantly. Then he stepped towards me. 'Jeanne, can't we –'

It all rose up, all of it, from further back than I could see. I screamed at him. I've never screamed at anybody.

'Stay away from me!'

His face went awry, as if I had slapped it. He spun on his heel smartly. His figure moved for once without eloquence as he walked away.

As we rode back towards London a few days later, I hardly had time to worry about the clumsy horse they had given me. Something in me accepted what Martin had said, but something fought it, too. You can't choose that easily. Just pick Sir Robert, head not heart? You can't split people like that, and I should know. Wasn't it what I'd tried to do all my life? Tried and failed, and what had the trying done to me? At that moment my horse pecked and stumbled, and I put thought aside, gladly.

Back at Burghley House, I went into the garden often, now that the days would soon be drawing in. It was as if everything smelt the sweeter for the sharp knowledge of how soon autumn would come. One day I found Sir Robert there, sniffing the last late rose; the damask with the musky smell, the one they had brought in from Italy that flowered for a second spring. There was a minute when I looked at him with a kind of horror, the memory of Theobalds before me. But he was so much the same – so small, so neat, so reassuring – that it was more a kind of appeal I felt, though luckily he couldn't see.

He seemed disposed to chat – asked me how the work was going, waited for me to fall in step as he strolled along the pathways, chatting gently of roses, and grafting and cultivation, and of the new strains that were coming to join the old varieties.

'You know my favourite story about the rose? It comes from the last century. That when the two great houses were squabbling for the throne, they met once in a garden. And everyone who followed Lancaster picked a red rose, and everyone who followed York a white.

'I doubt very much it's true. I suspect Warwick and the rest didn't do their business so prettily. And of course – as her blessed majesty likes us to remember – the red rose and the white are united in the house of Tudor today.

'But all the same, Jan, there does tend to come a time when people have to decide where their loyalties lie.' At the time I took it as a truism, and simply bowed my head respectfully. I should have remembered how wide was his network of information, and wondered if he was warning me.

PART IV

Change thy mind since she doth change,
Let not fancy still abuse thee;
Thy untruth cannot seem strange,
When her falsehood doth excuse thee.
Love is dead, and thou art free.
She doth live, but dead to thee.

Robert Devereux, Earl of Essex

When I was fair and young, and favour graced me,
Of many was I sought unto, their mistress for to be.
But I did scorn them all, and said to them therefore,
'Go, go, go seek some otherwhere, importune me no more.'

But there fair Venus' son, that brave, victorious boy,
Said, 'What, thou scornful dame, sith that thou art so coy,
I will so wound thy heart, that thou shalt learn therefore:

Go, go, go seek some otherwhere; importune me no more.'
But then I felt straightaway a change within my breast;
The day unquiet was; the night I could not rest,
For I did sore repent that I had said before,
'Go, go, go seek some otherwhere; importune me no more.'

Elizabeth I

Jeanne

September/October 1600

I suppose things went on as usual, those next weeks. I did my work, and ate my meals, and listened to the clerks' table stories. The cooks had begun to make the autumnal dishes – whole cabbages stuffed and boiled in broth, peaches steeped in wine, and plums dried and conserved as suckets. But I was not as hungry for them as I used to be. I went into the garden, as I'd always done for comfort, though when I got close to the rose garden, I tended to shy away. It felt as if I were a ghost, dragging myself around the place with the chains of the quarrel with Martin rattling behind me. Haunting the fringes of my own life.

It seemed as if all London was in waiting that autumn – even people who'd never heard Lord Essex's voice, or felt his touch on their body. He seemed further away from me, free, than ever he had done in imprisonment. Cut off from the world, I could imagine that he'd remember our meetings, few though they might be. Now he was surrounded by his admirers. And now, I had other things to worry about. The thought of Lord Essex was no longer so much with me.

More followers flocked to Essex House every day, and London was ringing with talk of it, and of the kind of men prepared to join that company. Anyone out of tune with the

authorities. Discharged soldiers home from Ireland, veterans of
the Azores and of Cadiz. Papists, so they said; and I couldn't
help but ask how that was likely to go down with Henry Cuffe,
or with the Puritan chaplain of whom people were beginning to
speak, an austere Mr Abdy? Rutland and Southampton and the
rest of the fantasticals were with him again, of course, each as
desperately short of money as he, each hoping to be carried on
his coat-tails back to the seat of power or else face bankruptcy.

When men spoke of Essex House they spoke also of a new
name, and one familiar to me. At first, it was with a sense of
incredulity that I heard Cuffe's name on others' lips – like meeting a creature from your own nightmares alive and walking the
streets. But suddenly Master Cuffe was being named as one of
Essex's party, almost as if he were a grandee. Suddenly, when the
wiser heads tutted over my lord of Essex's folly, they said to be
sure it was a pity he was advised so badly, and what about that
devil of a secretary? I felt like shouting that that picture was half
a lie, an image as distorted as you could see in the mirrors of the
queen's conjurer, Dr Dee. But the lie was spreading more
quickly than leaves on the wind, and knowing what I knew,
knowing the strings pulled behind the scenes, increased my
sense of unreality. I never saw Cuffe on the streets any more, and
small wonder, maybe. I didn't go near the booksellers' row, for
fear of who else I might see.

It was at the end of October that the blow fell; 30 October, to
be precise, and since I was the one who carried the message, I do
know it precisely.

Lord Essex had never abated his letters to the queen, and we
saw them all at Burghley House. They came more often, as the
day of the queen's decision grew closer, and more fulsome now
that Master Bacon leant over the shoulder of the one who held
the pen – '"shaming, languishing, despairing SX", indeed,' the
secret clerk snorted, as he read the signature on one. I'd come to
know him as a bitter man, with the scars on his face of foreign
injuries.

'"Till I may appear in your gracious presence, and kiss your majesty's fair correcting hand, time itself is a perpetual night and the whole world but a sepulchre ..." Very pretty.'

He couldn't let it alone. 'Look at this bit. He says if his creditors would only take his blood in payment, her majesty would never hear of his suit – oh, very likely. Still, at least he's getting a bit more open about what he really wants, none of this stuff about how he only writes in pure love of her majesty.

'Not that it matters. The queen will have seen through all that, don't worry.' The man sounded as though Lord Essex were his own personal enemy. But everyone in the house was beginning to sound that way, bristling with hostility. I thought that was the only reason that when, for form's sake, someone with clean fingernails and a decent cloak had to carry the letter to Essex House, the choice fell on me.

I could hear the noise from outside the gates. Not revelry, precisely. Just the hard clatter of a host of men who see no reason to hide their presence. Through the porter's lodge, I checked a second, in dismay. The courtyard seemed to be full of men and horses – men with tough scarred faces and stained leathers. Men with swords on their hip.

A couple of them broke off their talk to glare suspiciously at me and I ducked my head, hunching my shoulder to try and hide the badge of the Secretary's livery. One started towards me, and the porter hastily called a boy to take me directly to his lordship's study.

My heart was pounding, and not just because of the soldiery. The last time I'd seen him close to had been St George's Day. The day that we so nearly ... I didn't know whether he still felt any trace of warmth, I didn't know whether he'd forgiven me. The boy ushered me into the room and Lord Essex started up from his chair impatiently.

'Well? Come on, give it to me.' There was anger there all right, but not for me, myself. With the sensation of falling from a great height, I understood he hadn't recognised me. Hadn't even seen me.

He ripped the letter open and his face, already flushed, grew even more suffused. As he strode past me to the doorway, I could see that he was sweating heavily.

'Get their lordships! Southampton and Rutland. Tell them to come quickly.' He still hadn't so much as glanced my way, and I shrank back against the wall. The turbulent entry of the two lords sent me staggering into the tapestry. They must have been waiting close at hand to have arrived so quickly.

'What is it?' snapped Southampton. 'God's Breath, is it – ? What does she say?'

'Not she. He.' Essex was calmer now, his face growing pale and clammy. 'The queen's decision is relayed to me by Master Secretary. "For the time being, her majesty has decided to keep the tax on sweet wines in her own hands." Master Secretary says he is very sorry. You know, I really do find it very interesting that the letter comes from Master Secretary.' Southampton swore something under his breath, and kicked viciously at the pile of logs in the fireplace.

'She's keeping it to herself? For the moment?' Rutland asked. He seemed to me less angry than desperate, reluctant to relinquish hope completely. 'If she's not giving it to anyone else, then maybe there's still a chance that later … If you promise to abide by her conditions, absolutely?'

'Her conditions! The queen's conditions are as crooked as her carcase!' Essex's anger was none the less for having turned icy, I realised with dismay. His bitterness rose up in the room like a miasma. 'And believe me, my lords, I know what I'm talking about there. She –' It was Lord Rutland again who stopped him, with a nervous gesture of his hand towards me.

'Go. Get out.' Lord Essex did not look up. He had never once looked directly at me. This time I hardly noticed the soldiers in the courtyard. Their looks and their catcalls couldn't even touch me. It was as if I had gone into some other place, cold and lonely. As I turned into the street I looked up at the blank face of the house and I fancied that from behind a window a familiar brown head was watching me. But no doubt it was just my fancy, and in any case, instantly, I turned away.

I went back to Burghley House. It was my duty. And I didn't really have anywhere else to go, except the barren little room I'd long since ceased to think of as home, to dodge the landlady's eye and nurse my misery. In the courtyard there, Sir Robert's page was hanging around. He seemed to be waiting for me.

'I'm to take you to them, soon as you're back. What's going on, anyway?' I didn't answer, and he scampered before me along the gallery, to Sir Robert's study.

The old secretary was there, and the secret secretary, with a couple of sharp-faced men who were strangers to me, and not the sort of men I usually saw with the master, or not in public.

'Well?' Sir Robert asked quietly.

'I gave the letter to Lord Essex, sir.' I paused. I didn't quite understand what it was they wanted of me.

'What else? Come on, how did he take it?' It was the sharp-faced man.

'He seemed very grieved and sorry.'

'What did he say?' I told them the gist of it as best I could.

'Did he say anything about her majesty?'

I paused, but only for a moment. It was already too late for a denial, and I couldn't think of a good lie that fast. And, this was where I owed my loyalty. But afterwards I knew, it was partly the soreness of my heart speaking for me.

'He said her conditions were as crooked as her carcase.'

'Yes!' The sharp man said it with his fist punching the air, as though his side had just won a victory. The others murmured approval more restrainedly. I felt sick. I knew now why I'd been told to take the letter, rather than someone Lord Essex might view with more suspicion. The queen would hear those words as soon as they could find a way to tell her safely.

I'd understood my role in this great game by now, and it was one without dignity. I'd been used in the campaign against Lord Essex, but there'd never been any fine-wrought labyrinthine plot to involve me. Quite simply I was the old dog, expendable, sent into the boar's lair, to flush it out to where the younger, more valuable beasts waited to pull it down; I was the hawk sent up into an empty sky, just to see. Probably I wouldn't bring back any prey, but what did that matter? What had been lost, beyond a little of my time and someone else's ingenuity? A little of my time, and a little of my heartbreak, and what did that matter, really?

I leant my head against the cold window, as if I could see through the glum fading light to the autumn wreckage of the plants below. I had begun to feel sick, as the events of the last couple of hours sank into me. Lord Essex had sent me away without even noticing who he sent, and I couldn't pretend any longer that there'd ever been anything there for me. That any closeness I had dreamed had been nothing more than a silly girl's fantasy. Oddly enough, I felt more visible, more exposed, for the fact he hadn't even seen me.

I'd understood for some time, really. Since meeting Martin again, maybe. But although I'd learnt a lot in the Cecil house, I hadn't learnt to see myself clearly. Now I saw my figure as if reflected in a mirror – me, and not me – and the sickness grew as I understood what I could see. I'd played their game as surely as … as surely as Martin Slaughter, I realised, and yet I'd told him that he … Perhaps he had played his part more wittingly than I had done, but then he was an actor, used to the world of smoke and mirrors, to seeing himself so as to choose what others would see.

Sir Robert looked towards me. I felt his gaze on me, but I took it kindly that he didn't insist on catching my eye. 'That will do.

You may go,' he said quietly. 'Go into the garden, Jan.' He pronounced my name so softly, I could almost believe he was speaking it the French way.

Katherine, Countess of Nottingham

30 October 1600

It is Cecil who brings her the report, put together by some spy of his finding. They'd put it into writing, needless to say. No man alive would want to stand there and repeat to her majesty's face the words 'as crooked as her carcase', even to incriminate an enemy. Her face under the mask of paint is still as she reads, and I feel my face, too, stiffen and freeze into something like wood as I stand there and read over her shoulder. It's as though the guts have been kicked out of me.

Cecil doesn't enjoy it either, not personally. He doesn't have the absolute reverence for her crown his father did, but he is not a cruel man; perhaps that's what sometimes provokes her to flashes of cruelty. That, and the fact he was right about Essex all along, and for that alone she'll feel he owes her some apology. That, and for daring to have a vision of the future; a vision that, of necessity, will not include her majesty.

She keeps her eyes calm, and raises her brows slowly. I am proud of her, with the fierce pride I thought only my children could raise in me. 'Well, masters,' she says, 'it seems we have a while to wait before our treatment cools his lordship's temper. But we've cut off his supplies, and I'm confident that will ultimately bring him to our heels. A fractious horse must be bated of its provender before it will go more docilely.'

The spy begins to mutter something, and she snaps that if he's going to speak out of that ill-favoured face, the least he can do is to speak clearly. Cecil shushes him with a gesture; by this time he knows how best to break bad news to her majesty.

'We have all been concerned, your grace, by the number and the style of men Lord Essex seems to be gathering around him. His lordship, for all his abilities, is young enough to be influenced by evil counsellors, and these are not men with any motive to persuade him' – he gives a slight smile in acknowledgement of her metaphor – 'to take to the bridle lightly.'

The spy makes as if to speak again, but she jerks her hand to brush him away. Cecil is her man here: he believes as strongly as she does that peace in the land is the absolute necessity. Every time she looks at him she has to remember he is not Burghley, but he is his father's son in that much.

'We wait,' she says. 'We see. Either the boil comes to a head, or else it ebbs away. We'll know all that happens in the house, of course?' He gives the tiny bow of assent that means 'Trust me'.

She waves me away with the rest and I leave the bedchamber as quickly as may be. I'm almost running out through the Privy Chamber and the Presence Chamber, signing my own servants not to follow me. When I reach my own room at last, I lean my forehead against the cool window and find I'm breathing heavily. 'The queen's conditions are as crooked as her carcase' – to have to read that, in front of everybody! I find there's a tear trickling down my face. I want to go out there and tell them how she used to be, with her long red hair and the smile in her dark eyes and the way of moving – in the dance, on a horse – that made everyone else look clumsy. That when I first went to live in her house, I thought she was something from a story. I want to tell them that those other men loved her, Leicester and the rest, they did, they really did, and if they didn't distinguish the queen from the woman, well, that was all right. Neither did she.

I want to tell them all that even the quarrels were different, then. Standing behind her while she sat with Leicester or Hatton before her on their knees, I'd feel as if I were sharing her triumph, feel the delicious sense of power course through me like wine. Other women stood behind their husbands, but she ... I'd feel their eagerness to please like the scent on the mist curling round

the horses' flanks as we rode out early to the hunt, and I'd know
the reconciliations would be sunshine after rain, as sweet a
luxury of affection as though they'd lain together in ecstasy.

And Essex – yes, I'd tell them, even he! In another, warmer
summer I saw them once, when we were still basking in the
Armada victory, on one of those summer progresses through the
ripening country. I stood on the terrace and I watched them on
the lawns below, Essex half walking, half gambolling in front of
her as he expounded some scheme – oh, he was young, then, he
always had a scheme, but he didn't take himself so seriously. He
seized her wrist, in defiance of all etiquette, and laughed as he
tugged her towards the mound that looked out over the
surrounding country. Perhaps they looked like a child and his
nurse, but they looked like lovers too, surely?

I just heard his voice on the breeze. 'Come on,' he'd said.
'King of the Castle!' There's a sting in remembering that one
now, for who was to be king, precisely? But at the time she
laughed too, and moved as fast as her skirts would allow. And at
the top, as he stood behind and turned her this way and that way
to see the sky and field, all blue and gold, she leant backwards
onto his chest, like any girl with her lover, tumbling in the soft
shining piles of hay. They say she's a woman of head not of heart
– like her mother Anne, not her aunt Mary. I say, you can't just
split people, sheep and goats, that easily.

That's all gone now – there's a sting even in the memory. But
don't tell me Essex himself didn't feel her spell, once. Oh, he can
exercise a magic, but I tell you this: it went both ways. Armed
with that knowledge I compose my face, and set out to rejoin her
majesty. She's seated in front of the mirror – an act of defiance,
that – as a maid rearranges her wig to her gesture, carefully. She
does not move to catch my eye and I wonder exactly what she
sees.

Cecil

November 1600

In autumn, as the fruits hang from the pomegranate tree, brought in a pot in the hopes of coaxing it through the English winter, the tough skin splits so that from the underneath you see the dark red flesh and glistening seeds, like a woman's secret place. This is the time of year when the garden, like an ageing beauty, displays its few remaining charms with a shamefaced air, waiting for the visitor to spy out their paucity. There are a few late mulberries not yet moulding on the branch, with their musky taste and purple dye. In the kitchen garden a few yellow gourds cling to the withered vine, and the cabbages show green-grey. More colour here than in the pleasure gardens, come to that: my father sometimes grumbled I had low tastes, as a boy. Nothing out of its right order, was his creed, in nature or in society: sometimes I think he only purchased the new, late-blooming plants to please the queen, so that no one else would get ahead of him that way.

That's what he'd say about Lord Essex, were he here. Disnatured, is what he'd say. I came to the garden direct from the court, direct from telling her majesty.

There was never any question but that I'd tell her what Essex said. The game has to be moved on to the next stage, by what-ever means necessary. But that doesn't mean I enjoy seeing that slight brace of the back with which she meets a blow, and know-ing I have made it even harder for her to greet the next day like a queen, imperviously. God knows, no man has more reason than I to know her weaknesses, to know the squalls and the tantrums that ushered in each brilliant piece of diplomacy. You'd think I'd be like the mountebank at the fairground who knows how each trick is worked – and so I am, I've seen behind the curtain – and yet … I was born into the first flower of Elizabeth's England, and in some way she will always be Gloriana to me.

I have no appetite for this any more. There may once have been a moment when some tiny, surreptitious part of me would have expected to enjoy seeing Elizabeth humiliated – a moment when she was asking the whole court whatever she would do without her little pygmy. But I've supped too full of humiliation over the years to want to taste the dish again, even vicariously. I've watched the queen's face grow leaner and her teeth blacker, and I've seen her technique falter. I've seen the cracks appear in her façade and I've exploited them or papered them over as necessary – mostly papered them over, I'm happy to say. I know how much it costs her to put on that face, just as Lizzie in the last months would order her maid to lace her stays tighter, as if she would hold herself upright that way.

I could do nothing for Lizzie, I can do nothing for her majesty. Whatever the balm of flattery can do, she'll take from others, not from me. But I think Jeanne has played her last part in this story: she's been dragging around the house these last weeks as though she were sick. As though she were Lizzie. Gorges and the rest can do whatever is necessary. Gorges and Cuffe, my unwitting ally; no need to ask the countess what she's done about Cuffe, and not just because Martin Slaughter would tell me anything necessary. We are all on the same side, or nearly. I only hope Jeanne hasn't paid too high a price: I was told about the scene in the orchard at Theobalds, naturally. I would be little use if I could not know about a conversation like that, so close to me.

Then I think: but who am I to say her part is ended? How can I say what her future will be? The story may not have finished with her; she may be telling herself another version of the story. I look the thought square in the face: I accept the possibility. I only hope she won't prove like those caged birds we talked about, dying outside the safety of captivity.

Jeanne

December 1600/January 1601

London had begun to feel like an armed camp, or it did if you had got yourself attached to either of the opposing parties. The steward said I had better move into the house – the servants could set a pallet again. The dark came so early now, and it was hardly safe to walk late along the Strand with the badge of Sir Robert's livery. So at night I sat in the warmth of the hall, and found to my surprise that I was glad of the company.

I heard Essex's crew were growing ever more desperate, but what was it to me? I'd chosen, hadn't I? He wrote to the queen again before Accession Day, no doubt hoping to jog her memories of his glamour at the tilt, but I doubt if she was in any mood to receive his flattery. When the day came, some of the younger servants went to the festivities, but more of the household did not. It made no comment when I stayed away.

They had a play at court almost every day, that holiday, and when Twelfth Night came, the steward said a few of us could go along to see the show. 'Not that you'll see much except the back of courtiers' shoulders if you keep to your place and don't bother anybody, as I'm sure I trust you will do.' In truth, going to Whitehall always reminded me more of making one's way through a winding maze than it did going to a palace. So many alleys and passageways, courtyards and cubbyholes, half of them crammed with the traders and citizens who did business here every day, and all of them draughty. It took a lot of asking, and some arguing, before at last we made our way to the great hall, and shoved our way into the back of what was already a seething mass of humanity.

All I could see in front of me was a pair of blue broadcloth shoulders and the kind of ruff no one in town had been wearing these two years. A squire up from the country. I suppose the queen and Sir Robert were there, secure on a dais away from the mêlée. They had some kind of funny man to warm up the crowd, but I could hardly hear the words. If it weren't for one thing, I'd rather have been at home – the Lord knows, no one would notice if I slipped away.

The thought of that one thing was making butterflies in my belly. I'd known what the play would be, of course; I'd thought of who might be playing. But when I saw him it still felt like a surprise to me. Or, something had surprised my heart, because it seemed to be beating strangely. I caught a pageboy as he passed, and gave him a coin to tell Martin Slaughter I'd be waiting in the anteroom when he had finished his part. I couldn't for the life of me have stayed to watch. It would have finished me.

When he stepped through the door, his face was grave. None of the slight, sweet smile with which he used to greet me. Well, there wouldn't be, after the way we'd parted. After the things I'd said. For once, he seemed to be waiting for me to speak, and I wasn't sure what to say.

'I thought of you.' I paused. 'I missed you.'

His whole face seemed to concentrate, as if he were listening intently. Still he didn't speak.

'Martin, I'm sorry.'

Sorry for the things I'd said, sorry for my folly. For being so stupid as not to see where and what we all were. Pawns in the game but players too, with choices to make: and in the end we'd made the same choice, hadn't we? I opened my mouth, I almost began to pour out the silly story, but a tiny movement from him stopped me. There was just a trace of his smile now, though less assured than it used to be, and he was breathing strongly.

He half stepped towards me.

'But not yet – I'm not ready –'

He sobered instantly.

'No – I know,' he said with a fervency that surprised me. 'The Lord knows there is too much of this game still to play.'

'What do you mean?' I meant: Don't tell me you're still there; for all I hear, Cuffe now needs no urging. I meant: When I saw you playing here at court, I hoped at least that you were out of it.

He answered the thought more than just the words: I remembered how he'd always understood the things I didn't say.

'I am, I'm out of the Essex House set, anyway,' he said swiftly. 'I'm back to my trade, acting on the boards instead of off them. Just your straightforward freelance rogue and vagabond, no more mixing above my station with the nobility. Or their secretaries.' He flashed me the smile, but sobered instantly.

He cocked an ear to the great hall again. 'I've got to go. I'll be on in a minute. Will you – will you meet me tomorrow? We can't talk properly here.' I made myself nod, though my heart was beating uncomfortably. But then Martin himself sounded younger, less certain in his dealings than he used to be with me.

'Meet me at the eastern gate,' he said. 'No, not by St Paul's. We'll go for a walk – get right out of town.'

'But, Martin' – despite myself I was laughing – 'it's January. We'll freeze.'

He grinned. 'You little city girl. It'll be beautiful. You'll see.'

He'd told me, sometimes, about his long slow journeys through the English country, and how an actor in a strolling company got to know the banks and hedges of his land as intimately as a farmer, or nearly. How some make a kind of hobby out of getting to know every inn along the way – 'And Master Henslowe, he did nothing but fret about what was going on at home – bored us all to shreds with how the spinach in his garden should be coming up, and whether his wife would have got his stockings dyed!' But others chose instead to turn their eyes on the green book that lay around them – the plants you could crush and wedge into your boot to ease the pain of a blister, the tiny changes that told you to seek cover, since a storm was on the way. He'd said once, joking, that he would show me, but it was an altered country he showed me today. Snow had fallen in the night – I wasn't sure he'd be at the gate, but I went all the same. His face cracked into a smile of relief when he saw me, and he led me into a world where the very sunlight fell differently.

It was a world where every sense seemed heightened. Where the green of lichen on the tree trunks glowed emerald against the whiteness and a puff of wind blew fine snow dust out from the bushes so that it was like walking through a cloud. In the dykes the water had frozen into blue-green swirls, bubbled like the glass on a windowpane, except one pool where a long tendril of bramble blew in the wind to stir the surface, as a man might stir his spiced wine with his finger. It was so silent that when we stepped from path to snowdrift, we could hear that the crunch under our feet came differently. I didn't want to speak, but there were things we had to say. I waited for him to take the lead, but he seemed reluctant, today, and in the end it was I who broke the silence, nervously.

'You're right – it's good to be out of the town. Good to be out of all of it, I mean, really.' He was still silent, and I turned to him, anxious – prepared almost to be angry. 'Martin, you are out of it, aren't you? You're not still – I mean, Cuffe, everything I'm hearing –'

He flung out one hand to halt me, reassuring. 'I'm out. Well, out of that business anyhow. You know actors mix it by trade, we're never out of trouble entirely.' His grin faded quickly.

'But Jeanne, I'm not sure anyone in London is going to be able to stay out of it, the way that things are going.'

'Is it so bad? Really?' Bad, I meant, as nobles' quarrels were bad. Bad for the people like us, who could die without even knowing why.

'Oh Lord, yes. As bad as it can be. It'll come to blows. I can't see it ending any other way.'

'Real rebellion?' I almost whispered the word. 'He wouldn't, surely?'

'You know he would. He almost did, in Ireland. Take care of yourself if it comes, Jeanne. I don't suppose you could …?'His voice faded out.

'Could get away?' I shook my head. The house in the Strand, the lodging house at Blackfriars – the thought flashed through my mind of the Pointers in Twickenham. But I had nowhere to go, not really. He knew it. His hand brushed mine, just briefly. But there was something else – I was thinking aloud, in the way he seemed to make me. 'I don't want to go, anyway.'

He nodded, but the few feet between us seemed wider, suddenly. It had begun to snow again. The fat soft flakes came only lazily, but the white hill slope before us stood out, now, against a dark grey sky.

'We'd best get back. But, Jeanne …' He paused again, as if he were trying to decide what to say. 'You know, you're going to have to take risks again some day.'

I didn't want to understand him. 'You've just told me to take care! To get away.'

He made an actor's gesture of dismissal. 'You know what I mean. Though I'll admit right now it sounds odd, when we're standing in the eye of a storm that's going to break over us any day. But you do know what I mean.'

He paused, and when I didn't reply: 'What is it you're waiting for? For all the fears to go away? For a talisman to keep you safe for ever and a day?'

I managed half a smile as I shook my head. The dirty little bags of magic herbs, the lucky stones, were not for me. 'I don't have talismans.'

'Everyone has a talisman of some kind, even if it's a place or a tree. Here –' He reached out to catch a snowflake and made as if to press it in my palm. I looked down. It was melted already. 'Well, that's the way with talismans. There is no guarantee of safety. You just have to learn to trust along the way.' He seemed to have no more to say, but instead looked up at the darkening sky. 'We'd better hurry.' We stepped out faster and in silence, through a ghost landscape where the hoar frost coated each branch with menace, and the violet shadows were the only colour in a landscape turning to grey. We'd turned in the gate before he spoke again, and then it was with a casual air of normality.

'You're not the only one who loves a garden, you know. When I'm in London, I go to the garden by St Helen's, before dinner, whenever I'm free. Maybe I'll see you there, one of these days.' He didn't wait for me to answer, but instead just made me an actor's bow, and I stood there dumbly to watch him walk away.

February 1601

Once or twice, as January sobbed and blustered its way in and out, I had found myself by Bishopsgate, near St Helen's, and I looked in. But Martin Slaughter was never there, and in truth, for most of those weeks, the weather was enough to keep even the hardiest away.

It occurred to me too that an actor knows when to exit the stage, and Heaven knew these were tense times on the London streets, full of tales of clashes between Essex men and Essex's enemies. It did not occur to me, then, that this might be a private performance, for an audience of one, directed at me.

I spent a lot of time alone in the garden on the Strand, and in one way I was glad of the solitude. Something strange seemed to be happening to me. No doubt to the household I was much as I had been, but inside I felt like a young child. Naked, like a performer in an Italian comedy when he pulls the painted mask away. I wasn't sure if I was glad or sorry. It was like the pins and needles when a dead limb comes back to life. Once, I looked at the ground where the first green shoots were beginning to show: I wondered if the garden, too, was reborn each year only in pain and difficulty.

The first days of February brought a drier sort of chill, and
the gardeners wagged their heads with a pleasurable melancholy. 'If Candlemas be fair and bright, come winter have
another flight ...' But even the new light in the sky brought no
release from the dull ache of tension that was gripping me.
Gripping all of us, maybe. Even the old clerk exploded one day.

'Jesu! It's like waiting by a deathbed. In the end you just want
it to be over, since it can only end one way. If nothing else, you
want the surgeon to give you some idea – next week, tomorrow,
don't leave the room – and all they do is look wise, and bill for
another fee.'

I stared at him in surprise. Somehow I'd never thought of his
having a life outside these walls, where people close to him lived
and died. But wait – hadn't someone told me he'd been married,
once? I'd not been used to eyeing the people around me too
closely. It had always seemed safer that way. But now I felt ...
guilty?

It was the first Friday in February when the message came. I was
on my way back into Burghley House, just before dusk, when
the porter stopped me.

'There was someone asking for you,' he said, almost accus-
ingly. 'Well-dressed, well-spoken sort of fellow – thought he
was a gentleman at first, but he turned out to be one of them
players.' My heart gave a lurch within me. 'Wanted you to know
he'd be playing tomorrow, down at the Globe.' I nodded thanks
and hurried in with my face down, in case it should betray me.

The performance wouldn't begin till two next day. I didn't
pass the morning easily. It was barely dinner time when I was
headed towards the bridge, with the Globe's pennant snapping
in the breeze in front of me.

I hadn't been to a performance there in the eighteen months
since they built the place, and the rougher entertainments of the
Paris Gardens held no charms for me. But I knew the area

– every immigrant did. This was where you went to buy cuts of meat that made the English butchers roll their eyes, or find hose knitted in the continental way. This was the area of the stinking trades, the slaughterhouses and the tannery.

Close to, the theatre was enormous. I squeezed my way through the crowds, looking for a back way in. Martin Slaughter must have told the boy who kept the door that I'd be coming, for it was only a moment before he was standing before me.

I laughed a little to hide the effect the sight of him had on me. 'Goodness, Martin, you look very grand. Who are you playing – the king?' His velvet suit was a little worn, but it must once have been some nobleman's favourite finery.

'Which one of them?' he said, as lightly. I must have looked blank, because he added, 'You do know the play?' I shook my head.

'We're playing *Richard II* – and you had no idea? Well, maybe they didn't want to advertise this one too widely.' The truth was that there may well have been playbills handed out – I'd simply been too nervous to see. And some of my confusion must have shown in my face, because he went on to explain more slowly.

'My lord Southampton, and several of the Earl of Essex's friends, came to the performance yesterday. Oh, not this play – some comedy, it was, and I wasn't here, just the regular company. They told them, the lords, that they wanted a special performance of *Richard*, today.

'Well, the bosses protested, of course. That's so fast it's ludicrous, even if it weren't for the question of the play.' It must have been my fate, that day, to gape at him like the village idiot, but he'd obviously decided to forgive me.

'You saw it when it first came out? Or read it, maybe? Well, no matter, the printed version had all the important bits cut out.

'This play is about the moment that started it all off,' he continued, earnest now. 'Richard II pushed off the throne by his cousin, starting a hundred years of civil war, ended only by our beloved Tudor dynasty. An enfeebled monarch deposed, and the deposer presented as – well, maybe not the hero of the tale, but a man of honour, or something close. Now do you see?'

I did, of course I did, and the danger of what I saw appalled me.

'They depose the king?' I was working my way through it, slowly. 'With arms, with violence?' Martin nodded at me, the way a kind schoolmaster does when his pupil gets the right answer eventually. 'And the old king, Richard – they don't – is he –?' Again, Martin nodded. It struck me that he was apprehensive and excited, both at once, and, like the actor he was, registering both emotions clearly.

'Can you believe it – someone was saying they actually wanted us to put Richard into a red wig?' he said, inconsequentially.

'But why ever did they agree? And what are you doing? You're not even tied to the company.'

'Well, they were promised an extra fee. Rather a large one, actually – and those lords weren't to be gainsaid easily. As for me, I'm just a jobbing actor, you go where the good parts are and if you turn a company down one time, they may not ask you again too quickly.' He had dropped the bantering manner, and as he turned away his face looked older and more wary than the one I was used to seeing.

'No, I promise you, I'm just in this one as a player. Unless – well, perhaps you might say I owed their lordships something.' There was a shadow on his face and with a stab of guilt I realised – yes, for the first time – that I might not have been the only one who hadn't found decisions easy.

'And, of course,' he added, 'I do have … insurance, you might say.' He flung that reminder at me with an air of bravado, pointedly, as if daring me to remember that the subject of our quarrel had never entirely gone away. But I shook my head quickly, and he seemed to understand me. No trouble between us, not now, not with this other danger all around us. Now, the whole question of our anger seemed as outworn as the green wreaths after May Day. Now it was I, who'd always been the skittish quarry, who put my hand on his arm placatingly. He turned to clasp it with his own. It must have been the first time we moved to touch, or nearly.

I'd forgotten to ask again what part he was playing. It wasn't the king, either of the kings ('not for an occasional extra' – I could almost hear his voice in my ear), but it was one of their cousins, a Lord Aumerle. Loyal to the old king, even to the point of folly. I was glad of that, foolishly.

There was one line he had that struck me as true – something about having a hundred characters in one body – as I sat (for Martin had told them to let me through up into the gallery) brushing away offers of nuts, and gingerbread, and beer. Even the vendors were excited, and though the crowd was thinner than it might be, in this huge arena, they were roaring as if they were at a bull-baiting or a tourney. Tough men they were, for the most part, with more than one scarred face I recognised from the courtyard at Essex House. I turned my cloak badge in, so no one would challenge me.

A few lines did make me wince. About Bolingbroke, the young pretender, doffing his cap to every oyster woman and charming his way into the people's sympathy. Had Essex really found us that easy? And another, older, actor, playing John of Gaunt, had a speech about England that touched me. If you came here an immigrant you do forget – dodging the filth running down the streets, complaining about the weather and the taxes – you forget just how much it had meant to come here, and be free.

But I do remember that, as I gazed down from my height at the small figures under the big stage canopy, between the gilt lions and the great marbled pillars, I was puzzled, as much as dismayed. The main theme apart, I could see why the play would appeal to Lord Essex and his followers. This was a lament for the old chivalric England that probably never even existed.

The kind you tried to recreate, when you put a girl's flowers in your doublet and rode out to the tilt on Accession Day. It was a question about what a king was, once stripped of his majesty. As naked as – as a girl, if ever she put off the boy's clothes that had given her an identity.

What it wasn't was a triumphant hymn to king-killing, or so it seemed to me. What had it led to? Each side banging the other over the head, and shouting that they were putting an end to violence that way. The deposed King Richard sent for a mirror, to see if he still had the face of majesty, and I thought that in the aftermath none of them would recognise their reflections easily. As the play came to an end, and the actors gave those stage bows that seemed always to have an element of mockery, I thought that for everyone on the stage, for each of the warring parties, this venture into dissent had ended very badly. And as they knelt down on the stage for the prayers for the queen's safety, I wondered if I was the only one who felt that way.

And of course, there had been one moment struck me particularly. Hit home so hard, I had to turn my face away. King Richard's queen walks into a garden, and learns her husband's fate from the gardener's chatter. But before she does, the chief gardener is instructing one of his underlings, the way the head gardener at Burghley House might do any day. 'Go thou' he says,

> 'and, like an executioner,
> Cut off the heads of too fast-growing sprays
> That look too lofty in our commonwealth.'

The words had been written years ago, I knew they had. It was just a typically flowery poetic simile. But as I looked around the rapt audience, as they began to jostle their way out of the theatre, I did not understand how everyone else could hear them so hardily.

I got back to Burghley House to find the place in a fluster. The master had gone to court, and from there to a hastily called meeting of the Council. He would not be returning quickly. The old clerk came clucking towards me, when I appeared, like a hen with one chick and I was touched: I hadn't realised he had an affection for me. For a second I wondered, as I'd never let myself before, just what he saw when he looked at me.

The urgency of the moment pushed the thought away. 'What's happened?' I asked.

'Never mind that, lad – it's not what's happened, it's what's about to,' he said cryptically. 'That stage play you went to – oh yes, I know – wasn't far off a declaration of intent. They'll send for Essex to know what he means by it. Question is, will he go peaceably?'

All around us was a controlled bustle – not so much an ant heap disturbed, as a market where every stallholder has decided to pack up simultaneously. Papers being sorted and locked away in strongboxes, windows shuttered firmly.

Sunday, 8 February, morning

None of us slept very much that night – even those who had less to think about than I did. The gates of the great house were locked and barred, but they couldn't shut all the sounds out; and from well before daybreak – the cold late dawn that comes so reluctantly this early in the year – we'd heard in the still night the sounds of men and horses on the move. I'd slipped out into the courtyard when one cry woke me, and I'd found I was not alone to do so. Supporters of Lord Essex, coming from the south? Her majesty's soldiery?

'If they were coming from my lord of Southampton's, they'd not pass this way,' one of the secret clerks said. I think it was the first time he'd ever spoken, voluntarily.

By morning the master had not returned. 'It's coming, then,' the old clerk said – grimly, and yet with a kind of satisfaction. But it didn't come, or not immediately. Breakfast was served, albeit with scant ceremony, and some of the bolder spirits suggested going out to listen to the sermon, though the steward vetoed that one sharply.

For an hour, two hours, we hung awkwardly around, while the noise from the street told us the rest of the town was going about its Sunday. The boys among us were getting restive: what harm if they did go out, to see what was going on? The rest of London wasn't cowering behind its walls, was it? 'After all, I needn't wear my livery,' the brightest of the pages suggested, hopefully.

This time the steward agreed, desperate for news as the rest of us. The porter opened the door and the boy slipped outside, past the scandalised faces of the household's officers, in a scullion's shabby anonymity.

Tensely, we waited. Not more than a few minutes to reach Essex House; a brief while to gather what news he could from the crowd around the door, and then the same time back again. Maybe five minutes if he ran, and he would run, surely? He did: arrived panting, but rosy with self-importance.

'A party of lords – no, not the master – went inside half an hour ago. They didn't come out again, but from the sounds of it all Lord Essex's men are forming up inside the gates, and I thought I'd best get away.' His self-confidence faltered slightly, and the old clerk patted his shoulder reassuringly.

We looked at each other. Essex's men would be heading to the court and we lay right in his path. No one spoke, as we all strained our ears.

Ten minutes. Fifteen. Nothing. Could the boy have been mistaken? 'They were getting ready, honest they were,' he protested, almost tearfully.

'I suppose' – someone suggested hesitantly – 'they couldn't have gone the other way?'

Katherine, Countess of Nottingham
8 February, morning

The damned litter ride here last night, and me snuffling with a cold every inch of the way. It cost me a physical pang to leave my house at Chelsea, and not just for the warm bed that no one there would drag me out of. I'd had the feeling, which is absurd, that at least that was left to me.

But the message from Charles had ordered me to come to court at once, for safety. Then we none of us had much sleep last night – in fact, going to bed at all was little more than an empty gesture towards normality, a sign to the half-hearted that there is nothing in this rumour of rebellion. But on the whole I think Cecil and Charles had the best of it. They could stay up, watching, quietly. Last night the Council sent for Essex and he refused to come, saying he feared trickery, that he'd had warning there was a plot for his life. He refused to come, and that is enough, surely?

We could not afford to move too soon. No queen who plans to hold her throne can be seen to arm herself against her subjects until there is the direst necessity. Until it's clear she is defending herself against a few individuals, not threatening the rights of the majority. But before dawn, Cecil's spies brought word the courtyard of Essex House was filling up with men, and as her majesty broke her fast, with me standing behind her and trying not to sneeze too audibly, she agreed word should be sent to the Lord Mayor, to catch him before the sermon at St Paul's. He should let Essex in through the City walls and then close Ludgate behind him. He should prepare to defend the City. Essex House is full of angry swordsmen, and we at Whitehall are not an hour away.

They sent men Essex would not see as enemies – this much they allowed his fears – but sent them with the queen's full authority, to demand to know his intentions, and warn him that if he did not settle his complaints in the way of the law, things could only go gravely. Now she's set the maids to sewing, though I doubt there's a stitch there that won't have to be unpicked, but it gives the appearance of the ordinary.

I'd been watching for Philadelphia among the ladies. No sign, and I asked one of the maids in the end, quietly. The girl said that Lady Scrope had asked leave to retire from court a few days ago, and at first I thought, Thank God, she's learning sense at last. Then I thought, But where has she gone, and to keep what company?

Robert Cecil has done well. Not even Walsingham, when he was alive, could have arranged the flow of information more efficiently. Hardly have the first of the deputation's attendants come straggling back from Essex House – to say they were barred at the door while the lords alone were allowed in, with just a single servant – than news comes, from the first of the nondescript men Cecil's had posted all around London.

The lords are still inside the house – prisoners or hostages, effectively – but Essex and his friends are on the move. Cecil's man could hear the crowds inside the courtyard calling for the deputies' blood, and crying 'To the court!' Each one of us stiffens, imperceptibly, and Cecil jerks a command to one of his lieutenants. Orders will be going out to summon all available men from Westminster and the villages. But there is no denying, until the muster is complete, Whitehall is defended but poorly.

Several of the gentlemen around are putting hands to their swords, but the queen shakes her head to still them. 'The grace of Him who placed me on this throne will defend me on it,' she says clearly. But another one of those shabby men, who'd never have got past the guards without the Secretary's pass, is whispering in his ear, and the sharpness of Cecil's face does alarm me. The queen sees it too.

'What is it? Quick, man.'

'No, not that.' He'd know we were all expecting the enemy at the gates. 'They've gone to the City.'

Jeanne

8 February, midday

They must have gone the other way. But why, in God's name – why not the court, why into the City? Surely they can't think to take the Tower, with just a couple of hundred men?

'They must be expecting more troops there.' It was one of the younger officers who spoke, and the old clerk cried him down instantly.

'Get along with you! The City's always been queen's territory. They don't care for pretty faces and romantic battle cries, they just want things kept quiet enough they can go on making money.'

'All the same, he must think he'll get help there. There's no other reason for heading east.'

'Well, he must know whether he's been promised help or not,' another of the clerks said sensibly. I left them all squabbling there, and slipped away upstairs into my small chamber. A dreadful presentiment was beginning to take hold of me.

It wasn't that I wanted the rebels to win – how could I? Right and safety lay only one way, with the queen and the Secretary. But absurdly, irrationally, something in me fought against the growing conviction his dream had been nothing but folly ... What was I, I berated myself fiercely, a doting mother who calls everyone to praise her toddler's spirit, even while she smacks him and takes away his toy?

The door was pushed ajar. The old clerk stood there, and his rheumy eyes looked at me sadly. 'The boys have been out again,' he said, 'and one of them's come back already. Essex is going towards the City.

'He's going towards the City and he's crying out at every man he meets to join him, and hardly a one of them has. A couple more lords have brought a few retainers, but the City folk are pointing and laughing like it's the parade on fairground day. The pity of it, lad, the pity. Oh, he's wrong, wrong and dangerous. But all the same –'

Just then there was a noise like a rumble of thunder. We stared at each other, and ran back down to the courtyard, the clerk's old feet stumbling on the way.

'They're putting barricades at Charing Cross. Essex won't get to Whitehall easily.' The court had put up its defences, and we were outside them. I suppose I wasn't the only one to be struck by a sudden sense of vulnerability. Almost of hurt – they might have sent us to safety! – but I shoved that thought away.

'Did you hear what he's been saying?' It was one of the younger scribes, shouldering his way up to us and speaking indignantly. 'He's been shouting out that the master has sold the country to the Spaniards. That he's done a shabby deal, the Infanta will inherit the country.'

'No one really believes that, lad,' the old clerk said wearily. 'And you'd best take care – no one can speak of her majesty's death, unless it's treasonably.' There was a banging on the outer door, and the other of the venturesome pages tumbled in.

'He's gone to Alderman Smythe's house. No one knows why. But they're carrying food and drink upstairs.'

'All this fuss,' someone called mockingly, 'just for a dinner party!' A titter of jeering laughter ran around the courtyard, and the old clerk and I looked at each other miserably.

Cecil

8 February, midday

They will make for the City; it's always gratifying to see things work out as they were planned. But, if I'm honest, it is more than that: there must always be an element of doubt, no matter how carefully things have been handled, no matter how strong the assurances given. If I'm honest, it's more even than that:

when the trap that you have set springs shut, there is, there must be, a moment of fierce glee.

Gorges carried his argument that they couldn't take both court and City, we knew that early. His meeting with Ralegh on the river: two cousins meeting in secret, each trying to convince the other to change sides, or that's what it looked like. Where do you hide an acorn? In a forest. Where do you hide a real secret? Under a veil of pseudo-secrecy. The other plan, their first one, could really have been a danger: infiltrate the court with the lesser-ranking and less conspicuous men in the conspiracy; spread them out through every department of the palace, then move on a pre-arranged signal. A practicable idea, or nearly. But Gorges convinced them it would never work. He said what they needed to do, instead, was to confirm that there really would be support from Essex's allies in the City. He knew that would inflame his lordship, of course, to suggest that there might be any bound to his knowledge, or his popularity. I expect he hoped also to get the allies' names: he couldn't be sure we had them already.

Of course, when we sent the lords to Essex this morning, it will have flushed him out like a partridge from its covey. He'll have jumped to the conclusion we had a spy at his discussions, and it makes no matter he guessed rightly. When the truth works so well, there is no need to lie. Ralegh says their trouble is they'd been thinking too long, that dangerous enterprises never work that way. Well, it's not been my experience, but there are different sorts of danger. That's what he says, and there's just enough of a similarity there that I'd trust him to judge Essex's mentality.

Ralegh was laughing when he told me one of Essex's men actually tried to take pot shot at him. He must be burning to tell the queen: no harm in that, now, and I don't grudge him a little credit for that sort of bravery. For a moment, as I see the tension on her face, I wish I'd told her all already. I can see that now, swiftly, she understands, but she won't hold my reticence against me. 'Three people can keep a secret, if two of them are dumb,' that's what her father used to say. As did my own father, naturally.

We knew Gorges had won the first round, but there was still far to go. He's done well: he must have steered them all the City way as surely as the beaters drive the partridge, and of course the City was ready. Those clever, cautious men: for us to have a word in a few ears was really hardly necessary. Essex will be learning now just how he has failed to understand his own country. Cheer for handsome Lord Essex? Yes, of course! Turn out to watch his latest tourney? Absolutely. Risk your life for him, and your family's lives, and the butcher's or bakehouse shop you've built up brick by painful brick ... Don't be silly. All he'll have got is the gang of unruly apprentices who'll turn out for any fray. He's never understood that the common people want stability above all. As do I. As does her majesty.

The queen is speaking now. 'Well, gentlemen, if Lord Essex has leisure to dine, I think I shall do the same,' she says smilingly, and makes an imperious gesture, beckoning me. I bow, and offer her the support of my arm, as if my arm could offer any support of that kind she might find necessary. But for once, I don't imagine that her touch on it reproaches me. The pressure of her hand is firm and heavy. As we go into her private chambers, and the usual stately procession of pies and pottages, she signs to the bearer to fill my glass from her own wine vessel. We are neither of us drinkers, but now we both drink deeply. And, with the faintest inclination of her head, she acknowledges me.

Katherine, Countess of Nottingham

8 February, midday

They've turned their back on the court, which could have fallen to their hands like a ripe plum, and gone towards the City. At first the news strikes like a blow – instinctively you fear what you don't understand, and there must be some reason he had done it, some great waiting army of rebellious citizenry. But the suspense isn't long before another one of Cecil's newsboys comes panting in to where we all sit waiting, the pretence of sewing laid aside. It's a young lad this time, red-cheeked and eager enough, at the queen's impatient gesture, to gasp out his news to the whole assembled company.

'He was crying out, "For the queen, for the queen!" and calling that a plot was laid against his life.'

'Who by?' one of the men interjects, sharply, and the boy blushes, and does not look at Master Secretary.

'But, your grace' – he quickly picks up his tale again – 'thing is, you see, he wasn't getting any change, not out of the people in the City. Folks that were coming out of church, they just stared – some laughed – or looked away.

'You could see him starting to get panicky. He started out from his house with two hundred odd behind him, and that's what he's got now – just one or two more, maybe. He's gone into Alderman Smythe's house, but when he arrived at the front door, the alderman was trying to slip away out the back. I don't reckon he knows what to do next, I don't honestly.'

The boy has stopped like a mechanical toy run down, and is looking around him anxiously. One of the ushers steps forward with a coin, and they all turn towards the throne. The queen is looking inwards, with the mind's eye, and I am sure she can see what I can see, as if I'd spent the last few days in Essex's very study. The vague half-promises of support, talked up and talked over until they took on the appearance of hard reality, and none of the conspirators thought to check just how many fighting men, and on what terms, they'd get out of the hard-headed leaders of the City. Those foolish friends of Essex's, puffing him up until he saw himself riding at the head of a crusading people's army. He never did understand the people, really. Understand that, for all their cheers of admiration, or their squawks of sympathy, when it really comes to it what they want is stability.

'Wait!' The queen's call halts the boy as he's being pushed out of the pages' door. 'What was Lord Essex doing inside this alderman's house? Could you see?'

The child looks almost ashamed, for some reason. As if it were his own folly. 'They said – they said he was having dinner, Majesty. And he'd asked for one of the alderman's fresh shirts, because his own had got so sweaty.'

Several of the gentlemen around give a derisive snort, and I feel in myself the strangest mixture, of triumph, vindication and of ... pity? The image of Philadelphia passes over my mind's eye.

'Well, gentlemen, if Lord Essex has leisure to dine, I think I shall do the same,' her majesty says smilingly.

Katherine, Countess of Nottingham

8 February, afternoon

The afternoon is the hardest. We no longer believe the people will rise up, but the time passes so slowly. I wish I could have some word from Chelsea, or that I'd thought to leave instructions they should hide away my tapestries. Strange how, when a danger is surely passing over, that's the time you seem to feel it most acutely.

When the messenger boys come back to say Essex is still inside, still drinking, I begin to feel almost indignant that he's not making a better showing, that ours is all the activity. Cecil's brother is out now in the City streets, proclaiming Essex's treachery; and by the time Essex finally runs out, with his napkin round his neck, to understand at last that no support is coming, we here must have known it for hours. Our musters have raised three companies of foot and sixty horse, and the queen swears out loud she thinks of going with them, as they set out towards the City. They take it for bravado, which they call bravery, but I suspect that, like the rest of us, she'd be grateful for any activity.

Official messengers are arriving all the time now, from our forces in the City. They've set up barricades at Temple Bar. The Lord Mayor and the Bishop of London have done their duty. Charles, my husband, has ridden out at the head of a troupe, but I disdain to ask leave to see him off from the courtyard: what are Essex's few fools on London's own streets to a man who has often faced the Spanish? He'll be glad, I think, though he'd never admit it, that at last he can face Essex openly.

The February light is already beginning to weaken when we hear that Essex's followers have been stopped at the City gates on Ludgate Hill, but that he and the other lords got away to a boat and – 'To sea!' cried one gentleman, impetuously. I swear the discipline of the court has gone to pieces, but I suppose it must be forgiven for today. The messenger shakes his head.

'No, your grace. They were rowing upriver.' Every huntsman in the room knew what that meant. The quarry was going to ground, in Essex House, and it was there that he would be smoked out.

Jeanne

8 February, evening

'Smoke!' One of the boys was pointing eastwards, his nose snuffing the air like a hungry dog's.

'What's so extraordinary about that? London's keeping warm and having its supper, where's the story?' But the old clerk spoke without conviction. Through the dusk, the smell on the damp night sky was different, somehow, and we tumbled out into the street to see. There hadn't been a single moment, that afternoon, when anyone rang a bell and declared we could now go out in safety, but no one could hear the word from the City and still think it was a crime to go out in Cecil livery.

'They've not fired his house. It isn't bad enough for that – and besides, we'd see the flames,' someone said uncertainly. Without conscious volition, I found I'd broken away from the group and was running across the Strand, my breath coming sobbingly.

Outside Essex House the crowd was thick, but I squeezed and shoved my way through without remorse, until my path was stopped by a solid line of soldiery. I edged sideways until I caught sight of a sergeant, and then pulled the cloak forward to show him my badge.

'Let the young gent through. That's it, no further.' But at least now I could see. 'We think it's papers he's burning in there,' he went on, informatively. 'Southampton's been out, shouting down from the roof, doing a parley with our commander, and they're letting the ladies come out safely.' So it was 'Southampton' now, without his title – but only the surface of my mind took wry note of the liberty.

In my mind's eye I could see Essex in his shirtsleeves, staring-eyed and sweaty as the devils in a rood-painting, burning whatever might incriminate his friends and family. It must be of them he was thinking. For himself, he was damned to hell already.

It was something I'd always known about him – that he held to life but lightly. It was what he'd recognised in me, maybe. I knew, with a sick sense in my gut too strong to brook denial, that his urge now would be to fight – to die, as he'd see it, gloriously. But maybe – fiercely, I sent the thought winging to them – maybe the others wouldn't feel the same way.

They were telling people to move along, that the show was over, but I couldn't go away. My breath was clouding on the cold air, my eyes were stinging as I stared through the dark towards the house, but I could no more have left than I could have walked out yesterday in the middle of the play.

Vainly, I gazed around the crowd, somehow hoping that Martin Slaughter might be there. He wasn't, of course not. There was no reason he should be. And no reason for me suddenly to feel even more chilled than the night air had made me.

There was a low murmur from the crowd – almost a breathing, as if the mass of people had become one entity. A flickering light was moving along the ledge of the roof, a man holding a torch. I knew it was Essex. It had to be. The government commanders stepped forward to parley. Among them I could make out my lord Admiral, with his white beard, but the wind carried their words away from me.

The light on the roof retreated and vanished. The beast that was the crowd breathed in unison, quietly. We waited. No one told us what was happening. Why should they? My imagination traced a handful of figures down through the floors of the house and everyone present must have done the same, even those who'd never trodden that staircase in reality.

A door was flung open and there they were. A handful of men, dishevelled, falling to their knees. I could see Essex's face, glistening and ghastly, as he held out his sword, hilt first. Two soldiers stepped forward and took his arms – not roughly – but the Lord Admiral gestured them away, and the little group just stood there, for all the world as if they were debating where to dine after the play.

'They won't want to take him through the streets – too risky.' It was the friendly sergeant. 'And if it's the Tower they're after, they'll not get there tonight by water, not with this lot brewing up.' I followed his gaze and he was right. Black clouds were blotting out all trace of the stars, and a vicious rain had started to sting against my face. But some decision had been reached; the group was moving, with a kind of slovenly dignity. They were heading through the gardens, towards the river gate, and my eyes burned Lord Essex's back as they took him away.

Katherine, Countess of Nottingham

8 February, night

It's the small of the night when she wakes, shaking with chills. I hadn't returned to sleep in my own room but I'd had them set up a pallet for me, next to her majesty. I knew this would happen: she's always been cool in the face of crisis, even when she was a white-faced girl ordered to the Tower by her own sister and not sure if she'd leave it with her head still on her body. It's afterwards that there's the price to pay.

Now it's all over and it's clear who's won, this shadow of danger is looming larger every time the tale is told, by women who've never known what it's like to be really afraid for your life. So afraid you're sick with it, savage and lonely. As I set the girls to bring posset and furs I cast a cold eye on one who was thoroughly enjoying a flutter of panic half the afternoon; until I told her that she of all of us had nothing to fear if Lord Essex should seize control of the court. Not if the stories I'd heard of her goings on with him were true ... That silenced her, the pretty pert hussy.

I move over to the window while the girls are busy and I realise what awakened her majesty – and me. You don't live by the river all these years, in the palaces or at Chelsea, without developing a sense of its moods, and it must now be – 'Almost three,' one of the maids agrees. The turn of the tide. The time when those souls close to death go out with the waters, so they say. The time when they'll be moving Essex downriver to the Tower. For the few hours they held him at Lambeth, waiting for the water to quiet, he'll have been half hoping there was still some way out. Now he'll understand that, tonight, there truly isn't any.

That other time, as a girl, half a century ago, it was another early springtime day. I heard the stories from the ladies who'd been with her: how she scribbled and scribbled at a plea to

Queen Mary so that the waters had risen and they couldn't take her to the Tower that day. The water slopping under the boat as they shot the choppy waves under London Bridge, feet numbing under the sodden hems of their gowns, and her saying at least if we drowned now it would be easy. I wonder whether – if Essex had won, if we'd played that scene now – any of us would find the energy to fight for our lives quite so frantically.

If she'd been as rash, as credulous as Essex, she'd have been dead before she was twenty. All yesterday, as the news of idiocy after idiocy came in, she must, God knows, have been taken aback by his folly. But maybe, of all the people who'll hear the story of his foolish rebellion, she's the one who can best understand that panic, that slump of the spirit that makes decision impossible. But understanding is not always forgiveness, and this time it must not be.

Once she'd have called for Leicester and Burghley to sit with her through the long nerve-wracked night, but who is there to call for now? To comfort her, but also to help her hold her nerve, in those chilly pre-dawn hours that drain resolution away. It's not as if she had family – family closer than Charles and I. Please God Philadelphia and her husband weren't fools enough actually to have known anything about this conspiracy, but my Charles set the example there, when he arrested the men at Essex House but set the ladies free.

So that's why I'm still here, in the queen's outer chamber, though the fire is burning low in the grate and I haven't seen Charles since he returned in safety. Dreaming of the high-banked fires in my house, with apple wood to scent them sweet, and telling over the linen like a litany. I'm here so that, if she wants someone, she won't have to wait while they come to fetch me.

Cecil

8 February, night

There comes a moment, dancing the coranto, when you hold
your partner high. When just for that moment, the woman held
aloft seems of the air, weightless, and the tension of the man's
muscles freezes both into immobility. I swear that for that
second time itself seems to stop – as if, like the ancients dancing
for their gods, we have danced time itself into a lapse of drugged
security.

Well, when I say 'we', I've never been able to take part in the
coranto, naturally. But just now, a feeling of that moment comes
over me.

This is it, there is no turning back. As they take Essex downriver to the Tower he will understand that this time there can be
no forgiveness. That he, who is fond of boasting his lineage, is
the last in another long line of inheritance that stretches back
through our history. They've gone in ambition, or they've gone
in stupidity. They've gone for blind obstinate misguided faith,
or sometimes they have gone in innocence, with nothing but
their bloodline to make their continued existence an impossibility. But this they have in common: they go into the Tower with
the knowledge that getting out again will not be easy. Oh, people
are released from the Tower, of course they are. Sometimes after
just a comfortable token captivity, sometimes with the peril of
the axe so close they feel its cold breath on their neck the rest of
their lives, however long that may be. Like her majesty. But not
Essex. If ever I have understood the queen, I can say this with
certainty.

There was just a moment when I thought she knew. Oh, not
knew the details, not knew about Gorges, though even that is a
possibility. When a man has turned coat once he'll find it easier
to do so again, especially when both his new employers are on
the same side, or nearly. And I have to remember that anything

I can offer an ambitious man can be offered more directly by her majesty. A double agent's loyalties must be suspect to both sides: indeed, for a time I thought Gorges might have gone over to the rebels wholeheartedly. An agent buried deep in enemy territory is never sure where his cover ends and his life begins. The wear of the pretence is such it's almost easier to make yourself over into what you are pretending to be. Still, Gorges did well. He even managed to get back to Essex House before the earl, and release those lords the queen had sent who Essex had been holding hostage all day.

I do not know what brought the sudden suspicion of the queen to me. She was doing something quite ordinary – ordering the boy to bring more sweetmeats: now she is older she does let the release from tension push her into her own favourite gluttony. But she turned her head and I thought: She knew – knew, with a certainty beyond her politician's instinct, knew Essex would rebel, knew what the outcome would be. Knew, like one who had been planning long and carefully. As long and as carefully as me.

My mind reeled at the thought of it. If she knew, then all these months past ... If she knew, then even when she refused him the sweet wines tax ... God's Death, she's been baiting him like a staked bear. I know my father taught her the advantage of a long rope, that that way you can see if the puppy has really taken its training or just learned to obey when obedience comes easy. But to gamble so high, to do it so boldly ... It needs thinking about, closely. If I'm not wrong, if it's not my imagination playing tricks on me. The greatest mystery in all high policy is her majesty's mind, my father used to say.

It has been a day of revelations. To Essex, too, most grievously. He will understand now what he has done. He'll understand now what he is – and what I am, maybe. Or maybe not – perhaps it is too much to hope that at last, after all the long years, he'll understand what harm and what good we would each bring to our country. He will never understand how much we have in common – how close I come to understanding his lurches of spirit, his collapses into uncertainty. And what does his understanding matter anyway?

But after all those long years – after the attacks, and the approaches, the insults, and the silences – after all those years when my tongue has been stilled from saying what I really feel, by prudence, by tact, by suitability, after all those years, I feel as if I have been set free.

PART V

Gardener: 'Hold thy peace.
He that hath suffered this disordered spring
Hath now himself met with the fall of leaf.'

The Tragedy of King Richard the Second, William Shakespeare

My tale was heard, and yet it was not told;
My fruit is fall'n, and yet my leaves are green;
My youth is spent, and yet I am not old;
I saw the world, and yet I was not seen:
My thread is cut, and yet it is not spun;
And now I live, and now my life is done.

from 'Elegy for Himself' by Chidiock Tichborne
(written in the Tower on the night before his execution)

Jeanne
Wednesday, 11 February 1601

The rebellion had been on a Sunday; on Monday the proclamation of Essex's treason was printed, and Tuesday it was the word on every street. Translations of all the important documents would be sent to every court in Europe that seemed disposed to pity Essex; that was why they needed me, no time for plants today. Wednesday the peers were sent for – only they could try one of their own – and instructions were being prepared for every preacher in the land, what they should say in the sermon on Sunday. How they should make clear Essex's guilt, and give thanks for the preservation of her majesty. But the mood in London was subdued – and at court too, I was guessing. When Sir Robert had finally come home for a few hours' respite, his grim face and bloodshot eyes didn't look like those of a man who'd won a victory.

'Does anyone get tried for treason – and then get off?' I tried to sound idly curious, but the old clerk's eyes were full of pity as he looked at me.

'Never, lad. Don't even think of it. A "trial" is just what they say. What they mean is a demonstration, to prove to everyone he's guilty and wrap the ends up neat and legal. And besides, what's Lord Essex going to say? That he disobeyed the queen's direct order and went waving swords around the capital just to pass the time of day?'

'He said he believed his life was threatened. He said he never meant any harm to the queen's majesty.'

'He said, he said. That's always been Lord Essex's trouble, he's a sight too fond of saying. And don't you forget' – this time, his eyes were sterner, and he wagged an admonitory finger at me – 'who was it he said wanted to murder him? The master, that's who. I know it's hard, but don't forget where your loyalties lie.'

I bent down over my pen again, but the old clerk hadn't finished with me. 'You know what the old master, Lord Burghley, said? In a Council meeting, it was, and he took out his Bible and showed Essex the passage. "Men of blood shall not live out half their days." What's Essex now? Not long past thirty, and three score and ten the good book says.'

I crouched down lower over the book in front of me, but my hand was too unsteady. There was nothing I could add without spoiling the page, and now even that was swimming before me. I mumbled something about needing to piss, and left the room hastily.

I suppose, like a child, I'd been still hoping it wouldn't happen, that I'd wake up and find it was all a dream. You'd think a child who'd seen what I've seen would know better – but it had all seemed so civilised, at the end, as they left Essex House that night. I suppose I hoped that meant the violence was over, for ever and a day – even while I worked on the papers they'd use to kill him, oh so civilly. When I'd stumbled out of the clerk's room and puked my guts up in the privy, I went to the steward and told him I was sick. I looked bad enough that he believed me; or maybe I wasn't the only one sick those days. I went back to my lodging house, where the landlady pretended to be thankful to see me. But she wanted to talk it all over, of course, to get the gossip from Burghley House hot and spicy, and it was only by pleading a fever, and the danger of infection, that I got away.

Perhaps it really was a fever: I threw myself down on my bed, and let the shaking take me.

They gave me two days' grace and the weekend as well before Monday morning, but then the steward sent a messenger, early. There were piles of papers needed translating; the lawyers, examining scores of the rebels, were producing more and more statements. Unless I was really gravely sick – and the tone said, I'd better not be – then I should come into work at once. The trial of Lord Essex was to take place on Thursday.

I walked to the great house in a kind of trance. Twice I saw a brown head I thought I recognised, and that was the one thing that could rouse me. Or the turn of a shoulder that for a second I thought spelled Martin Slaughter, but it wasn't he. I suppose it was no surprise that an actor who'd taken part in that *Richard II* might find it prudent to be out of town these days – even an actor who had insurance. Even one who had done service to the men, and women, in authority. Accidents happen, at times like the present. If a man of no great name is snatched up by the system, it may not always be convenient to release him easily. The manager of the company had been brought in for questioning, though to everyone's surprise he had been set free.

But I looked for a brown head anyway.

Thursday, 19 February 1601

I thought at first it would be like the last hearing – then I saw it wasn't. This was terrifying, the more so for the grandeur of the place, Westminster Hall, and from the cramped upper chamber where the clerks huddled, I could see light falling the way it does in church, and snarling stone beasts, and roof timbers that must have been old when this queen's grandfather crossed the sea.

Two of our clerks were joshing with the Westminster boys, and they, enjoying their role of host, made no bones about opening up flasks of ale, as if they were settling down to a play. But I clung like death to my share of the tiny window, my fingers gripping the stone. Craning, I could just about see the judges on a bench below the dais chair, and the peers lining up on either side of them, to make three sides of the square. The doors were flung open and they led in the two earls, Essex and Southampton. The commoners would be tried with far less ceremony.

In front of them paced a uniformed officer carrying – I saw it with a twist in the guts – an axe, its blade turned outward and away from them. They kissed each other's hands and embraced – of course, in the Tower they'd have been held separately. He was dressed well, as I saw with an odd sense of relief, and looking around him proudly. I could see Cecil's brother, the new Lord Burghley, among the peers, but there was no sign of the Secretary.

They listened to the indictment against them. 'Do you plead Guilty or Not Guilty?'

'Not Guilty.'

Sir Henry Yelverton was speaking first, sonorously: '… very rebelliously to disinherit the queen of her Crown and dignity … my Lord of Essex can no way excuse nor shadow this, his rebellious purpose, nor turn action to any other intent … a man's own conceit and an aspiring mind to wish honour …' He wondered they didn't blush to be so forward as to stand their trial without confession; he might have been telling off a child in the nursery.

The Attorney General came next, detailing every gift, every office Lord Essex had had of her majesty. 'But now in God's most just judgement, he of his earldom shall be Robert the Last; that of a kingdom thought to be Robert the First …'

That was to suggest he'd wanted the crown himself, and didn't he, really? That was the thought we'd all tried to suppress, that was the thing no one until now would say. The other clerks applauded the hit, as if it were a mock duel in the sporting gallery.

But this was a game Lord Essex, too, could play. The Attorney General was acting the orator, he said, and abusing their lordships' minds with slanders. Could he and Lord Southampton not answer the charges as they heard them, or they might not remember properly.

I didn't understand; I had to understand. I looked up frantically, and found the old clerk peering over me.

'They have to answer all the charges together, at the end, one by one and in the right order. They're not allowed to write them down, either. I know, I know, but in treason trials, it's always done that way.'

The examinations continued; the men who'd egged Essex on. Not blaming him now, precisely, but trying desperately to suggest it was all a misunderstanding and they at least had meant no harm, whatever those above them in rank might secretly have planned. Francis Bacon was one of the leaders of the prosecution, and he spoke especially eloquently. One Ferdinando Gorges deposed that the rebels' plans had been laid three months and more, and told of a meeting where information was exchanged, between himself and his cousin Walter Ralegh. I could see Lord Essex's face grow pale, and then fiery. He demanded Gorges should be called before him, and asked the court 'to consider who they be that testify this against me. They are men within the danger of the Law, and as such speak with a desire to live, but I think they have much to answer for between God and their souls and me.'

All day it went on, until I felt as if my brain were floating away from my body, though when someone tried to offer me the ale flask, I pushed it away. Then a name roused me – or perhaps it was the hiss through his teeth of the old clerk above me. Yes, that was it ... Cecil's name again, and from behind a screen our master himself stepped forward, theatrically.

He can't have known it would come to this – could he? – but he was speaking as well as if he'd conned his speech in play. Or perhaps, as he stood opposite Essex at last, he was saying the things he'd waited all their lives to say.

'The difference between you and me is great; for I speak in the person of an honest man, and you, my lord, in the person of a traitor. The pre-eminence is yours, but I have innocence, truth of conscience and honesty to defend me. I protest before God, I have loved your person and justified your virtues. I told her majesty that your afflictions would make you a fit servant for her, attending but a fit time to move her majesty to call you to the court again. And had I not seen your ambitious affections inclined to usurpation, I would have gone on my knees to her majesty to do you good; but you have a wolf's head in a sheep's garment.' His voice was shaking slightly.

I'd almost missed the accusation that had moved the master so deeply. Essex claimed Sir Robert had said to one of his fellow councillors ... that no one in the world but the Infanta of Spain had the right to the Crown of England? It sounded more than unlikely. But Cecil was falling on his knees, and demanding that they fetch the councillor – Sir William Knollys, it was – and that he shouldn't be warned what the matter was but fetched out of her majesty's presence if necessary. That they should tell the queen if she would not send Sir William, then he, Cecil, would rather die at her foot.

It was Sir Robert as I'd never seen him before, flamboyant as Essex himself, but speaking with a terrible sincerity. It was as if a quiet brook had burst its banks. As if we'd never seen him clearly before.

Sir William came, looking flustered, as well he may. Yes, he remembered the conversation, about that banned book on the succession, and the Secretary had just been saying what impertinence in the author, to place the claim of the Infanta so high ... Lord Essex flushed scarlet as Cecil turned on him again.

'I stand for loyalty, which I never lost. You stand for treachery, wherewith your heart is possessed. I have said the King of Scots is a competitor, and I have said the King of Spain is a competitor, and you, I have said, are a competitor. You would depose the queen. You would be King of England ...

'I beseech God to forgive you for this open wrong done unto me, as I do openly pronounce, I forgive you from the bottom of my heart.'

Essex was rallying. 'And I, Mr Secretary, do clearly and freely forgive you with all my soul, because I mean to die in charity.'

The peers went out for half an hour, and their return was anti-climactic, except for the ceremony. All twenty-five of them, from the lowest in rank upwards, placed their left hand on their right breast and said 'Guilty'. Not that anyone expected them to say differently.

The Lord High Steward faced the earls, where they still stood proudly. 'You must go to the place from whence you came and there remain during her majesty's pleasure, from thence to be drawn on a hurdle through London streets, and so to the place of execution, where you shall be hanged, bowelled, and quartered. Your head and quarters to be disposed of at her majesty's pleasure and so God have mercy on your soul.'

A minute ago my lord Essex had said he knew it was no time to jest, but he cracked one all the same. That in life his poor quarters had been at her majesty's service all over the world; and it was only fitting they should still be so in death. He declared that never would any man die more cheerfully.

The blade of the axe was turned towards them as they paced out, firmly, to be walked to the Tower. One phrase he'd used was sticking in my mind. 'I owe God a death,' he'd said. I didn't understand it, but it made a kind of protest in me.

Cecil

Thursday, 19 February, night

Of course it's long dark when I get home, and the torch boy dares make a grimace of incredulity when nonetheless I turn towards the garden. But I employ no stupid children in my house: he looks again, and realises this is not the day to flout me. Just as well – out of the savagery in my breast tonight I could tell the steward to order him whipped, and I could do it gladly. But I am a civilised man – all I do, when once the door is unlocked and we're out in the faint moon, is to take the torch from the boy's hand and order him away. At least if I stumble in the darkness there will be no one to see.

The crunch of the gravel under my feet sounds loudly on the still air. I pick a path less with my eyes than with my memory. But the very forms of the plants are different in the darkness – a flowerbed bled away into shadows, a bush grown into a bogey – and the strangeness, as much as the quiet, begins to soothe my ragged nerves. Forgive me, would he? Every soul under God has need of forgiveness in the end, but for what I have done against Essex, let no soul here on earth judge me.

My eyes are growing accustomed now, and I can make out the harsh straight line of the clipped hedges of rosemary. I crouch down, settle the stem of the torch into the earth, like a child making a sandcastle, and brush the flat of my hands over the crisp spikes, though the air is too cold to set the scent free, and I have to crush the needles between my fingers to carry it away with me.

The flame of the torch flickers on a clump of snowdrops, just beginning to drop their heads: there'll be daffodils here later. I press further, delicately, with the palms of my hands and the sharp spears of their first folded buds press back at me. After the daffodils, the fritillaries, still under the earth: a garden in winter is like a coded message that only a gardener can read clearly. I press down on the earth again, and well tilled though it is – my labourers know their work – a mixture of clod and pebble meets me. Essex and his ilk were always fond of picturing the Cecils, the pen gents, as new men, themselves as the ancient and honourable aristocracy, but this is older than either of us. A garden is about the future and the past too: always has been, always will be.

The chill of the earth is seeping into my bones: they'll be surprised when I go back into the house with my knees all muddy, like a schoolboy. We are finding new ways to label and define our plants: will we ever be able to see humans differently? To look at Essex, and see not just a catalogue of virtues corrupted into vices, but a different compact of possibilities? To say that, just as a garden has its exotics and its native wildflowers both, its clipped neat hedges and its flowery meads, so people can be one way or be another and to be other does not have to mean to be at enmity? In the garden a fountain spurts water from a hidden jet, and we aren't up in arms at the deception – instead we exclaim at the novelty.

If my father were here, he'd say that the moonlight had got into my brain. Now he is dead I'm having a new house built for myself across the Strand, and I wonder if, when I move there, his voice will be with me as frequently. My father would say that the only change is decline and the only future is eternity. That God has ordained the order of things, and the fantasy of improving it is as impious as the attempt to destroy. God and the queen love unity. So do the people, the godly. It is only those with malicious and private purpose who seek to corrupt and destroy what is manifest so clearly. Better to hold my mind to the now and the necessary. I have won a victory today, and if I feel I bared my heart to the whole court, I did no more than what was planned and necessary. I brush the earth from my hands as I move back to the house, turning my thought to Mr Abdy Ashton.

It is true, tares have to be torn up, or they would choke the garden. My father would have said it, and my gardeners would agree. But the battle between thistles and garden flowers is not personal. Was it personal, with Essex and me?

Katherine, Countess of Nottingham
Friday, 20 February 1601

They'd have killed Charles as well as Cecil if they'd reached the court, and they were all set to storm the court until Gorges turned the idea away. Gorges – I *wonder*, now. Ralegh's cousin, isn't he? But too many cooks haven't spoiled this broth so far: it takes warp and weft to weave a cloth, anyone can tell you that much, or anyone who's worked with fabrics. We will not need to speak of this: if Cecil still has any games afoot with Gorges he can certainly play them out without any help from me.

One of the rebels admitted it, about Charles. He said if he and Cecil were killed it would have been just 'a fillip matter', that nothing would be made of it. I told that to Philadelphia; oh yes, I went to see her – a little red about the eyes, a little worn about the cheeks, but not nearly as worried, or as guilty, as she should be.

'I owe God a death,' Essex said as they took him away, and asked if he could have his own chaplain, some Master Abdy Ashton, with him for his last days. I wish I could have been there and could say: Everyone owes God a death. And anything special that you owe, right down to the silks on your back, you owe to her majesty. She gave them to you, didn't she? The silks and velvets, the sleek horses, the chef in your kitchen and the malmsey in your cellar, and the offices that made men bow down before you. I tell them over, like an angry litany. 'Only merchants count the cost,' you said once, when she tried to teach you the price of your wars, and we all knew people remembered there'd been merchants in her mother's – my grandmother's – family.

Of all the things you have, your earldom is the only one that wasn't a gift from the queen. No, her father gave that to yours, and now you pride yourself on your old nobility? Aye, there's a few drops of old royal blood in your veins, but what you've never understood is, it takes more than that to make a monarchy. If it didn't – well, they used to whisper my father was born at a time my grandmother was very close to old King Henry. It used to be a joke that my hair was as red as the queen's, but of course she got hers from her red-gold father, whereas for me ... People didn't finish that thought, prudently.

And who is this Ashton, anyway, that you want him so particularly? Some black-winged crow of a Puritan preacher, I suppose, who'll help you fling yourself into the fantasies of guilt and repentance as eagerly as you once flung yourself into the games of power and glory. Folly! But I suppose you'll find a kind of escape that way. I don't think any the better of you for it. I'm old enough, just, to remember the bigots and the bloodshed before you were born, with the smell of burning flesh from the faggots and the stakes in Queen Mary's day.

You want this Ashton, this Abdy, do you – and why should you have what you want now, pray? You wanted Henry Cuffe once, and much good his advice did you. The wheel comes round; another day, another dear friend to advise you, and you too blind, too in love with your own magic, to understand that the dear friends have their own lives and their loyalties, and that other hands may be spinning the wheel, hands you cannot see. But it's possible this Ashton, too, is someone for whom Robert Cecil will find a use, and that is as it should be.

Jeanne

Saturday, 21 February 1601

I'd been having the dreams again, of being young, and small, and unable to move, and the screams, and the knife in the belly. But what came next was almost worse. The night-time dreams I'd learnt to cope with. I could shut them down into a dark hidden place and walk calm-faced through the day. But what happened now – as my landlady banged on the door to ask if she should send for a physician, or if I was going out to work, as I got shakily up and went out into the streets – left me no safe place by night or day.

The private horrors started slowly, like something just seen out of the corner of your eye. It was as if I were seeing two worlds at once. As if the ordinary world were a thin membrane, fragile as the skin on warm milk as it cools, and under it the flames like the hell in a rood painting, and we were all about to tumble down into the nightmare below, but somehow only I could see it. I don't think I could have told anybody else – not just for fear they should think I was mad, but for very pity.

I don't understand. I don't understand. I don't understand him, I don't understand me. Or Cuffe, or – anybody. The trial was on the Thursday; the next day I went to Burghley House, but I may as well not have bothered, for all the useful work I did. It's as if my real being is somewhere else, crouched and waiting. Waiting for what, I do not know, but the words that come to me are 'to be set free'.

He's the one who's supposed to lack freedom, of course, but he seems to be finding his way. Perhaps that's the root of my misery. On the Friday we heard they'd sent Dr Dove to him – an honourable cleric but a man with a fine eye for the political side of the story.

Be sure he'd been briefed by the Council – they needed more than the peers' verdict of Essex's guilt: they needed confession, they needed repentance, if they were to carry the feelings of the people with them and win through to safety. And, of course, they needed the names of any sympathisers who might still be at liberty. Torture was out of the question – they didn't ever rack peers – so they had to try another way.

Dr Dove got nowhere; my lord still held to it that he'd meant nothing wrong, that he had in no way offended God Almighty.

I saw the note Cecil sent back, when they'd sent him word. 'Try Ashton,' it said briefly. I knew of this reverend, this Abdy Ashton – he was probably there when I went to Essex House, I'd heard him asked for at the trial – but I hadn't understood him as the enemy.

They'd have taken him aside before he went to Lord Essex, shown him both the carrot and the stick. And Ashton knew his man; he went in thundering that Essex had dishonoured God and pulled down upon himself the notes of infamy. That his lordship's refusal to reveal the details of his plot just protected his associates – atheists or Papists, and discontented riff-raff – and left them a danger to the queen's majesty. That he was guilty of ambition and of self-deception, and of hypocrisy, since whether he'd admitted it or not, his real end must have been to seek the crown for himself. It would have been that accusation that touched Essex most nearly.

Be sure we heard exactly what Ashton said: the man wrote it all down, so the Council could see how well he'd done their work. I expect he touched it up a little in the retelling, but perhaps not much. These zealous preachers, after all, pour out their phrases every Sunday.

'If by a true confession and unfeigned repentance you do not unburden yourself of these sins, you shall carry out of the world a guilty soul before God, and leave upon your memorial an infamous name to posterity.' Ugh! Perhaps it's easy to see why Essex fell into the trap. But – he fell so completely.

He didn't just tell Ashton what his own plans had been; he went on to try and prove that his confederates had been worthier men than Ashton implied. He proved it by naming them precisely. He didn't just fall, he flung himself down the ladder into the trap, as if impaling himself on the spikes at the bottom would be some bid for liberty.

By Saturday morning he'd convinced himself it was his duty to see all those who'd sympathised with him restrained; the only way to protect her majesty. He sent for Sir Robert and my lord of Nottingham to hear his confession for themselves. You can be sure they went eagerly. They didn't even need to take a clerk. He wrote down his confession himself, quite readily. He said that he was the greatest, the vilest, the most unthankful traitor ever born; but he was none the less ready to blame all his friends, for all that he blamed himself so freely. He had them bring Cuffe before him, so he could blame him to his face – told Cuffe he'd been one of the chiefest instigators of all his, Lord Essex's, disloyal course, and I couldn't help but think, what, wasn't he a grown-up, then? Nothing more than a leaf in the wind? I'd blamed Cuffe myself for his evil counsel, but this … You know Cuffe wasn't even out there, on rebellion day? They said he stayed in his room, sunk in melancholy. They made that sound the worst of all, that he hadn't even the courage of his convictions, that he was just a scurvy 'book traitor', but surely Sir Robert couldn't think that way? Maybe he could: the prosecutor's papers, that called him the seducer of the earl, went through stamped, without query. The old clerk showed me a letter in Sir Robert's own hand, that Cuffe was a subtle sophister and showed his baseness in that he wasn't even confessing his treason freely. The old man must have seen my horror.

'Well, they have to blame somebody,' he said. 'They can't lay it all on the earl himself – after all, he's a grandee, and it would reflect badly on the queen's majesty. And after all, it's not as if Lord Essex were rushing to take it all on himself.'

It was true. When they went to the Tower to take his confession, his lordship even warned them of the danger in his own sister Penelope.

I do not understand it. Before the trial I'd suffered for the violence all around, and for the knowledge he must die, and for the division in my own loyalties. This was different. Like a dog with a bone I worried at the difference, walking the streets all the day Sunday.

Out of Bishopsgate and up, past Bedlam and the butts, past the Curtain playhouse to the north; south again over the bridge towards St George's Fields, and turned again. From the country itself I shied away. I needed the bustle of people around me. As I paced, I argued it out with Lord Essex, as if he paced beside me. His zeal for his religion struck no chord in me. He was a sure Protestant; well and good, so was I. (So, unfortunately, was the Reverend Ashton – but so was Sir Robert, and so was her majesty. And so, I supposed, was Martin Slaughter: it wasn't a subject on which we'd spoken much, but it was one on which we seemed to agree.) It was why my parents had died, but the fury of a faith was for me an absence, not a presence. I cherished the empty space; the massacres had bred in me no desire to kill Papists as some Papists had killed, but a shudder for all religious frenzy.

Thus far I was as Jacob had raised me. As England had raised me. But I knew, even without understanding it, that for others it was different. That wasn't the problem, surely.

Before, I'd seen it as a contest. Strife against stability, energy against order. Heart against head, maybe. Never really that cut and dried – I was not that unsophisticated – but in the end, to be decided, as definitely as the prize was decided at the tilt, on Accession Day. Once I had chosen – and in the end the choice could only go one way, I was Cecil's servant, wasn't I? – the other had to be excised, however painfully. Perhaps not as cleanly as a surgeon cuts out a tumour, more like a schoolboy gouging out a knot from a piece of wood. But excised at last, leaving me scarred perhaps, but still me.

I'd thought I was past this. I'd made my choice, I'd under-stood my dreams of Lord Essex had been built on a fantasy. And Martin and I were ... friends again, weren't we? So why now did I feel I had a whole new hill to climb if ever I were to be able to name that *friendship* honestly? Why did Essex's betrayal of his allies leave me so sick and angry? No, more than that – so guilty? I'd thought Martin was betraying Lord Essex by encouraging Cuffe's dangerous folly, but then hadn't I betrayed Martin by blaming him so harshly? And where was the greater treason: anything Martin might do against a great lord who hardly even knew his name, or my hurting someone who – I pushed the thought away. We were ... friends again, weren't we? All I knew for sure was that I felt sickened by the spinning of wheels I couldn't even see. I passed by St Paul's – I was circling by now – and though the booksellers' stalls were closed I thought of that pallid-faced figure in his foolish black finery and I thought of him – yes, even of Cuffe – with a kind of pity.

As I went through the streets, it was as if the citizens around me, the merchants and the housewives, were just children, dancing on the edge of a well, and I couldn't tell them the truth any more than I'd wake a sleepwalker suddenly. By the after-noon I'd started moving slowly, as if the weight of my thoughts were bowing me down, and I knew people were beginning to stare at me.

I found my steps had led me back to the garden where I used to go with Jacob – what, only four years ago? It seemed an eter-nity away. The gate was locked but I could peer through. Whoever had it now had replanted the periwinkle seat with chamomile, so that at this season it stood brown and bare. The rosemary bird had been let grow into a great ragged bush – and of course, I'd now seen better topiary. The vines were bare over the arbour, and there were cabbages where some of Jacob's rarer herbs had grown. But all the same I rattled the gate, as if I could shrink back down and have the world again bounded by those low hedges. As if somewhere between the pond and the pea sticks, I'd find security waiting for me.

My eyes were full of tears, and I could feel my face beginning to go awry.

My walk was turning into a stumble, and when I passed the end of the street with the slaughterhouses, the smell made me turn away. I was remembering – what? Yes, years ago, and Dr Lopez, who had been so kind to me. I didn't know if I were grieving for Lord Essex, or for my own folly, or with the sheer fatigue of the discoveries I had made and those I sensed still ahead of me, but everything I saw said pain, and every pain was inside me. I bit my hand so as not to cry out when a stray dog in the streets cringed away from me. Even the eyes of the landlady's pampered spaniel, when I got back to my lodgings, seemed so full of grief I had to set my lips, though I daresay he was just lamenting he'd get no more tidbits that day. I'd bought a pasty, though I'd not be able to eat. But I scooped the dog up, and carried him up to my room with me. He snorted with pleasure as I fed him, and I buried my face in his warm fur.

As I sat on the bed, too tired to get inside it, I was footsore and worse than chilly. But something had been gained. I knew myself a little better now – knew I couldn't just choose a side, like in a game of chess, knew that surely as the fallow ground in winter, I had different impulses working inside of me. Knew I had to follow where they led, and knew too, with a fresh shock of shame, that if it was true for me it was true for others, that I'd judged too easily, up till now, in blindness and vanity. Knew maybe somewhere underneath this knowledge, there was something that would set me free.

Tuesday, 24 February 1601

I was back at work on Monday, and packing my inks up at the
end of the day when the old clerk came in with a face of misery.

'She's signed the death warrant,' he said. Neither of us spoke.
There was nothing more to say. But I found comfort in knowing
here was another Cecil man whom Essex's charm had touched,
and as he left the room he dropped a hand on my shoulder,
uncharacteristically.

As I passed out through the lodge, the porter called me.

'That actor fellow was here again.' His tone spoke a mixture
of grudging respect, the result, no doubt, of a large tip, to soften
a player's lack of good solid respectability. He handed me a
folded note, and I shoved it still sealed into my pocket,
unheedingly.

I knew I had to see Essex, knew it with a certainty beyond
reason. It wasn't about him, or not precisely. It was about me.
I'd felt what I felt for him, however foolish the roots of the
fantasy, and for once in my life I had to face my feelings squarely.
Lay them honourably to rest and go on the freer to the next stage
of my journey. I never asked whether, with only a day or two left
on this earth, Lord Essex would even want to see an unimpor-
tant secretary, a boy–girl with whom once or twice, in a dull
moment, he had flirted idly. Instead I set myself to the how of it,
as if this were no more than an exercise in practicality.

To get into the Tower was not so hard. The place wasn't built
as just a prison, it was an armoury, a mint, and a warehouse. A
royal palace, when necessary. Guards watched the gatehouses,
but what use was a guard when he had to nod through a small
army of workers, and a score of delivery wagons each day? I
could go in with a load of firewood, or ale, or hay, I could probably walk in waving a handful of papers, or a school book for one
of the officers' children, or a paper of pills for one of the beasts
in the menagerie. To get into Lord Essex's rooms themselves

would be a different story, but I could hide until dark fell and surely there'd be some opportunity.

It was absurd, it was childish, and a part of me knew it. But as I lay in my bed that night, all I understood was that I had to be there, with a hunger more acute than any pang I'd ever felt in my body.

I decided to go in soon after dinner time. Too early, and I'd have to try and loiter there all day, without anybody noticing me. Too late – too close to curfew and the closing of the gates – and someone might ask themselves why I was going in when everyone else was headed the other way.

The stallholders outside were busy. There were surely more people around than usual, drawn by the sweet sickly smell of catastrophe. There'd be even more the next day. I found an old man selling pastries which didn't look too poisonous – an old man with a face that looked sharper than most – and loitered as I forced myself to chew it down appreciatively. These people know everything that's going on.

'What's the latest?' No need to specify. He didn't pretend to misunderstand me.

'They're building the scaffold now. They took the timber in at daybreak. You can hear hammering when the wind is right. But' – he shot a sly sideways glance at the badge on my cloak – 'you'll know more than I do, I daresay.'

'We don't know everything, grandfather! Not the way you lot do, on the ground here. Which rooms have they got him in, anyway?'

'Right over there – that tall bit, see?' He pointed across the grey waters of the moat, and I stared at the great fortress eagerly. Beyond the low, solid outer wall an inner, higher, wall reared up, set at intervals with turrets and it was one of these – on the north-eastern corner, the citywards side – that he was indicating.

'They call it the Devlin Tower – the devil's tower – after some old Robert the Devil who was held there once. Got another Robert the Devil in there now, that's what I say.' As he cackled,

I pressed a coin into his waiting palm and turned away before the conflict on my face could be seen too clearly.

I told the soldier at the gatehouse I had a message for the Lieutenant's deputy, and he nodded me through. I didn't even have to say it was from Sir Robert – it was that easy. Across the bridge, and I could hear the sounds of feeding time from the menagerie below. In through the first gateway. To my left a cobbled road led between the two walls, lined with tidy offices, and I turned up it, walking purposefully. My heart was thumping as I could see his tower just ahead of me.

But at the corner I received a check. The two storeys of the tower were set with small arched windows, but there was no sign of an entrance. Of course – I should have expected as much. Access only on the inmost side, for greater security.

To turn right around might look suspicious, if from any of those windows someone was watching me. I ducked into a doorway. I could hear a burst of laugher from above – clerks, no doubt, while their supervisor was away – but none of the inner doors opened and after waiting a moment, trying not to think just how close he must be, I braced my shoulders and stepped out again – task done, message delivered – and walked with all the confidence I could muster back the way I'd come.

This time, I took the path that lay straight ahead from the gatehouse, and the number of carts and people around told me this was the right way. A short distance on, there was an archway cut into the inner wall, and the heart of the Tower lay before me. But to the northeast, I saw with dismay, a solid mass of buildings lay around the foot of the Devlin Tower – what, did I have to find my way through them, and then maybe realise I was mistaken again, under the eyes of all the people working there? No – that can't be right. Think, Jeanne. They're not going to drag him in and out through wardrooms and kitchens and stables, are they? It wouldn't be safe and it wouldn't be proper – not with all those official visitors coming to see him, especially.

I strained my eyes upwards – yes! A walkway ran around the inner wall. Now all I had to do was find the stairs up. But as I rounded a corner I stopped in dismay.

In front of me was a platform, about breast high, made of crude new planks. I'd have guessed what it was for, even without the big baskets of sawdust that stood nearby. I'd never been one of those who flock to executions, but everybody knew that much. They'd scatter the sawdust thickly enough to soak up his blood, next day. The thought drove me on, as I raced up the staircase. The Devlin Tower lay right before me, only yards ahead, but two guards barred the door.

For the first time I froze. In the two years since I'd first met Lord Essex I'd sailed through many barriers, but instinct and experience told me this one would be different. These would be intelligent men, hand picked and hard briefed that it was as much as their life was worth to let anyone in without the proper authority. And for the first time, too, it really came home to me that it might be all my life was worth, here, to be caught out in a lie.

I stood there, paralysed, like a rabbit in a snake's eye. Was one of the guards already beginning to stare at me? It was almost with relief that I caught a bustle of footsteps behind me and went down into a bow as a party of expensive cloaks swept by.

'Jan! What in the world?' said a voice I knew well. 'Are you looking for me?' It was Sir Robert, and he was holding out his hand, assuming I'd brought some message, urgently. But as his gaze hardened on my face his hand dropped, and he glanced over my shoulder with a flash of comprehension.

I didn't say anything. There was nothing to say. Either he understood, or he didn't, and if not then I had no words to explain. Silent as I, he regarded me gravely, gesturing his companions to pass on. A finger and thumb massaged his forehead and briefly, the gesture jolted me back into the outside world, it was so familiar to me.

The moment stretched on. His eyes found mine and, for the first time since I had known him, I looked straight back at him. Stared, really. If I'd learnt some things in the past weeks – learnt I was the stalking horse, the decoy – then somewhere I'd learnt, too, that the only way was to play the hand of cards they'd dealt you. To accept you would be used in the great lords' plans, and use that knowledge to forward your own goals. To forge your own autonomy.

He said something, half under his breath. It might have been, 'I suppose I owe you that much.' And then: 'And after all, who knows?' – as much to himself as to me.

A quick crook of his finger brought one of the guards forward, but for a second I hardly understood what Sir Robert was telling him.

'Ten minutes, nothing given and nothing taken away. Ten minutes and one of you – you're the senior? then you – to stay.'

Without another word to me, he turned down the stairway. I will never know whether he acted from compassion or calculation. Both, maybe. He was a man who'd learnt to use even his most private impulses in the service of his country. They'd got so much information out of Essex already, but this man of all others knew his lordship capable of surprise and there was always the chance he was a lemon they had not yet squeezed dry.

It had been only a few days since I'd seen him in the courtroom, but the first thing I thought was that he'd changed. Perhaps it was just that I expected the nearness of death to have put some mark upon him – but it wasn't that, precisely. It was something else, something I mistrusted, and I stared it in the face, his face, even as he was saying 'Janny!' He sounded surprised, but not too surprised; I think he sounded pleased, but I don't know. I was too busy staring at the invisible enemy.

I'd never realised how much I hated that saintly look. That glow, of the fool who dreams of martyrdom as a goal, not an outrage against their humanity. I'd never used the word hatred to myself, when I saw it on a preacher's face of a Sunday. But I hated it when I saw it now. No wonder he hardly thought to ask what I was doing there. It seemed natural to him the whole world should come to admire his sanctity.

'I wanted to see you again,' I said lamely, conscious of the guard who had slipped in behind me. 'Before ...'

'Before tomorrow, yes, of course. I'm glad to see you, Janny. I wish I could see all those I knew before, in the days of my vanity.'

I couldn't believe he'd said it. He sounded like one of those hellfire Puritan preachers, if there's no one in authority around to sweep them away.

'I mean' – I said it brutally – 'I wanted to see you before you die.' I swear that just for a moment there was a flicker on his face, and I knew I had to fan it the way you do a tiny flame, before the fire has had a chance to catch. 'I mean,' I stumbled again, more gently, 'I'm sorry, I'm so sorry, that it ended this way.'

'No! No, you mustn't be sorry, Janny. I thank God for it every day. God knows what danger and harm it would have brought to the realm if we had succeeded. I didn't understand. My folly and my vanity blinded me. My sins are more in number than the hairs upon my head, but the Lord saw to it that our intents went astray, and now Mr Ashton has shown me the right way. I am become another man.'

A gust from the window ruffled the papers on his desk, and he turned to weight them, carefully. This was no prison cell they had him in but an apartment furnished adequately enough, if hardly with the grandeur he was used to.

I looked at him in something like despair. I wished with all my heart I could be out of that room, up with the crows on the battlement if necessary, just to think what it was I needed to say. Why had I come here? What had I been hoping for – some sort of quietus? Some reassurance, if not that he was all right, then at least that I had not missed the chance to serve him in any way?

Well, I had it now, didn't I? Against all the odds, against all reason, here he was, telling me all was well with him, even though he was to die the next day. Die in the straw, like an ox in the shambles, to lie in cold earth and to rot ... 'No!' I almost shouted it at him, and the guard half started forward. 'I won't let ... It can't be ...'

Not, I can't let it happen. Not that, precisely. More, I cannot stop them swinging an axe into the flesh of your neck, just where your skin is whitest when your hair falls away. Your blood will pour out like wine from a fountain and I cannot stop it, even though I cannot bear to think that the sawdust will soak up all your glow and all your energy and all your fantasy.

But I can try to stop you dying with a lie on your lips, the only lie that matters. I can try to stop you swearing that this is right, that you don't want to feel the spring as it quickens, and the firm flesh of the next pretty maid to come your way, and eat strawberries and dream a future for your country. I can make you admit that life is the great gift of my God, or yours, or the God of your Papist allies, or even of your precious Abdy.

He's looking at me with the ghost of that gleaming smile of his, underneath the sanctity. I take heart from it. There must be something that can touch him. I gaze round the room again as if for help, as if the decent furnishings might offer me something irresistible with which to tempt him, but even if we were the palace itself, I know that trying to urge pleasures on him will not be the key. There is nothing martyrs love better than to wave the pleasures of the world away. Absurdly I found I was wishing Sir Robert were there, with all his long knowledge of Lord Essex. I know this man so little, really. I pushed the foolish thought away.

The guards by the door are wooden-faced as toy soldiers, but I swear I could think they were urging me on. No one in this country really wants him to die – yes! That's it.

'But my lord, the country …' Without conscious thought, the right word had come to me. I had the key in my hand now, and I would turn it remorselessly. 'My lord, we need you. England needs you. We all know hard times lie ahead' – even here, I couldn't bring myself to name the queen's death directly – 'and there has to be someone with a vision, someone who can see beyond the everyday.' Fleetingly I thought again of Sir Robert, but I stamped down the idea of disloyalty. 'You say you're not the man you were. Think of the ways the man you are now might find to serve her majesty!

'My lord, you have to live – or at least, you have to try! If you fail, you fail, but at least then you will have done your real duty. My lord, is there nothing you can say? Is there no way?'

I could feel something growing in him, as surely as shoots were growing under the ground. I tried again.

'My lord, think of the horror of it – a civil war. My lord, think of the play.' *Richard II*, and what can happen when the ruler is weak and the succession uncertain, but more than just the play's message came flooding over me with that memory. I saw a slim brown figure, and a familiar face under actor's paint. But I also saw the eagerness on the faces of the crowd at the Globe that day, and the smell of spiced ale on the damp wind, and the noise, and the frenzy. He felt it too, I knew he did. I had run out of words, but I stood there staring at him with a frantic intensity.

In the midst of my outburst, he had half turned away. I could see he was tugging at something on his hand, but he would not look at me directly.

'There is a ring – a ring that she once gave me.' The queen's ring, then. There could, here, only be one she. 'She said it would always stand as a token of what there was between us. That it was a pledge I could call on, sure as money in the bank. I suppose' – his face twisted in a spasm of self-mockery – 'I must have been complaining of my poverty.

'If you got it to Lady Scrope at the court, the lady Philadelphia, then maybe –' Now he was the eager one. 'Sister-in-law to the Lord Admiral – you'll have seen her, surely?'

I hadn't, but I wouldn't have said so for the world. Already the brief flame I'd kindled was fading. Lord Essex shrugged, and the gleam of energy in his face died away.

'But it was a long time ago, that gift, and I expect her majesty only gave it because she didn't want to give me money. She always found a way to say no gracefully.'

'It's worth a try! Anything is. Give it to me, my lord – I'll get it to Lady Scrope, or else to her majesty.' Eagerly I started forward, but the guard was in my way.

'Easy, now, lad. Nothing given, nothing taken, that's what Sir Robert said. I'm sorry, my lord.'

Essex made a graceful little gesture with his hands, slipping the ring back on his finger. 'No matter, soldier. You're just doing your job. There, now, Janny. I hope you're satisfied. I tried, didn't I?'

I stared at him, speechless, afraid the bile that was rising in my throat was going to spew out of me. It wasn't only the disappointment, it was the guilt washing over me in waves like the tide of the sea, a wild reverse of feeling so abrupt it made me dizzy. What had I done? What gave me the right? He'd been content to die and had I taken that comfort away?

'You see, Janny?' He was speaking to me as to a child, gently. 'When you walk out of that door, nothing goes with you, except the love that made you come to visit me.' There was the faintest possible emphasis on door, and from behind the guard's shoulder, he shot his eyes to the window, meaningfully.

I don't know how I got out of the room in the end. The guard helped me, unwittingly.

'My lord – I'm sorry – the bell will be ringing shortly. This lad had best be on his way. They'll be locking the gates,' he added in explanation, as we both looked at him blankly.

Lord Essex half held out his hand to me, than let it drop. Heaven forbid the guard should get any ideas that way.

Back along the walkway, and down the short flight of steps. Don't rush so as to draw attention, but it's safe to move fast and openly. Past the scaffold with barely a glance and across the green, just another visitor at the end of the day. It's only as I approach the inner gateway that my pace slows. This is the dangerous moment, but there's a steady trickle of workmen and delivery vehicles heading home, and that will help. The luck is with me – there's a vintner with a load of barrels trying to get in, the fool, and the guards are fully occupied swearing at him that the Tower is closed for the day. I lounge in the lee of an empty cart, glance around as if I'm cursing the delay, then shake my head and turn determinedly to my right, up the alley between the walls, shaking my head as if to say, Better things to do than hang around here all day … I feel as if someone's drawn a target on my back, like the circles on the butt they use to practise archery. I'm braced for the shout, the 'Hey, you, what are you doing?' but no one tries to stop me.

There are lamps in the alley, but it's easy enough to dodge between them. The patch of deep shadow at the foot of Devlin's Tower reaches out to embrace me. Eagerly I stare upwards, where a crack of the window is still open to the night air – what did he do, complain of a smoking chimney?

How am I supposed to let him know I'm here? I can't risk a shout. A bubble of hysterical laughter rises in my throat. Perhaps this will be the end of the adventure – I'll just stand here all night, silently, until they open the gates again in the morning to let in the spectators to see Lord Essex die.

Like a gift from nowhere, the memory of that June day in the gardens with him comes back to me. The Lord alone knows what sort of dove's call I can make, but I give it a try. 'Whoo-hoo …'

The sound that answers me seems loud as a shot. It's the chink of metal on stone. It seems as if every door in the alley must open and men come out to see what's happening, but no, I'm alone in the darkness as I grope around the cobbles frantically. Oh God, if there were one thing more absurd than to stand all night waiting, it would be to fumble until dawn, fruitlessly.

Thank Him, thank Him, the ring is there under my trembling fingers. I look at it almost incredulously, plain wrought gold surrounding a dark carved head. It seems as though it should be more extraordinary. With the token clutched safe in my hand I speed, openly this time, back towards the gate where the guard is standing, key in hand. Good naturedly, he waits a moment.

'Cutting it a bit fine, aren't you?' I grimace, and clutch my chest, melodramatically, coating a layer of fake panic onto the real terror below. As I walk more slowly across the drawbridge, I hear the Tower shut behind me. Safely past the outer gate and the minute I am out of sight, I'm running as if my own life depended on it.

I'm not even sure why I'm running – don't know how much faith I put in his romantic story, the kind of thing lovers tell themselves at night, that fades in the cold light of day. But it isn't day, it is night and I am running: running for my own salvation, running for all those others I'd not been able to save. Running to be set free.

When the first stitch comes in my side, I slow down enough to think more calmly. Of course you don't run from the Tower to Whitehall, not if you're in a hurry. There are steps down to the river, just nearby, and with luck there'll still be a waterman waiting for trade, to take me the direct way.

There is a waterman – a sullen fellow, but burly enough, I am pleased to see. He hardly waits until I am well in the boat before pulling out onto the river, but almost at once I can see the reason for his alacrity.

'What is it? Why are we going so slowly?' I can hear the faint rhythmic splash as the oars dip in and out of the waves, but we seem to be labouring only to stand still. 'What is it,' I try again, 'the tide?' He only grunts in reply; the fellow seems barely to speak English, or perhaps he just doesn't want to let a fare get away.

I sit in the prow, in an agony of frustration, every muscle as tense as if I could push the boat upriver that way. Dear God, long minutes have passed already, and even the creek mouth where the Fleet joins the Thames is still an eternity away.

I have to sit it out that far – by now, they would have locked the City gates for the night and once inside, I could be trapped till break of day. But the minute we're past Blackfriars and the mouth of Fleet, the minute we're outside the walls … What time do they retire for the night at court? Surely not early. For several long minutes more I endure, eyes fixed on the eddies in the dark water, almost glad of the cold for taking my mind off the way that time is ticking away. But it is no use, I can bear it no longer.

'Let me out – onto those steps over there. Let me out, I say!' He only grunts again, and in desperation I make as if to seize an oar. This time he curses at me – I assume it's a curse – in some uncouth language. Hibernian, maybe. But he is pulling over to the bank at last, and holding out his hand for money. It takes most of what I have in my purse, and still I leave him shouting after me. Up the dark lane between two tall merchant houses. It is as muddy as a ploughed field; I slip, and go down hard on one knee, into the drain running down to the river, with the smell of filth rising up to me.

Into the broad street, with only the chink of lights behind shutters to keep me company. Run a little, walk a little. The cobbles strike hard through the thin soles of my shoes, and the soaked leather is rubbing me.

Run a little, walk a little, feet like sponges, pierced with burning wires, breath coming sobbingly. Sometimes I think that I hear footsteps behind me, but whenever I stop to listen, the wind carries them away. Left onto Fleet Street, past Essex

House; can I turn in there, and find someone to help me? The thought of the explanations makes my heart quail within me. And in any case, all London knows that Lady Essex has spent days trying to get into the queen's presence to plead her husband's case, and been turned away as if she were a nobody. They are broken reeds there – more broken than me.

There are the walls of Burghley House looming up on the other side, and I know an impulse to turn in there, throwing my problem into the lap of the old clerk. Or Sir Robert himself, maybe. I snarl at my own folly. This is a game I have to play alone, since there is no other player on exactly the same side as me.

Past the walls of the new house Sir Robert is having built; past York Place, where I'd visited Lord Essex that day. Charing Cross, and the straight run to the palace lies ahead, with the tilt-yard to the side. For a single second, the smell of rosemary comes back to me. But I wrench my wits away: now for the hardest part of the journey. By day the palace is like the village square, but at night it withdraws into its own privacy. And getting into the palace is one thing – it will be another to get anywhere near the queen's majesty.

The guard at the gate was as solid as an ox, and as impossible to push out of the way. I suppose it wasn't the first time he'd heard a lunatic saying they wanted to see her majesty. And every frantic word, as I pleaded and protested, made him more determined not to let me even as far as the outer courtyards, where every scullion can go quite freely.

Perhaps if I'd said at the start, coolly and confidently, that I was here on an errand for the Secretary? Too late for that now – the trick had failed me when I needed it most – and, sweat-stained, begrimed and teary, I hadn't realised how my looks would be against me. It was with some relief that the man turned away from me to bow low to a little cortège approaching.

'You're so set on seeing the queen – perhaps you'll make do with one of her ladies?' he said sarcastically. True words spoken in jest: I ducked under his restraining arm and stepped in front of the litter, peering in at the window eagerly. Heavens be praised – it wasn't one of her pretty junior maids, out for a kiss and a compliment, but useless for anything of gravity. Lined, experienced and haughty, a face not as old as the queen's but almost as shrewd looked back at me.

'My lady – I beg you – it's urgent, truly, truly.' The guard gave a click of exasperation and reached for me, only to be checked by a jewelled imperious finger.

'Urgent for whom, young man? For you, or for me?' Clear, uninflected, authority-packed, it was the voice of the true great lady.

'For the queen's majesty. And for Lord Essex,' I added desperately.

Her hard old gaze sharpened on me. 'I think I will hear more of this. No' – to the protesting guard – 'you've done your duty, I'm sure, but this is on my responsibility. Follow me, young man. And all the rest of you, wait here for me.' Her heels tapping on the paving stones as she set off across the courtyard towards a doorway, she paid me no more attention than if I'd been a dog at her heels, and I followed just as obediently.

'Now then – first things first. Who exactly might you be?'

'I am – I am Sir Robert's man.' Invoking his name here and now would surely come back to haunt me, but I'd do it anyway … But I must have waited too long, for like a hawk she was on to my hesitancy.

'Indeed? Then doubtless you'll know that the Secretary is even now with her majesty.' Caught in my own trap I just gaped at her, my eyes welling, shamefully. Thank God I hadn't said that he'd just sent me. 'Come now – what's the real story?'

So I told her – or told her the bare bones. I couldn't think what else to do, and perhaps her habit of command had laid a spell on me.

'Let me see this famous ring.' It looked dull and old-fashioned in her hand, and she eyed it dispassionately. 'You can leave this with me.' I must have started forward to snatch it back again, because a flash from her eyes stopped me.

'What did you think I was going to do? Usher you into the queen's presence?'

'My lord said – I was to give it to the lady Philadelphia – Lady Scrope,' I corrected hastily. I had the feeling I had startled her.

'For Lady Scrope, is it? Then you can certainly entrust it to me.' She turned her head and the flickering candlelight showed hair that still held a glint of red in the grey. Did she mean? – she must do – I gazed at her dumbly. Her tone sharpened, as if her patience were running out.

'I said, you can leave this to me.' A gleam of amusement, like winter sunshine, softened her face momentarily. 'You don't, after all, have very much choice. A word from me will have you thrown out into the gutter, or worse. And without me, you or your precious ring have so little chance of reaching the queen tonight, you might walk into the kingdom of heaven more easily.'

She looked at my face, and relented just a little. 'I dare say in the end you'll understand that you've not done too badly. I assure you I will do what is right, and you've fulfilled your promise, as nearly as might be. Neither you nor his lordship were really pinning too many hopes on this, I trust?' She held up the ring, contemptuously.

I shook my head. I knew there was an ambiguity in her words, but great waves of weariness were washing over me, churning my gut as though I were on the sea. I'd been chasing a chimera through the streets of London. I wished I could go to sleep, and the thought of waking did not interest me.

The old lady – I still didn't know her name, but her air of authority made her old to me – nodded her head sharply, as if satisfied, and gathered her skirts to sweep out of the room. 'Go home, child,' she said, not unkindly.

I jerked out a bow, and stumbled after her back towards the
gate. I was not going home – I was not sure where home would
be. I was going, if I could find a better waterman to take me,
back to the Tower, to find a corner where I could crouch down
for the rest of the night, and wait for the events of the next day.

Katherine, Countess of Nottingham

24 February, night

It's done – no it isn't, that's the trouble. I still could take the ring
to her majesty. No decision's been taken, not one thing has
happened yet, to stop me doing just that – or nothing outside my
head. I tell myself it's too late at night to disturb the queen, but
of course that's just idiocy. It's the fear that's gripping my guts
and rising in my throat; oh, not at dealing with the boy, that was
nothing, I hardly saw him for the anger that was in me. What,
Essex get away with it, would he?

The fear is at what I have done. Am doing. Will have to go on
doing, every hour and every minute through this night until
dawn has come and I know the guards will have brought Essex
from his cell and there's no doing anything different, for
anybody.

I plump down onto a stool and wrap my arms around my
belly. So, what, I change my mind? I put everything I've worked
for away? I take the ring to the queen and then what, pray? Do I
really think she'll call the whole thing off, for a piece of trumpery jewellery? Always assuming the boy's story was true anyway.

All that would happen is it would make tonight harder for
her, give her a heavier load of regret to carry. And she'd blame
me for putting that on her, I know she would. Anyone knows
that, who was around when they forced her – when Charles
helped to force her – to sign the death warrant for the Queen of
Scots. I'll never forget the day they told her that had been done,

and her shrieking out one minute that she'd lost her sister-queen, and the next, that Mary should have been dealt with secretly.

And if she did call it off, for God's sake, then what about Essex? Is he just quietly going to go away, and cause no more trouble to anybody? No: this is, it is, my duty. But when I take a gulp of wine it's like vinegar in my mouth and I'm shaking as if I had the sweat. My cold turned to an ague, maybe. I wouldn't give the ring to Philadelphia, for her to decide, even if she were at court. This one is for me. Only I thought I'd done enough already; but what had I done, really? A word to a player, a hint it would be as well Lord Essex were encouraged to show his hand quickly. Later, a present to that same actor, but what of that? His father served mine faithfully. And he's a decent, sensible man, who'd see why this was necessary.

My old nurse always said a secret untold would turn sour in your belly. Years ago, I'd have to make her words into a goblin story to take the fright away for Philadelphia, but who is there now to tell a story for me? Think; think of something else – what her majesty should wear these next days. Not crimson, no, nothing red, blood-red. The blackwork sleeves, perhaps. The fine needlework reminds me of the Queen of Scots and her endless embroidery, but that's just an irrelevancy. No – nothing funereal. The white knitwork kirtle with the pink tufts, or the carnation and white? No, the beaver colour with green she had last winter. It wouldn't do for her to look too gay.

I want – who do I want? Charles? This would be even harder for him than for me. It's foolish, at my age, but the thought of my parents washes over me. My father, not as he was at the end, doting on his young mistress, but how he used to be. It's too silly, at my age, but I feel more like a child now than I have for fifty years – a child, or an old lady. It's silliest of all, when you consider the facts, but do you know what I wish? I wish Philadelphia were here to comfort me.

The ring is still lying there on the table. I feel as if it is looking at me. Into my box, with my children's first teeth, and a lock of the queen's hair, and a piece of unicorn's horn that Robert Dudley once gave me. I will, I must, get rid of it soon – into the river, maybe. But not right now. I've done all I can do for now, and it feels as though the effort may be the death of me.

Jeanne

24 February, night

It was the longest night of my life. Or maybe the shortest, I don't know. As I bowed myself out behind the tapping of the dowager's heels – past the porter, who pretended hardly to see me – I suppose I thought the night's adventures were at an end. My whole being was focused on the Tower. Like a dog shut out behind a door I yearned to be near him – not from love (I understand that word better now) but more as though I wanted an answer. I needed to tell him that I had done his bidding, that I had done my best. I wanted him to tell me he knew it, that I wasn't guilty. That I was free. Oh, I knew it wasn't going to happen, but if I could get as near as possible, if I could spend myself just that bit further, then even the pain itself might ease the tightness in my chest to some slight degree.

I hadn't enough money left for boat fare in my purse, though this time the tide would have been with me, and the river passage would have been quick and easy. I hardly remember the walk for I think I'd passed beyond weariness by then, but in the end I reached Blackfriars and the western edge of the City. My room wasn't far away, but I could no more have roused the landlady, made some glib explanation, than I could have made conversation with a red savage, if one had appeared in front of me. Besides, every muscle – every clenching ache from my shoulders through my spine – told me I had to be by the Tower when dawn broke.

How to get around the City walls? To circle up through the north, and in the dark without a light ... My heart sank within me. Down by the water, there'd be cargo boats moving, to take advantage of the tide. If I tried them all, surely I'd find one who'd give me a lift to the City's eastern wall; if not for the few coins I had left, then for very pity. The fourth boat I tried had been carrying hides, and it smelt like a tallows merchant, but the owner, though silent, must have been kindly. He let me off by an old water stair, and told me as long as I went quietly, no one was likely to see.

I'd planned to huddle down in some doorway, but in the end, the cold defeated me. Towards the small hours of the morning a dank wind came up off the river that seemed to stab to my very bones. I didn't dare go far, but if only there were somewhere I could get out of the air. Behind loomed the great bulk of All Hallows, and though they'd have locked the body of the church for sure, there might be a porch. Maybe even a bench where I could stretch out, without the chill of a stone floor striking through me.

I don't know which was more comforting – to be out of the wind, or the presence of sanctity. Sunday mornings with Mrs Allen, and feeling the sun warm through my clothes as we came out into the daylight, after. Christmas, when the church was ablaze with lit candles; and the well-known words of the litany. I hadn't thought of these things for a time, but now I mouthed them over, telling each sonorous familiar phrase like – like my grandmother, in the first part of the century, before all the changes, might have told over the beads of the rosary.

Heretically, my mind roamed over the church as it must once have been, before the old queen's father had the saints and the painted statues stripped away. I'd seen some of what had been saved from the wreckage – the odd torn page come up for private sale, or two Books of Hours in Cecil's library. Calendars and offices, painted borders of poppies and pansies, and tiny figures disporting themselves among wreaths of ivy. Prayers to the Virgin, the queen of heaven robed in blue, enthroned with her baby on her knee, or seated on the grass like a simple country girl while the angel came to whisper in her ear. Her long gold hair, and the faint flush on her cheeks. My mother, Maman, letting me help comb her long hair, and the feel of daisies in my fat fist and my mother seated on the grass, pointing out the pimpernels and speedwells to me ...

I hugged the cloak, the thick black cloak with the Cecil insignia, more tightly around me. I wondered if it had been a bright scarlet, if it would feel any the warmer. There was something about the feel of the wool under my fingers, something that made it less familiar and ordinary. I heard a voice in my head – could it be my father's, speaking from my memory? 'Here, Jeanne, feel my cloak. Now feel this silk – do you feel the difference? It's beautiful, *hein*? Fit for the nobility.'

The press of the wooden bench under my back was like the feel of the deck as we lay, on the boat that brought us to England, Jacob and I. I had taken care not to think about these things for years. It was as if the different parts of my life had been like the compartments in a garden knot, and now the different plants in each were breaking through and running riot inside me. As if the new space inside my head, the space that effort and exhaustion had made, were being filled by something both foreign and familiar.

Perhaps there'd once have been a statue of the Virgin, looking down above my head. Perhaps, in the darkness, there was one still, watching over me. I thought of how small a part women had played in my life, and for the first time I saw that as an oddity. Maman gone so early, Mrs Allen who had never managed to play a mother's part to me. For a moment I thought of the old queen, absurdly. I had not known much of the kindness of women, and I hadn't known how to be kind to myself. Here in the empty dark I faced the knowledge squarely and without pity. The nearest thing I'd found had been in a man who knew what it was to play a woman's part. I wished I knew where in the city Martin Slaughter was this night, and whether he was thinking of Lord Essex. Or of me.

In all those years alone in the world, I had always kept fear at bay. Too much feeling had been a luxury, but now terror washed over me. Men had died screaming for less than I had done, and who was there who would save me? I thought Sir Robert had always wished me well, but I knew that he had other games to play. I thought of Martin Slaughter, but what would he be able to do if the old lady gave me over to the authorities? He was no all-powerful lord but a cog in the machine, like me. And what price even a lord's power, today?

To think of Lord Essex brought no comfort. He was already a ghost to me and not because he was to die the next day but because the man I'd imagined I'd been close to had never been alive, not really. But thinking of Martin Slaughter did bring some relief. A kind of warmth, a feeling that beyond this night-mare of the dark there would again be the warm ordinary light of day. Cog he might be, but he seemed to pick his own path through the world, and to do it surely. There were lessons I could learn from Martin Slaughter, things that he might teach me. In the silence, it came to me I'd already begun to learn and this fear was part and parcel of the tutor's fee I had to pay.

I saw it, like a pattern laid out in front of me. I saw that every-thing that had happened had worked out as the government – as Sir Robert – had planned it to. England would keep its good order, and how could I be sorry? I knew what bad order could do. I'd tried to disrupt the pattern but I doubt I'd succeeded, and it didn't matter. I'd done what I was supposed to, I'd been true to what was in my nature, and that was something, too. You can graft old apple stock onto new, you can train pears into fan shapes against a wall, but any gardener knows in the end plants grow as they have to, and any attempt to thwart that need will fail eventually. My head would always be with the Secretary, but I could no longer pretend I didn't have a heart as well. If I had a future after this night's work then perhaps I could start again and live as I was meant to. Live, in the understanding that other people had their own life's vision too.

You are always close to death in a church, but I truly under-stood now that there is birth, too, in the story. I felt – if not a sense of being comforted, then at least, like the moment a doctor's opiate starts to take effect, a faint sensation of relief ahead, of where comfort might be. In those Books of Hours I'd seen, skeletons dance through the Office for the Dead. As a child I'd peered at them fearfully. But as sleep came closer I remembered there'd been other pictures from the Calendars, too – the hopeful sowing into the bare autumn fields, and the blos-soms and courting couples of May.

Wednesday, 25 February 1601

'They won't do the disembowelling bit anyway. They never do for peers – don't want anyone to hear them screaming. It would spoil their dignity.' It had been the gangling clerk's attempt at comfort, and in fact it was comforting in a way. I'd always shied away from executions, or floggings, or even bear-baitings, even when it had set me apart from the boys all around, at a time when what I most wanted was to seem like one of the pack.

When the time came to execute Cuffe, he wouldn't be so lucky.

This execution I knew I had to attend, but it wasn't in the hope of witnessing a reprieve, not really. The cold of the night had cooled my brain, and I understood I'd been chasing a chimera – and making Lord Essex chase it too, may God and he forgive me.

So now I was taking refuge in the details, like a wife smooth-ing the pillow for a dying husband. I wished they could have sent for a swordsman, like they did for Anne Boleyn, so he could kneel upright, not lie down on a chopping block like something out of the butchers. But they didn't do that even for Jane Grey, nor yet for the Scots Queen Mary. So now it was dawn, with the

dank, will-sapping, cold of February, and on this Ash
Wednesday, this day for repentance, they'd erected a platform
under the wall like something set up for the acts in a fairground
so all the spectators could see.

Not that there were so many spectators: orders of her majesty.
They said it was a favour begged by Lord Essex himself, that he
might die privately. I wasn't so sure: if he'd had the chance of
bawling his remorse before all London, he might well have
seized the opportunity.

That was what they were afraid of, of course. They were
afraid the mood of a big London crowd would swing back too far
towards pity. As it was, they'd sent two executioners – what, in
case one couldn't bring himself to do the job? And when Sir
Walter Ralegh arrived, being Captain of the Gentlemen
Pensioners, even this hand-picked crowd murmured so loud he
had to go away.

It was soon after seven when we heard footsteps. The crowd
had gone so quiet we could hear them clearly. He was all in black
– a velvet cloak over a satin suit: was he afraid if he shivered in
the cold, we might think he was shaking? A black felt hat which
he took off as he bowed to us all. I found my nails were biting
into my palms; not because I was hoping for a reprieve – any
more than he was, I knew with certainty – but with wanting him
to do this well. To die on behalf of those others I'd known, who'd
had to die without dignity.

One of his servants sidled next to me, perhaps drawn to a
familiar face. He told me Lord Essex had been up all night praying, and he looked it; with that pallid look only the ginger-haired
have. But he'd found what he had been praying for. He'd never
really believed my fantasy, after all. I hadn't damaged him too
badly, and as he began to speak my hands unclenched themselves, slowly.

'I beseech our Saviour Christ to ask the Eternal Majesty my
pardon; especially for my last sin: this great, this bloody, this
crying and infectious sin, whereby so many, for the love of me,

have ventured their lives and souls and have been driven to offend God, to offend their sovereign, and to offend the world. Lord Jesus, forgive it us, and forgive it me.

'I beseech you and the world to have a charitable opinion of me for my intention towards her majesty, whose death, upon my salvation and before God, I swear I never meant. I desire all the world to forgive me, even as I do freely and from my heart forgive all the world.'

He turned to take off his gown and ruff, but he wasn't used to undressing himself – how should he be? Confused, he called for his servant Williams, and I felt the boy beside me stir as if to move forwards. But I grasped his arm to hold him still, and the ruff was off, eventually. The chaplain whispered to him – what, not to be afraid? – and he answered gracefully. Said he had been diverse times in places of danger where death was nonetheless neither so present nor so certain as here, and that therefore he desired God to strengthen him, and not suffer his flesh to have rule over him.

The executioner knelt and asked for his forgiveness. It's the tradition, but it is horrible to me. 'Thou art welcome to me. I forgive thee. Thou art the minister of justice,' Essex said. He knelt down in front of the block, and the straw under his knees rustled comfortably.

He took off his black doublet to show the waistcoat underneath, red as blood. They offered him a blindfold but he waved it away.

'O God, creator of all things and judge of all men, I humbly beseech Thee to assist me in this my last combat. Give me patience to be as becometh me in this just punishment inflicted upon me.'

With the chaplain leading him, he repeated the Lord's Prayer. Some spectators joined in, though some looked away. Some were sobbing – not that this was a hysterical market crowd, but the childishness of those words touched me to the core.

'Our Father ...' He repeated for a second time the bit about forgiving his enemies. The chaplain prompted him again and said over his belief, the Credo. This was being dragged out almost unbearably.

'O God, give me true humility and patience to endure to the end. I ask you all to pray with me and for me, so that when you see me stretch out my arms and my neck on the block, and the stroke ready to be given, it may please the everlasting God to send down his angels for me.'

He lay flat in the straw and fitted his neck into the groove, turned his head sideways. I could almost feel the unaccustomed edges as if on my own flesh. They say Katherine Howard sent for it to practise with, before her execution day.

One of the divines told him to begin the Fifty-first Psalm: it was in everyone's mind that he would not be allowed to finish it. He knew it too.

'Have mercy upon me, O God, according to Thy loving kindness, according to the multitude of Thy compassions, put away mine iniquities. Wash me thoroughly from mine iniquity, and cleanse me from my sin.'

Perhaps he couldn't endure it any longer, but he flung out his arms and cried: 'Executioner strike home. O Lord, into Thy hands I commend my spirit.' At least, that's what he was saying. I completed the words in my head.

He was still talking when the axe swung down. He didn't move or speak again, I thank God, though the first stroke seemed to only strike into his shoulder and the crowd groaned in sympathy. It took three strokes in all before the head was severed completely. The executioner held the head up by the long hair, in a ritual gesture of triumph, and called out 'God save the queen!' but it was in silence that we all moved away.

I walked back to my lodging like someone in a dream, looking neither to the right nor the left. I have an idea that someone spoke to me – the merchant from the house next door – but if so, they got no answer. I'd never expected the ring to work, that much was a certainty. I don't know whether it even reached the queen; I don't know whether the whole tale itself was just another of Lord Essex's fantasies.

But one thing I did know: he'd asked to be returned to her favour a dozen times before; a dozen times he'd shown she couldn't safely agree. This much I knew – and I almost felt I'd come to feel a bond with her, or perhaps that was just another of my mistakes – Elizabeth was not the woman to gamble her country's fate on a trumpery piece of jewellery.

As I flung myself down on my bed full clad, I understood at last that my mad run yesterday hadn't been born of hope. I'd been running as you run in a nightmare when the wolves are at your heels. Running, as you run in childhood, to run your confusion and your fears away. Running out of my mouth the taste of betrayal; that I no longer even wanted Essex alive and free, that I no longer believed in his vision nor felt his spell. Running to do his bidding, to give him this one last feeble chance, not out of love but pity.

I slept like the dead and I must have slept for hours. When I woke, the light was fading in the sky, and I found to my surprise that I was hungry. I ran down the stairs, not even pausing to wash my face, then caught myself up as I reached the street, paused a moment, then retraced my steps more slowly.

In my room I checked there were no peering eyes, then got a knife and levered up the loose floorboard where I kept my money. I took something else up, too – the fingered note the porter at Burghley House had given me.

In the street I went direct to an inn where food would still be served, though the place would normally be too expensive for me. I craved food, strong and savoury. They brought me a slice of salt beef and mustard with the wine, while I waited for the broth, and the mallard boiled with cabbage, and the coney stuffed with pepper and currants and steaming with gravy. They brought me a dish of warmed sweet cream, with rosewater and ginger to make it spicy.

The landlord asked curiously if I'd had good news, and for a moment I blushed crimson. Half London was looking over its shoulder today, and I was behaving like a small-town spend-thrift up to town for the holiday. I paid my bill and went out, down through the Exchange towards the Pawn, where the milli-ners sold their ready-made garments, pausing only at the seam-stress' booth and the apothecary. By the time I got back home I could feel exhaustion coming like a lover to claim me. I slept at once, and dreamlessly.

Epilogue

For though the Soul do seem her grave to bear,
And in this world is almost buried quick,
We have no cause the body's death to fear,
For when the shell is broke, out comes a chick.

From 'Nosce Teipsum', Sir John Davies

Cecil

Thursday, 26 February 1601

It is one of those bright early days when you can fool yourself winter has really gone, and spring is here to stay. Lizzie used to have a ritual for days like this. She would go around the garden, pouncing with triumph on anything already out – snowdrops, a sprig of witchhazel, the fat sweet early violets – and bring them into the house, gloating over them, as if to salute their bravery.

My man tells me that this morning Jeanne stopped to buy violets, on her way.

Of course I've had someone following Jeanne – for everyone's safety, you might say. That ring, now: I doubt it would have done harm even had it reached the queen, but as so often in the course of these events, my intervention was unnecessary. The countess will never mention it, and neither will I. Some gardeners dislike the self-sown plant, the happy accident, but that has never been my way. And after all, I think we might safely agree that the process of Essex's end had a momentum of its own – a snowball, rolling unstoppably down the hill, once given the first push by his folly.

It was a good man I've had to follow Jeanne, these last two days. She won't have had any idea he was nearby. He was too discreet to show any surprise when he told me what he saw this morning – or too experienced to feel any, maybe. The only time he blinked was when I asked: Did she look pretty? That did shock him, oddly enough, or perhaps shocked him coming from me.

So: I have let her go, or the machinery let her go, and now I have other fish to fry. Next week would not be too early to send an approach to James, discreetly, discreetly. We are in the endgame now of her majesty's reign, but there is every hope it will be possible to move on in safety. I plan for the future, but I find myself also bound to the past, as surely as Essex with all his outworn dreams of chivalry and glory. A nice irony there, no doubt. I shall appreciate it, eventually.

I will take care not to think of Jeanne again, not unless it is necessary, though if she continues with Martin Slaughter I suppose she may come my way. I wish her well, I hope her happy – to know yourself is the most valuable education: those old men, with their manuals of advice, that's what they should say.

But that is all. It must be. I shall go into the garden, and smell the witchhazel, and I will go to the bed where the violets grow, and I will not let myself be overwhelmed by the memories. Now that my father is dead I am laying out my own garden at the new house across the Strand. This place belongs to my brother now, but no doubt I will still walk here frequently. I will not be able to stay away.

Lizzie.

Jeanne

26 February 1601

I woke to a morning of sharpness, but of sunshine. A morning when you know the ripe of the day will offer just an hour or two's pledge that spring is on the way. That though it's felt as though the ground would be frozen forever the thaw must come eventually. A morning that might tempt any Londoner to take the air. I yelled to the kitchen boy to bring me hot water; yes, I'd pay the extra fee.

The fine soapballs I'd brought last night were scented with lavender. I'd bought and I'd bought, yielding to all of the shopgirl's suggestions, and some of my purchases were strange to me. A water with chamomile and wormwood in it, and a paste of alum to rub under the arms. A linen bag to rub over my teeth, filled with ashes of rosemary. A tiny twist of paper filled with orris root powder had cost more than the rest put together. I rubbed it over my chest and behind my ears, gingerly.

I pulled the linen shift over my head first, and only the fineness of the fabric gave me pause. I shivered a little, as the silky coolness touched my skin. The whalebone stiffness of the bodice felt not unlike a doublet, though I had an impulse to clutch at my bare expanse of chest, in all its immodesty.

As I reached for the petticoats I gritted my teeth. I was moving into unfamiliar territory. As I hooked them into place they fell too limply. Oh yes – 'the bum-roll', as the assistant had told me, grinning mockingly. Man, woman or hermaphrodite; I could even manage a brief giggle, now, over what she must have thought of me. A top petticoat with a coloured panel at the front; dressing as a man, I'd had it easy. I yanked my way into the dress until a snagging of the embroidery made me halt, and then I went more slowly. I turned to face myself in the glass, and a woman looked back at me.

It would be a day of promise, outside. This time of year, when February is turning to March, every day brings something new. In the garden there are the first of the Lent lilies, and the swell of bud on the grey apple branch, and the men are taking the sacking off the tubbed olive trees. When we walk out into the fields there will be new buds on the primroses, lamb's tail catkins shaking yellow in the breeze, and the first of the celandines a golden glory. Even if the tall trees are still bare, there will be the red filament of blossom on the young elms and new leaf sprouting on the little hazels. Spring starts from the bottom up, and that seems right to me.

Just for a second I thought of Burghley House, where every tree was a known friend. I knew in my bones Sir Robert would be out there, noting every new bud with his careful eye, whatever else might claim the Secretary's attention on such an important day. But the garden at Burghley House was not the only garden in the City. In the churchyard at St Helen's some City father had paid for them to plant up the nodding bulbs of spring, in honour of his wife's name day.

People would be out early today, alive in the spring sunshine. Even yesterday, as I went about my purchases, I'd felt a kind of tremor in the blood. Sometimes, in the garden, I'd wonder where the spring *comes* from – pushing blindly through the frozen earth, fighting the cold every inch of the way – but something of the same was happening in me. The spring comes too slowly to register as a miracle until suddenly it overtakes you on your way. This was a day when you could look at the bare boughs of a tree, and know that the sap was working secretly. The dress I'd bought was apple green. 'Made it for a young lady up from the country,' the tailor had said confidingly. 'But the money isn't there to settle the bill, so I can let you have it cheaply.' Perhaps it was light, for so early in the season, but the panel on the underskirt was the pink of blossom, the fabric was embroidered with sprays of tiny leaves. I fingered it delicately. I'd seen a girl yesterday on her young man's arm, face aglow with a warmth that had nothing to do with her thin clothing, and as I gazed in the mirror now, she seemed to be smiling along with me. I'd had a sense I'd never really felt before, of how much pleasure was to be had in this city – if you knew how to take it, and how to share it, maybe. Of how men and women did lean together, laugh together; and if there were still secrets and shadows in their world, well, sometimes they laughed anyway.

In the country soon, those first fragile pokes of primroses will turn into fragrant platefuls of the palest gold, and curved green spikes will spring up overnight; the cuckoo pint, the Lords and Ladies. Then the moment when the world at your feet becomes a carpet of emerald, and cherry is white on the trees. A moment when the spring looks back at you from far down the road ahead, and she too is laughing over her shoulder, kindly.

There is a portrait of the queen at the house on the Strand, a treasure of the Cecil family. She wears a low-cut white dress, edged with gold and embroidered with spring – heartsease pansies and cowslips, honeysuckles and gillyflowers. A rainbow showed in the sky overhead, to admire a timeless beauty. She herself might be old now, but the portrait would shine out for all eternity. The embroidery on her skirt, of watchful eyes and listening ears, told a darker story, but I pushed that thought away. I pulled fine wool stocking up my legs, stepped into shoes of red Spanish leather. We were none of us spies today. Not in a world where, as the weeks move on, we'll be seized by the first scarlet advance guard of poppies, and the gold of the buttercups will make rich men of us all. When summer will bring days when the air itself is so heavy you should be swimming in it, languorously. Oh, the summer may be bad again, sure enough, the harvest poor and the people sulky. But there'll still be a few days like these. There will be.

I turned to face the glass again, and I was pleased by what I could see. Even my face seemed to have more contours to it – or perhaps it was just that, in all those years, I'd taken care never to look too clearly. I took the ruff from its box – yes, I'd bought that too, though only a small one – and pinned it to the collar, unhandily. It framed my face like the petals do the gold heart of a daisy. Tentatively, I fluffed a bit of my hair forwards onto my cheek. It was still boy-short, of course, but it would grow eventually. For the first time, I dared to see a future ahead of me.

The light coming in through the window seemed to put courage into me. The gillyflowers the queen wore weren't in season, but I'd buy violets from the flower woman that would smell as sweetly. I'd tuck them into my bodice – the queen wore her flowers for symbols, but I wanted ornament, modesty. But when I went to St Helen's churchyard, to find Martin Slaughter, I would be as fine as she.

General Historical Note

The story of a plea, sent by Essex on the eve of his execution but kept from the queen, was first suggested in 1620 in John Webster's *The Devil's Law Case*. It was however later in the seventeenth century when, in the anonymous *A Secret History of the Most Renowned Queen Elizabeth and the Earl of Essex*, the story of the ring was established in the form we know it today. Essex, so the story goes, passed the ring out of the window to a boy instructed to take it to Philadelphia, Lady Scrope, who would get it to the queen. Alas, the boy gave it instead to Lady Scrope's sister, the Countess of Nottingham, who physically resembled her, but whose husband the Lord Admiral was Essex's mortal enemy.

The countess in malice kept the ring, confessing to Elizabeth only on her deathbed. 'God may forgive you, but I never can', said Elizabeth bitterly. The tale never went away – features largely, indeed, in the 1939 Bette Davis and Errol Flynn film, *The Private Lives of Elizabeth and Essex*, though by this point the Countess of Nottingham no longer figures, as she had done in the eighteenth and nineteenth centuries, as Essex's discarded and vengeful lover. The ring itself – gold, with a cameo of the queen – can still be seen in the Chapter House Museum of Westminster Abbey. But sadly, for all its long history, its near-contemporary credentials, the tale is surely apocryphal – no more than a romantic story.

The Countess of Nottingham was known to be in Chelsea in January 1601: there is no evidence she even returned to court in

February. Moreover, two years later, grief at the countess's death was believed to have played a part in hastening the queen's own end. That cold the countess suffered in January 1601, a cold her husband mentioned in a letter to Cecil, may have marked the start of a long decline. She died on 24 February 1603, to be followed within weeks by her royal mistress. The news of Elizabeth's death was carried north to Scotland by the countess' brother, Robert Carey, who bore with him by way of proof a ring originally sent by King James, and thrown to Carey out of a window by his sister Lady Scrope. Another token ring, another story.

The execution of the Earl of Essex had marked a further decline in Elizabeth's already failing fortunes. Her godson John Harington observed how, alone, she would pace her rooms in rage, thrusting into the arras with a rusty sword. For their part the people, it was said 'were weary of an old woman's govern-ance'. The question of Elizabeth's successor, with the frantic canvassing of more than a dozen possibilities, had long been a topic of secret speculation, but though few knew it, Essex's death was a turning point. Literally within weeks, Robert Cecil (aided by details of Essex's correspondence with Scotland, wrung under interrogation from Henry Cuffe) took advantage of his rival's disappearance from the scene to begin his own negotiations with King James, always in the deepest secrecy.

Cecil kept his loyalty: the condition for his support was that Elizabeth should not be menaced or deposed during her life-time. But when she finally died James – belying the widespread fears of confusion and civil war – succeeded to the throne of England 'without so many ripples as would shake a cockle boat', as Cecil himself put it complacently. In gratitude for his vital part in these negotiations, the new king would eventually create Cecil Earl of Salisbury. The Earl of Nottingham, too, prospered under the new regime. Within months of his wife's death he had married again, a woman forty years his junior, and was getting something of a reputation as a court dandy. But while

Nottingham lived to be almost ninety, Robert Cecil died before he was fifty – due in large part, his contemporaries believed, to his unhealthy habit of eating fruit every day.

Private letters show Cecil's grief at the loss of his wife and sensitivity to his disability. The abortive progress of Essex's rebellion is of course a matter of historical record, but so too are all the incidents I describe in the course of his turbulent relationship with the queen, and with the Cecils. Even the thunderstorm in which Essex set off for Ireland is a matter of historical record, as is the queen's visit to the dying Burghley, while Essex's one-man Garter ceremony – even the public comment about the wicked ways of London watermen, even the touring theatrical manager Henslowe's concerns about his spinach and his stockings, back home – survive in letters and diaries. Lord Burghley, Sir Walter Ralegh, Lord Essex's father and most notably Francis Bacon were indeed among the many who wrote manuals of advice, from which the maxims I use were taken. Wherever possible, and especially on public occasions, I have tried to use the recorded speech of these very public personalities, while letters quoted are drawn from actuality.

The government's role in the demonising of Henry Cuffe is explored in Lacey Baldwin Smith's book *Treason in Tudor England: Politics and Paranoia*. Smith suggests that Essex's rebellion was reconfigured into a more acceptable stereotype by making it less a reaction to the pressures of those fraught years, or an unpardonable lapse into folly by one of England's premier peers, than the results of evil counsel. The fruit of a base man's 'motiveless malignity', in the term Shakespeare used to describe Iago just three years later. Cuffe was sentenced to death in March 1601 and, unlike his employer, suffered the full horror of hanging, drawing and quartering, protesting to the last that he had been victimised.

As concerns other details of the plots I suggest, the more one reads about the late sixteenth century and its infinitely complex network of spies and informers, the more almost *anything* comes to seem a possibility. Francis Bacon's role in Essex's downfall was a cause of widespread discussion and debate even at the time, with allegations he had been poisoning the queen's ear against his former patron, and disapproval of the double role – as Essex's advisor, and as his accuser – that he seemed to play. The suggestion of the leaked letters, however, is my own – though, again, the trade in such potential sources of spin was well established: at one point Francis Bacon was known to have been writing letters purportedly exchanged between Essex and Francis' brother Anthony, the real purpose of which was to be displayed to Elizabeth as 'evidence' of Essex's fidelity.

Sir Ferdinando Gorges, a follower of Essex's and a cousin of Ralegh's (and, later, a founding father of the state of Maine) did indeed speak against the rebels moving on the court as well as the City and did, on the day before the rebellion, hold a meeting with Ralegh. We cannot know exactly what loyalties Sir Ferdinando carried to that meeting, nor exactly what was said there: though it is recorded that Gorges told (warned?) Ralegh that Essex had been 'making his house into a Guard'; and went away to inform the earl that he was in danger, a statement that could only foster Essex's suspicions. Gorges did indeed release the hostages contrary to Essex's orders and subsequently gave evidence against Essex at his trial. Nonetheless, in the world of sober fact it is certainly possible that he was merely half-hearted in Essex's cause rather than actively suborned against him. I might offer a putative apology to him, as to Bacon, for aspersions cast, if it were not that the latter at least fits very uneasily into the 'injured innocent' category.

The role played by Jeanne is obviously invented with her character, but that apart, there are only a few, and I hope comparatively minor, ways in which I am aware actually of having contradicted the known historical record. The 'Rainbow' portrait of Elizabeth that Jeanne describes was probably painted a few months after the end of this story. Elizabeth did not visit Theobalds in the last summers of her reign: her travels in those years took her mostly south of the Thames. Her comportment there was much as I have described, but her last journey north-wards had taken place a few years before. After that, Theobalds had to wait for a royal visit until 1603 when King James stayed there on his journey south, liking it so well he took it from Cecil in exchange for Hatfield, where another great garden, designed by the Tradescants, would soon be underway. In July 1600, however, Theobalds was visited by one Baron Waldenstein, whose diary records its many splendours – now, alas, long passed away.

The Cecils' passion for their gardens is in general well docu-mented. In 1597 Lord Burghley gave Elizabeth a copy of John Gerard's revolutionary *Herbal*, with eighteen hundred hand-painted colour illustrations. The collection and classification of new plants was a great obsession of the age: Anna Pavord's *Searching for Order* paints a riveting picture of the work of men like Matthias de l'Obel (writing as Lobelius: no prizes for guess-ing to which flower he gave his name); of John Gerard, whom Pavord describes as 'a plagiarist and a crook'; and indeed even of the Twickenham nursery gardener Richard Pointer.

On a more practical level these decades marked a great turn-ing point in garden history: Francis Bacon was only one of many who wrote on the subject. Anyone wishing to monitor the seasonal progress of the gardens described here, however, should remember that while on the one hand England was at this point in the grip of the 'little Ice Age' of particularly hard winters, the English calendar had not yet been reformed on European lines, so that Jeanne's February 1 would correspond to our February 11.

The name Martin Slaughter features several times in the theatrical records of the period. I first encountered it as that of an actor fined for having falsely represented himself as belong-ing to a licensed theatrical company. But an actor variously called Martin Slater or Slawghter also figures extensively in the documents of the Rose playhouse, as a sharer or partner in the

Admiral's Men, the company patronised by the countess' husband, Charles Howard: numbered in the first list of the company in 1594, quitting them in 1597 taking with him five books of plays, which had later to be bought back from him. In 1599 he was in Scotland, with an English troupe.

In an age when everyone traded information, the employ-ment of actors in espionage circles was not uncommon, as the career of Christopher Marlowe shows. It might be though that Jeanne's cross-dressing is likewise a tradition from the world of the stage and only from that fantastical world: we are all, of course, familiar with it from Shakespeare's plays. In fact, the conceit of the young woman who dons boys' breeches can be seen in a number of real life cases from the 'Roaring Girl' Moll Cutpurse to the maid of honour Mary Fitton. I first came across it in writing about Arbella Stuart, one of Elizabeth's potential successors, who donned male dress to flee abroad when her cousin King James forbade her to marry – but that too is another story.

Elizabeth and Essex

The relationship of Elizabeth I with the Earl of Essex has always baffled historians: the more so, perhaps, because it does not show either participant in the most attractive light. In 1928 Lytton Strachey's *Elizabeth and Essex* was the last book to be written specifically about the subject and though Strachey's analysis is very much of its era, it is a little hard to claim that we have moved on in any real degree. Recent work done on Essex's political role in the decade one historian calls 'the nasty nineties' has had little impact on our understanding of his private relationship with the queen. With all our supposed new elasticity in terms of personal relations, this is still a case that both worries and intrigues today. Had I been writing a biography rather than a novel about Elizabeth and Essex, I would of course have paid far more attention to the political part played by other faces and other forces than I have been able to do here; and perhaps that might have cast an alternative light on the events that ushered in the seventeenth century. But I do not think I would have understood the personal situation any differently.

It was Elizabeth's great favourite the Earl of Leicester – Essex's stepfather – who introduced the teenaged Essex into Elizabeth's favour; he was still only twenty when, in 1587, he was given Leicester's old job of Master of the Horse, which meant he was by her side whenever she rode out. Perhaps Leicester, now a white-haired fifty-five, knew he himself could no longer offer Elizabeth the warm flirtations they had once enjoyed: perhaps he wanted to provide a counter-attraction to the dashing new Captain of the Queen's Guard, Sir Walter Ralegh. If so the device worked: 'At night', it was soon reported, 'my Lord is at cards, or one game and another with her, that he cometh not to his own lodging till birds sing in the morning.' Essex was the queen's 'wild horse', whose very gaucheries may have seemed fresh to a palate jaded of more practised flattery. 'Very comely and beautiful', as an attendant reported to his one-time guardian Lord Burghley, he was tall and intense, at once educated and athletic – the model, probably, for Nicholas Hilliard's swooningly romantic 'Young Man Amongst Roses'. But a prominence based on his personal attractions was never going to satisfy a man who saw himself as England's champion – as the last representative of the old code of chivalry.

Over the next few years chance favoured him – or, just possibly, injured him, in allowing him to climb faster and further than his experience and his abilities really justified. The Earl of Leicester died in 1588, within weeks of the Armada victory, leaving Elizabeth so distraught she reputedly locked herself in her room, until her councillors were forced to break down the door. Leaving her, perhaps, more inclined than ever towards Leicester's stepson and surrogate. The stage was being emptied: the queen's chancellor Sir Walter Mildmay died in 1589, her spymaster Walsingham in 1590, Christopher Hatton in 1591 while in 1592 Ralegh was disgraced for having made an illicit marriage with one of the queen's maids of honour. (Essex, in 1590, had married the widow of his hero Sir Philip Sidney, but the queen had forgiven him – the more readily, perhaps, since he did not allow marriage to cramp his sexual style.) By 1591 it was already being said that Essex was 'like enough, if he had a few more years, to carry Leicester's credit and sway'.

In 1591 and 1592 he persuaded Elizabeth to allow him to command the forces sent to help the Protestant Henri IV against the Catholic League. In 1593 he became a Privy Councillor: greedily gulping down influence and honours, in the memorable

image of one contemporary, 'like a child sucking on an over-
uberous nurse'. Even Burghley, early in the decade, seemed to
be hitching his son Robert's wagon to this rising star. Yet with
all this in 1592 Essex was described as being 'of all others, the
most discontented person of the Court': convinced, as he
complained to his sister, that 'I live in a place where I am hourly
conspired against and practised upon'. He was already in indi-
rect communication with King James of Scotland.

He was far from alone in his concern for the country's future
– and his own. Elizabeth had been right to fear, as she always
had done, that men's eyes would come to turn towards the rising
sun. It is, of course, only hindsight that tells us the queen
survived until 1603: as far back as 1589 Essex had been writing
that her death could not be far away, and anyone who has ever
sat by a protracted deathbed knows how fraying to the nerves
the experience can be. These were the years of intense speculation about the succession: speculation all the more desperate for
the fact that it had to be conducted in the utmost secrecy. These
were the years of debate – in which Essex would play a contro-
versial part – about the very nature of monarchy. And perhaps
some of Essex's frantic ambition might be put down to the spirit
of the times – the *fin de siècle* atmosphere as the end approached,
both of the queen's reign and of the long Tudor century.

The fifteen years between the Armada and the queen's death
make up the bulk of what is now often spoken of as Elizabeth's
'second reign'; in which her grip on the country did begin to
slacken, in which her council did seize the initiative. The queen's
urge towards vacillation which had once served her so well had
now become a disability. She, who had always encouraged and
manipulated a measure of competition among her courtiers and
advisors, now feared that if her councillors united she would be
unable to stand against them. To Essex, her hesitation was anathema. 'I shall never', he wrote, 'do her service but against her will.'

If we are to see Essex as a man of vision (albeit a vision, aristocratic and militaristic, that we do not admire today) and a man

of principle (albeit living proof that the first thing a principle does really is to kill somebody) then his very strengths must have made the situation more frustrating. In so far as he was, as John Guy has called him, 'dazzling but paranoid', it can only have fostered his paranoia. Josephine Ross in her book on the queen's suitors, *The Men Who would be King*, points out that in many ways, Essex resembled Elizabeth's first love Thomas Seymour in his vaulting ambition and his death on the block: another man of 'much wit and little judgement'.

The Cadiz expedition against Spain in 1596 represented the height of his reputation as a soldier, but the conduct of the expedition, and the division of the glory, was a source of controversy. From the end of that year the court was increasingly divided into factions. One Lord Grey wrote of how Essex demanded he should choose sides: to be friendly towards Robert Cecil was to be his, Essex's, enemy. The earl's relationship with the Cecils had not been one of simple uninterrupted hostility, at least during old Lord Burghley's lifetime; nonetheless he clashed with them over everything from control of patronage to foreign policy. And soon Essex's anger seemed to encompass not only the Cecils, but almost everyone in a world which was failing to give him the influence he felt his due. By the time he went to Ireland, one observer wrote, Essex's greatness 'was now judged to depend as much on her Majesty's fear of him as her love to him'. His appointment there was a poisoned chalice, as he knew himself, but he was trapped by his own insistence on his role as England's warrior: 'tied by my own reputation to use no tergiversation'. His unscheduled return from Ireland is well documented – how he caught the queen 'newly up, with her hair about her face' – as is his cruel comment that her conditions were 'as crooked as her carcase'. Elizabeth's comments were almost as telling: she said to Sir John Harington that 'by God's son, I am no queen; that man is above me'; and declared she would not renew his lucrative grant of the duties on sweet wines because 'corrupt bodies, the more you feed them, the more hurt they do'. But the earl still kept the people's sympathy. Though the exact site of his imprisonment in the Tower is not known (the 'Devereux Tower' actually takes its name from another source), it is recorded that two headsmen were secretly ordered for his execution 'because if one faint the other may perform it'.

Elizabeth, it seems, finally turned against Essex when he seemed to threaten her sovereignty. Nonetheless she had, until this point, indulged him to an extraordinary degree. In 1928 Lytton Strachey suggested that the queen half liked Essex's arrogance, his apparent hostility. The fashionably Freudian analysis seems a little too easy now, but it is true that though Elizabeth early declared that 'it was fit that some one or other should take him down and teach him better manners', she nonetheless never brought herself to be that somebody. But then Strachey described an Elizabeth whose 'sexual organisation was seriously warped'; filled with 'a deep seated repugnance to the crucial act of intercourse' but nonetheless, 'filled with delicious agitation by the glorious figures of men'.

At the centre of her being, Strachey wrote, 'desire had turned to repulsion': her decision to execute Essex he sees as the final resolution of a lifelong trauma. 'The wheel had come full circle. Manhood – the fascinating, detestable entity, which had first come upon her concealed in yellow magnificence in her father's lap – manhood was overthrown at last, and in the person of the traitor it should be rooted out.' Strachey's book attracted some dissent even in his own day. His friend Virginia Woolf – whose own *Orlando*, the extraordinary story of the young man-woman embraced by the ageing queen, was in some ways a companion piece – disliked it: and with some reason, Elizabeth's admirers might say. But has the picture Strachey painted been altogether superseded today? It is true, as he points out, that Elizabeth was a woman who had vacillated over all the most important decisions in her life, from the question of her marriage to the executions of her cousins Norfolk and Mary. Yet she ordered Essex's execution without apparent doubt, as if instinctively – unless, as she later claimed, it was her council who pushed her to the act. It is certainly true that in what one might call her professional capacity she did mistrust that militaristic aspect of masculinity Essex represented: one field in which a female ruler was seriously disadvantaged, in the sixteenth century.

In the personal sphere, Essex's feelings are even harder to gauge than those of the queen – if, that is, one is to assume that he was anything other than wholly cynical in his relations with her. Strachey wrote that he was lavish in the protestations of his love: 'That convenient monosyllable, so intense and so ambiguous, was for ever on his lips.' 'Affection – admiration – exasperation – mockery – he felt them all by turns, and sometimes, so it seemed, simultaneously.' Bewitched, bothered and bewildered by Elizabeth, in other words, as so many had been: but Strachey saw Essex suffering under the conviction that Fate had reversed the ordained gender roles, 'and the natural master was the servant'.

Perhaps his feelings changed over the fifteen or so years in which they knew each other. The Elizabeth Essex first knew was, after all, the Elizabeth of Tilbury: he was there as she rode, in her breastplate and finery, to make the great speech that is still remembered today. By the end of those years, foreign visitors were describing a queen with yellowed teeth and red wig, who felt it necessary to stuff a perfumed silk handkerchief in her mouth before greeting them, pulling open the front of her dress to display a 'somewhat wrinkled' bosom.

It is a picture that haunts – that lends a sour note to Essex's lavish claims that he had been 'conquered by beauty'. True, this was a rhetoric still commonplace among Elizabeth's courtiers and borrowed from the older tradition of courtly love poetry. But if you read the letters Leicester or Hatton wrote to Elizabeth you feel, rightly or wrongly, that under the hyperbole you see genuine feeling. Read Essex's letters to the queen and they seem redolent only of fantasy.

It might be argued that the role Essex fulfilled for Elizabeth was less that of lover than of surrogate son. The son she never had with Leicester ... (Or, in some eyes, did have: several narratives around the dawn of the twentieth century saw both Essex and Francis Bacon as Elizabeth and Leicester's secret offspring.) There may be an element of truth in this picture of frustrated maternity – it would help to explain just why, before the last unforgiveable denouement of their story, she had already forgiven him so frequently. There was Elizabeth's own remark that his conduct in Ireland was something she would not have overlooked even in her own son: there was the undeniable echo in his furies of a toddler's tantrums.

To me the picture does not ring entirely true – or not when stated so crudely. If this was indeed a mother/son relationship, there was surely an element of the incestuous in it. I do indeed believe that Elizabeth's indulgence of Robert Devereux, Earl of Essex, was the fruit of her long love for the dead Robert Dudley, Earl of Leicester – but in many ways I see a doomed attempt to *recreate* the earlier relationship (as, with rather more success, the queen used Robert Cecil to replace Lord Burghley). But with Elizabeth – as her contemporaries knew – it is never safe to explain anything simplistically. That 'deep and inscrutable centre of the court, which is her Majesty's mind', as Francis Bacon put it, still retains its mystery.

Select Bibliography

The two non-fiction books I have written about the Elizabethan era – *Arbella: England's Lost Queen* and *Elizabeth and Leicester* – included more extensive lists of sources and suggestions for further reading. The fifteen books below, however, are ones I found particularly helpful in researching this story.

Borman, Tracy, *Elizabeth's Women: The Hidden Story of the Virgin Queen* (Jonathan Cape 2009)

Guy, John (ed.), *The Reign of Elizabeth I: Court and Culture in the Last Decade* (Cambridge University Press 1995)

Jardine, Lisa and Stewart, Alan, *Hostage to Fortune: The Troubled Life of Francis Bacon* (Victor Gollancz 1998)

Kenny, Robert, *Elizabeth's Admiral: The Political Career of Charles Howard, Earl of Nottingham, 1536–1624* (Johns Hopkins Press 1970)

Marcus, Leah S., Mueller, Janet, and Rose, Mary Beth (eds.), *Elizabeth I: Collected Works* (University of Chicago Press 2000)

Martin, Trea, *Elizabeth in the Garden: A Story of Love, Rivalry and Spectacular Design* (Faber and Faber 2008)

Pavord, Anna, *Searching for Order: The History of the Alchemists, Herbalists and Philosophers who Unlocked the Secrets of the Plant World* (Bloomsbury 2009)

Smith, Lacey Baldwin, *Treason in Tudor England: Politics and Paranoia* (1986, new edition Pimlico 2006)

Weir, Alison, *Elizabeth the Queen* (Jonathan Cape 1998)

(on Essex)

Devereux, W. B., *Lives and Letters of the Devereux, Earls of Essex, in the Reigns of Elizabeth, James I, and Charles I 1540–1646* (John Murray 1853)
Hammer, Paul E. J., *The Polarisation of Elizabethan Politics: the Political Career of Robert Devereux, 2nd Earl of Essex 1585–1597* (Cambridge University Press 1999)
Harrison, G. B., *The Life and Death of Robert Devereux, Earl of Essex* (Cassell & Co. 1937)
Lacey, Robert, *Robert, Earl of Essex: An Elizabethan Icarus* (Weidenfeld & Nicolson 1970)

(on Cecil)

Handover, P. M., *The Second Cecil: The Rise to Power 1563–1604 of Sir Robert Cecil, later first Earl of Salisbury* (Eyre & Spottiswoode 1959)
Loades, David, *The Cecils: Privilege and Power Behind the Throne* (The National Archives 2007)

Five related gardens

Hatfield House (Hertfordshire)

The notable garden created for Robert Cecil in the early seventeenth century may not itself have survived the years – but even without the collection of rare plants built up by John Tradescant, the beds of roses and iris, the clipped low hedges of box and aromatics, still cast a powerful spell.

Burghley House: The Garden of Surprise (Lincolnshire)

At once thoroughly modern and robustly Elizabethan in spirit, this new water garden was inspired by descriptions of the garden at Theobalds; with statues, grottoes and other 'conceits' – like hidden jets of water to soak unwary passers-by.

Kenilworth Castle (Warwickshire)

A recent re-creation, based on contemporary descriptions and complete with fountain and aviary, of the garden the Earl of Leicester built for Queen Elizabeth's visit in 1575. Impressive for its painstaking accuracy.

Lyveden New Bield (Northamptonshire)

House and garden were left unfinished when Sir Thomas
Tresham died in 1605 (and his widow sold the trees in the
orchard to Cecil for Hatfield). What remains is a wonderfully
evocative landscape of ruins and waterways, now under restora-
tion by the National Trust.

Penshurst Place (Kent)

Eleven acres of enclosed garden, much as it was originally laid
out by Essex's connection Sir Henry Sidney. Within easy reach
of Hever, with its hedge and water mazes, and of Sissinghurst,
where Vita Sackville-West's famous twentieth-century garden
was nonetheless a great source of inspiration for me.

Fact and Fiction

The idea for *The Girl in the Mirror* came to me on the M25 – junctions 7 to 9, if you want to be precise. I can't quite say that it came to me in a flash (though we were in a spring lightning storm) but it came fully formed, all the same, as if someone had just handed me a kicking, breathing baby.

After what felt like years experimenting with one historical novel, I'd come to the conclusion that it was unlikely to happen, or, at least, not immediately, so I suppose I was actively looking for a story. Cursing the fact that in the late-Tudor period (which I knew better than any other) all the best tales had already been told. Brooding on the fact that while (as Virginia Woolf said) 'it is the stories of women that fire my imagination', there was only a prohibitively limited sphere of action open to most women in the sixteenth century. Reflecting that a ruling queen was the great exception but I'd already written about Elizabeth and Leicester from a factual standpoint, and the problem with Elizabeth and Essex is that you don't really want to stick around that relationship for the space of a whole book …

And there it was. A background of Elizabeth and Essex, but the protagonist an invented character, a girl who gets to operate with the freedom of a boy. She had in some way to be cut off from the society around her, and history provided the answer to that – she'd be a Protestant refugee. The name (Musset, from de Musset, like the poet; a clan of eccentric Essex fishermen and sailors) was there in my own Huguenot ancestry.

It really was that simple, or that serendipitous; the first idea, anyway. I was on the way to Hampton Court to see their new recreation of a Tudor garden: was it coincidence that I decided shortly after, that gardens should be an important subtext to my story? Over the next few days, as I was walking or driving, other understandings about the major characters came to me just as easily.

That was utterly different from the way my earlier attempt at a novel had behaved. There, if I'm honest, I'd been chipping away at a lump of intriguing historical fact, unable to let go for long enough to find my actual story. A commissioning editor once told me that it's harder for someone who has written factual history to move over to fiction than it is to go the other way. I'd already made one major change in my writing career, from showbusiness journalism to historical biography, and found the two spheres weren't as different as people claimed. The skills you need to make readers accept the gaps in our historical knowledge are the same as the ones that turn a fifteen-minute interview with Michael Douglas into a double-page story in the *Guardian*. You call up the cuttings, you draw on your own past encounters with the star – you write around it, basically. But there is no writing around in fiction. It's another matter entirely.

I had the situation for my novel, and we all know 'what happened next' – not just historians, but anyone who's seen Helen Mirren or Glenda Jackson playing Elizabeth on TV. Essex leads a rebellion against the queen and she orders his head be cut off ... But that didn't tell me where my refugee was going to be left – the emotional journey of the story. There is, heaven knows, a kind of historical fiction that consists largely of drama-tising real-life events, adding and embroidering only where necessary. But I seemed to have landed myself instead with the kind that uses those as a jumping off point, leaving me with the power and responsibility of invention as surely as if I'd been writing a piece of modern chick lit, or a detective story. Leaving me to understand the real nature of what was going on in my tale

– what I was writing *about*. About a girl unable – like so many of us, like other characters around her – to shake free of the demons of her past. About finding the courage to become the person you are meant to be.

Slowly, I had to learn to trust the novel-writing process itself. A cliché, I know, but it did often feel as though I were taking down dictation, one episode at a time – disconcerting in a way, but reassuring in another, since I found one scene was actively showing me the way to the next. But that didn't mean it wasn't scary. Writing factual history, there is always a great deal of sheer donkey work. You can ease yourself into the book each day by research or simple transcription of events, and that does cushion you. It stops you from having to feel – to commit. Fiction, it seems, has no equivalent – you're 100% there or you're wasting your time. Or, worse, doing actual damage by forcing the story along a path it would not have taken naturally.

My non-fiction had been about Elizabeth and her day, so I already knew my background. That meant I could start writing fairly quickly, though there would be a million places where I'd have to go back and do more work – in many ways you need a more detailed understanding of a period for fiction than for factual history.

Those details would be as accurate as I could make them. That's one of the deals I made between fiction and history. So too would be my picture of the big public events … though that taps into the question of whether you believe there is one inalienable historical truth and I'm not sure I do, actually. But that doesn't lessen your responsibility to tell the truth *as you see it* – and you'd better be sure of what that truth is going to be. You don't have the luxury of giving the evidence for and against, and then leaving an open verdict as you do when you're writing a biography. Different characters may see different versions of the same event, but you can't put footnotes in a story.

There are the deals you make with history – and then there are the deals history makes with you. Something strange happened to me, towards the very end of the time I spent writing this novel. I'd long before found a name for Jeanne's actor acquaintance – Martin Slaughter – when I'd read a brief mention of two actors charged, as rogues and vagabonds, with having falsely claimed to be members of a licensed troupe. Borrowing the bare name, I'd made 'my' Martin Slaughter what I needed him to be: present in London on certain dates; attached, then not attached, to an established company. I was actually revising when I decided more colour was needed for the theatre scenes. I knew actors well enough from my journalism days – spent more hours than I care to remember backstage at the RSC – but I'd never been a student of theatrical history. So I raided a friend's bookcase, came up with the *Documents of the Rose Playhouse* – and as I read it, the hairs on the back of my neck began to rise, just slightly.

The history of the real Martin Slaughter, in so far as it is known, fitted my invention precisely. Joining the right company – the one under the protection of the countess's husband – and leaving at the right moment exactly. Of course there is the obvious psychological explanation – I'd read this information before and forgotten the details, until my subconscious reproduced it when necessary. Except that the book (edited by Carol Chillington Rutter, published by Manchester University Press in 1999) is not one you pick up at any airport bookstall, and until now I'd barely had occasion to register the location of the Rose, let alone hunt out the details of its company. As Charles Kingsley wrote in *The Water Babies*, this is all a story and you shouldn't believe a word of it, even if it is true. But sometimes – even for the person who's written both – it can be hard to keep an eye on the dividing line between fact and fantasy.